Death of Kings

Book Four
of
The Abyss Walker Series

by

Shane Moore

A New Babel Books Release
381 High Point Drive

Holiday Shores, IL 62025

www.newbabelbooks.com

Genre: Fantasy / Series

ISBN: 978-1-63196-021-5

Revised Edition; First printing.

Printed in the United States of America.

Other Abyss Walker Works

Table of Contents

I would like to thank Mr. Tolkien and Mr. Gygax.
for unlocking the door.

SHANE MOORE

1

A Gittledorph's Luck

"What a battle! Boy, humans sure know how to enter-tain!" Stieny thought to himself as he strolled from alongside the lower edge of the arena wall. People were slowly making their way out at the east exit, and the attendants, or whoever they were, were checking on the large swordsman. Stieny had figured the man was doomed when the twelve or so dwarves rushed him, but such fury! The giant man roared like a lion and cut them down one by one. He didn't parry, he didn't even seem to defend any of their strikes. The ones that managed to stab him died quickly. In fact, they all died quickly, but the ones to cut him died first.

Stieny swung a thin loaf of bread around like a sword, mimicking the battle as he recalled it. The small halfling paused to take a tiny bite from the end of the loaf and watched as two men; both dressed in white robes, lifted the man on a stretcher and hauled him down the corridor.

The others started piling the bodies of the dwarves and the men together after they removed their armor and cloth-ing. It was a gruesome sight and the little halfling re-exam-ined his loaf, thinking his appetite might have been ruined. But he quickly dismissed the notion. Eating was one of his more favorite hobbies. The little thief would not allow it to be ruined. Munching on the hard bread, Stieny followed the procession along the edge and down the polished, stairs of the arena.

As he made his way into the streets, the people mingled around, some waiting for coaches, others patronizing the local vendors that had set up small portable stands selling everything from bread and cheese to small "good luck" trin-kets. Amazingly enough, the trinket merchant seemed to be doing well, so Stieny made his way through the crowd toward his stand. The stand was a simple one. It was about seven foot tall and made of wood. It had a large rectangular bottom that acted as a table with two poles on each side that rose up supporting a large flat wooden sign with some writing on it. Stieny wasn't very good at reading common, though his talents at thieving often gave him insight to the meanings of languages he didn't speak, and deciphering them took time. The little thief stood in line and munched on his loaf of bread. His tiny mouth and small teeth chewed in delight as his small hands fumbled the small knife in his pocket. It shouldn't be difficult to cut the trinket seller's purse. Stieny would flash a silver mark in the man's face, and while the fool stared at the coin, Stieny would relieve his purse. Of course, the halfling would buy a trinket. After all, they might really be good luck.

As Stieny contemplated his heist, he was jolted from behind roughly and stumbled forward. Frowning, the halfling turned around and saw a short fat man glaring at him. The man wasn't short as far as Stieny was concerned, but he was short by human standards. He wore a brown leather jerkin stained from sweat and grime and his tattered breeches were dark blue. He wore a pair of old walking boots that had his big toe sticking out of one and the other was missing the heel. Stieny readjusted his shirt and glared at the man. "Excuse you, sir."

The fat man chewed his lower lip and looked the halfling up and down. "You a dwarf or some smelly kid?"

Stieny placed his hands on his hips incredulously. The fat man didn't seem too threatening, and calling him a dwarf was a downright insult. Dwarves were smelly, drunkard warriors, all of the things the halfling was not. "I beg your pardon, but I am no dwarf, thank you very much," Stieny said as he shook his head from side to side.

The fat man inched forward. His bright yellow teeth and fetid breath made the halfling lean backwards in disgust. "You getting smart with me?"

Stieny frowned and began glancing around him for a possible escape route. The little thief didn't want to have to run, he figured the trinket seller an easy mark but getting clobbered by this fat thug was not on his list of things to do either. "Of course not, good sir. I wouldn't want you to get confused."

The fat man paused for a moment and frowned, thinking about what the halfling said. Then he reached down and poked Stieny in the chest roughly. "You making fun of me, dwarf? Cause I hate dwarves."

Great. Just when Stieny thought he had an easy target in the trinket maker, some fat drunken lout had to decide he looked like a dwarf. Other than height, he no more resembled a dwarf than a dragon. "Look, sir. I have no intention of making fun of you. Truth be told, you look to be of little or no fun at all. Now if you please, I would like to stand here in line unmolested," Stieny said, cursing his luck as a crowd of people began to pay interest to the two of them. If too many people watched him, he would not be able to safely remove the trinket keeper's coin purse.

"What's going on here?" said a stern voice from the crowd. Stieny turned and looked, keeping one eye on the fat maniac in front of him. The halfling saw a human step from the crowd with a much shorter woman. The man wore a brightly polished suit of plate mail armor with some religious symbol on his chest. He had a long flowing violet cape and his shoulder length blonde hair bounced around his head as he walked. He had bright blue eyes that commanded respect while they seemed to look into a person's thoughts.

The woman was much shorter wearing a bright green suit of leather armor that hugged her features well. She had long blond hair that hung down behind her in a thick braid that revealed her thin pointed ears. A white ash bow was strapped to her back and a large quiver of arrows with bright green fletching. The woman wore a short sword that was strapped to her thigh and a boot dagger that was fastened to the outside of her black knee-high boots. Stieny didn't say anything as the pair walked up. The halfling had learned long ago the best policy was silence first.

The fat man immediately began stammering. "Nothing, My Lord. I was just leaving."

Stieny watched the fat smelly man duck into the crowd and decided that it was a perfect time for him to make his exit also. The thug had ruined his score and he had no inclination of hanging around to speak with this lord, whoever he was.

"No so fast," the elf said as she hooked her polished white ash bow around the halfling's neck. Stieny thought about drawing his thin dagger and cutting the bow string to make a run for it, but decided against it. Elves were typically twice as dexterous as humans, and he didn't want to risk being caught in a foot chase. Not to mention being held responsible for cutting her string. Elves were weird like that. Stieny had relied on his wit many times in the past, and would do so now.

The little halfling lifted his hands in the air disarmingly and turned around slowly. "What? I have done nothing wrong, My Lady."

Alexis flashed a knowing smile as she lifted her bow from the halfling's neck. "I am not your lady, halfling. But, you can call me Overmoon. And he," she said, gesturing to the man in the polished plate armor, "...is Apollisian, a man that is not to be trifled with."

Apollisian gripped his platinum holy symbol that hung from his neck and frowned, becoming more and more distant from the halfling and the elf. Alexis didn't seem to notice.

"What may I do for you, Lady Overmoon?" Stieny asked, bowing deeply as his eyes darted into the crowd looking for his escape route.

Alexis leaned down and stuck out her hand. "For starters, you can place the razor knife from your right pocket into my hand and place however many purses you have in your left pocket into my other hand."

Drat! The damnable elf not only knew where he kept his knife and stash, but she had made him cross his arms. It was not difficult for a skilled thief as he to make any slight hand movements and throw dirt into her eyes, or slide the coin purse up his long sleeve, or any other tricks he knew. They all were near impossible to perform once your arms were crossed. Stieny sighed, gently placing the razor knife and coin purse into her hand as she asked. With her hands full of his stuff, he would make a bolt for the crowd. It was unlikely she could throw down the knife and draw an arrow, notch it, and fire, before he could vanish into the mass of people. But again to Stieny's dismay, she kept a hold of his hands while he held his own knife and coin purse. What a dirty rotten trick!

Alexis smiled as she watched the anguish on the thief's face when she didn't let go of his hands. Thieves were all so predictable. The elf glanced back over to Apollisian who was gripping his holy symbol in his hand and shaking his head. "What is wrong?" she asked, keeping an eye on the halfling.

Apollisian shook his head. "It is as if Stephanis can't hear me. I can feel him, but I cannot seem to use any of his divinity. I do not want to release this thief unless I know he is not evil. I'll not pardon a law-breaker of any crime, if his heart is black."

Alexis shook her head. "This one is fine. Other than opportunistic, I think he is a model citizen."

Stieny glared. "Opportunistic? Lady, I am a well-trained meticulous planner. I never let opportunity guide my path. Why, even suggesting such a thing is downright insulting! Never in all my day..."

"Can it, squirt," Alexis interrupted. "This purse obviously isn't yours. So, I am going to hang on to it for you. If I can't find the owner, I will see it goes to a nice church. As for punishing you for taking it, I instead offer you a way to help the community, instead of stealing from it. Not to mention, you can actually earn your money for once."

"Of course the purse is mine," Stieny said, feigning insult. "How could you even nsinuate that I...?"

"The thong that holds the purse to a belt has been cut recently. The coin purse has a bright red embroidered "A" on it. The bright red means nobility here in Beykla, and you are certainly not nobility in this country. Third, I bet you can't tell me how much money you have in it," Alexis said with a wry grin. Stieny slumped his shoulders and took a deep breath as he stared at the dirt-covered street in defeat. "What is it you want me to do?"

Alexis smiled triumphantly. She turned and saw that Apollisian was deeply engrossed with something. His knuckles were white from tension as he gripped his holy symbol roughly. His eyes were closed, his face was red, and sweat was beading upon his forehead. She turned back and spoke quickly to the thief. "Listen carefully. This will be quick. I have other matters to attend to. There is a man being held in the coliseum. His name is Jude. He is a large man, larger than most. He fights with a great sword. He shouldn't be too hard to locate. All I need is for you to find where he is being kept and bring the information back to me at the Blue Dragon Inn. I will be in the common room for one hour after twilight each night for the next week. I expect a report from you each night. To keep you from being arrested I will give you a gold crown to live on. After you complete your task, and I manage to speak to the man, I will pay you ten gold crowns. Any questions?"

The halfling's eyes lit up! Ten gold crowns! A single crown was like ten gold in Beykla, let alone ten of them. And all he had to do was break into the arena and find some large swordsman. Stieny figured he knew who they were talking about already. The little thief held out his hand and batted his brown eyes.

Alexis placed a single gold crown in his hand and watched his eyes light up. "Remember, I want a report each night on how your task fares."

The little thief nodded. "It shall be done as you ask, Lady Overmoon. And in the future, if you have any tasks that pay as good as this, please come calling."

Alexis smiled and nodded as she quickly shifted her attention to the troubled man behind her.

Stieny made his way into the street, mingling with the people. The elf hadn't been as bright as he initially suspected Stieny thought as he tossed a small purse into the air with an embroidered red "A" on it. The coins jingled as he stuffed the pouch back into his breeches pocket and headed back toward the arena.

"Are you okay, Apollisian?" Alexis asked as she placed her warm hand on his wrist. The paladin looked down at her beautiful green eyes.

He managed a weak smile. "Yes, but I cannot make contact with Stephanis. Something is wrong, terribly wrong. I need to go back to my room and pray. Perhaps I have done something to earn his disfavor."

Alexis nodded as they moved through the crowd. People quickly moved from the pair's way, suspecting they were royalty or at least nobility. Elves didn't travel with common men. Apollisian glanced down at beautiful Alexis. Her twinkling emerald eyes seemed to shine in the bright sunlight and her golden hair was a frozen cascading waterfall of the purest amber. She was an amazing creature. "You do not think Stephanis is angry with me over hiring the cutpurse? I could not manage to tell if he was evil or not."

Alexis shook her head as she gazed back up at the handsome Apollisian. His blonde hair bounced around his chiseled features and his bright blue eyes were like steel over a deep chasm. Never had she seen a more immaculate being. Alexis shook her head clear. She could stare at his stunning face for eternity. The elf placed as much of a reassuring hand on the paladin's forearm as she dared in public. "I am sure he is not angry with you. You were having troubles before we even hired the thief, remember? Relax. Let us go to our rooms. I will order you some warm soup and see you to your bed."

Apollisian smiled at the notion, and then nodded distantly as they made their way down the street. If this was what being without Stephanis was like, he wasn't sure he could give up his god for Alexis. Being with her was like filling one half of his soul, while being without the divinity of Stephanis was like emptying the other half.

The pair made their way to the inn, while the halfling ducked into an alley near the arena. Before he tried to investigate the coliseum, he needed to go shopping first.

Delania watched the black-haired man that gave her the crimson robe dart around the corner and disappear into the masses of the street. She bunched her hands into the soft, velvety fabric and held it to her face. Never had she felt such a sensation. The cloth was soft and soothing. She quickly lifted the garment up in front of herself and examined it, searching for a way to put it on. She slid her arms into each sleeve slowly, savoring every inch. The fabric was heavy, and a little too small, but the way the velvety interior brushed against her skin gave her goose bumps. Delania examined herself in the robe, holding her arms out in front of her. The garment seemed to shimmer in the sunlight, something the succubus had not gotten used to yet. She channeled a weave of magical energy into the bright red "R" that was on the left breast of the garment. She intricately wove the flows around the threads, easily twisting and turning them, until the "R" transformed into a "D." She severed the weave neatly, making the alteration permanent. Bunching her long black hair up, she tucked it under itself into a bun and boldly stepped out into this new world. There was much research to be done on how she got here, and how to remove the necklace that the fool imp, Kornicus had placed on her neck.

As she stepped into the street, she was amazed at the vastness of this new realm. In the Abyss, the clouds hovered a few hundred feet above the surface, occasionally dipping down to burn and scour the blasted landscape. But here, the clouds seemed miles away. They floated along on unseen currents, slowly shifting and changing, unlike the violent gusts of sulfurous winds of the Abyss. Squeaking carts and the hum of voices and animals permeated the air, instead of deep growls and screams of the damned. Delania moved across the street and stopped a man that was walking along a stone walkway. The man was of average height and his head was shaved. He stared at the ground as he walked and carried a small basket of some green leafy substance. She stepped in front of him and the man stopped immediately.

"Hello," she said, raising her hand up vertically in an awkward greeting.

The man glanced around nervously as if he wanted to flee. Beads of sweat immediately formed on his forehead as he stammered. "Y-yes, Mother?" the suda said in a terrified voice. Never had he been greeted so. He was not to speak to a Mother, unless they asked him a question, but not speaking was also a crime. Plus he had no idea if this woman was a mother. She wore a Mother's Robe, yet she had no jewelry and no shoes. The terrified man hoped he had answered correctly.

Delania noticed the man was afraid. She had spent an eternity witnessing fear. Yet, the idea a spawn would have fear here, on their own realm, never occurred to her. "Are you afraid?" she asked looking around for some demon that might swallow the man up.

The suda began to shake visibly. "I fear that I might fail to answer correctly, mistress."

Delania tried to smile disarmingly. "Nonsense. As long as you are truthful, I am not displeased," Delania said, seemingly more nervous. The beads of sweat had transformed into small streams that began to trickle down the sides of his face. "Do stop sweating. It is annoying me."

The suda felt his knees go weak and give way from under him. He dropped the basket and hit the stone walkway hard. His head suffered a fair blow and a small cut formed on his forehead from the fall. Delania kneeled before him and cradled his head. She had never seen someone lose consciousness before. In the Abyss, it was impossible for a spawn to pass out. The demons enjoyed that fact when they tortured them. Fearing the man was dead, she shook him lightly and gently patted his cheeks. The suda slowly came to and Delania felt his body tense as he stared up into her red eyes. "I thought you had died," she said soothingly as she ran her hand over his shaved head. The short stubbles tickled her and she enjoyed the sensation.

The terrified suda didn't move. Not only had he fainted, she was cradling him in her arms. Her bright red robe was loose fitting and her sallow white bosom was mashed together creating the most inviting cleavage he had ever seen in his life, yet he knew if he glanced at it for, even a moment, he would surely die.

"What is going on here?" a soft, but stern, voice demanded.

Delania looked up and saw a woman standing in the street with her fists planted on her hips. The woman was heavy set and tall, compared to the other women Delania had seen since arriving here, which to say was choice few. The woman was wearing plate mail armor and a long blue cape. She had a long sword strapped to her side and a disapproving glare on her face. Delania smiled as she cradled the terrified suda and gently stroked his head. "The spawn fell. I don't know why, but when I rubbed his head like this...," Delania said, demonstrating how she stroked the suda's shaved head, "...he awoke."

The large woman seemed uninterested in the story. "What sept do you belong to?"

Delania frowned. Sept? What was sept? She shrugged her shoulders. "I do not know. What sept do you belong to?"

The woman growled and grabbed the suda by the collar and roughly jerked him up. She turned and glared at Delania. "I do not take kindly to being mocked, Mother, if that's what you are. Where are your shoes?"

Delania felt a fire beginning to rage inside of her. This spawn had taken her man from her. She longed to stroke the stubble on his head, yet this fool spawn was denying her.

"What is going on here?" asked another voice.

Delania watched as a second woman clad in plate armor approached. This woman was much shorter, but also wore a blue silk cape and a long sword.

"I don't know. This Mother, if she even is one, was sitting in the street, clearly showing this suda affection, a blatant disregard for law," the fat woman said.

The other woman in armor shook her head from side to side. "Who are you? What sept do you belong to?"

Delania felt the fire begin to roar. "My name is Delania. I do not belong to any sept, whatever that is. I demand you return the spawn to me or face my wrath," she said coldly.

The suda began to tremble again and shook his head slowly from side to side. He didn't know who this woman was, but crossing the guard was a bad idea. The honor guard of Aquabar wore pendants that protected them from magic. Only the most powerful Mothers could affect them, and then the results were not always full strength. Plus the honor guard, or sword mistresses as they were called, were deadly warriors that could kill in an instant with their enchanted blades.

The fat woman chuckled. "You dare to threaten me, child? Now you are under arrest with this suda here," she said as she motioned to the smaller sword mistress. "Bring her with us."

The shorter woman stepped to Delania and roughly jerked her to her feet. Both women gasped as Delania stood to almost six foot tall. She looked down at the sword mistress' grip on her red robe and she felt the fire roar.

"Unhand me, spawn, or die," Delania said calmly. The suda hung his head low and cowered on the ground, not wanting to see the gruesome scene that was about to unfold.

The fat woman growled and drew her long sword. "You have threatened a sword mistress's life. The penalty for..."

Delania channeled a complex weave of magical energy directly into the woman standing next to her. The weave was so intricate that it contained thousands of tiny strands that instantly roared into life. The woman released her grasp of Delania and dropped to the ground, clutching her chest and moaning in agony. People on the street who had paused to watch the execution of the strange black-haired woman now backed away as they saw the complexity of the weave that struck the shorter sword mistress. The fat woman, unable to see the magical flow, still realized that her enemy was no novice. She raised her sword and charged.

Delania channeled again. This time she shaped the energies around the fat sword mistress' body. Bright blue rings erupted from the air surrounding the woman, binding her. Hundreds of rings formed, until a thick single ring that stretched from the fat woman's ankles to her chin held her fast. Delania neatly severed the weave and turned her attention back to the shorter woman, who was struggling to stand. She reached down and grabbed the sword mistress by the hair and violently pulled her face to hers. Her bright red eyes were ablaze with anger. "I am taking this spawn with me. Hinder me further and I will see you dead," Delania snarled as she cruelly tossed the weak woman back to the ground. "Come along, spawn," Delania said as she interlocked her arm around the arm of the terrified suda. "You must show me where you live."

Reena turned to Lance as she watched the display on the street. "Ramasiel tells me you are a sorcerer. If that is true, tell me what you saw."

Lance stared at the ground. "I saw nothing, Mistress Reena. I am not allowed to set my eyes on any woman."

Reena slapped Lance across the face. The sharp blow staggered him. "I am no fool, suda! I see your tricks. There is something about you that Ramasiel hopes to use to propel her to the senate. Tell me what you saw."

Lance rubbed his stinging cheek. "I saw the dark-haired woman channel a flow into the woman next to her and then she sent out a spell to hold people."

Reena smiled and stroked Lance's face affectionately. "Good boy, Lance. Now what did you notice about the flows?"

Lance frowned? Notice about them? What was there to notice? They were a thousand times more complex than anything he had seen before, and that she severed them when she was finished to keep them from unraveling, but nothing seemed to jump out at him. "I am not sure what you mean, mistress. I noticed the weaves were complex and that she severed them to make them permanent."

Reena's jaw dropped. "Complex? Are you serious, fool? They were more than just complex. They were incredible. Ramasiel herself could maybe weave that many strands at once on her best day, let alone two spells in the same day with not so much as a strain!" Reena said as she glanced back into the street to watch the strange black-haired woman disappear down an alley. Then it occurred to her Lance had mentioned severing the weave. That was a trick only the more powerful sorcerers and sorceresses could recognize and only the most powerful could perform. She whipped around. "What do you mean severed the weave? How do you know of such things?"

Lance shrugged. "I figured it out when I was a boy."

Reena slapped him again across the face. The slap echoed down the alley. "Do not lie to me, suda! I do not have to tell Ramasiel of how you were accosted by some street thugs. I could mention how I caught you trying to sell her robe to escape the city."

Lance rubbed his stinging cheek. "I assure you, Mistress, I am not lying. I would show you if I were not shielded."

Reena chuckled. "I bet you would try. What other secrets do you hold, Lance? "

Lance shrugged. He noticed how whenever Reena was angry or displeased with him, she would slap him and call him suda, but when she wanted to know something, or get him to talk to her, she would speak soothingly and call him by his name. This one was more cunning than Ramasiel. That was for certain. What she lacked in magical prowess, she made up in deviousness. "I am not sure of what knowledge I have that is considered a secret with your culture," Lance said.

Reena leaned close and pressed her firm body against Lance's, pinning him to the brick wall of the alley. She breathed her hot breath against his neck and lifted her leg between his as her hand gently groped his coal black hair. She leaned closer until her soft lips rubbed his ear as she whispered into his. "We need to work together, Lance. I can free you; teach you things that would take you years to discover on your own. All you need to do is be my eyes and ears around Ramasiel."

Lance's mind raced as did his pulse. He had no feelings for Reena, but the raw physical attraction he had for her was powerful enough to get his blood racing, let alone the idea of her teaching him. He wondered if Reena was trying to trick him, but Lance knew the mistress hungered for the robe as much as Ramasiel hungered for a scepter among the senate. He quickly formulated a response. "I will do as you command, without fail, Mistress."

Reena smiled seductively. "Good. Now, Ramasiel will undoubtedly command you to do certain tasks. Carry them out completely. Do not hesitate regardless of what it is. Even if it is against me, just be sure to inform me of the task. I will deal with it accordingly. She will undoubtedly teach you things also. A suda that can weave spells is almost unheard of. She will no doubt loose your shield on certain occasions to eavesdrop and the like. Be wary. Other Mistresses and Mothers will have wards to guard against such things."

Lance smiled and looked the woman in the eye. She started to slap him but smiled instead. "How I wish to teach you more than magic, but I'll not have you fall prey like my last tuda. In good time, you will be mine. Then I'll show you what magic is really used for."

"Ego? What is an ego? Some great scholars of mytime defined an ego as a secular part of a three tiered consciousness. They believed that the first part of this tier controlled basic needs, or drives. Hunger-sexual desires, etc. The second part of this tier controlled how to satisfy the first part. If you were hungry, you looked for food. The third, and final, tier determined the ramifications ofthe second. Simply trying to wrestle a deer from the jaws of a lion would be an action the third tier would dissuade the second tier from attempting to satisfy the drive of the first.

But, though this sounds great in theory, how does it apply to oneself? I discovered that the first tier is a constant. These drives never go away, they are always present and guiding us. Thus, in my mind, they simply cannot be a tier at all, but an equal constant. An equal point of a triangle, if you will. My intelligence determines in what manner that I need to satisfy these drives, but not as a higher tiered conscious, but simply as a two way point-the second part of the triangle. And, the third is simply wisdom. The greatest minds in the world, often fall prey to a lack of wisdom. The third point of the triangle can be summoned up into discretion-the greater part of valor.

No, there is no secret tier, or greater labels for the human mind. The drives are simply all linked together into a single consciousness. It is the minds of fools that attempt to assign labels and tiers to a singular plane that needs not defining. Red is, red. It cannot be broken down or assigned separate values. It is unfortunate that the brains of the world muddy the waters of truth, with labels and titles, when they simply should be focusing on the bigger picture. For even the king of Beykla, fell prey to his own clouded thoughts."

-Lancalion Levendis Lampara

2
A Spirited Charge

The warm winter sun shone down lightly through small gaps in the thick rolling clouds. A chilling breeze stirred occasionally, blowing the limbs of leafless trees. Amerix and Vlargcar had been prisoners for three nights, their arms and legs stretched out, forming an "X" across the flat wooden horse-drawn cart. They were stripped down to their small clothes and each chilling breeze brought hundreds of tiny goose bumps on their exposed flesh. Amerix had learned that the leader of this band was known as Meirgan, some kind of a bounty hunter. Amerix didn't speak common, but he was able to discern the man's name. The wizard that was with him would sometimes use some sort of spell to ask questions. Amerix learned that apparently the entire kingdom of Beykla was looking for him. The king had posted thousands of wanted posters for his capture, or execution, offering a reward that many considered would break the crown. This Meirgan and his wizard, Tallnok, were especially pleased because there were no men left in their group and they only had to split the enormous reward three ways. The wizard was undoubtedly intelligent. Amerix clearly recognized that just by listening to the man speak. But it was obvious the fool wizard was not very wise. He loved talking about how he specialized in catching men by using hold spells and other dweamors. That explained a lot to the old dwarf. In his long life, he had been particularly resistant to magic, all dwarves were to some extent. But this mage's skill in certain forms of dweamors made him more powerful in those areas, thus his capture.

Amerix went out of his way to make the interrogations unpleasant for the wizard. He had no real reason to hide anything from the human, but took a personal pleasure in confounding him. Amerix had frequently told Tallnok that he liked him, only to immediately follow the statement up by saying he would like to kill him. The coward wizard's face would redden and he would get all in a huff trying to feign bravery. Meirgan had thought Amerix's continued taunting was an attempt to get the bounty hunter to slay him. Meirgan assumed that he was afraid of the torture he was to receive when they dropped him and the orc off at Central City.

Amerix didn't fear death. He had faced death more times that the fool bounty hunter had seen sunrises. But, he feared facing death without a weapon in his hand, and dead enemies at his feet. That was how a warrior was supposed to die, not by having his intestines slowly pulled from his body and rolled onto a reel while he screamed himself into oblivion. Though, the challenge of enduring the torture without uttering a sound seemed a close second to dying in battle. Then even in death, he could have some sort of victory. But the poor whelp; what kind of deviate plan did they have for him? They asked a lot of questions about the boy. Amerix always felt the exalting rush of hate when the wizard asked about the orc. It was revitalizing to feel the incredible emotion raging through his veins. Amerix often envisioned the pair, mistreating the orc, just to get his own hackles in a rise.

Early in the journey he had tried to speak to the orc, who was chained to the wagon behind him in the same fashion, but the beatings quickly deterred him. It was not the pain, but the loss of consciousness that the dwarf hated. He never knew how long he had been out and where he was when he came to.

Vlargcar, on the other hand, despised his captors and tried to bite them as often as possible. He frequently tested his chains by pulling on them until a large vein in the side of his head threatened to burst. Then he only paused long enough for the dizziness to subside. The wizard had cast some spell to enable himself to speak orc, but Vlargcar refused to speak with him. The larger man had beaten him until he became unconscious more than once, and Vlargcar had vowed before Durion, that he would feast on the man's brains. And Amerix couldn't say a word, because the damn bounty hunter couldn't speak orc or dwarven, and Vlargcar didn't speak a lick of common. The dwarf rules about not eating anything that you could talk to was clearly not in effect.

Vlargcar handled the cold weather well, but as they rode north, the weather began to take a turn for the worse, getting colder only at night first, and then the days, too. The trees went from having leaves to having few or none and their shapes were different. Vlargcar figured it had something to do with the location, but he had never actually contemplated that other lands would have other trees. He had always assumed that the trees in Beykla were the same as trees in other places in the world. The trip to the plateau was proof that that assumption was false. Amerix had told him fantastic tales of lands to the far north, where there was no summer. He said it snowed all the time and the land was covered in great sheets of ice; sometimes you thought you were walking on ice that covered land, when instead you were walking on a floating island of sorts. The old dwarf also told him of lands to the south where it seldom rained and there was no winter. There were no trees, just endless hills of sand and every day was as hot as a furnace. He had heard of a land that was covered in a shallow layer of water infested with sink bogs and large snakes and lizards that could swallow an orc easily. All of these fantastic lands captivated Vlargcar and as soon as he was away from these wicked humans, he was going to adventure off and Amerix would show him these wondrous places.

Vlargcar lifted his head and stared at the wizard riding one of the fourteen horses tethered to the rear of the wagon he was tied to. The man seemed out of place on the trail and was always stretching and shifting in his saddle. Next to him, he could see his and Amerix's equipment that was bundled up on the rear of one of the horses. The bright long sword, Songsinger, was nowhere to be seen, but the orc's eyes feasted on his two swords, dangling loosely from the dark brown bundle. He could almost feel the hilt of the blades in his hand.

Vlargcar closed his eyes, letting his head fall back against the hard wooden cart. Fantasies would get him nowhere. All he really needed to do was think. He was always the smartest orc in his tribe. He could remember things for long periods of time.

Vlargcar flexed his arms and pulled against the iron chains that held his manacles. He strained, pulling as hard as he could, but the chains did not move. Sighing in defeat, he closed his eyes and drifted back to his fantasies about far away distant lands.

Stieny peeked his head out from under thick folds of icy laundry that was being hauled into the coliseum on a large wooden cart. The heavy woolen sheets were frozen stiff and their weight made breathing difficult for the little halfling. Fortunately the night sky made him near invisible under the woolen mass. Stieny gazed at the passing street urchins that scrambled to gather their hats, bags and other means to beg money. Humans had no shame. Why would anyone resort to such demeaning notions as to sit and beg for handouts? Stieny never belittled himself. He always found ways to get by without doing foolish, underhanded deeds. Granted, hiding out in a frozen linen cart and sneaking into a coliseum wasn't exactly glamorous, but there was a certain level of danger that made the task adventurous and besides, he was thinking of skipping town. Gold crowns or not, it didn't seem worth the task. But when he considered the fact that the coliseum was filled with murderers, rapists, and hired thugs, he changed his mind. After all, these men were in this prison-like structure for a reason. They were ruthless and deadly. They were captured and forced into bondage within the walls. Stieny was sure they would escape if they could. But he was going to show how much more skill he had than they. Not only would he break into the building, something even the bravest villains didn't try, he was going to break out, something the hundreds of prisoners had no chance of doing. It was a way for Stieny to redeem himself in his own eyes, after getting caught by the elf, and the human, and by being duped by the dragon into believing the serpent could capture his soul. He would never fall for that one again.

The cart squeaked and creaked as it was hauled down the long stone ramp under the great coliseum. The driver dismounted and spoke to the guard standing outside a thick wooden double door. The guard was dressed in thick leather armor and held a long spear-like weapon with a wicked hook on one end. He and the driver exchanged words briefly before the guard turned and opened the thick wooden double doors. The driver returned to the cart and drove the team of horses through the stone gates.

As the wagon made its way into the expansive room, the warm inside air washed over the halfling. He scrunched his flat wide nose at the smell of sweat and mildew of the coliseum. There was little or no air circulation in the bare chamber and the floor was made of hard packed dirt and the walls were made of thick gray stone. There were many several sconces on the rough walls that held flickering lanterns between old tattered tapestries hanging from the ceiling by rusted iron hooks.

Stieny slowly slipped out the back of the cart and climbed under the bottom of it, sitting on the thick wooden axle. The driver exchanged a few words with a fat chubby man with a limp that approached when they entered the chamber. Stieny didn't pay much heed to the fat lame man as he spoke to the wagon master. After a brief exchange, the pair tugged at the heavy frozen blankets, pulling them from the cart and piling them up in a corner near the base of the wall to thaw. The halfling deftly made his way along the dark shadows of the expansive room, taking steps with each cough, or the sound of the frozen blankets made as they were tossed onto the ground. He reached the far end of the room and slowly crept to the wooden door that was partially left ajar by the chubby limping man. Stieny watched the two men until he quickly slipped from the shadows and into the door without the faintest sound.

Once through the small door, Stieny gazed down a long corridor to his right and left. There were many other hallways that extended in both directions off of the main one he was currently in. The ceiling of the passage was made of stone, but with thick wooden rafters embedded into the walls that seemed more part of decoration than of structural function.

Stieny made his way through the complex maze of passages and hallways, often hiding in a crate or barrel to escape notice from a random guard that seemed to be roaming the halls. The halfling was more than annoyed at the fool man. Who in their right mind wanders corridors in this time of the night anyway? Humans were so unpredictable.

After many hours of diligent searching and marking the walls with a small piece of burnt wood to keep from getting lost, Stieny had narrowed his search down to two locations. In one location a large human slept in a fancy room at the top of many flights of stairs. The room was anything but lavish, though there were no locks on the door, and no guards outside of it. The large man surely looked like a gladiator to him, but not necessarily a prisoner. The other room was at the deepest part of the compound, down a long dark corridor that was not guarded either, but was shrouded in well over twenty large iron locks. Of course Stieny was well acquainted with the intricate workings of almost all kinds of locks and these were no exception. Inside the room was a man who seemed a prisoner by every definition of the word. He wore dark gray prison rags and slept on a hard wooden cot hanging from the wall by a narrow chain that creaked under the large man's weight. He had no pillow and no blanket and had his thick muscled legs curled up tight into his chest as he slept. The bars of his cell were thicker than any of the bars that the halfling had seen since he entered the coliseum. Stieny decided that this was the so-called Jude. Crossing his short stubby fingers and taking a deep breath, he crept to the edge of the cell door. The halfling estimated the length of the prisoner's arms and quickly stepped the appropriate distance away from the bars, in case the man was faster than he. Stieny hadn't lived as long as he had by taking chances.

Swallowing again he whispered the name the elf had given him. "Jude."

The halfling hated making contact until he was sure the man was the one he was looking for. He had checked the entire room for some kind of roster, or something of that nature, but he found nothing save for some old bread and bit of cheese, which hit the spot. He thought as he patted his soft, plump little belly.

The big man did not stir so the little thief whispered a little louder. "Jude."

Nothing. Not even a mumble from the large man. Stieny would have thought him dead, if he hadn't seen the man's chest rise and fall with each breath he took. Stieny pulled at his collar and stretched his neck. "Jude," he said in a normal voice, yet the big man did not stir. Stieny rubbed his own head vigorously in frustration, ruffling his curly hair. The things he did for ten gold crowns. Stieny turned from the cell and looked around for something to throw. He picked up a fair-sized stone that had chipped from the wall. He scooted back into a dark corner, behind the desk and tossed the rock into the air, measuring its weight. The little thief then forcefully hefted the thing into the large man's cell. The rock hit the sleeping prisoner right in the forehead. The blow made a hollow thud sound and the man jumped from the cot, rubbing his head and cursing loudly.

Jude sat up from his new cot and stretched his sore muscles. They were somewhat fatigued, but he felt pretty good overall. He couldn't believe how much food he had eaten. The three heaping plates of roast and potatoes had filled him well, but left him wondering about the implications of this whole Mershul business. Jude doubted he was one of the cursed men, but he could not deny the similarities of what he experienced on the battlefield with the feelings Copel had described to him, let alone his incredible appetite. As Jude reevaluated his room, it was apparent his captors were more concerned with him escaping. The walls were now made of stone, instead of metal bars and the door was made of thick wood that was reinforced with thick iron bands. The hinges to the door were on the outside of the room, and the edges of the door were covered by a stone lip, preventing him from manipulating the locking bolt. There was small window about head high that was covered with thick iron bars, and a second window at the bottom of the door, where his captors slid food, and other items, to him. Jude wasn't sure if it was day or night since the room was always dark, faintly lit by a flickering lantern on the far wall that seemed to be running low on oil.

After eating the heaping helpings of food he lay back on the hard wooden cot and rubbed his cold arms. There was little heat down in this part of the complex so he tucked his legs up to his chest and quickly drifted off to sleep.

Jude awoke to a sharp stinging pain in the middle of his forehead as if he had been struck by a fist. "What the bloody hell?" Jude yelled as he stood in the dark rubbing a small knot that was growing by the second. He scanned the room and found a small rock that was lying in the middle of the floor of his cell. "Who's there?" he called out as he stooped to pick up the rock.

To his surprise a feint squeaky voice called out from the shadows. "It's me,...uh...Chester...lar..kin...son. Yea, good ole Chester Larkinson, your old pal," the squeaky voice said.

Jude rubbed his forehead and leaned against the bars of the upper window of his cell. "How ya been, Chester?" Jude called out.

Stieny couldn't believe his luck! Who would have thought of all the people in the world, this guy had a friend named Chester Larkinson. "Uh, I'm doing good."

Jude frowned. It sounded like the squeaky voice was hiding under the desk, but he didn't see how any man could manage to squeeze under it. "How is the wife doing, Chester?"

Shoot! A wife, Stieny thought to himself. He had to invent a person that already existed that had a wife. He didn't know what this Chester's wife's name was. "She's uh, good. Been doing the thing she does, ya know. All the time. Sometimes I say to myself, why don't you stop doing that thing honey, but boy, does she like doing it," Stieny said as he felt the beads of sweat beginning to trickle down the side of his chubby face. He had to figure out how to get this guy to say his own name.

Jude scanned the room for any other hidden silhouettes, but he found none. As far he could tell, he could see everywhere into the room, save for under the desk. What this squeaky voice wanted was beyond him, and Jude began to wonder if he wasn't imagining it. He had heard how people who are confined, or locked away from contact with other people, start to talk to inanimate objects. "Yep, she sure liked doing that. Say Chester, you mind fetching my boots from over there in the corner, behind the door? My feet are cold."

Stieny froze. How was he going to get the man to say his own name and keep from moving from behind the desk? "I'd love to help ya', pal. But you see I wouldn't want to get the guards mad at me or anything. You know how they like to call you names when they get mad at ya'."

Call you names? Jude rubbed his head gently. He had to be imagining the voice. He turned and sat back down on the hard wooden cot.

Stieny wiped the tickling drops of sweat from his brow when the man turned around. Perhaps this man had a nickname that was short for his real name. Maybe Jude was short for Judedacious, or some other crazy human name. "So pal, they still call you your nickname back home?"

Jude lay back onto the cool wooden cot, trying to ignore the voice. "No, they don't have a nickname for me. It is just Jude. Now go away, voice, and leave me to some sleep."

Ah, it is Jude. The halfling thought. Sometimes he surprised himself with his wit. Who could outsmart him? He was a genius. Now all he had to do was return to the elf with the information and he was ten gold crowns richer. Life was good.

Stieny waited for the large man to fall asleep and slipped from behind the desk and back into the alley. He carefully relocked the many large iron locks that sealed the large man's cell and made his way back the way he had came.

The cold winter air was the first greeting the little halfling received from a job well done as he slipped into the dark veil of the night shadows. There were not many people walking around on the street so he elected to not be seen.

The little thief had been in this town for almost a week, and he was yet to see another of his kind, meaning anywhere he went was well noted not the kind of notoriety a spindly thief such as himself prefers.

Stieny slipped into the common room of the Blue Dragon Inn. To his surprise the elf was sitting at the table, sipping a warm cup of cider. She was wearing a snug-fitting deep forest green cloth sleeping suit. It had a deep neckline that teased at the mountainous cleavage that could almost be seen. Her normally long braided blonde hair, hung loosely at her shoulders as she leaned on the thick wooden table. The little halfling darted over and scooted the chair across from her out from under the table and climbed into it. Alexis smoothed her angel thin hair from her face and pinned it behind her ears. She smiled and poured some cider from the flask into a small wooden cup and scooted it across the table to the halfling. Stieny smiled nervously and sipped the warm fluid. His nose and cheeks were red from the cold temperature outside and the warm cider hit the spot.

Alexis let him finish his sip and gave him a questioning look. "How goes your search, Master Gittledorf?"

Stieny nearly choked on the hot cider. How did she know his name? Had he told her? No he didn't think he had. Was she a mind reader? Some of the sorcerer elves were mind readers. He had read about it in the story books. "How do you know my name?" he asked.

Alexis smiled disarmingly. "Unimportant. What is important is how your search goes. Have you a good lead?"

Stieny reached into his pack and pulled out a small weathered parchment. He produced a pen and ink, and quickly scribed a small map of where he had been, how to get there, the times the watches change shifts, and the location of Jude's cell. He blew on the ink until it dried and pushed the thick parchment over to the elf.

Alexis picked up the paper and examined it. The halfling had extraordinary mapmaking skills, including a fine eye for detail. She wondered how many similar establishments the little thief had broken into or out of in his life time. In truth, the paper was more than she ever hoped for. Not only had she proof that the human was being held, but she had proof of exactly where in the compound he was. Alexis neatly rolled the parchment up and slid it into an empty ivory scroll tube that was in her backpack sitting at the foot of her chair. She then tossed the halfling a fat leather purse that was bulging with coin.

Stieny snatched up the coin as quickly as it landed on the table and hopped down from the chair. He got onto his tip toes to fetch his wooden cup of cider. After downing the warm drink, he sat the cup back on the table and tipped his hat. "Goodnight, elf. A pleasure doing business with ya'."

Alexis smiled as the halfling made his way to the door. "You gonna' count your pay, Master Gittledorf?"

The halfling shook his head from side to side. "Nah. You running with fancy pants tells me you are a person of your word. Besides, I can tell by the weight of the bag, you overpaid me by two silver."

Alexis's smiled faded into astonishment. She had indeed added two silver as a tip in case the halfling managed to complete the task on the first night. But he could not have seen her add the two coins, because she had filled the purse before she came down from her room. She watched the little thief as he slipped out of the common room door and into the cold dark street. The little halfling sure had some amazing talents. Too bad he wasted them on thieving.

Alexis gathered up her belongings and made her way back up to her room. She was concerned with Apollisian. Since the encounter with the thief in the afternoon, he had been praying without pause to his god. He said his link with Stephanis had somehow been severed.

He couldn't explain anymore than that, other than he could use his god's divine power. Alexis didn't understand such things, but she was concerned for him just the same. He didn't eat supper and hadn't so much as left his room. She brought a small loaf of bread and some cheese, in hopes he might pause from his prayer for a moment to eat.

She made her way up the stairs and gently knocked on his door. He didn't respond so she pushed her way in quietly. There on the bed, Apollisian lay in his armor, clutching his holy symbol fast asleep. She quietly placed her pack on the floor and set the food on the desk. She shuffled over and lifted his feet onto the bed, removing his thick leather boots. He was such a handsome man. His think blonde hair was unkempt from the long hours, but seemed to cascade away from his face in an amber waterfall of unexplainable beauty. He was such a fascinating creature to her. It was amazing that such a noble man lived, let alone the fact that he was human.

Alexis gently unfastened the leather straps to his greaves, hoisted the heavy metal plates from the bed and placed them onto the floor. She did the same with the other parts of his armor, including his breast pate. She marveled at how he could walk around in the thing, it must have weighed twenty pounds by itself.

Alexis stared at the sleeping paladin. She loved him. She was sure of it. She knew that she would love no other man for the rest of her life. Such was the way of an elf. When he died, she would spend the rest of her life suffering the gravity of that loss. But as she stared at the beautiful sleeping form of Apollisian, it seemed such a small price to pay.

Alexis neatly pulled the covers of the bed up and tucked them around Apollisian. She leaned forward and gently kissed his firm lips. His breath was hot and his touch seemed to ignite a fire inside of her, but she kept her composure. Alexis picked up the flickering lantern and walked to the door. "Goodnight, my paladin," she whispered, as she closed the door and went to her room for the night. Tomorrow was going to be a busy day.

Bodrell awoke to an aged man dressed in a white robe dabbing his forehead with a damp cloth. His vision was blurry and he felt a terrible fire in his chest. He knew he was in a surgeon's tent, yet he had difficulty thinking and comprehending. The tent was abuzz with mumbled speech and moans of pain. Bodrell closed his heavy eyelids, unable to keep them open for any long period of time. It hurt when he inhaled and he weakly lifted his arm to the bandage that covered his chest. A strong arm quickly seized his wrist, moving his hand back down to his side.

Bodrell offered no resistance and started to drift back into a deep sleep.

"Will he live, Doran?" a voice asked.

Bodrell recognized the name. Doran was the army's high cleric. He was powerful and wielded much divine power of his god. Bodrell couldn't seem to remember who the head cleric's god was. Why didn't they use their divine power to heal him? He was a general, and though he expected no special treatment, he knew the king gave the clerics orders on who to heal first, starting with the highest ranking officer.

Bodrell heard the aged cleric's raspy voice as it seem to fade farther and farther away. "I do not know. His wound is stabilized, but I am afraid infection has set in. He has a strong fever and I have administered all the medicines that I dare. Only time will tell."

Roars of battle and the sound of steel ringing against steel echoed down the large stone corridor. King Theobold had launched an attack just before dawn on the second day of the battle and had managed to push the dwarves back past the stairway. They stubbornly clung to a small defensive line just before the large cavern that extended deep into the mountain. Since breaching the door, the king's army had suffered more reasonable casualties, unlike the first day of the battle. He had lost over three men to every dwarf, but today, reports were about two to one.

This was still an unacceptable number, but as long the ratio continued, Theobold was certain for victory. He had many of his huge barrels of oil and kerosene brought in from the supply wagons and established light sources behind the front battle lines. The dwarves had made several unsuccessful attempts to extinguish the fires, and all but the battle line was retreating into the cavern. There were about two thousand dwarven soldiers holding the line and they were no longer rotating in and out. They were pushing against the humans with great ferocity.

Theobold rubbed the burning pain in his leg from the dwarven bolt that struck him in the first battle. He had the wound properly dressed, but the surgeons mentioned that somehow an infection had set into it. Almost all of the wounded men reported such infections. Theobold suspected poison initially, but no poison could be found on the dwarven weapons they seized. Theobold and his officers were perplexed by the event, but his mind was focused on the battle at hand. He absently fingered the large thumb-sized puncture in his leg armor. The dwarven crossbows were powerful indeed. He had been in a few battles since he took the crown, and never had any arrow or bolt pierced his thick enchanted mail before. The dwarves seemed to be great weapon smiths also. Theobold's sages had discovered that every weapon they had seized had the same mark in the metal. The strange rune looked something like the human letter "S" with a few smaller runes around the outside of it. The sages reported that they thought the symbol was a house symbol or some particular creator's symbol. The Beyklans knew little of the dwarven culture, and there were few weapon smiths in the Stoneheart clan. As a whole the people were artisans and craftsmen. The thought of the dead men, women, and children of Torrent Manor haunted his mind. Tell their families that the dwarves were artisans and craftsmen. As far as he was concerned, the dwarves as a people were nothing but wicked warmongers that needed to be cleansed from the mountains.

Theobold rose from his soft plush easy chair and limped to the brick mantle that had been constructed in his lavish tent. One of his attendants quickly shuffled to the wooden stand next to his chair and refilled his wine goblet. The king leaned on the hearth and stared at the warm fire that cracked and popped as it burned. He seemed to be cold as of late and didn't seem able to stay warm. His thigh ached and he often felt light-headed, but he managed to keep his mind focused on battle tactics. His men were making the final push to the large cavern. The task of creating enough light inside the expansive region was a new task that he and his sages needed to work out. Theobold's personal tactician had proposed leaving a main force at the entrance to the cavern while many smaller patrols scouted the perimeter. Some reports showed the grotto at three miles in diameter. Rooting out the dwarves would become more dangerous and more difficult the farther into the under mountain they ventured. Theobold was sure, he had all but crippled the clan with the number of the bearded folk he had slain, but crippling the dwarves was the least he wanted to do. Theobold wanted every last one on a pike, rotting in the sun. The loss of the Torrent was a grievous scar on his place in Beyklan history, and he would not be remembered as the king that weakened his proud nation. He would forever be remembered as the great avenger of those lost.

A sharp, shooting pain in his leg that danced from his thigh to his groin roused Theobold from his thoughts. He grabbed his thigh with both of his hands and cried out, falling on the floor. An attendant rushed into the room and helped the king back to his chair. "Shall I fetch the leech, Sire?" the attendant asked worriedly.

Theobold waved him away. "No. No, thank you. I will be fine. Back to your station," the king said as he gently massaged his throbbing scar. In moments, the pain that ran up from his wound to his groin fled as quickly as it came. Theobold shook his head from side to side as he stretched his leg and tested it by timidly placing weight on it. The wound seemed healed and his leg held him fine. He had no idea what had caused the pain, but he assumed it had something to do with the toxins on the dwarven blades. It must have been on the crossbow bolt heads as well. It was irrelevant at the moment. If he had been poisoned, Theobold had many days before he would be stricken down and the king was not about to let the bearded demons escape.

Theobold limped from his tent, though he felt no pain in his leg. It was more the lingering memory of it that caused his limp. Several of the king's attendants began fastening his long red silk cape to his shoulders, while others brought his sword. Theobold rolled his shoulder back, allowing the heavy crimson cape to fall over the back of his shoulder so his attendants could fasten his long sword to his side. While the men kneeled before him, fastening the leather scabbard to his hip, he accepted his brightly polished brass-colored helm with a sleek red plume that erupted from the top. The thin hairs of the plume blew in the cold mountain wind as Theobold slid the great helm atop his head. Strapping the wool chin strap under his clean shaven chin, Theobold began to march toward the damaged wooden doors of the entrance to the dwarven compound. The thick heavy wooden doors that lay in front of the entrance, pulled down by his men, were covered slightly with blown snow. The bright red blood that had turned the snow and ground into a crimson muddy bog the previous day had all but been erased by the snow that had fallen the night before.

Light clouds of black smoke drifted out from the entrance to the dwarven stronghold and up from the thin slits on the internal battlements. The strong smell of blood mixed with smoke and kerosene filled the dark passage. Shouts of men drowned out the few dwarven war cries and the shrill ringing of steel had lessened. As the king made his way into the entrance he was met by a large man wearing light leather armor. The man seemed as wide as he was tall and wore a thin leather cap that had wide straps hanging down from his chin. He wore a long red cape, similar to the one the king wore, but not nearly as ornate, and had two bright red stars pinned to each side of his collar. He carried a great two-handed sword that was fastened to his back with the thick worn pommel and hilt jutting out behind his head. His long messy brown hair was dirty and greasy and he wore a three day old beard. The large man bowed deeply as Theobold approached.

Theobold's polished brass-colored armor glinted in the sunlight that poured into the mouth of the corridor. His flowing red cape flickered in the mid-day breeze as the heavy metal greaves clicked on the stone floor of the corridor with each step. Several wounded soldiers that were sitting on the stone stairway awaiting the surgeons to examine them struggled to their feet when they recognized Theobold.

The king watched the large man kneel for a moment before commanding him to rise. "Report, Captain Westwood."

The captain stood from his bow and cleared his throat. He didn't care for Theobold as king, and had voiced his opinion to many people many different times. The most recent time resulted in thirty days of extra duty and the loss of his third star, but Westwood didn't seem to mind. But the one thing the captain hated more than the king was the dwarves. His wife's brother had been a soldier stationed in the Torrent Manor and had been found by this army in a horrid state. The crows had feasted on the corpses that were left from the battle, a grizzly scene that Captain Westwood kept in his mind every second since they started engaging the dwarves. "We have pushed the dwarves back into the cavern, sire. The thin resistance line they formed to delay us has been defeated. My men are finishing up with the dwarven stragglers who we managed to back into a small alcove just to the north of the passage."

Theobold grinned slightly. "What is stopping us from invading this cavern, Captain?"

Captain Westwood could not contain his elation. Though he despised the king, his men had defeated the first wave of dwarven defenders. "The only thing that we wait on, Sire, are your orders. My men are prepared to charge blindly into the darkness, cutting anything under five feet tall into small unrecognizable pieces."

Theobold smiled, looking past the captain at the group of soldiers walking back toward the entrance and another group that seemed to be cheering and hollering. "I hope the men are not all sporting with the cornered dwarves," Theobold said, turning his gaze back to the large captain.

Captain Westwood's smile faded from his face. "No, Sire, I have many refueling the lighting kegs, others gathering the dead and dying for the surgeons, while others still sharpen their blades and get a bite to eat. I would like to rotate in a fresh garrison, My King."

Theobold pondered the captain's request. "How many do you have left at the front, Captain?"

Captain Westwood frowned. "I have about four thousand men from six garrisons. I broke them down into three groups and assigned what would have been the fourth to other duties. The men are tired, sire. They have bled this cave red for you."

Theobold's smile faded. "Bled the cave red for me, Captain? Are you some fool? Most of these men fight the dwarves because of the Torrent and Central City. They care little for me or my politics. They care nothing for the northern nobles or the southern rebels. They care nothing for how my name will be recorded in Beyklan history and they care not, Captain, for relations with the Minok elves," Theobold said sternly. "These men bleed and die to vanquish the bearded foe that mercilessly attacked and killed their countrymen. I will not rob them of that glory. Take the men who have the slightest wounds and assign them to non-fighting duty. When you are finished, I shall replace that number with fresh men. The rest of those who have yet to see the inside of this Stephanis forsaken mountain will be set to building light pyres and scouting runs."

Captain Westwood stiffened. "Yes, Sire. It will be as you command."

Theobold looked past the captain and walked down the corridor toward the sounds of fading battle.

"Ignorance. It is a powerful tool when used by the ignorant. An ignorant man may kill his lover, a best friend, or even a brother all from the supposed belief that is not factual. The ignorance of the truth is as dangerous as a blind man trying to navigate a briar patch when he does not know he is blind.

All men are ignorant of many things. It is the wise that understand this and move slowly. The brash often bring doom about themselves and those around them.

Theobold was ignorant of nearly every aspect of his kingdom, the plotting of his advisor, the wisdom in his son, and the belief that the clan of artisan and craftsman dwarves would bow down and place their own thick wrists into shackles devised by his own arrogance. No, the Stonehearts were not an ignorant people. They knew full well the task they were setting upon and the levity of it."

-Lancalion Levendis Lampara

3

To Stand for Something

Tharxton ducked a wild slice from a human longsword and sent his massive hammer into the man's chest. He let out a winded cry as his ribs snapped and sliced his internal organs. The dying soldier gurgled in protest as he drowned on his own blood while yet another filled his place.

The dwarven king had led the final stand before the humans would have free run of Mountain Heart. His clerics had sealed the clan's precious works deep into a stone vault some weeks earlier. He had anticipated the upcoming retaliatory strike after the disaster at Torrent and Central City. Just as he had predicted, the proud Beyklans would not stand for such a humiliating defeat and fearless attack on their cities. It took some time for the young king to convince the elder council to prepare for fleeing their home of two thousand years. Clan Stoneheart had been in the Pyberian Mountains long before Beykla was established as a governing nation. It had originally been a colony of Aboe as the southern kingdom searched for resources. The forests of Beykla had been riddled with thousands of orc tribes and once the tribes discovered the pink-fleshed invaders, an age-long conflict had been created. It wasn't until about fifty years ago when the humans, at the aid of the elves, had managed to drive the orcs from the forests, though a few tribes remained.

Clan Stoneheart had persevered since the sea just north of Beykla had once been a human fertile farming settlement known as Balfour, before it sank into the ocean. Yet now Tharxton's clan seemed to be on the verge of becoming wiped out, just as the orc's had. The young red-bearded king had no doubt that in another hundred years the Minok elves would be next. The disgusting humans would not rest until they ruled all the lands in their entire kingdom. Then what? The damn fools would probably try to conquer the world next.

Tharxton deflected a sword thrust with his thick, armored forearm and brought his stone hammer up, catching the human attacker just under the chin. The man's teeth shattered in a crimson spray as he fell backwards, clutching his broken jaw and toothless maw. But before Tharxton could enjoy his handiwork, another damned human soldier filled the gap.

"Good shot, Sire," Targavian bellowed, as he drove his armored fist into a crippled soldier's unprotected face. The man fell dead from massive skull injuries and the old general ducked a wild long sword slash, backing further into the passage. "I think this ploy worked, though I must admit I would have enjoyed it more, had I a chance to survive."

Tharxton felt the pang of guilt. He knew he and the remaining dwarves that stood at the front line were doomed to die unless they could somehow defeat the entire remaining human army, a task his clan in full strength was unable to do, let alone four hundred of his brethren.

Tharxton proposed the idea of leading the soldiers into the dead end cavern to allow the women folk and children the chance to get to Stormghast, a great stone entrance into the under mountain. Deep into the under mountain was the only chance his people had of surviving. The humans would not be able to follow regardless of how many barrels of kerosene they brought with them. The things of the under mountain were ten times more deadly than anything the fool humans had ever encountered on the surface. Once you were in the endless caverns and passages of the deep earth, things changed. The simplest of sounds could ricochet off of stone walls for miles, alerting hundreds of would-be predators. Tharxton worried that his own people, despite their ability to see in the dark, would perish in the trials the under mountain would bring upon them. But what other chance did they have? The Beyklans had no intention of accepting any surrender or negotiating a treaty. If they had intended on keeping the treaty that was proposed to Tharxton, they would not have brought the entire western army.

The dwarven general ducked another slice that came unsettlingly close to his neck. His blistered face from the cold breath of the white dragon was glistening from sweat and his eyes were sunken and tired. He and his brethren had been fighting for almost seventeen straight hours. Tharxton was unsure if he could feel his hands and his body bore more minor cuts and scrapes than he had endured since his birth.

The human launched another slice. Tharxton let it slide past, pinning the blade against the stone wall and striking the man in his knee with his heavy hammer. The man let a shrill cry and dropped to the ground, clutching his leg that was bent backward behind him. Before Tharxton could deliver a killing blow, two men stopped fighting and carried the man from the battle. The dwarven king watched out of the corner of his eye with astonishment as they hauled the crippled man away. Tharxton chuckled to himself at how he managed to eliminate three men without killing a single one. The soldier must have been important, he surmised perhaps an officer or something.

The battle raged on for hours more, well into the afternoon. Tharxton had taken a serious hit on his shield shoulder and could no longer hold the protective device. General Targavian seemed as strong as ever, yet he was covered from head to foot with dripping crimson gore. He limped on his right leg and favored his left arm, but because of the dead human's blood that covered him, you could not determine how much of it was his own. Tharxton's numbers had been cut in half and they had backed further into the narrowing corridor. The dwarven king had selected this passage because it had been an old mining shaft and he knew it became narrower the farther you went into it. That made it an ideal passage in which to make a final stand due to the fact that as their numbers dwindled they could still create a line of defense.

Targavian ducked a wicked axe strike from a large man that had pushed his way to the front. The man seemed to be someone of importance by the look of the bright red star on the collar of the red tunic poking out from under his thick plate armor. The heavy axe hit the stone wall of the mine shaft, sending a shower of splintered rocks over the dwarven defenders. "Well, I'll be dipped in orc skins," Targavian bellowed in half-laughter.

Tharxton stole a quick glance over at the old general as he ducked and parried a large human that attacked with cunning precision. "What are you blabbering about, old general?" Tharxton asked between breaths.

Targavian smiled and giggled. "Look at the wall where this axe just hit."

Tharxton ducked a jab from a short sword and brought his ten pound stone hammer down on the man's foot. Blood splattered out on both sides of the soldier's boot as bone was crushed under the force of the blow. The man screamed and fell to the ground. Tharxton thought about finishing the man off, but instead he stole a glance at the wall. To his surprise, he saw the bright amber glimmer of a gold vein. "Well I'll be clean shaven and six foot tall," Tharxton said, as he chuckled. "All those years we searched for gold in this shaft and a damned human finds it by accident."

Targavian roared with laughter, much to his axe-wielding enemy's dismay. "I tell ya, Sire, 'tis the funniest thing I think I ever experienced. Plus, this fool has no idea what the hell I am laughing about. Look at him," Targavian said as he ducked a wild chop from the large man. "He thinks I am laughing at him and he goes from skilled fighter to wild bar room brawler."

Tharxton found himself and many of the other dwarven soldiers laughing. Laughing! Here they were, fighting an endless enemy with no escape possible and they were laughing. Tharxton figured his end was near. He had to be delirious. It was when he watched as two more soldiers carried off the man with the crushed foot that he was still thinking clearly. Tharxton stopped laughing immediately. "Targavian, I have an idea," he said with deadly seriousness.

The old general lost his smile as he cut down the large axe-wielding man. "This better be good, Sire. You gone and ruined a perfectly good laughing fit. I don't get those except for every twenty years or so."

Tharxton deflected a sword slash from his right. "Do not kill the humans unless it is an easy strike. Try to cripple them!" Tharxton yelled.

Targavian nearly lost his head from a sword slash as he looked at the young king in awe. "Do you not think we have a difficult enough challenge, Sire? Shall I close my eyes and stand on one foot as well?" Tharxton stepped into a strike, batting it down with the back of his gauntlet and crushing the soldier's knee. Just as before, two soldiers dropped out of battle and hauled the man from the front lines and took him away. "I have crippled three men today. Each time two other soldiers have taken the crippled man and hauled him from the battle. By crippling one, I defeated three."

Targavian pondered the idea for a moment. "I'll give it a try, Sire," the general said. "Pass the orders down the line, brothers. We may find a way out of this yet." The other dwarves began to cripple, rather than kill, the human invaders. It was slow going at first, with many dwarves falling under the wave of the endless human onslaught. But as each dwarven defender fell, the remaining warriors backed down the ever narrowing passage, keeping their line tight, and allowing them to kill many more humans than they would have been able to. The dwarves fought for the remaining part of the day, crippling as many of the soldiers as they could. It was near sundown, or at least as far as the dwarves could tell, when the Beyklans pulled back.

"Sire, I think they are pulling back," Targavian said, sidestepping a sword strike from a human soldier before retreating back down the corridor.

"Aye, I guess they realized we are more formidable than they expected," Tharxton said, turning his heavy hammer upside down as he leaned on the blood-mottled shaft.

Targavian frowned when the humans only backed about one hundred yards down the tall stone corridor. "Sire, I suggest we find as many shield bearers as we can find and bring them to the front."

Tharxton, who was resting his weary head on his black, frostbitten hands, looked at him. "Why do you suggest that, General?"

Targavian regarded the humans for a moment, then turned back to gaze at the end of the tunnel that was only a few hundred feet behind them. "We are down to about two hundred men, Sire. The passage has a much lower ceiling from here to the end. The humans would have to crouch in some places to battle us. How would you deal with such a force?"

Tharxton scratched his red-bearded chin. He imagined the humans firing bows or crossbows into his ranks. He and his brethren would have nowhere to retreat, and with the humans at the wider part of the passage, Tharxton could not lead a charge to assault their archers.

"Shield bearers!" Tharxton called out as he slowly shook his weary head. Targavian nodded in agreement and stepped back into the exhausted ranks of the last surviving dwarven defenders. The old general wondered exactly how long his brethren would last before they all were slain, or the humans ran out of arrows. He didn't expect to survive the campaign when the king suggested it, but given the amount of casualties that they forced the humans to suffer, he had begun to hope that he would live to see victory. It was crushing reality of his rapidly approaching death that seemed to weigh a little heavier on him than before. Regardless of when he died, the humans would remember the day they battled Clan Stoneheart. He would see to that personally, regardless of that cost.

"Sire, the dwarves' front line has withdrawn into a wide cavern that narrows the farther our troops advance. As we kill them, they simply withdraw deeper, maintaining their front line integrity," the captain reported.

Theobold limped to the mouth of the large cavern and stared into the expansive blackness that seemed to devour the light from his oil pyres. The pain in his leg had intensified and he often felt dizzy and cold. "What of the dwarven population? It is obvious these remaining soldiers were making a stand to offer the women and children a chance to flee."

The captain ground his teeth. He had frequently voiced his displeasure for the king and his family, but it was times like this that he fought the urge to draw his sword and slay the wicked ruler where he stood. But he was a soldier before all else. "Scouts have been dispatched, Sire. We have located several dozen passages from this cavern, but they have not been able to determine if the helpless women and children fled down them or not," the captain said, hoping to get through to him.

The captain's concerns had no effect on Theobold. "I want a report as soon as the scouts determine anything. Until then, set up kerosene pyres at the mouth of each passage from this cavern. Dispatch four-man teams down each corridor until we locate the rest of the bearded vermin. As for the dwarven soldiers that are holed up in the passage, withdraw the troops and fetch the archers. If the dwarves won't charge into our front lines, then we will launch arrows into their cowardly bodies, until either we run out of arrows, or they are all dead."

Captain Westwood nodded. "Sire, what if we run out of arrows before they are slain?"

Theobold pondered the question for a moment.

"After the archers exhaust their supply of arrows, count the remaining dwarves. Triple their numbers and post a guard. The little bastards will either charge our men, or we will guard them until they die of hunger and thirst. Either way, I do not want a single bearded demon to walk from that cavern," Theobold said wickedly.

The captain nodded and bowed. "As you command, Sire."

Theobold limped back up the passage to the entrance of the dwarven compound where his tent was. His fever was getting worse and he needed some herbs from the leeches. He had hoped the clerics would soon discover why they could not converse with their gods, but it didn't bother the king much. He figured if his clerics couldn't use their divine might, neither could the dwarves. Good with the bad, he surmised. Good with the bad.

Arrows panged and clanged against the thick iron shields of the dwarves. The well armored shield bearers held their large tower shields with the bottom of them flat against the stone floor of the cavern. Arrows occasionally dug into a dwarven soldier and his cry of death was the only thing that echoed in the eerily quiet corridor. Tharxton crouched directly behind one of the shield bearers next to Targavian. Tharxton did well to suppress his fear. When he felt afraid, he would look over at the iron-faced general, who looked angry enough to charge into the human archers at any moment. Tharxton fed off of his strength and courage. "How many have fallen since the barrage?" the young king asked.

Targavian shrugged. He had started counting the moans of death, but stopped at fifty. He decided that he might lose his nerve if he kept counting. Targavian had been a general for some time, and had participated in many battles, but never had he faced such hopeless odds. He gazed in wonderment at the ferocious bravery his young king possessed. Had he been the same age as Tharxton, Targavian knew he would not have the courage to face such a foe. In truth, had it not been for his young king, he would have ended his torment by running into the wicked barrage of arrows. A quick death was always preferred to whatever horrors the humans surely had in store for them. "I stopped counting at fifty, Sire, but by the look of things it is well above that number," the general said, glancing at his dead and dying brethren. "Too many of us and not enough of them is a better answer, Sire."

Tharxton nodded. "I agree, General. But until we weather this storm of wood and steel, we can do nothing but speed along our defeat. I pray that the humans are not able to craft new arrows too quickly, since there are few trees on the mountain, and there are surely none in Mountain Heart."

Targavian nodded, and then winced. He slowly reached over and pulled a bloody arrow shaft from his right shoulder. He tossed it over the tower shield. "That stung," the general said with a grunt.

Tharxton leaned as close to the general as he dared. "Are you okay, General?" he asked worriedly.

Targavian nodded as he held his hand over the wound

that began to leak bright red blood over his heavy armored shoulder plate. "Aye, I'm okay, Sire. But too many more of those, and I'll be bitchin' to Leska personally about letting these fools invade our home."

Tharxton felt a wave of relief. If Targavian died, he wasn't sure how he would keep himself together, let alone his men.

"Your wound is severely infected," replied the leech that was wearing a white robe stained with dried blood. "If it is not treated soon, Sire, I am afraid it could become life threatening. We already have had well over fifty men die from related infections. I think there is some kind of chemical in the ore that the dwarves used to forge their weapons."

Theobold groaned. He didn't have time to get sick. He was on the cusp of a great victory over his bearded enemies. "Why didn't anyone from the Torrent Manor get this illness?"

The leech rubbed his clean shaven chin and pondered for a moment. "I suppose the relative few survivors from the Torrent had not been wounded by the dwarves, but had perished in the fire. There was a paladin that survived a battle from the renegade general Amerix, but we know how those knights manage to avoid such afflictions. It is said, the truly powerful paladins can even cure disease in others."

Theobold batted the leech's hand away from his leg and sat up from the cot. "I do not need a lecture on the whole damned order, leech," Theobold said angrily. He remembered his meeting with that paladin. Apollisian was his name, if he remembered correctly. He hated having to show any respect to the damnable church. Had the northern nobles not had such influence, he would disband the self righteous order once and for all. As it was, he had to dispose of a valued duke in Central City, because he wouldn't abide by the paladin's wishes before the dwarves attacked. The event had worked out to his benefit, though, because it allied the north against the dwarves. That was something he had been seeking for over ten years. Theobold was king, but he knew of many kings in history that had been removed from the crown by going against his people's wishes.

The leech bowed slightly and tried to hide his disgust for his king. He had not realized how wicked his king was until this campaign. It used to be customary to offer captured enemies medical care, until the war was over, but Theobold had executed all prisoners that he happened upon. "Sire, I must warn you..."

"Stow it, leech!" Theobold shouted angrily, rising from the wooden canvas cot he had been lying on. He limped over to the bench that contained his clothing and armor. "I'll not pack up and leave a battle with my army so close to victory!"

"As you wish, Sire," the leech responded disarmingly with another slight bow.

Theobold quickly slipped into his heavy plate armor and stepped from the warm surgeon's tent. The frigid winter mountain air quickly made him shiver as he plodded up the small slope of the summit toward the entrance to the dwarven compound. It had snowed again the night before and many of the wounded soldiers that were not able to fight were spending their time digging out supply carts and entrances to tents. He had spent most of the night in the leech's tent, getting healing herbs and other treatments, but they seemed to only ease his suffering, rather than cure any of his aliments. He was concerned about his infection, but he hoped to finish the dwarves off in the next few days. His first general, Bodrell, seemed to be making a recovery from his infected wound, which gave Theobold a belief that the toxins in his leg merely needed to run their course.

Theobold slowly made his way into the entrance of the dwarven compound, finding himself unconsciously admiring the great craftsmanship it took to create the intricate carvings and designs that were sculpted into the solid stone. His head felt heavy and his eyes burned from the fever that raged through his body, but he forced each foot in front of the other. Theobold marveled at how his condition worsened when he left the tent and walked outside, but he recalled a few times in the past years when he was sick from the flu. If he went outside it seemed his fever always kicked up a few notches and his nose seemed to run more than usual. But now the only difference was that his nose wasn't runny at all. He felt just as lightheaded and dizzy as a normal cold leaves you, save that he wasn't sick.

Theobold stepped carefully, trying to keep one foot in front of the other without showing any signs of dizziness. He knew that if the battle turned sour, the morale of his men would be crushed if they thought him sick, or incapacitated in any way. The young king smiled as he walked alone down the wide stone corridor of the front lines of the battle. His father always surrounded himself with servants and advisors. Had he surrounded himself with the like, his fever would have been readily apparent to those people and try as he might, the word would leak out. Theobold always recalled how enraged his father would become when a closely guarded rumor or family affair managed to leak out in the populace and he would be forced to address the issue publicly. Theobold avoided all of these problems by keeping only one advisor and next to no personal servants. Now he could make his way through the ranks of his men without them suspecting he was battling the sickening effects of the wicked dwarven metals.

As he approached the mass of soldiers that were at the front lines, just inside of the massive cavern, Theobold saw hundreds of his men that were wounded and only a few that were dead. Many of the soldiers bore a single, but crippling, wound. Some of the men had toes or fingers missing, some had deep gashes in the back of their legs and many others had a single wound on their knee. Very few had any injuries on their upper bodies, suggesting the dwarves were injuring them intentionally. Why the bearded demons were not slaying the soldiers outright was confusing to the fever-stricken king.

Theobold gently rubbed his aching forehead and ran his hand through his sweaty brown hair. He could hear intense fighting deep in the passage and echoes of commands given by his sergeants. Theobold leaned against the cavern wall and rested his hot forehead against the cool clammy rock.

The cold stone felt good against his skin, but he allowed himself one brief rest and then quickly pushed past the injured and toward the looming figure of Captain Westwood.

The large captain was standing with his thick muscled arms crossed under his chest, surveying the crude map his scouts had made of the tunnel. The thick parchment was pulled taut across a thin flimsy board resting on a wooden spool that the army had hauled rope on. Now the empty spool was the only support for his small command outpost at the base of the expansive carven. The captain was careful not to smudge the charcoal sketches of the cavern, though he doubted the accuracy of the map. His scouts were not trained or even practiced in mapping underground terrain and he could not be sure of the marked slopes or exact directions they posted. He was, however, sure they got the initial dimensions correct, as they often worked in circular patterns when in the forest. Captain Westwood's eyes took the sight of the map in, occasionally leaning forward to inspect some squall that had been written carelessly when the light of the lamp that rested on the edge of the table would flicker or fade. It was his men that shot up to attention that made him pull his weary brown eyes from the poorly made map and turn around. To the captain's surprise he met the pale, hallow face of King Theobold.

"Sire!" Captain Westwood called out. "What brings you to the front lines?"

Theobold pressed his thick tongue to the front of his mouth and stammered before speaking. "Report."

Captain Westwood cleared his throat and slowly straightened his posture. The damned king looked as if he was drunk. His men were dying while his despicable ruler drank himself into a wobbling stupor. "The dwarves realized that we were going to wait them out after we exhausted our arrow supply, so they mounted a charge. We managed to cut their numbers down considerably, but they still were able to make their way to one of the north passages. The passage travels upwards so we do not think it is an escape route, but merely an attempt to get our men to chase, then they will spring some trap."

Theobold slammed his fist down on the make-shift table, toppling the thin wooden plank. The weak lantern fell and crashed onto the hard stone floor. The lantern was protected by a thick set of iron bars that surrounded it to keep it from breaking from such falls, but the jolt extinguished the flame. The nearby pyres that were lit gave off a weak light source, disguising the obvious contempt that Captain Westwood held for his foolish liege. "Who blasted cares if we spring a trap? It can't kill all of our men! The longer we allow these foolish rogue dwarves to run amok in these caverns, the more of a chance we allow them to escape," the king shouted angrily.

Captain Westwood kneeled down and slowly picked up the lantern from the hard rocky floor of the cavern and handed it to one of his men to re-light. The soldier nodded and quickly ran to the pyre a good distance away. The young captain strained to keep his comments to himself. Speaking out against the king when the king was not around was a league of a difference when speaking out against him to his face during a war. This could likely result in his death. "Sire, I have dispatched a large patrol to root them out, I just haven't ordered them up the tight narrow passage."

Theobold roughly grabbed the large captain by the top of his thick metal breast plate and pulled him closer. "I want that patrol up that passage and I want those remaining dwarves' heads on a pike by the end of the night tomorrow or I will find a suitable head among our own to place there. Do I make myself clear, Captain?"

Captain Westwood nodded slowly fighting with all his contempt to not reach out and snap the damnable man's throat.

Theobold released the captain's breast plate and staggered past into the heart of the cavern toward a second gathering of troops, unbeknownst to the murderous glare that was set upon him by the large Captain Westwood.

The thick heavy arrows shifted and became light thin

ones as the barrage continued long into the night. Though there was no sun to rise and set here in the under mountain, the dwarves long ago had learned how to discern the passing of the day without its aid. Tharxton had taken a smaller shaft just above his right knee. The smaller, lighter arrow quickly shattered when it struck his finely crafted mail, but the arrow still delivered a hard bone-crunching pop when it hit, and the dwarf king was sure he would have a thick bruise from it. When the arrows became smaller and less frequent, he shifted over to Targavian. The old general had suggested taking turns holding the great shields and rotating the men into some kind of a sleeping schedule.

Though the dwarves would only get two hours of rest, they seemed refreshed and their morale seemed higher. Now Tharxton and Targavian were standing on the shield watch and no arrows had rained down in almost an hour.

"I say when they start shooting again we charge them and fight our way out of this cursed passage. It was a good idea to come here when they were trying to cut us down, but now they haven't sent any soldiers in at us in almost a day and a half and I don't like standing down here for their target practice," the old general said as he held the heavy shield upright facing toward the mouth of the long corridor.

Tharxton nodded, holding his shield upright as well. "I agree. It seems to me that they are running out of arrows since they are no longer using the thicker, larger ones."

"Aye, especially since they have been sparing in their volleys. I'll rouse the men and we will be ready to make the charge, but what of the wounded who can't make the run?" Targavian asked.

Tharxton took his eyes from the old general and stared sadly at the hard cold stone floor but did not answer.

Targavian patted Tharxton on the shoulder as he handed the heavy tower shield to another dwarf to carry. "The right decision is always the hardest, Sire," the old general said as he got up and started back into the darkness.

Tharxton stopped him by grabbing his shoulder. The old general turned and faced his young king with admiration and sadness knowing the weight of the decision that rested on his shoulders. "Targavian...," Tharxton started. The old general paused to hear what his king had to say.

"Targavian, ask for ten volunteers to stay back with the wounded. Be sure to tell them that we are not coming back to get them if we make it out. Tell them that we are going to make our stand at the Stormghast."

"It shall be done, Sire," Targavian said as he disappeared into the darkness to rouse the remaining soldiers.

As he spread the word of the battle plans to the remaining one hundred and twenty able fighters, he had an abundance of volunteers to stay back with the wounded and a few offered to wrestle for the right to stay behind. Targavian smiled at the bravery of his brethren. If the humans had one hundred soldiers with the valor that these dwarves around him had, he and his clan would have been defeated long ago.

After picking ten dwarves at random to stay behind, he advised them to move the wounded to the very rear of the cavern and to spread the dead out behind them now, making sure they looked as if they died where they fell. Many dwarves were angry at leaving their dead, but

Targavian explained that by leaving the dead here, it left less of an indication that the wounded had fled to the rear of the passage. The soldiers quickly complied and soon the dead were strewn about and the wounded were taken to the deepest part of the cavern. Tharxton ordered all water reserves to be given to the ten remaining dwarves, since no one knew how long they were going to be at the end of the tunnel.

It was mere minutes later that the arrows started again. Tharxton gave the command and the remaining dwarven soldiers rushed head-long down the passage with the shield bearers in the front. Hundreds of arrows clanged and splintered against the large heavy shields, and an occasional dwarf fell to the smaller thin shafts when it managed to pierce the chain armor between the thick dwarven plates.

As the charging bearded marauders neared the edge of the corridor, the human archers had all but fled and a flood of soldiers were filling the gaps of the corridor, trying to create a semblance of a battle line. But the small tightly formed dwarven battle group hit the men on the far side of the corridor like a bull into a crowd.

Tharxton ducked and slashed, killing his enemies now trying to quickly force his way through the ranks. Targavian roared as he swung his twenty pound war hammer in great sweeping motions, clearing out the human invaders in droves. The mighty dwarven maul splattered heads and bodies, covering the old general and the dwarves next to him with bright coppery smelling gore. The humans shouted commands that Tharxton couldn't understand, but their voices seemed frantic and scared so the dwarven king fought on, cutting down soldier after soldier.

A deep dwarven voice echoed from Tharxton's left. "I am through! I am through!"

Tharxton's heart raced. He and his men might actually manage to get through these lines and make a stand at Stormghast after all. Though that was the plan, he seriously doubted it might work. "To the Tallengard!" Tharxton screamed as he managed to break free into the open ranks of the corridor. Half of him wanted to turn and cut more of the human invaders down, and the other half wanted to run for Tallengard, but he had to hold open an alley for the other dwarves.

Soon all of the dwarven soldiers were sprinting to the narrow northern corridor leading to Tallengard. The dwarves could get to Stormghast by way of Tallengard, the mining guild's headquarters, with a small exit shaft. Like many of the Mountain Heart passages, Tallengard's entranceway and small rear escape passage was rigged to collapse. Rigging passages to collapse was the dwarves' oldest method of defense. Invaders could seldom ever burrow as fast as the dwarves could flee, so when the battle wasn't going their way, clans would often cave in their own tunnels, and they would usually do so with their enemies in them.

To Tharxton's surprise, the humans didn't give immediate chase, save for a few stragglers that quickly turned back when they realized the rest of their company waited back at the passage they had just came from.

The young king led the dwarven charge through the

large cavern, their heavy armored footfalls jingled and echoed off of the smooth rocky walls. The remaining dwarves ducked around giant stalagmites that rose hundreds of feet into the air from the floor. The colossal rocky pillars seemed like a bulbous ringed tower that had merged with the stalactite hanging above, creating a great tower that rose into the darkness of the cavern's canopy. As the remaining dwarves scampered up the narrow stone steps to Tallengard, Tharxton stood by at the stair's base, gazing into the endless darkness. His brown eyes darted back and forth, hoping against hope that the humans would not pursue them right away, and give his tired, wounded, and hungry men a small reprieve from the hellish battle they had partaken in. Tharxton's soldiers had not eaten and slept little in the last three days, all the while fighting for their lives and watching their brothers and clansman get cut down one by one.

After the last dwarf rushed up the narrow stone stairs, Tharxton gave the dark cavern a final glance before heading up. When the dwarf king reached the top he was stricken with grief by what he saw. Sitting on the hard smooth stone floor of the large meeting room of Tallengard, sat the remnants of his wounded, exhausted army. His soldiers seemed to collapse when they got a chance for rest, and many had blood trickling out from dents and puncture wounds in their hard thick plate mail.

His clansmen were mentally and physically exhausted. Tharxton could hardly blame them. He wanted to give up as much as they did. His hands that were still recovering from the dragon's breath were often numb and tingling, he had hundreds of small wounds from the human's swords that had pierced his thick plate armor, and he had not slept in days. The young king hobbled to the thick door secured by a sturdy wooden timber. He patted the dwarves on the shoulder as they finished, clearing his throat as he addressed the chamber. "My brethren, I address you now as your comrade in battle, not your king. We have stood against an insurmountable foe, and made them pay. We backed ourselves into a suicide maneuver to allow our women and children a chance to retreat into the under mountain while our brothers fell dead around us. We are tired, injured, and weak. I know we have little left to fight the bastard humans with. I understand if no one volunteers for the next assignment, but I will ask for them anyway. I need ten brave brothers to remain here in Tallengard while the rest of us make a final stand against the humans at Stormghast."

The dwarves all muttered amongst themselves in confusion. Some shook their heads in disbelief while others glanced around to see who was going to volunteer to stay behind and lose the glory of slaying more of the pink-skinned invaders.

Targavian forced his old weary bones into motion and struggled to his feet. He leaned on his massive hammer for support as he spoke. "My King, why must any men stay back here? Why not all of us stand side by side and send as many of the bastard human scum to the depths of the Abyss?" the old general asked. Many more dwarves mumbled amongst themselves in agreement.

Tharxton smiled and raised his weak arms out in front of him and motioned for the room to quiet. "My brothers, I know we all want to stand at Stormghast, but I want to take more than just our fair share of enemies. I want to take them all."

Targavian twisted his neck with his meaty hand, popping it a few times before he rested both hands on the heavy hammer. "My King, how will we kill them all?"

Tharxton smiled as he walked to the south wall of the mining chamber. He removed a large golden key from a leather strap tied around his neck and held it aloft in the dark room for all to see. "This is the key of Stormghast," he said as he inserted it into a small key hole in the stone wall. As the golden key was pushed into the dark stone, hundreds of runes started to glow, illuminating the room. The runes were many, and took up most of the southern wall.

"What sorcery is this?" Targavian asked under his breath.

"Not sorcery, but divinations," Tharxton replied. "We

have little time before the humans regroup and send patrols looking for us. The mass of us must get to Stormghast. The other ten must remain here in this chamber." Tharxton pulled a small hourglass from a wooden chest and set it on the stone ledge next to the golden key. "When the hourglass runs out of sand, this key is to be turned. It will collapse the beltway cavern."

All of the dwarves in the chamber gasped out loud. Targavian grumbled and ran his blood-stained hands through his beard nervously. "I have never heard of any key that would collapse the beltway cavern," the old general proclaimed.

Tharxton ignored the old dwarf. "I have no time to explain how it works, but our old king passed the key down to me when I was made king, and he said it was given to him by the king before him, and so on and so forth. There are three clan members in every generation that are keepers of it. One holds the key, two hold the word. The word has something to do with Leska. In case the key is lost, the two keepers of the word can activate it without the key. The Nameless was one of the word keepers, but he is no more. We have no way of telling whether or not the magic will work, but we are all doomed anyway. Let's take as many of the damned humans with us. Do we want them following our loved ones into the under mountain?"

All of the dwarves jumped to their feet with renewed vigor, raising their weapons in defiance. The old general smiled a wry smile and hefted his weighty hammer of his right shoulder. "The king needs ten volunteers. I suggest...," before Targavian could finish, ten dwarves raised their weapons high in the air. "It is settled then. Your highness, your troops are ready. Lead us to victory."

"What is honor? It is that in which no man can take from you and that in which no man can give you. Some say, it can only be achieved as a gift to yourself.

But that still does not explain what honor is. Some believe they have honor, when others believe that they do not. In my travels I have heard the saying; 'there is no honor among thieves.' Is this true? I guess it all comes down to what a man determines is honor.

It would seem to me, that honor is a codified body of core beliefs that are inflexible and follow some unwritten edict that a man will, and often must, follow. What is honor for some, is surely not honor for others, but if both have the same codified beliefs, then they would view each other as honorable.

There could be honor amongst thieves, but I doubt many would recognize this truth, save for other thieves.

One day I had to make a decision based off of honor. In one hand I could damn all of Terrigan for my personal benefit, and the other, I could damn a single soul for the benefit of hundreds of millions. Though in truth, either choice was an honorable one."

-Lancalion Levendis Lampara

4

Fevered Arrogance

"Sire, scouts report that the dwarves are massing at a large iron gate at the east end of the cavern. The iron gate is over thirty feet tall and we suspect that it is where the dwarves all fled to after we punched through their defenses," the heavily armored Captain Westwood said as firelight from the many lighting pyres danced across his polished plate armor.

Theobold stared off into the darkness of the cavern in a feverish stupor. Sweat no longer beaded on his forehead and his pupils were dilated from the fever. "Send the remaining ground forces against them and crush the bearded fools!" the king commanded.

Captain Westwood coughed in surprise. "Sire, there are less than two hundred of them, why send the entire remaining ground forces against them? If it is some kind of a trap, we will have no units to halt a flanking maneuver."

The king growled and kicked over the makeshift table that had been set up to display maps of the cavern. "Do as I command, knave!"

Captain Westwood became more suspicious of the king's uncharacteristic tirades. "Sire, I forgot to mention, the dwarven king is at the front of the chamber calling for you, saying you are a coward and that you do not have the honor to meet him with two hundred of your own troops, that his finest men could defeat you any day," the captain lied, hoping to lure to the king into the fray.

Theobold went into a furious tantrum, kicking the already downed table and swatting lanterns as he cursed loudly. "No honor! I'll show that little bearded bastard honor! I'll show him the honor that was shown to the men and women of the Torrent Manor!" the king said as he stormed off into the darkness of the cavern followed by a troop of officers that were trying to reason with him.

Captain Westwood smiled triumphantly and made his way back down the corridor toward the entrance to the cavern. He hoped to stop by and see General Bodrell. The general was surely doing better, and this battle was obviously soon to be over. Perhaps he would get lucky and the fool king would charge in against the dwarves. Regardless, some fresh mountain air would surely do him good.

Tharxton led the remaining soldiers to the base of the thick iron gates of Stormghast. The gates had been constructed thousands of years earlier. They showed scars of battle from invasions past, but never before this day, had the door stood behind the dwarven clan as they fought to their last. Now, the remaining warriors of Clan Stoneheart stood beaten, bloodied, and bruised before the ancient portal, but, as those who fought before them, the sturdy clansmen knew not defeat until they had exhaled their last breath. Now they gripped their weapons with bloodstained gauntlets and their weary eyes squinted into the darkness at the approaching onslaught of human invaders. The young king could see thousands marching toward them. Many bore great pyres atop of wooden stanchions to light up the cavern and he knew his men would have no chance getting close enough to one of the pyres to extinguish it. The humans would no doubt expect the dwarves to try and fight in the dark, where they could see and the humans could not. The approaching swarm was endless as their numbers seemed to span each edge of the great cavern. The young king doubted his final stand would last long.

Tharxton swallowed hard and wiped his sweaty brow with his cold gauntleted hand. His reign as king had been a short and ineffective one. He did not secure peace with the Beyklans as he had hoped to. He allowed a rogue general to take leadership of his brethren, and he permitted an army of humans to not only invade, but defeat Clan Stoneheart in their very home. For the young king, death could not come soon enough.

Targavian, on the other hand, considered his young king a great success in the face of inedible defeat. The old general knew it was nearly impossible to defeat an army the size of the one the humans sent against them. The fact that they were making their final stand where they were and that the women and children of Clan Stoneheart had managed to safely pass Stormghast was victory in itself. Now he stood ready to deal out more death to his pink-skinned enemies. The old general had slain hundreds of humans in the past few days with little sleep and no food. The prospect of dying and finally getting some rest didn't seem quite so bad, though he surely would rather enjoy rest that he could wake from.

The dwarven general glanced down at the heavy iron shield that hung from his left arm. The battered metal plate was dented and warped from the battles of the last few days. Glancing down at his heavy war hammer that rested against his side, the old general tossed the shield to the cavern floor. The iron plate clanged and bounced off of the hard stone.

"General, are you all right?" one dwarf called out.

Targavian chuckled and flexed his weary hand. "Of course I am. It is just that I don't plan on doing a lot of defending, only a lot of killing."

The gruff response seemed to excite the fervor among the remaining defenders and many dropped their shields and began to mumble light-heartedly amongst themselves.

Targavian glanced over at Tharxton who seemed to be reflecting on his failures rather than raising the morale of his men. Being the seasoned veteran he was, the old general took the opportunity to spark a little life in the battered troop. "Come on, my brethren. You all sound like a bunch of belly-aching gnomes!"

The dwarves all grumbled protests at the insulting comparison. The remaining dwarves were the most skilled battle-hardened dwarves in Clan Stoneheart. Alone and rested they could have surely defeat a thousand men.

Targavian let the insult sink in for a few moments. "We all here have fought in battles we figured to lose, yet we did not, or we wouldn't be here. The reason we did not lose was because we didn't give up. I don't care if we die today, I surely plan on it, but I'll be damned if I open my arms and welcome their swords into my belly!" the general shouted. "And if one of the cursed pink-skinned babies gets lucky enough to stick his sword there, I'll be sure to split his soft skull for his trouble before I die."

The other dwarves began to turn their defeated grumbles into shouts of defiance. They began to whoop and holler, pounding their bloodied and dented weapons against the stone floor of the cavern, taunting and daring the humans who out-numbered them more than three to one to come on and taste defeat.

Tharxton raised his dark brown eyes from the depths of his own despair and churned the fiery pits of vengeance in his own heart. He, too, had not killed enough of the enemy today.

Theobold staggered through the dark cavern in front of his entire remaining ground forces. His bright polished brass-colored plate armor glinted and shone in the flickering firelight of the many pyres that were being carried with the army as they rapidly advanced through the meandering cavern. The army of nearly four thousand men often had to break formation to navigate around a giant stalactite that had merged with a stalagmite creating a colossal stone pillar that erupted into the dark ceiling of the great cave.

Theobold was not concerned with a flanking maneuver. He still had about three thousand soldiers outside of the compound. Though some of them were hurt and injured, they were still trained in the art of war and could be roused if need be. What confounded the king was the fact that as he marched deeper into the cavern, he seemed to become weaker. His leg was almost numb and the tingling in his toes had turned into a faint tickle. He felt light-headed like he had been drinking for some time, but at least he had stopped sweating. Theobold figured that meant his fever had managed to break and he would soon be recovering from the poisonous dwarven ore. He surely felt worse today than he had since getting infected, but he was not about to let a little nausea prevent him from witnessing the greatest military victory of his tenure as king.

As the army neared the far western wall where the scouts reported seeing the dwarves massing, they could hear pounding of metal on stone and shouts of what sounded like anger. As they approached and the pyres lit up the cavern around them, they could see almost two hundred dwarves standing with their backs against the giant iron doors. They were all bloodied and wounded, some worse than others, and many had tossed their shields down to the ground. Theobold thought about calling for an interpreter to come forth and offering the dwarves a chance to surrender, but he thought against it. Killing them all seemed much more appropriate. "Kill them," Theobold said weakly as he drew his long sword from its scabbard.

The front soldiers let out a cry of battle and charged into the dwarves with weapons high.

Tharxton nervously gripped the pommel of his hammer with both hands, flexing his fingers in anticipation of the upcoming battle. The humans seemed to be a sea of never ending bodies that were swarming down on him and his brethren. His eyes shifted through the darkness as he tried to identify the leaders. He figured he would target the human's military officers and kill them, hoping to disorientate their commands. He worried little that his death might lower the morale of his brethren. They all figured they were going to die anyway, and there were little tactics involved. They were simple going to keep their backs to the wall and fight until they were overwhelmed.

The young red haired dwarf king scanned the front lines of the humans as they stood some fifty feet away. The soldiers were poorly armored, and looked nervous and tired. It was obvious they had never made war in an underground cavern and it seemed as if they expected Tharxton's small resistance to triple in size and crush them. The young king began to worry that they knew of the trap, but quickly decided that if they knew, they would not have came into the cavern. Tharxton imagined that they expected a trap, he surely would have, the fool humans just simply didn't have a clue about the death they were going to suffer.

Tharxton glanced down the row at his brethren. They were all gripping their weapons tightly and some were growling. They were clearly anticipating killing as many as they could for defiling their sacred homeland.

The humans made some kind of command and they charged in. Tharxton held his hammer back and shook it vigorously and just as the first soldier came within his reach, he ducked a sword strike and let the hammer fly. The heavy weapon hit the man in the chest, crushing all of his ribs and knocking him back through the air. But just as the first man died, two more took his place.

Targavian roared as the humans charged, and then he charged, meeting his surprised foes before the front dwarven lines. He brought his massive hammer around in a circular motion and the incredible weapon struck the first man in the head, killing him instantly, knocking him into two more, and clearing a path. The old general took a sweet breath of the cool under mountain air and quickly roared again, battering another three soldiers before they could react to his savage attacks.

All down the line of bearded defenders it was the same, scores of humans lay dead around an unbroken vicious dwarven line. The battle raged on for minutes which seemed like hours upon hours as the dwarven defenders slowly began to succumb to the sheer numbers of human enemies that they faced. Tharxton frequently called out commands for the lines to tighten after a defender fell, keeping the humans from forcing a wedge between them and creating a flank on either side of the line. Targavian, however, raged his own personal war out in front of the dwarves, completely surrounded by human soldiers, who were more than reluctant to step in front of the savage dwarf's deadly hammer.

Tharxton attacked furiously at any human that appeared to be giving orders while making his way to a human that was garbed in brass-colored plate armor and standing toward the front lines, barking commands. The man seemed to be drunk and was having difficulty standing without swaying, but the soldiers seemed to obey his commands without question. The young king had taken many hits, and he wondered if he would manage to make it to the odd leader before he too fell prey to the human's blades.

For what seemed like an eternity there were no sounds in the cavern except for the shrill ringing of steel upon steel and the cries of death and dying. The dwarves fought like possessed demons, some even bringing down a killing blow after being run through by an enemy sword, but one by one, the brave bearded defenders fell. There were almost a thousand or more dead humans littering the cavern floor, but the dwarves could not keep their pink-skinned foes from forcing a wedge between their comrades at the stone wall. Tharxton and his brethren soon found themselves in the middle of a swarm of human invaders. The brave dwarves formed a tight circle, keeping their backs to each other as they tried to limit the fronts each dwarf would have to face, but as the battle raged on, they were forced to make several small groups of twenty or more to fight for their lives.

Tharxton ducked a wicked slice that felled one of his brothers, and then lashed out with a ferocious strike that split the human's skull. Pink gore erupted from the man's head and spewed out, covering the dwarf king and many other humans that were nearby.

"Die, you baby-killing bastards!" the dwarf king screamed as his heavy hammer came down, killing another human soldier.

Several dwarves were trying to fight their way to the area where Targavian's wicked shouts of war still erupted into the bloody cavern.

"Rally to Targavian!" Tharxton bellowed, as he bulled his way through the mass of human enemies.

The old general heard his young king's voice and screamed out, spewing blood and spittle into the air as his massive hammer claimed another enemy. "Aye! Come to me brothers! There be a lot of killin' to be done over here!" the general said with a sadistic grin.

Tharxton ducked several slices, and felled another human as he and his soldiers reached the wounded, but savage general. "We are here, Targavian," Tharxton called out as his hammer cracked the spine of an unsuspecting human that had been battling the general.

Targavian quickly shifted his attacks and melded into the circle of remaining dwarves, about thirty strong. The old general chuckled as he crushed the leg of an enemy soldier. "'Tis good to have you, My King. I was getting lonely killing them all by myself."

Tharxton deflected a sword strike with the metal shaft of his hammer, shattering the thin blade. "It's getting lonelier by the moment, my old friend. We are all that still stands."

Targavian glanced around sadly as he caved in the rib cage of another foe. "It appears our numbers do dwindle, Sire."

Despite the wicked death that was sure to come, Tharxton found his spirit soar as he fought alongside his long-time friend. "Don't you get weak on me, General. By my count, I am at least thirty kills ahead of you."

Targavian scoffed. "What? You have surely gone mad with fatigue to count so poorly, sire. No matter. I will double your kill total by the time we are finished here, and you still will be standing at the edge of Leska's garden waiting for me to finish."

Tharxton smiled through his blood mottled face as he started to respond. Targavian turned his side away from the young king and felled two more soldiers with a single stroke. When he ducked a slice to his right, the old general turned to dispatch the foe, and when he turned around once again, he saw the young king face down on the cavern floor. Blood poured from a fresh wound in the back of Tharxton's plate armor and streamed into a rapidly growing crimson pool under his belly. "Sire!" Targavian called out in disbelief. "Protect the king!" the general screamed, as he stepped over Tharxton's body. Several of the remaining dwarves moved in a defensive position around the felled king, some taking unneeded hits to make the maneuver.

"We make our stand here, brothers!" the general called out as he brought his massive hammer down in an overhand strike that crushed a soldier's head, violently forcing the shoulders of the dead human deep into his chest. Targavian wanted desperately to kneel and check Tharxton, to staunch his bleeding or to hoist his head as he passed into the afterlife. He wanted his king to die in comfort, rather than face down in a pool of his own blood, but the seasoned general knew such comforts were not possible.

Targavian let the frustration fuel his anger. He roared out more ferociously than before, swinging his incredible hammer with such power. He seemed to sweep his enemies down in front of him like a scythe that cut rows of wheat. The enemy soldiers that witnessed the horrific general and his devilish hammer cried out in terror at the mad savagery that they faced, some trying to turn their back and flee as the soldiers behind them tried to push forward to the fighting. Targavian ignored the thousands of human soldiers that still swarmed around him and his twenty five dwarven defenders. Had he, or his comrades, paused to ponder the number of enemies they faced, they would have likely lowered their arms and hoped for a quick death. Instead, they battled on fearlessly, focusing on the enemy in front of them, rather than those who they could not reach.

"I say we charge down the passage and kill as many as we can," Desklan said, stroking his bright yellow beard with his blood-streaked hand. "It only takes one of us to turn the blasted key."

The other nine dwarves that stayed behind in Tallengard looked at each other in indecision. They had been keeping their promise and staying in the small mining headquarters, despite the fact they could hear the battle in the cavern below them.

"I don't know," Hewless said, as he stroked his green

streaked blonde beard. "Maybe all ten of us are needed for something to set the magic off," the timid dwarf reasoned.

A few of the other dwarves nodded uneasily as they glanced around at each other, and some looked up at the hourglass that was about to run out of sand.

"Let's just wait the last few minutes to turn the damned key. Then we can charge down the passage and lay waste to as many of the pink-skinned bastards as we can," Korinthalion said as he waved his hands around in the air violently.

"I don't think that is a good idea. The battle will be over by the time the sand runs down," Desklan argued.

"The hell it will," Korinthalion retorted. "Even if the king and all of his clan are dead, there will be one hell of a bitchin' battle to be had when I get my ass down there!" the foul mouthed dwarf spat as he grabbed his crotch in an insulting gesture.

The other dwarves that were not accustomed to Korinthalion's mannerisms, mumbled to themselves. The young hot-headed dwarf shot his head their way and gestured again, purely for effect. "Here's another one for you dainty-hearted rock huggers!"

"Enough, Kor," Desklan said, shaking his head from side to side. "There are enough enemies out there for us to fight; we don't need to be fighting each other."

"Then let's get off our asses and go fight them!" Kor responded, adding another gesture to taunt more comments from the others.

"Enough," Picard said softly. To the other's surprise, Desklan and Korinthalion quieted down. They were hot-headed in their own right, but both admired and looked up to Picard. Picard was a Stoneheart. Even though he was not royalty, he was a Stoneheart by birth, and his family did hold the crown, making him somewhat of a celebrity among the clan. "We will hold a vote. All those in favor of going down and fighting early, raise your hand."

Before Picard could finish, Desklan and Korinthalion shot their hands in the air, glancing at one another as if it were a race. Soon the others followed suit until all hands were in the air.

As Picard glanced around, he stroked his red beard, trying to discern who would stay behind with the key. "Since we all want to go out and fight, who will stay behind and turn the key?"

A small thin dwarf shot his hand in the air, but did not speak. Desklan nodded and flexed his grip on his flail.

Korinthalion grinned wide. "Hot damn. Let's get the show on the road, brothers. I got some blood to spill."

Picard narrowed his eyes as he looked the dwarf up and down. He did not recognize the dwarf from any of the military units and the dwarf's armor was new and undamaged save for a few recent scars from the human invasion. The newcomer was shorter than the average soldier, almost as short as Hewless, and he was thinner than any soldier he had met. He started to ask the dwarf his name, when the others lifted the heavy bar that was holding the door and started down the stone passage to the cavern below. Picard gave the dwarf a suspecting look as he disappeared into the passage.

Mylaneia exhaled a deep breath of relief as Picard and the others made their way down the thin passage into the heart of the cavern. She could not bear to let Tharxton fight the humans without her, but the thought of shaming him by donning armor and weapons prevented her from keeping to his side. She had no idea how vicious the war was going to be. She saw friends and family members cut down before her very eyes, and she expected to die several times over the last three days. She fought on the forward lines when the humans first burst through the front entrance to Mountain Heart and stood her ground in the cavern with the dead end, fully expecting to die there also. Through the leadership of her lover and king, Tharxton, she and the rest of the soldiers were able to fight their way through the enemy and flee to Tallengard. Now her lover and her king faced what seemed like an inescapable death in the cavern of her home.

Mylaneia was not a warrior, though she often pretended

to be. She found herself wanting to run out into the battle, pleading with the humans to spare the life of Tharxton and the others, knowing full well they would not. She found herself praying to any god she thought would listen to save her beloved Tharxton, though she knew in her heart his life and death were out of their hands. Instead, she bravely stood her ground, alone in Tallengard, patiently waiting for the horrifically slow hourglass to drain its sand so that she could turn the key to cave in the beltway cavern. How the collapse would aid her and her clan was beyond her. The beltway cavern was the long corridor just on the other side of the entrance to Mountain Heart. Other than sealing the humans without escape inside the cavern, she found little benefit to them. Of course by sealing them in, they too were trapped, but she had accepted the inedibility of her death.

Moments dragged on, until the last grain of sand fell into the bottom of the hourglass. Mylaneia took a deep breath and wiped the sweat from her brow as she turned the key. The heavy golden key was fluidly smooth in the stone wall and grew warm as she slowly forced it around. Suddenly the runes on the wall began to light up, each one glowing so brightly she had to shield her eyes. The runes lit up the room in a shower of ephemeral light that rocketed out beams so bright, that its whiteness consumed all shadows in the room. Then in a flash there was a quiet thunder. A ripple of nothingness washed over Mylaneia, knocking her to her backside, and sending her rocketing across the room. Her unconscious form thudded limply against the far wall as the room went completely dark, as if nothing had happened.

Desklan charged into the mass of human invaders that were a few hundred yards away from the narrow passage that led to Tallengard. His heavy flail bounced and clanged across the human bodies, sending out showers of blood and spittle, and making a melon breaking sound when the efficient weapon struck a head.

Hewless' calm, timid demeanor was cast aside when he

met the human invaders. He transformed into a savage beast that leapt onto the soldiers' back and bit at their necks and gouged at their eyes, quickly leaping away before they could hit him.

Picard kept his attacks precise and fluid, using the trademark hammer that most Stonehearts used, keeping his breath for fighting, rather than wasting it on battle cries.

But Korinthalion on the other hand, had as much fun screaming and taunting the humans with obscene gestures and cat calls as he did killing them. It didn't seem to bother the incorrigible dwarf that his enemies couldn't understand him, the fact that he understood himself seemed to be entertainment enough.

The four, followed by the other five that stayed behind at Tallengard, save for Mylaneia, cut a path toward where they suspected Tharxton and the others were. Picard's crew was awestruck at the humans' numbers, but pressed on, trying to get to their king. It wasn't long before they found themselves surrounded and fighting for their lives, unable to force their way through the human ranks any longer. Had Picard and his crew another twenty or so dwarves, he surmised they may have been able to cut a path, but now they were doing good to stay alive and three of the nine had already fallen.

Targavian took a wicked strike in his left shoulder and he felt red hot sticky blood pour from the deep wound and drip down his arm into his hand. Though he could still use his wounded arm, he had to abandon it because he didn't want the slippery blood to get on the pommel of his hammer. A small amount of blood would make the massive weapon impossible to hold. As difficult as it was to use one-handed, Targavian knew he had little choice. Without the use of both hands, it didn't take long for the humans to score many more hits against the dwarven general. He was too slow to wield an effective attack that would keep the Beyklans defending, and he had no way of defending himself. Since he was attacking with one hand, he had no choice but to accept the hits and keep fighting, knowing that his death would soon follow his king's.

Targavian accepted a strike to his leg as he brought a killing blow from the hammer down on the human's head. He felt a deep stab penetrate his back as the hot stinging tip of the sword drove deeper into him. Targavian knew that the only way that a human was able to stab him in the back was because all of his brothers had fallen. The old general felt a wave of acceptance wash over him. He stood over his fallen king alone in the darkness of the great cavern, surrounded by thousands of enemies. He took a deep breath and ducked low under the human's strikes. He grabbed his heavy hammer with both hands and swung it in a circular motion, spinning around. The mighty weapon cracked against the legs of the soldiers that surrounded the wounded general. Bones splintered as the hammer cashed against the human's legs.

All around Targavian, humans fell. Again and again, the lone dwarf swung his massive hammer, circling his body, making heavy swooping sounds as the mighty weapon cut the air. But as abruptly the general swung his axe, the blood-soaked pommel slipped from his grasp and rocketed into the mass of the soldiers. The fleeting weapon killed a final man as it collided with his chest. The old general savagely drew a small knife from his boot and stood over the fallen king. "Come on, ye' bastards! I am gonna' take one more of ya's with me!" Targavian screamed.

As he finished his taunt, there was a flash of light through the cavern so brilliant that it seemed to burn into Targavian's eyes. He involuntarily turned his head and covered his face with his knife arm, expecting the humans to pounce on him at any moment, but he heard their shrieks and wails as well. The old general grunted in pain as he snatched Tharxton's limp form from the chamber floor, and hoisted it over his shoulder. He turned to where he thought the south part of the cavern was and ran as fast as he could, bumping into human soldiers as they rolled around on the ground wailing in pain. As Targavian ran, something hit him in the back. It was like quiet thunder and then a ripple of energy that sent him hurtling headlong through the darkness. He fell

to his belly and dropped Tharxton as the power of the unseen force knocked him along the cavern floor. He came to
rest near a rocky wall that the lone dwarf could only guess
was near the southeast edge of the chamber. The old general
sat up and weakly rubbed his eyes with his good arm and
felt around on the ground for Tharxton with his weak one.
The wounded limb had lost a lot of blood and was going
numb so Targavian resorted to trying to get his vision back
while he heard the humans as they started to recover from
the blinding light. The old general opened his pain-stricken
eyes, but his vision was poor at best. Everywhere he looked
he saw a bright yellow spot in the center of his vision, but
he could see out of his peripherals as long as he didn't look
at what he was trying to see directly. The general pondered
what the light was as he scanned the cavern floor for Tharxton. It seemed like an hour had passed since they started
fighting, did the light have something to do with the key?

A strange rumble in the earth roused Targavian from
his thoughts as the sound of rock grating on rock filled the
cavern. The old general curled up in a ball and lowered his
head. Now the cavern was going to collapse and the deaths
of his clan would be avenged.

Theobold sat atop a bright lighting pyre that was almost
fifteen feet tall. He surveyed the battle from a little over fifty
feet away and basked in the upcoming victory. There were
about ten remaining dwarves and they stood guard over
one of their fallen that he suspected was either a general or
a king. Theobold hoped it was the cursed dwarf king, but in
his fever-induced stupor, he couldn't seem to force his mind
to recall what the cursed bearded ruler looked like. He knew
he had met the squat little beast, but for the life of him, he
couldn't recall the damnable dwarf's face. Though short of
hair color, Theobold figured all of the dwarves looked the
same anyway. It wouldn't be long before the last few were
dead, and he could inspect their bodies and revel in his great
victory.

It was a commotion to his left that drew the weary king's attention. He saw several more of the dwarves erupt from some smaller passage and attack his flank. Theobold was nervous at first, thinking this was the great counter assault he had been warned about, but it looked more like a joke than anything. Theobold couldn't count more than ten of the enemy, though he found himself struggling with what number came after ten. He was sure he knew it, but fatigue and hunger must be keeping his mind from thinking correctly. Next, Theobold expected to have some hallucinations. He had those before when he had a bad fever, and he took some coldroot and in a few hours the fever was gone. Coldroot, that was what he needed. How he could remember coldroot and not what number came after ten was beyond him. Funny how fevers worked like that.

Suddenly there was a flash of blinding light that seemed to bore into his brain. Theobold felt an excruciating sting in his eyes, but the pain was numbed by his fever so he hardly even covered his face. He could hear the cries of his men as the light blinded them. "Some fool dwarf trick," he muttered to himself. One last card the bearded demons would try to play before they were crushed. "Stand your ground, men!" Theobold commanded as he rubbed his eyes vigorously. "The light is nothing more than a cheap parlor trick. The bearded fools are no doubt trying to escape at this moment. Steady yourselves...," Theobold was cut off as a quiet thunder rushed over him and he was hit with an unseen power that splintered his lighting pyre and sent him hurtling through the air. His body landed against the hard clay floor of the cavern and he scooted to a stop. Pain shot from his right arm and shoulder as the king sat up, struggling to see in the dark cavern, as he rubbed his dizzy head. All the pyres were out, save for small patches of burning oil that were spilled when they were tipped over, giving the cavern an eerie orange flicker. Theobold rubbed his head and strained his ears as he heard a loud grating of stone on stone. Confused, he glanced up to see he was sitting next to a great stalagmite that erupted from the cavern floor and disappeared into the darkness. As he gazed at the towering rocky peak, two bright yellow spots appeared on the stalagmite about twenty five feet up from the cavern floor. Small rocks and debris began to fall from the stone tower as it began to move and shift. To the king's horror and surprise, a giant boulder-like being stepped from the rocky pillar. The two bright yellow spots were a pair of glowing eyes. The creation had a flat rocky head and two thick, jagged arms that hung down from broad stone shoulders. The beast had no hands, but its arms ended in a pair of giant hammer like appendages that it raised over its head.

Theobold kicked out and scooted back as his eyes remained fixed on the earthly apparition that was before him. The yellow-eyed monstrosity blinked once, then looked down at the cowering king before him. In a lightening quick and violent motion, the stone beast brought its anvil like hands of pure stone down, crushing the human king in a pulp of fleshy mass. The rock beast then turned its flat rocky head toward the remaining human army that was fleeing in terror from two other beasts just like the one that crushed the king.

Most of the humans turned back toward the entrance to the cavern that was several hundred yards away, but as they started to flee, a second rumble came from deep inside of the earth and the beltway cavern collapsed, sending a shower of rocky debris and dust into the expansive chamber. The two thousand remaining human soldiers screamed in terror as the giant rocky creations hunted them down one by one, crushing them with their massive feet and fists.

"It often strikes me as odd how a leader of men can take the credit for success or failure of the others they lead. Sure they can motivate their people to perform to a slightly higher standard they might not normally achieve. But in reality, the people have to have the initial motivation to do the tasks they perform. A good leader helps inspire their men to greatness, but they can also inadvertently inspire them to fail.

I was wiser, yet more foolish than history's leaders. I elected to lead an army that had no inspiration to achieve more than they might normally, nor could they perform any less. I discovered a way to lead a massive group of soldiers I was completely able to calculate their entire capabilities. A bane for some men, but for a man of my preferred calculations it was a sweet compliment to my quiet genius."

-Lancalion Levendis Lampara

Of Suffering and Fire

Great endless fires of thick, syrupy magma drifted along giant seas of red and black. The dark crimson skies held two types of thick billowing clouds, one was a scalding gray stream, and the other was a dark black, but both were mostly soot and ash. Floating islands of mountainous rock, some as large as kingdoms and others as small as fishing boats, drifted along the slow currents that flowed through the magmatic oceans. The air was so hot, that thick ripples of heat distortion waved around endlessly like ethereal currents of water. This world was the elemental realm of fire. Once the realm of Flunt, the God of Fire, now was devoid of its omnipotent ruler. The God of Fire had been destroyed by Dicermadon, King of the Gods. The creatures of the realm carried on as they had done before, but the magic of Flunt no longer maintained the small rock walkways that acted like passages between land structures. The creatures that could not fly or swim were doomed to be prisoners on their respective terrains.

Suddenly the dark red sky lit up as a clear white light formed high above the surface. Small dwarf like creatures with bright red skin and beards made of fire that flickered as they walked, gazed upwards in astonishment toward a brilliant flash as it shifted and changed high above the lakes of fire. Elementals, and all of the other beings that dwelled in this fiery existence, paused to watch the shimmering spectacle. Great gouts of lightning and balls of fire spewed out of the shining sphere as it plummeted toward the molten seas at unearthly speeds. The sphere struck the thick magma with such a tremendous force, that a great wave over thirty foot tall shot out from the collision. The rolling swell rumbled as pieces of rock and stone that were floating in the sea collided against the rocky shores and great drops of thick magma showered the land. The scalding melted stone washed over the beaches of the rock islands and receded back into the sea, leaving bright spots of magma that rested in small holes and pockets on the dark rock-strewn shores.

The sphere slowly rose to the fiery ocean's surface after its mighty plunge. Bright flashes of lightening flickered from the sphere as it floated on the top of the molten sea. Gallant oceanic beasts that dwelled in the fantastic oceans rose to see the bright spectacle. Then as quickly as the sphere appeared, it ruptured. A flash of blinding light from inside of the globe washed over the land and the oceans of magma. The ruptured sphere was replaced by the bright red form of a naked body with hundreds of dazzling black spines that splayed down its backbone. Two magnificently sculpted leathery wings, much like those of a bat, were neatly tucked under each other and curved with the hunched form, extending well past the top of its head and below its rump. The beast had a thick tail that was covered with the same black spines that protruded from its back. The broad appendage had a spine at the end of it, much like a scorpion's stinger.

The monster stood erect slowly, standing on the surface of the molten ocean without sinking. It was well over thirty feet tall. Its head had two thick black horns like a ram that spiraled around each other several times until the tips pointed out to the side of its skull. Two more spiraling horns, much like a gazelle, were fixed into thick sockets on either side of the creature's forehead and pointed backwards. A third set of horns, much like a bull's, protruded from in between the ram horns and the gazelle horns, and shot forward above the creature's eyes. The beast had massive muscular haunches like that of a bull, including cloven hooves. There was a jewel-encrusted golden ring on each of its fingers that shone like a beacon in the bright air of the blistering realm.

Dicermadon opened his eyes and marveled at his new form. He was twice as powerful as he was before. The once God king, turned devil, could feel vast pulses of rippling hate coursing through his new body. A deep guttural laughter shot out from his throat and echoed across the plane. The devil extended his hand out in front of him and sent hundreds of thousands of magical weaves into the air. The weaves began to rip and shape the land, creating walkways, traps, mountains and valleys out of the rocky earth that dotted the fiery seas. The beast stood motionless for months, creating and shaping the land. Even the most powerful beings that dwelled in the plane of fire dared not approach Dicermadon. All but one.

Renagargus, the great red dragon, opened his bright yellow eyes. The resilient amber orbs that had seen the passing of countless millennia, blinked in confusion. Renagargus was the oldest and most powerful of all dragons. No dragon could match his strength, his size, his ability to wield magic, nor his breath. Renagargus was a red dragon, the only species of dragon that could breathe fire. The great red's breath was so hot that he could melt mountains if angry enough. He could have easily conquered the world, had Flunt not banished him here, to the elemental plane of fire. Here, beings could not be harmed by his fire, on the contrary, the beings here often are healed by the soothing heat of the blistering plane. Left to using his size and ability with magic, the wicked and cunning dragon had started to dominate even here, creating a castle for himself to live in and enslaving the lesser races that dwelled around him.

The great red was creating an army to one day send out and conquer this realm, since he could not rule his native plane of existence. Flunt noticed the dragon's new army and fortress and attacked the great red. Renagargus, despite his size, his power, and cunning genius mind was no match against the god. The dragon was defeated and sealed in his castle where he had resided for the last two thousand years. He had used his magical ability to see beyond his prison to monitor the events of the plane, but up until recently he had been bored with the everyday happenings. The dragon mainly focused his time and energy to try to develop a spell to create a portal that would take him from one plane of existence to another.

He knew how to move about each plane by creating individual portals, but he could not form the weaves needed to transverse the planes. Flunt had laughed at him, saying the dragon's mortal mind could not comprehend the trillions of weaves needed to perform such tasks, and if the elemental gods themselves had the ability inherently, they would not be able to do it, but the great red tried everyday anyway. What else was he to do in his prison? But now, the ancient dragon sensed something different. Something had changed, but he couldn't pinpoint exactly what. His scrying showed nothing out of the ordinary, but the plane of fire was almost endless by definition, and it would be near impossible to search everywhere.

Renagargus stretched his long scaled neck and yawned. His gaping maw contained hundreds of jagged black teeth that were serrated on both ends to cut and tear the flesh of his enemies. The dragon plodded to the edge of the single expansive room he was kept in. How he longed for a bed of gold and jewels to lie in. How long had it been since he rested in a lair of his own? He was just a young dragon then. It was about the time the metallic dragons started to appear. The great red wondered how they came into existence. All of the chromatic dragons, or dragons with color in their names, like red or green, basically ruled the lands around them including humans and elves. They were worshipped like gods. Then came the metallic dragons – the gold and silver. They appeared and began to battle Renagargus and the others. Though they were young, it didn't take them long to increase in numbers and mature. What made the metallic the most deplorable to the chromatics was the fact they allowed the humans to ride on their backs while they fought. Not only did Renagargus and the others have to deal with the dangers of fighting one of their own kind, there was always some wizard or sorcerer shooting fireballs and other spells at them. This era was referred to as the Dragon Wars, and as far as Renagargus could recall, the period of history was forgotten by the humanoid races, save for some of the elven societies. The great red soon found himself wondering if the other chromatic families still existed, like the Quieness, or the Achts. These were questions that he hoped would someday be answered. If the families no longer existed, it was of no matter. It simply left more of the world for him to rule.

Dicermadon outstretched his thick muscular hand. The bright red appendage had only three fingers tipped with wicked long black talons and he was unaccustomed to such anatomy, but it took the former God King little time to adjust. His newfound power that coursed through his body made him long to create beings that would be subservient. The former God King could feel the power of Flunt pulsing through him, almost as if the God of Fire still existed somewhere deep in his conscious, but he easily ignored the sensation as he used his new ability to create the beings of his world. The red devil focused his thoughts and sent millions of magical weaves into motion. Commanding and controlling so many would have been impossible, even for the elementals, but now, now he could do it consciously but with great effort. The strain was mighty, but he struggled through it.

Dicermadon formed the first being, crafting its hellish form in a likeness of himself. It stood nearly twenty feet tall and was as equally as wide. The beast had bright red skin covered in small wisps of hair-like flames. It's head was flat and wide with long pinchers like that of a stag beetle that hung from its lower jaw in front of its mouth and extended down almost to the beast's waist. It's body was sculpted muscle and each arm ended in two large crab-like pinchers instead of hands. The only armor the beast wore was a black onyx loin cloth, like that in which Dicermadon fashioned for himself, that hung down from its wide belly.

Dicermadon held the body together with his left hand which had its three fingers outstretched while he wove a net of magical energy to meld into the being, making it permanently flesh. His right hand grasped the very essence of the plane of fire and instilled it into the beast's body. When he was finished, the beast opened its bright yellow eyes.

"You shall be called, Donathuku," Dicermadon boomed as his unearthly voice carried across the plane, sending its inhabitants scurrying for cover. "And you shall reign over hate, controlling all lesser devils."

The crab-like beast growled as it studied its form. "I will obey, Master. I will rule the lesser devils with ruthless authority, and all that fail will be consumed for their weaknesses."

Dicermadon smiled at his creation. "Go Donathuku; make your lair about this world of fire. I will call upon you soon and you must be ready."

"I exist to serve, Master," the large red beast replied as it bounded off across the mountainous terrain.

Dicermadon smiled as his creation lumbered over the hard rocky wasteland of the plane of fire. He then focused his inner thoughts on fear. He focused on the fear he possessed inside the fear of Ecnal, and what threat he posed on all of the gods. The former God King harnessed that fear and amplified it, mixing the emotion with millions of weaves, just as he had done when he created the devil, Donathuku. This time the weaves formed a smaller, manlike form. It was about eight foot tall and had a corpulent belly that hung down over its waistline. The devil's skin was red, like the others, but was covered in large bulbous boils that leaked and drained over its skin. The devil had no hair, save for small thin black wisps that protruded from its head that flickered in the scorching air of the plane of fire. As Dicermadon looked harder at the forming devil, he noticed that the black wisps of hair were not hair at all, but were dark sable adders that spit acid and hissed at him when he leaned too close. That fat-bodied form clung to a small scythe that it held in its left hand and a wicked black leather whip with nine long strands attached to it. The long whip strands were barbed and dripped yellow syrupy ooze. The devil lacked any real expression and merely stood there, even after Dicermadon had instilled its essence in it.

The former God King didn't smile at the form, merely frowned in awe at its unusual composition. "You shall be called, Mortigalus. You will preside over fear and hate, striking it deep into those that have none of it, and you will exploit and increase it in those with it. You are my task master in the world of the soulful." The chubby devil said nothing in reply. He merely nodded his portly head and bounded off while the snakes atop his scalp hissed and snapped at the former God King.

Dicermadon created another devil to reign over pain, just as he created the other two devils, but much to his surprise this one took on a form so small, he wondered if he had erred in its creation. The being took shape at about five and half foot tall. But as the weaves settled in and took form, the former God King smiled in satisfaction. The devil took on a human female shape. She had long black hair that flowed around her like she was standing in an infinite breeze. Her bright red eyes shined like those of a succubus feasting on a dozen souls. She smiled a sinister fanged smile and cracked the small whip that she held in her right hand. She was dressed in a revealing black leather smock that ended just below the end of her buttocks. She wore no underpants and her bright red skin seemed to almost glow in anticipation of the torment she would be allowed to inflict on the world of the living.

Dicermadon smiled and marveled at the devil of pain. "You shall be called, Amirillion, and you will reign over pain. You will seek to increase tenfold the pain of others and inflict it without remorse on those with none."

The small framed she-devil smiled and licked her supple lips with a forked snake like tongue. "I will obey out of my lust for pain, My Master."

Dicermadon smiled at his creations. He had created the three powers of suffering and fire, and they were wicked. Soon, he would see just how wicked.

The proud white equestrian champion pranced forward throughout the lush Beyklan countryside. Her sallow mane bounced as she trotted and her long hair-covered hooves hit the soft ground, becoming neither bogged, nor dirty. She left no trace that she passed by and disturbed nothing. The very underbrush seemed to bend away from her and the biting insects dared not land on her hide. Her bright shining white coat glistened in the morning sunlight as its rays poked through the thinning Beyklan canopy. The beast seldom, if ever, came this far north into the corrupt lands of the humans. Though now, she was called out of duty.

Unicorns seldom ever came near the borders of Southern Beykla, let alone tried to navigate its thin forests that were littered with its impure hearts. Occasionally the proud equine might stumble across an elf maiden that might be pure of heart enough to converse with, yet the northern lands were filled with high elves, not the supreme nobles like the grays. Unicorns enjoyed the company of the few proud sylvan cultures and enjoyed solitude least of all, and that was what this trip into Beykla was a journey into solitude, but the proud animal could not deny the call of its heart. Something or someone was calling out to it, asking for freedom, for salvation. The equine was so moved that she could no sooner ignore the voice, than she could turn her back on an innocent. She had been tracking the voice for several months, and it seemed the calling was coming closer to her as she was to it. Then strangely, the voice became silent and started moving away. Fearing the being of pure goodliness was injured or enslaved, the equine ran day and night until she could pinpoint exactly where the voice had been coming from. She could still sense its presence, but it no longer called out to her.

Ehleeshuh, the proud unicorn from the lands far south of Beykla, known to humans as Tyrine, had tracked the sensation to a human caravan that was traveling north along a dirt road. She had secretly followed the band, watching as she tried to learn about them before rushing in.

There were three humans, though the band had picked up a few as they road north the last few days. They hauled an old dwarf and a young orc in chains. The humans were well armed, wearing light chain armor and carried well-crafted swords. One of the humans seemed to be a spell caster and the others were merely swordsman, but she detected no fear among them, only deadly confidence. What was strange to the equine was that the only fear she detected came from the orc. Ehleeshuh was familiar with orcs, and fear was not an emotion they experienced. In fact, the orcs didn't even have a word for it in their language. The emotion was as foreign to them as friendship, yet there laid a young orc, chained to a cart and riddled with fear. She thought she detected a calculating determination about him, but she could not tell.

On the other hand, the dwarf, who was also in chains, held nothing but remorse. For what, she had no idea, but he seemed resolute in his current predicament, almost a form of relief. The only worry she detected in the bearded prisoner was fear and concern for the orc, which really confused her. Dwarves and orcs were as bitter enemies as were elves and orcs. The two species had hated each other since the beginning of time. What confounded the poor unicorn further was that the only good she detected in the whole lot came from the green-skinned menace. The dwarf was a multitude of swirling grays, varying from horrific black to blinding whites. The humans all had dark souls, yet the only inherently evil being, the orc, had a white heart certainly not pure, but positively good without doubt. A good orc? If Ehleeshuh had the ability for laughter, she would have fell over and rolled around in hysteria. She must surely be tired to confuse her senses like that.

Yet despite all of her findings, it was a sword in the pile of equipment that she sensed the call from. The band stopped and camped in the cold autumn night after starting a fire. Ehleeshuh fought her urge to rush out and impale the humans when they defiled the forest by chopping down live trees for lumber.

They then discarded their trash and other waste haphazardly about their campsite. She reminded herself that she was here to investigate the call for help, not teach an incorrigible group of humans about respecting nature. She would watch and wait. The voice would sense her close by and call out to her, and then she would rescue it and be on her way. If a few of the evil humanoids died in the exchange, well she would not lose any sleep over their well-deserved deaths.

Vlargcar stretched his neck to try to see his two swords. He longed for them, to feel their hilts in the palm of his hand. He knew the humans that were enslaving him and Amerix were wicked. They had to be. He and the dwarf had done nothing wrong. Vlargcar realized why his people hated humans so much. They were an immoral and ruthless race. Though, when he thought about it, he was unsure why they hated elves and dwarves so much. He figured the dwarven and elven revelation would come later. He would have to remember to ask Amerix about it when they escaped. Escaped. Yes, the young orc had to devise a plan to get free of his chains somehow.

Vlargcar flexed his ever-growing arms and tested the thick iron chains that bound him. But to his disappointment, they did not budge. He turned his head and looked over at Amerix, but the old dwarf merely laid his tired head back against the hard wooden cart. Great gouts of white mist erupted from his mouth as the dwarf exhaled into the cold autumn night.

Most of the leaves had turned brown and a few of the trees had lost more than half of them. The moon was high in the night, silhouetting the empty bare branches like thin rigid snakes that danced in the cold autumn breeze. The orc sighed and turned his head back to the weapon cache. He could not find Songsinger for anything. He wondered what the humans had done with the magnificent blade. The thought of the pink-skinned weaklings holding the sacred sword by the pommel enraged him. Vlargcar felt the anger bubbling up inside of him. The cold autumn air no longer felt cold to his skin, and the thick unyielding iron chains did not feel as heavy. How dare they touch that sword? It was Amerix's sword!

Vlargcar flexed his taut, corded muscles against the iron chains that held him. He felt the chains tighten and raise from the wooden cart. They jingled and popped as the orc pulled them tight. Vlargcar let the rage boil inside of him. He was not aware of the splintering wood of the cart, nor was he aware of the humans shouting and rising up from the sleeping rolls and grabbing clubs. He was not aware of the thin magical rings that encircled his form, but fell away like butter on the side of a hot skillet. All he was aware of was the rage and the fact that he needed to escape the chains he was in. Never in Vlargcar's short life had he felt power like he now felt. He was stronger than he had ever been. The wooden car splintered and popped under the tremendous force he applied to it. The orc felt the boards begin to crack and break, then he felt nothing.

"What the bloody hell was that?" one of the guards asked, as he held the blood-soaked club high in the air over Vlargcar's unconscious form.

"Beats me, but I ain't never seen nothing like that. Did you see the chains go taut?" Another asked as he inspected the iron bindings, almost expecting to see some damage to them.

"I tell ya' what, that orc is trouble. We should have just killed it when we had the chance," the first man said as he watched the wizard approach and examine the orc's tattoos carefully.

"What ya' lookin at, Tallnok?" one of the men asked as the mage ran his finger across the strange markings in the orc's hide.

As Tallnok's bare finger slid across the edge of the dark black tattoos on the orc's hide, a blistering shock tore through his hand. Tallnok jerked his hand back in surprise and cried out in pain. He immediately stuck his finger in his mouth and sucked on the end of it, quickly pulling it out and examining it thoroughly. There was no burn marks or cuts, but it still hurt tremendously.

"You okay, Mister Tallnok?" one of the men asked.

Tallnok gave him a dirty look as he fumbled through his pack. "I am just fine. I think I am able to handle these simple runes," the mage said defensively.

The man shrugged. "Runes, huh? I just thought they were a bunch of tattoos."

Tallnok pretended he knew exactly what the runes were and did not answer the man. He instead pulled out a quill and ink and began to scribe down the symbols in his scratch book. After he was finished, he slammed the book shut and made his way back to the burning embers of the campfire. He shoved the book into his pack and pulled out a second one. This tome was much older and was worn from extreme use. The book appeared to be exceptionally old and seemed it would fall apart if treated roughly. Yet, Tallnok flipped through it veraciously, thumbing down one page, then rapidly up the other. The mage was sure he had seen similar markings before in his studies, but he could not place a finger on it.

Meirgan walked over and guzzled wine from an intricately gilded flask. The golden hews and precious jewels sparkled in the bright moonlight. The bounty hunter awkwardly wiped the excess drool and wine from his mouth and belched, as he stuck one of his hands into his pants and scratched. "What are ya' doing, Tallnok?" the bounty hunter asked, as his drunken breath washed over the mage.

The wizard waved his slender hand in front of his face to fan Meirgan's foul breath. "Nothing, Meirgan. Why do you bother me so?"

The bounty hunter took another swig, but this time he belched when he was finished. "Cause that's why I pay ya'. Besides, I am hoping to make some money from that orc, and you didn't look too happy when you was fingering his shoulder," the gruff bounty hunter said disrespectfully. "Something I need to know about?"

Tallnok arched his eyebrow as he held his place in his book with his slender index finger. "If you would leave me to my work, Meirgan, I could better answer that question for you."

The sound of men shrieking and the thunder of hooves roused the two from the fire. Meirgan drew his sword and rushed to the carts where the dwarf and the orc were held while Tallnok neatly tucked his tome back into his pack and slipped a single silver ring on his index finger. He did not have time to don the ring in the first encounter with the pair, and he was sure he would need the item in future encounters.

Ehleeshuh stared at the source of the calling, but she could not tell whether the orc or the dwarf was the one calling her. In truth, she couldn't understand how either could have sent such a strong message, and neither was extremely pure. She guessed perhaps they had somehow masked their true hearts. She knew of such beings that could do that. It was in the next moment her queries were answered.

"Ehleeshuh, thank you for coming," the feminine voice echoed in her head. It was the first time she had actually heard a voice. The other times it was a powerful emotion, then it became a sense, but it had never been a voice before.

The proud unicorn shook her head in confusion and fear, snorting quietly in the cold autumn night. Thick clouds of her hot breath erupted from her nostrils as she tossed her head.

"Ehleeshuh, my name is Songsinger. Look, you may see me now," the voice continued.

Ehleeshuh lifted her head and stared at the weapons cart, where she now saw a magnificent blade that was stacked with a pile of moderately crafted long and short swords. Its hilt was made of gold that glittered in the pale moonlight and its thin blade was like polished chrome. The weapon was a diamond among rocks in the weapons cache.

"I have called for you since I was carried by the dwarf. Amerix's heart was hardened for some time, but I have watched defeat soften it. The orc's name is Vlargcar. Remember it. The green skin's heart is pure, but undecided. It is not our way to rescue either, they are not worthy, and are not innocent. I was served for a time by a paladin named Apollisian Bargoe of Westvon Keep. I have no further need of Amerix and I need you to take me to a druid's grove near the sea in Southern Beykla. Can you serve me, Ehleeshuh?"

The majestic equine snorted again. She was not aware of any druids that lived anywhere that far north. The Sylvans had abandoned the land to the humans and the denizens there, but she could not deny the feeling of ultimate good that radiated from the magnificent weapon. She had heard of the name, Songsinger, though. Surely a weapon of such renowned power would have been known to her, but it was not. The fact the sword knew her name told her that her inclination about the weapon's inner heart was correct. "I shall serve you proudly, Songsinger," the equine champion thought to the sword.

"My thanks, noble Sylvan. First, perhaps we could rid Terrigan of a few of these vile beings," Songsinger suggested.

Ehleeshuh pawed at the ground for a moment before approaching the campsite. Her fantastic equine form slipped in and around the underbrush as quietly as a breeze and her ivory hooves made no sound and left no trace that she had passed. When she neared the thick heavy wooden carts where the dwarf and the orc were kept, she saw a few of the humans trying to repair the thick wooden cart the orc was attached to. The orc was bleeding from a deep cut on the side of his head and he was unconscious. The three human guards were ignoring the cart which held Songsinger. She could see the magnificent blade gleaming in the night. One of the guards' eyes caught the gleaming sword as he tested the strength of the repaired wagon.

"I think it will hold now. I'm not sure how the blasted orc managed... When did that get there?" the man asked the other guards as he pointed to the bright polished hilt of Songsinger.

"Whoa! That wasn't there before," the man said as he lifted the fabled blade from the cache.

Ehleeshuh rocketed from the darkness of the forest and charged the men with blinding speed, her thick ivory horn leveled with her head. Her powerful muscles rippled under her fine white coat as her thick ivory horn stabbed deep into the man's sternum. Every rib in the guard's chest shattered from the tremendous force of the blow. As he was lifted from his feet, Ehleeshuh hoisted her head, snatching Songsinger in her mouth. The gallant equine did not have time to stop without running into the heavy weapon cart, and to the other men's disbelief, her sleek powerful equine form simply dissipated into a white swirling mist that vanished as it collided with the wagon.

The body of the dead guard landed on the ground and

thudded against the thick wheel of the cart, while the unicorn reappeared on the other side, never missing stride as if the cart weren't even there.

"It's a unicorn!" the guards called out as they fled back to camp. Ehleeshuh never stopped running; she continued on well into the next day, carrying a very thankful Songsinger in her mouth.

"Procreation. This term is coined by men to pave a life path for society. It is good for men to meet wives, marry, and have children. Their children will learn this value, and do in kind. They will be well balanced and grow into fine upstanding members of the society and carry the thoughts and the will of the government in which they serve under. It teaches men and women that following this model is the norm and those who do not must have an internal flaw.

Have you ever seen an elderly man that has never married and had no children? Did you ponder how horrible his life must have been? Or question the quality of his character that he could not attract a mate? Or perhaps he had some flaw in his body that prevented him from fathering children? Yet, few of you would ever imagine that he lived a full and completed life that he enjoyed very much.

In my life I was never one to conform to rules or standards, or a supposed belief that the will of the people, or government, was a model to live by. My name is Lance Ecnal. I forge my own path and it is my own god given right to do so. I will love who I wish, marry who I wish, when I wish, and if the notion so takes me, I will have children. But I will do none of these things for status, recognition, or a misguided belief that I need to do this to be whole. I will simply do them because I want to."

-Lancalion Levendis Lampara

6

The Heart of a Demon

Reena grabbed Lance by the collar of his shirt. "Get moving, suda. We have to get back to the tower if we are to convince Ramasiel of our story."

Lance stepped out into the street and walked north toward the red tower that jutted out higher than most of the other towers in the fantastic city of Aquabar. He kept his head down, though he wanted to look around and see where the dark-haired women went. He dared not speak of his conversation with her to Ramasiel or to Reena. Perhaps he might be able to use her to escape this god-forsaken city. It was obvious that the dark-haired woman was not from this cursed country. She didn't even look like any of the other women.

The trip went quickly for Lance as he imagined how he might use the dark-haired woman to escape and he began to wonder if he might even be able to use Ramasiel and Reena against each other, too. Reena surely seemed surprised that he knew about severing strands to make them permanent. She acted as if that was some safeguard secret known to the powerful, but the idea struck him as odd. Perhaps they just guarded such knowledge. Lance was quickly finding out that knowledge was power in this city.

As Lance pondered the events, he found himself standing outside of Ramasiel's chamber. Reena straightened her dress and stared around at the ceilings and the like, searching for magical devices that might be on them. When she was satisfied there were none, she straightened Lance's shirt with both hands and stared at his face. Lance looked away, knowing that he was in the tower and if he dared so much glance at her chin, he would be in for the beatings of a lifetime.

"Now let me do the talking, suda," Reena said as she whispered in Lance's ear.

Lance nodded as he tried to ignore the warm sensation

she created every time she whispered in his ear. She always seemed to know how to make his body tingle. He supposed she practiced such things. Lance took a deep breath and whispered back. "Yes, Mistress."

Reena smiled and watched Lance for a moment then turned and rapped her delicate fingers on the hard oaken door. The door opened inwards slowly, guided by a flow of air and Ramasiel sat comfortably in her red velvet chair. Sitting across from her was a mistress of the blue sept. She was not held by any means, but the blue was surely terrified, as would most be if they sat across from the powerful Ramasiel.

Lance felt the urge to test the shield that held his inner power at bay, but he did not, knowing that Ramasiel or Reena would be able to sense it, and that always meant a beating. He was just getting able to walk without a limp from the last one. Instead he tried to watch the three out of the corner of his eye without actually looking at them.

"It seems we had an event unfold in the streets while you were away, Reena," Ramasiel said as she crossed her arms under her thick, firm breasts that were pressed together and showing through the center of her low-cut red gown.

Reena found it deplorable how Ramasiel seemed to wear such provocative clothing when she was around women of other septs. It was as if the Mother was more interested in attracting the women she dealt with, than the affection of the tudas. "What event do you speak of, Mother? Is everything in order?" Reena asked disarmingly.

Ramasiel fumed. "Reena, how do you ever plan to move above your station, if you cannot establish the simplest of informative networks?"

Reena curtsied and bowed her head. "I do not know, Mother. I have set a small group about, but I must confess I had not the opportunity to speak with them as I was bringing back your suda."

Ramasiel frowned. "What suda? This one?" she asked as she pointed disgustingly at Lance.

Reena nodded. "Yes, Mother. He had been accosted by a street thug and your robe was damaged, but I took it to the tudas in laundry. I commanded them to repair it immediately."

Ramasiel looked disappointed that Lance was accosted instead of trying to escape. "Oh bother. Do flog this suda for getting my robe damaged. Tell him next time, I will have a day set aside for nothing but his torment," Ramasiel said as she sipped wine from a golden goblet that sat on a polished oaken table next to her velvety red chair. The mother held her long polished fingernails away from the cup in a dainty fashion as she turned her attention back to the blue mistress.

The woman in blue shook nervously, but did not take her eyes off of Ramasiel. Her hands fidgeted in her lap with her bright blue dress. Ramasiel set the golden goblet down and crossed her legs, causing the high-cut ankle length dress to slide to the side, exposing her slender but muscular bronzed legs. "Do continue."

The blue mistress swallowed and cleared her throat. "Well, Mother, witnesses said the woman stole a suda, severed a weave as powerful as any in Aquabar, held a sword mistress with a complete bar, then simply walked away."

Ramasiel sat back in her chair and thumbed her supple lip. "What is wrong with this story, Reena?"

Reena frowned, trying to hide the fact she knew it to be truth and hoping that she was not seen by any of Ramasiel's agents. Reena doubted it, since they would be focused on the dark-haired woman and not her. She had been lucky, but she would not allow the same mistake to happen again. Next time, she would take the alleys. "Well, for starters, Mother, few others can cast a complete barhold."

Ramasiel smiled. "Very good, Reena. Now, Marlana...," Ramasiel said as she thumbed her bottom lip again. "...care to tell me what really happened in the street?"

Marlana shuddered. "Mother, I have told it all as I saw it. I could tell nothing else, or it would be false."

Ramasiel smiled wickedly and turned to Reena. "Leave us, Reena. This mistress must be taught how to tell the truth."

Reena curtsied again and bowed her head before turning and leading Lance out of the chamber. When the door closed, Ramasiel sent a weave of energy around Marlana, holding her arms and her head fast. "Follow me," she said as she led Marlana into her private chambers.

Marlana was nearly sick with fear. Ramasiel had a reputation for killing mistresses of other septs, claiming they wronged her somehow, and the red mother was too powerful for most to oppose her. Marlana knew her Mother could not rival Ramasiel's power, so she was helpless to defend herself from the ruthless red.

"Lay on the bed," Ramasiel commanded.

Marlana obeyed, but fell backward since she could not move her arms or her head. The soft red silk linens enveloped her and caressed her skin as she lay frozen on her back. She stared up at the intricately gilded plaster ceiling of the bed chamber. Why Ramasiel would kill or torture her here confused the blue mistress. Surely she would not want the blood to disturb her bed chamber.

Ramasiel slowly unbuttoned her blouse and let her robe fall around her feet exposing her naked body. She climbed onto the bed and leered over the shocked and horrified Marlana. "I have a use for you, Marlana. Serve me well and I might keep you around for a few days, before your untimely death."

Marlana wanted to cry out in disgust, or try to fend off the woman, but the bindings of the spell held her fast. All she could do was endure and hope she did not displease the red mother. She knew if she did not perform as commanded, her death would be much more horrific than any deed she would have to carry out.

Reena led Lance down the curved narrow hallway of the tower. The very structure itself was magical in nature, since the inside was much more spacious that the outside measurements would allow. From the outside, it appeared as if the tower was about one hundred and fifty feet in diameter, but on the inside it was at least twice that. When Lance focused his eyes, he could almost see the hundreds of thousands of weaves it must have taken to create such a fantastic structure.

The halls of the tower were lined with sorceress after

sorceress. Most of them were from the red sept, but a few wore the robes of others, sometimes a blue or a yellow, but Lance was unable to really see the women since he was not allowed to look upon any of them. The long walk back down to the bottom of the tower took about an hour. Lance's legs ached from the hundreds of flights of stairs and almost welcomed the confines of his cell, so he could sit for a while.

Reena unlocked the heavy iron-barred door and bid Lance to enter. As he did, she gently patted his bottom and closed the door behind him. Lance didn't flinch; he had grown accustomed to such unwanted fondling from the mistress. He sat down on the hard wooden cot and rested his head in his hands as Reena disappeared around the corner and started back up the stairs. He was not sure how the small framed woman was able to move up and down the many flights of stairs and not be tired. He also knew that she seldom slept. He suspected it was some benefit of a charm she wore. She was always covered in so many weaves and auras; he could not discern one from the other, though he was beginning to understand a few different weaves, even when linked together. What aggravated Lance was that he needed to learn faster. He had been a prisoner here for so long, he was beginning to look forward to the women's praise and feel bad when he disappointed them. Being called a suda seemed to bother him mainly because the women looked at him less, instead of being a suda. By no means did he wish to endure the operation that made you into a tuda, but the fact remains his values were changing. Lance knew that whatever brainwashing techniques they used were working on him.

Lance lay back on the hard cot, kicked his feet over the edge and put his hands behind his head. He stared at the dark gray stone ceiling and thought about Jude. Where was the swordsman now? He had probably accepted Lance as dead and had gone about with his life. He hoped so. The thought of Jude trying to make his way here and rescue him made his heart sink. Jude would be more helpless here than a baby in a den of wolves. Yes, a sword was no weapon against magic; you needed magic for that. That is exactly what Lance decided he was going to do in the morning. He was going to devise a plan tonight before he went to sleep, and in the morning he was going to set it in motion. There was enough plotting and backstabbing in this tower between the women, he should have no problem slipping in a few of his own plots unnoticed. Who would suspect a slave, after all?

Lance pulled his small itchy wool blanket up around his shoulders and curled his knees into his chest to keep them under the frayed bed covering. He grinned slightly for the first time in months as he drifted off to sleep.

"I don't live anywhere, Mother," the suda said nervously as he tried to walk behind Delania.

Delania growled in frustration as the fool spawn seemed to refuse to walk. He would lag behind her and when she would slow down for him to catch up, he would go slower and when she would stop he would stop. The spawn never made any attempt to run away and he kept staring at the ground. "Why do you keep stopping? I grow tired of waiting for you to catch up. If we keep this pace, you will grow old and die and I will have to find a new spawn to capture."

The suda shuddered. "I am sorry, Mother. How would like for me to walk?" he asked as his heart paused to see if she was going to kill him for being displeased.

Delania scratched her head and felt her skull, surprised to not feel her small horns that normally protruded from there. "I want you to walk next to me of course, or at least in front of me. How else are you going to take me to your house?"

The suda shuddered again as he quickly stepped in front of Delania. He had never heard of walking in front of any mistress, let alone a Mother. "Mother, I do not live in a house. I reside in the blue tower, under rule of Sarafine," he said, fearing Delania was testing him in someway.

"Sarafine?" Delania said in confusion. She knew spawns lived in houses, sometimes great stone houses called castles, but in towers? "Is that your mother, this Sarafine?"

The man's eyes welled up with tears and he collapsed on

the narrow side street and said, "Mother, please end my life. I am not of your tower. Please have mercy on me."

Delania frowned and jerked the man to his feet while the other women who were walking in the street began to take notice. "Get up, fool. I have no intention of ending your life, I just got you. This deed needs to be in a secluded area, and that is where I hope to go."

The suda stifled his sobs and led Delania down a side street to an old, dilapidated brick building. "Mother, I will not betray my sisters, no matter what you do to me."

Delania paused. "What do you mean? I am sure you will enjoy what I do to you," Delania said with a confused look on her face. She didn't understand; she thought all spawns enjoyed the act of love making. It never occurred to her that one might not want to. She looked herself up and down as she stood next to the building in the ally. She was sure she was attractive by human standards. Perhaps she was a bit too tall, but she was sure her other features were more than adequate.

As Delania examined herself, she did not feel the thick powerful strands that quickly wrapped around her. Her arms and legs were suddenly held by ten thick bars of flickering blue light. A second weave of green energy descended down and covered her head in a thin shroud to keep out sound, while a third, murky-white shield slammed into her with tremendous force, sealing her off from any inner power she might possess. The succubus almost chuckled as three women burst from the run-down building. One wore a bright white robe, and two wore thin yellow gowns.

The suda jumped to the side. "Careful, sisters! She is powerful, I think she is a Mother!"

The three women quickly hoisted the frozen form of Delania, took her into the brick building and closed the rickety door.

"Were you seen?" asked the burly man holding a heavy wooden club as he looked out into the alley from a small hole carved into the door.

The woman wearing the white robe shook her head from side to side. "No, I do not believe we were," she said, turning to the young man that led them there. "That was very dangerous, Sidney. I hope she is worth the risk." The woman examined the shielded Delania.

The suda smiled nervously. "I think she is worth it. Anyway, she was going to kill me soon. I didn't have much choice."

Delania fumed. That fool spawn thought she was going to kill him? That would explain a lot of his odd actions. She easily forced a razor-thin strand of energy through the shield undetected and severed the weave that prevented her from speaking. "I wasn't going to kill you fool, I was going to bed you."

Sidney jumped against the wall as the woman in white took a step back in surprise and horror. The other two women fired a more complex weave at her, but Delania quickly dismissed them with two more strands of energy that she forced through the shield, severing the weaves the two had sent at her. She then severed the hold spell that bound her and she simply stepped through the invisible shield. The three women gaped in awe and horror, and changed their tactics from capture to kill.

Delania frowned as the lethal strands rocketed toward her. She created a thick net, disrupting the spells the three women hurled at her like a strainer disrupting a small trickle of water.

The large man lunged forward with both hands on the club. Delania snarled and sent a thick fist of air, striking the man in the groin with such force that his pelvis snapped. The thick man dropped his club and toppled forward as he ran, sliding past Delania to come to a rest at the far wall. There, he kicked and screamed in pain, holding his genitals.

Sidney backed away to the far wall and slipped through a small trap door that led into the alley. Delania hurled all three women, pinning them against the wall with their arms and legs spread wide. She pushed the straining weave around the room and to the astonishment and horror to the three women, Delania severed the weave. "I should kill you all!" Delania screamed with her fists tight against her side.

"Please make it quick, Mother," Tonya pleaded, hoping

that she and the others would die before they were forced to betray the other sects.

Delania scanned the room for the spawn that had taken her into the alley, but he was nowhere to be found. "That little rat managed to escape!" she snarled as she kicked over a chair looking for him.

Tonya gulped. Who was this woman? She knew of no blue septs that had a mother with the symbol of a "D" not to mention she knew of no tower that had a Mother as powerful as this woman, save for Ramasiel in the red. Yet, Tonya doubted even Ramasiel could create such a net as to unravel any spell that was hurled at it. The white glanced over at the yellows, who were also pinned against the wall. They seemed more terrified than she was. "Why would you want to bed Sidney, Mother, when you could have almost any suda you wanted?" Tonya asked, hoping to enrage the woman enough to kill them. But to her disappointment, the woman propped the chair back up and scooted it in front of her.

Delania sat in the chair and crossed her legs as she picked at her teeth. "He was handsome enough, don't you think?" Delania asked calmly.

Tonya frowned in confusion. "What tower do you reside in?" the white said, hoping to insult the Mother by suggesting she did not rule a tower.

But Delania merely smiled as she answered. "Why does everyone think I live in a tower? I just got here."

Tonya started to get worried that she could not enrage the woman. It was obvious they were not going to escape. The sect's only chance for survival was for them to be killed, yet their captor seemed uninterested. "Why don't you kill us, bitch? Are you too weak to stomach it?" Tonya taunted.

Delania chuckled. "All I wanted was to make love to Sidney. You are the fools that brought an adder into your bed."

"Sidney would never make love to you, slut!" Tonya snarled. "He loves his wife. No matter what you made him do with you, it would not be love."

Delania frowned. She knew spawns sometimes took mates when they were alive, but how could she make love to him and it not be love? It was then it dawned on the succubus that making love was a phrase the spawns must have reserved for some special meaning to cover the same deed. Spawns were the strangest creatures and humans were the strangest. "I see. I didn't know he was married. It seems every man here acts differently than I expected. I assumed him to be some kind of a slave."

Tonya couldn't believe her ears. This woman was no Mother, that was for sure, unless she was putting on some kind of charade to try to get Tonya and the others to admit what they where up to. But the woman didn't need admission, and she was clearly powerful enough to kill them all if she wished. "Of course he is a slave. Every man you see will be owned by someone. Do you not know where you are?" Tonya asked, leaving off the title Mother purposely in attempt to read the woman's actions in case she was trying to trick them, but the woman gave no reaction to the exclusion of her title.

"Sure, I know where I am. I am on Terrigan, the land of the living. You are a spawn, uh, of the human type I am pretty sure, as is everyone else in the room," Delania responded as she gestured to the two yellows and the unconscious burly man.

Tonya's jaw dropped. Spawn? Terrigan? The fool woman called her human, but that is what she clearly was. "You talk as if we are human, and you are not."

Delania giggled again, something she was not accustomed too, and she decided she liked doing it. "Of course, I am not. I'd show you my true form, but you would probably die in fright."

Tonya tensed. Perhaps this being was from another realm. That would explain her power. "Are you female?" Tonya asked, unsure of what significance that had, but she truly believed the woman was not a Mother. No Mother would belittle herself by giggling, regardless if the queen herself offered the crown.

Delania giggled again. "Yes, why else would I seek to bed a man? Anyway, that is on my list of things to accomplish first while I am here. Do you know where I might find one that I might purchase and experience the joy of love?"

"You cannot simply bed a man and experience love," Tonya said, unsure of why she was even getting in this conversation with the deadly woman that held her captive. "You have to be in love."

Delania frowned. "So you are saying in order to make love you have to be in love. But how do you get in love?"

"You ask the question that will take time to answer, perhaps weeks. I do not know who you are, but it is clear we have mistaken your identity. Perhaps you will accept our humble apologies and release us, so that I might make a formal introduction. This land is dangerous and if you do not understand the rules, you will make many enemies," Tonya said, hoping the woman would release her and the others.

Delania chewed on her bottom lip for a moment before dispelling the net and the shield. "If you try to ensnare me again, I will kill you. I have battled risers a hundred times more powerful than you three combined," Delania warned.

Tonya let the warning slide away, unsure of what a riser was. "Do not worry. I promise we offer you no threat. I am Tonya of the Whites. She motioned to the yellows. They have not earned their names yet, but are named in their septs."

Delania frowned in puzzlement.

"Do not worry. I will explain everything. First and foremost every woman, except the honor guard, belongs to a sept. They are divided into colors, including black and white," she said, gesturing to herself. "Each sept has a powerful leader, known as a Mother. Here in Aten, men are nothing more than animals. They are used as slaves and a choice few are used as reproduction. We, in our secret sect, believe the treatment of them to be wrong so we set as many men free as we can and smuggle them out of the country."

"Each tower with a color is a sept's tower?" Delania asked.

"Yes, and each tower has a leader called a Mother," Tonya answered.

"How does one become a Mother?" Delania asked.

"One can become one in many ways. The simplest way is to outmaneuver the current Mother politically, but a few have done so by force," Tonya responded.

Delania smiled as she imagined taking over a tower. She always liked the color blue.

Alexis woke in the morning with dry cotton mouth. She rose from her soft bed and stumbled to the wash basin across the cool room while gently wiping the sleep away from her eyes. When she reached the basin, she fumbled with the ceramic pitcher and slowly poured water into the wooden flagon that was left for her. The water was chilly and felt good on her parched throat. Autumn was in full swing and the air was growing dryer every day. When she had finished drinking, Alexis brushed her long golden hair and braided it. She sat in front of the small mirror in her lavish room and hoped Apollisian found her as beautiful as she imagined she might be to his eyes. The elf knew she was attractive to her own people, but she was not so sure what humans valued in a mate. With elves, the value of a mate almost had the same certain qualities with only small variances with each individual elf, but humans on the other hand, were very radical in their different likes and dislikes. Alexis realized she was too short as far as humans went, and she was somewhat commanding and needy. She realized her station as royalty was surely intimidating, but she could not tell if the cool paladin was intimidated by it or not. The affair was tiring, and she wished it was over, yet she often found herself smiling at she thought of falling in love with the thick-headed man.

After Alexis finished brushing and braiding her hair, she slipped into her leather armor and slid on her light backpack. After stringing her white ash longbow, she slipped from the room and quietly stepped down to Apollisian. When she reached the outside of the paladin's door, she paused to look herself over and straighten her shirt tail. With a soft rap of her knuckles, she waited for the paladin's voice. But to her dismay, the paladin did not respond. Alexis knocked again, a little more forceful than before when she heard a pitiful, faint voice that said, "Come in." The elf poked her head inside the thin wooden door and saw Apollisian still lying on the bed where she left him. He was still wearing his same small clothes and it did not look as if he had moved from last night. He had a thin blonde shadow across his face from lack of shaving and his hair was unkempt and oily.

Apollisian didn't look at her directly, but sat up from the bed and ran his hands through his dirty hair. "He is gone."

Alexis didn't know what to make of her champion. He had fearlessly battled against a horde of dwarves that killed almost every man that stood against them. She had stood by him when a league of undead apparitions had surrounded her Vale on all sides and Apollisian would not even show the tiniest amount of fear. But now, the fearless paladin sat defeated on a bed because he lost something he could not touch or see. Alexis did not know what the bond between he and his god was like, she had no such bond with any of the divine, but she imagined if it was even remotely similar to the love she had for him, she would rather die than lose it.

Alexis sat on the bed next to him and placed a comforting arm around his chiseled muscles. He was hot to the touch and his skin was clammy, but he felt good to her. "It is early. Shall we go to see the human that ran with the Abyss Walker?"

Apollisian turned suddenly and looked her dead in the eye. His steel blue eyes seemed hollow of any feelings but raw anger. "Did you not hear me, elf?" he growled. "He is gone!"

Alexis pulled her arm back quickly. She had not anticipated his verbal barrage. "Elf, am I? Have you so forgotten my name? A name I gave you to speak out of love. A name never spoken by anyone of your race before."

Apollisian rose up from the bed in anger. His fists were clenched at his sides and he towered over the much smaller Alexis. "Do you think your worthless ideals, your misguided belief that some innocent boy is a harbinger of doom, matters even in the most diminutive form? Stephanis is gone! Do you not hear me? Gone!"

Pain tore through Alexis as the cold dagger-like words from the man she loved stabbed into her heart. Instead of recoiling from Apollisian, she responded with an attack of her own. "Worthless ideals? Misguided beliefs? Apollisian, it is not I that has misguided beliefs if you are fool enough to deny me as I stand before you! I will turn my back on the entire Pantheon and curse them to the Abyss for you!" Alexis said as her voice began to crack and tears started to well up in her eyes. "To hell with Stephanis, or any other god if they were to take you from me. Are you too ignorant to understand the depths of my love for you? I am not some barroom harlot that has feasted her eyes on you for a few moons. I have traveled with you day and night for many seasons, faced certain death against a horde of dwarves and then faced a league of undead just to be at your side. I have turned my back on my family and my heritage to stand next to you. Do you not love me? Would you not do for me as I have done for you?" Alexis asked in a tearful explosion.

Apollisian glared at Alexis with a fiery anger that could have scorched the moon and stars. How dare she try to place his god before her? Yet his anger, rage, and desolation seemed to melt away with each tear that fell from her deep emerald eyes. Soon his frown faded and his tone softened. He gently pulled her into his arms and hugged her for all the support she had given him since they met. He realized at that moment, that he loved his god, but that love was a moon cast shadow to the love that he felt for her. Though she often had her own agenda, Alexis followed him throughout his journeys with little complaint. "I am sorry," he said softly into her long pointed ear. "Without the touch of my god, it is as if my soul is lost in a dark nothingness. But without you...," Apollisian paused and took a deep breath. "Without you, not only would I lose my soul, my heart would be forfeit as well."

Alexis hid her face into Apollisian's strong chest. Part of her felt foolhardy and selfish for her tirade, but part of her felt overjoyed at his admission of love for her. The two sat back down on the bed and held each other for several minutes in a teary embrace. Finally, Apollisian pulled her away and stared compassionately into Alexis' deep green eyes. "I do not think it is necessary to speak with Jude."

"But I agree he has been wrongly imprisoned," Alexis

interrupted as she wiped tears away from her cheeks.

Apollisian raised his hand to silence her. "I do not disagree completely. Yet, there is a much greater issue here. As a paladin, part of the wisdom that comes with the title is to weigh the greater good and fight to achieve it. Stephanis has left me, and I have not violated his word, therefore it is safe to say others have lost him as well. I must speak with my order here in Central City. If they too have lost Stephanis, I must return to the central church at Westvon and speak with the high priest. Such a cataclysmic event will surely require a great quest."

Alexis frowned. "How is the loss of a link with Stephanis such an immediate problem?"

Apollisian jumped up from the bed and started pouring water into the small porcelain tub that was in the room. "Think of the sick and injured that will die without the divine powers he instills in his followers."

Alexis nodded in understanding. "What shall we do?"

Apollisian removed his shirt and started unbuttoning his breeches. "You can go back to your room and get ready. If you wish to stay here, I suggest you find a priest to marry us before I finish undressing."

Alexis blushed and turned her head as she started out of the room. "I'll be ready in a few minutes."

"Given my need for a bath, better give me at least ten," Apollisian chuckled as he turned his back and started pulling his heavy breeches over his feet.

"Trust me, better take twenty," Alexis said with a playful smile as she closed the door to the paladin's room.

Jude awoke in the small stone cell. He had spent the last four days and nights there, allowed only brief periods of time outside of the cage to perform manual labor. Most of the work involved heavy lifting, loading and unloading. He was always carefully watched by ten or more armed guards and he never saw an entrance or exit that offered a path of escape. Jude had performed the tasks with little prodding, though he often fantasized about killing the guards and running from his confines. The guards must have sensed his anger, because they always stayed clear of him and kept their hands on their swords. Jude would occasionally overhear one of them saying something about Mershul and what was he going to fight next.

The jingling of keys drew the large swordsman's attention to the heavy iron cell door. Jude watched apathetically as Copel walked into the room and tossed the heavy brass key ring on the small wooden desk that sat against the far wall. The chubby old man limped over and pulled a sturdy chair and sat down, folding his hands in his lap and staring right at Jude.

The large swordsman lifted his head as his powerful arms gripped the bars in front of him. "What do you want?" Jude growled.

Copel didn't smile or frown as he inhaled deeply, and then exhaled slowly. "Was I right about your appetite?"

Jude's knuckles turned white as he gripped the iron bars with both hands. The thick corded muscles in his arms bulged and the round veins in his arm flexed. "So I was hungry. Let me out of this cage and I will show you a Mershul," the large man taunted.

Copel sighed. "You are going to fight tonight, Jude."

Jude didn't respond immediately. He just kept his iron-like gaze locked on the retired champion. "What, more dwarves?"

Copel shook his head. "No. It seems you dispatched them too easily last time. Despite your money making potential, the magistrate wants you to die so they have captured three orcs for you to face."

Jude's face showed little expression, but his stomach knotted up a bit. He had become hard since his arrival in the coliseum, but facing three adult orcs would be a challenge for any fighter. Orcs were vicious, ruthless killers. They were not always the most intelligent of warriors, a fact that kept them from ruling lands very long, but in an arena, there was little opportunity for cunning. But as Jude thought about the encounter, he became less concerned. Death was not a bad alternative when faced with the prospect of life in the arena.

"You don't seem worried," Copel said as he picked at his teeth with a small wooden splinter from the old desk.

Jude shrugged his muscled shoulders. "Why should I be? Won't change nothing. I could be excited as hell to kill some of the green skins, or I could be terrified. Neither emotion would help me much."

Copel nodded and sighed. "I had a messenger check on your friend."

Jude's eyes lit up for the first time in weeks. He lifted his head and pressed it against the cold iron bars. "What did you find out? Is he alive?" Jude asked eagerly.

Copel shook his head from side to side and tossed the splinter from his mouth onto the cold stone floor. "Nope. The man said the elves had executed him."

Jude's heart sank. He let his hands slowly slip from the cold iron bars of his cage and he eased himself down on the hard wooden cot. "What proof do you have?" Jude asked in more of a growl than a whisper.

Copel stood from the chair and stepped toward Jude's cage. "None, really. Said he talked with the guards that brought you here and the elves supposedly told them he was executed. Apparently, the elves are responsible for the charges against you."

Jude didn't lift his head as Copel rambled on about the murder at the inn. Jude knew the assassin had slipped into their room and there was no way the magistrate could have thought that he and Lance were responsible, but the mention of the elves explained a lot. They rambled on about Lance being some Abyss Walker or something like that. It mattered little to him now. Jude had suspected that his friend had been killed. How the boy had been confused with some elven enemy was beyond him, but Jude knew the fool always managed to stick his neck in any problem that looked interesting.

"Is it true you defeated Amerix the Slayer?" Copel asked after he finished talking about the murder at the inn and Jude obviously had not been listening.

Jude raised his head up from his hands. "Who?"

"Amerix the Slayer, the tall grizzly old dwarf that led the

battle against the Torrent Manor and Central City," Copel stated flatly.

Jude narrowed his eyes. "So the old dwarf had a name, huh? No, I didn't defeat him. We barely managed to keep the demon from killing us. I was lucky to knock him off of the bridge, and even then the damned dwarf nearly took me down with him. I swear I saw him cutting his armor away as he fell. The bearded demon is probably still alive somewhere, killing a few men as we speak."

Copel smiled. "Close. Rumor has it he was captured by Meirgan the bounty hunter and is being brought back to Central City for a public execution."

Jude flinched as he heard the name Meirgan. That ruthless bounty hunter never failed to get his man regardless of how elusive or difficult the quarry may have been. Jude despised the man. He was neither interested in guilt or law, only the amount of gold that was paid for the capture. The bounty hunter's reputation was well deserved if he managed to capture Amerix.

"Meirgan, huh?" Jude asked.

"Heard of him?" Copel asked when he saw Jude's reaction to the name.

Jude nodded slowly. "Yeah, but I didn't say it was good."

Copel nodded slowly and stared at the floor. "Some are calling for a rematch between you and the renegade, but the kings officials fear that if Amerix defeats you, the people will want him to be a champion."

"You mean when," Jude responded.

"What?" Copel asked.

Jude cleared his throat. "I said when. When he defeats me. There would be no if. That dwarf is the meanest fighter I have ever seen, and probably will ever see. He has the strength of three men, the ruthlessness of a cold-blooded killer, and the cunning of a thief who makes a living stealing from dragons."

Copel didn't argue the point. A man who could fight as well as Jude was able to tell when he was beaten. But the old gladiator had a difficult time imagining someone as mean as Jude described. "You make him sound invincible."

Jude looked up from his cot. "I have no doubt that that demon dwarf is alive only because he just doesn't want to die yet."

Copel didn't respond he just sat in the chair staring at the floor with his legs wide in front of him. "They will be coming for you soon. Coming to take you to the arena."

Jude sat for a while before looking back down at the stone floor. "What do you want to tell me, jail keeper?"

Copel winced at the title. He had tried many times to warm up to Jude. The young man reminded him of himself many years ago, but the large swordsman would not allow it. This was something Copel probably wouldn't have done either, making the retired champion feel even closer to the swordsman. "Well, if ya' don't make it, just know I was rooting for ya'."

Jude didn't respond, he only nodded his head as his cell door to the room that held his cell burst open. Several guards pushed past Copel and opened his cell, putting Jude in shackles. Jude didn't fight as he was taken from his room and led down the same group of corridors to the weapon room, or war room, as the other prisoners liked to call it. It was where they kept the weapons and armor for the gladiators to wear.

Jude nonchalantly strapped on some field plate mail armor and a great sword. He slipped two small daggers into his boots before he was led out of the room and up to the ramp. Jude winced and covered his eyes as the bright evening sun fell on his sensitive eyes. He tried to think of how many days it had been since he smelled fresh air and felt the kiss of the sun, but he could only remember the last battle instead, something the young swordsman figured was another way to make the fighter want to fight. It was like he had a brief moment of freedom before he was forced to kill or be killed.

The heavy metal portcullis on the opposite side of the arena began to rise and the chant of 'Jude' began to echo through out the stadium. Each time Jude fought, more and more spectators had gathered and now he imagined the arena was full. Copel would always stop in and tell Jude what he was fighting before the fight, and he had learned that none of the other prisoners had that luxury. Jude suspected it was trivial at first, but after a few fights, he found himself mentally preparing and planning how to defeat his opponent. Jude soon recognized the value of such information so he never mentioned the old champion saying such things to him.

The orcs screamed guttural growls and charged from across the arena. One had a thick, overweighted, poorly balanced orc axe, a weapon Jude would have been afraid of a few months ago. Now he had learned how to battle such weapons and the once menacing seemed to offer him little threat. The other two had crude looking battle axes with only a blade on one side. None of the three orcs wore armor as they charged across the dirt-covered arena with reckless abandon.

Jude slowly drew the great two-handed sword and leveled it out in front of himself with both hands. The fool orcs were charging right next to each other, making Jude's defense all the easier. As the three neared Jude he stepped into them, throwing off their timing and disrupting their charge. Jude stepped to the right orc, drawing his attack. The green-skinned beast swung his axe at Jude's midsection with tremendous force. The middle orc swung his heavy axe over his head, bringing the slow blade down at Jude's head, while the third orc had to swing around the other two because he could not reach the swordsman.

Jude rushed between the middle and right orc, swinging his great sword at an orc's head while just passing under the slow overhand strike of the middle orc. The orc's crude axe bounced harmlessly off the back of Jude's breast plate as his great sword hit the green-skinned foe in the neck. The ring of metal on bone echoed throughout the arena and the crowd mumbled in awe as the orc's head sailed through the air.

The middle orc turned and hoisted his axe for a second attack, while the other orc managed to circle around again. Both of the green-skinned foes were in front of Jude and the third orc's body lay twitching in the throes of death. Drool and spittle dripped from the green-skinned monsters as they anticipated cutting down the large swordsman. They growled and gestured, while Jude tried to keep his composure and not give into his Mershul rage. The strong need was there just the same, like an itch that he was ignoring. It never went away; it only grew stronger.

Jude had dispatched the second orc unconsciously as he fought the urge to give into the rage. He was barely aware of its lifeless form as its blood spilled to the ground around his feet. The third orc circled the large swordsman, unsure of himself and seeking a weakness in the large human. "Come on," Jude mumbled, daring the orc to attack, but the green-skinned foe kept his distance.

Jude angrily hoisted his heavy two-handed sword over his head, the blade pointing high in the sky, and growled in anger. He was not really angry at the orc; killing had become a way of life for him. He was angry at the crowd. How dare they rape him of his soul by forcing him to battle for his life? The orc was unsure of the human's intentions and backed away from the large devil's reach. When Jude kept his sword aloft for a moment, the orc stuck out his head and growled back, thinking the display was a measure of strength. Instead Jude brought his sword down in blinding speed and released it out in front of him. The heavy sword sliced through the air and embedded itself into the hilt in the chest of the startled orc. The green-skinned monster's growl quickly turned into a bloody gurgle and it fell dead.

The crowd roared as Jude started back toward the gate. He didn't bother to acknowledge the crowd, check to see if the orc was indeed going to die, or even to retrieve his sword. He simply turned and started to slowly, yet purposely, march toward the south portcullis he was led out of. The large man's apathy seemed to ignite the coliseum. Loaves of bread, flowers, and copper coins began to rain into the arena from the stands. Jude didn't flinch as he was occasionally hit by the tokens of appreciation and started back down the long dark ramp that led to his cell.

After Jude removed his weapons and armor, he was escorted down the dark unidentifiable corridor and back to his cell. The guards hastily closed the iron cage and hurried from the room.

Though Jude wore no armor and had no weapon, they feared the monstrous man by reputation alone. Jude eased himself down on his hard wooden cot and lay back, staring at the dark gray ceiling of his cell. He had counted the cracks and lines in the stony roof hundreds of times, but tonight he did so with a smile. The large swordsman breathed deeply and exhaled slowly, relaxing his muscles as he felt the rage slowly fade from his body. It was the first time since he lost control in the arena that he had controlled the rage. Though he had not been injured, which made containing the rage much easier, Jude considered suppressing it a victory nonetheless. Rolling over, he pulled the thick wool blanket over his wide shoulders. The rough material felt warm in the cold cell and soon the large man drifted off to sleep.

"Great events bring about great change in a person. I was surely changed by my stay with the women of Aten. They forced me to become a critical thinker, a self-servist, and a vengeful monster. I later rectified the wrongs they had taught me, but I was forever changed by their wickedness. It took the rest of my life to get to know the man who looked back at me from the other side of the mirror. He and I were once great friends, but when I looked upon him after my stay with the witches, he seemed more akin to someone I once knew.

Many men and women experience this sort of change in their lives. Most often it is when they come back from war. They know they are different. They see it in their own actions and see it in others' faces when they look at them. They know they have changed but what makes the transition difficult is that person cannot recall the way they were before. Sure, they understand they have laughed at this joke before, or smiled at this humorous event, but what strikes them as odd is that they can't recall what it was like to think that way again – to have a thought process that enjoys such mild humors. It takes a person a long time to get to know the stranger in the mirror, but like old friends, if you spend a little time around them, you will see they haven't really changed that much."

-Lancalion Levendis Lampara

7
A Web of Sorceresses

Tonya quickly made her way to the wounded man that lay near the base of the wooden wall. She knelt down and felt his pulse, then rolled him on his back and propped up his feet, placing her overcoat under his head.

Delania frowned and bit at her lower lip, still unaccustomed to not having her narrow fangs that jutted from her mouth. "Is he a slave?" she asked.

Tonya did not look up as she answered, stroking the wounded man's cheek. "No, his name is Henrious. He was once a slave and then became a gladiator fighter for the Diltz Quest."

Delania felt an odd feeling seeping into her chest. It was somewhat of a heavy feeling that she could not place her finger on, but she could tell it revolved around the injured man. The succubus rose from her chair and kneeled by the injured man, using her superior knowledge of the human anatomy to help, rather than torture. "Cover him up. This will help prevent his body from going into a shock from his injuries."

Tonya wanted to argue, but the power of the strange dark-haired woman kept her silent. Instead she obeyed and removed her overcoat from behind Henrious' head and covered him up with it.

Delania smiled, feeling the heavy feeling lift when she helped the injured man. She rationalized that perhaps she had guilt for hurting him. "What is a Diltz Quest?"

Tonya was still concerned the woman might be a spy or some powerful mother sent to root out their underground network, but since the others had escaped and the question had nothing to do with them, she answered. "It is a ceremony and contest in which natural born Aten males battle to the death to appear favorable to certain Aten suitors."

Delania frowned as she tried to comprehend the purpose. Tonya recognized the woman's confusion. "Aten women only reproduce with men from the Aten bloodline. They are considered the most valuable slaves and only the most powerful Mothers have any. Once a year, suitors looking to reproduce will go to the Diltz Quest seeking out the most powerful, most appealing suda to bed."

"What is a suda?" Delania asked. "I have heard that term used before."

"A suda is a male slave that has not been turned into a eunuch. After that event, they are considered a tuda. The men are severely beaten and brainwashed over a period of several years until they wish above all else to be turned into a tuda, often betraying other men to earn the coveted title," Tonya said sadly.

Delania pondered the thought a moment, recalling similar torture methods that she used in the Abyss on spawns that were destined for the lake of the damned. "I assume that the men without hair are called sudas and the men with a little hair are called tudas."

Tonya nodded. "Yes, the length of one's hair is a symbol of status among the Aten women. The longer your hair, the more powerful you are, though it is clearly symbolic. You have to be careful, though. If you grow your hair too long, a more powerful mistress, or even mother, may challenge you for a right to power. That could prove deadly," Tonya said as she finished looking the injured man over. "I must get him to a cleric; his injuries are severe."

Delania stood and slapped her hands together to brush away the dust and dirt from the abandoned building. "It was interesting meeting you, Tonya. I hope you are successful in your future endeavors."

Delania walked out of the building oblivious to the confused stares of the white mistress. She deeply inhaled the fresh afternoon air, beginning to relish the lack of the sulfur and silt that the air of the Abyss. She turned back quickly as she stood in the doorway. "One more thing, Tonya. How does one join a sept?"

Tonya was reluctant to answer. She stammered a bit as she tried to think of a response that would dissuade the strange dark-haired woman from injuring or enslaving men. "I don't know why anyone would want to join such an evil and wicked band, but if they were so inclined, they sometimes accept powerful outside sorceresses who hate men, but...," Before Tonya could finish, Delania had hastily turned and started back down the alley.

Delania pondered the many new revelations about the living world. She could not bed a man without being in love with him, save by force, and that course did not appeal to her. But how was she to make a man love her? That was another problem entirely. She guessed it took time and exposure. Second, she was interested in perhaps getting a slave and making him bed with her, but she wasn't sure if that constituted force. But regardless, the best way to makecontact with a man, having one love her, and getting one into her bed, was to join a sept. So that is what she set out to do.

Delania figured she first must have a target man in mind. She stood on the edge of the streets in the shadows, watching the many hundreds of sudas as they performed their daily tasks they were set out to do. Yet as long as she watched them, she could not distinguish any traits that made one stand out from the others that showed he might fall in love with her. Some were handsome, and others well-built. It wasn't until her sinister blue eyes fell upon a tall thin man walking slowly toward the market that Delania couldn't figure out why he caught her eye. He was surely handsome, but he was not well built compared to some of the other sudas. His dark black hair was merely stubble on his shaved head but it was when he turned to cross the street that she caught his eyes – those horrifically beautiful emerald eyes. Delania immediately recognized him as the slave she first met when she arrived in the world of the living. The suda had given her a robe that Delania was now sure he was beaten for. Why would he do that?

She pondered this as her eyes never faltered from him. Then it dawned on her, perhaps he had the ability to love her. The succubus had never had anyone do something self-less for her before in all of her existence and as far as she knew, the suda gained nothing from it. Yes, she must follow this suda and join the rival sept he belonged to and purchase him away. Delania knew that only if she was a mother would she have the right to call the slave hers. The wicked succubus contemplated taking over the sept the suda belonged to, but she knew it was a red sept, and Delania really liked the color blue.

As the dark-haired, green-eyed suda made his way into the market, Delania turned north up the cobblestone street to the large blue stone tower that extended far into the sky.

"Get up," the deep voice whispered excitedly.

Lance opened his tired eyes and rubbed them lazily. His cell was still dark and he suspected it was early morning. As he sat up from his pile of straw, he smelled the sweet honey-eyed smell of perfume and immediately recognized it as the kind Reena wore. "What's going on?" Lance asked quietly.

"The witches are bringing in new slaves," the man, Markus, from the cell next to him answered.

Lance smiled at the words witches and slaves. Lance had grown to appreciate the way that Markus fought back against the women. He was told he had been killed, but a few weeks later, there he was. Markus would obey them for the most part, and would pick the times to be disobedient. Though he would be severely beaten, Markus always made it a point to push against the rules the mistresses gave him. And whenever they were in their cells, Markus never referred to any man as a suda or tuda, and the mistress were always witches, and a mother was always 'the red bitch,' or 'blue bitch,' whatever her order might be. The man always managed to keep his wits, never despairing despite the trials he had endured. "How many?" Lance asked.

"At least three, maybe more," Markus answered.

Lance didn't respond, but merely pondered what the other men had thought when he was brought in. He often found himself trying to imagine which of the new slaves would make it the longest, and which ones would become tudas the fastest. The young mage had learned you never could tell by looking, it took a while to judge their character before you could make an accurate prediction. Lance would have guessed Markus to fold early because he was educated and seemed refined. He knew about etiquette and heraldry and most slaves who were once noble were converted or killed the quickest, but Markus never cracked. Lance would often ask the man how long he had been a slave. Markus would respond to the hour and then ask Lance how long he had been one. When the young mage could not answer right away, Markus would shake his head and call him a tuda boy, which was the term used for a slave who was near completely brainwashed and was soon to be a tuda. Lance soon learned that the label helped him and other slaves mentally fight the battle that they would inevitably lose. The witches would do good to kill him; his heroics made their job much more difficult.

"Four," Markus sounded out loudly.

Lance shuddered. They were prohibited from speaking and Markus surely said it loud enough so they would hear.

"Quiet, they will hear you," Lance whispered as loud as he dared.

"Watch and learn, tuda boy," Markus answered with a smile.

One of the mistresses stormed over. She wore a bright red robe that had a blood-stained tear in the shoulder. It looked as if she had endured a sword cut but had been healed by a cleric. Her hair was fairly long and blond, wrapped in a tight bun about her head, which was odd compared to the other women who always wore their hair down to show the level of their status. Her skin was an almond color and her bright evil eyes were light brown like the desert sands. Had Lance laid eyes on her at any other time in his life, he would think her stunningly beautiful.

But now, she was the epitome of death and torture.

"Who said that?" the blond woman demanded.

The slaves were all silent; no one dared speak out and

Lance tried not to look at Markus in hopes not to give him away.

"I will have to fetch a cleric to weave a net of truth, and then we will see who said what!" The blonde haired woman said before she stormed off fuming with her fists at her side.

"What are you doing?" Lance whispered to Markus.

The man chuckled and waved his hand. "They have their hands full enough to mess with us. I have managed to break a rule and they can do nothing to discover who it was."

"What about the net of truth?" Lance whispered nervously.

Markus waved his hand in dismissal again. "There is no way they are going to spend the money to employ a cleric to cast a powerful spell just to figure out who broke a minor rule. It isn't cost effective. All they can do is endure it, just like we are forced to endure their treatment of us."

Lance smiled as he thought about the man's logic. It seemed sound enough until he spied Reena making her way toward their cells. The dangerous woman paused in front of Lance's cell and folded her arms under her breasts. Her tight red silk blouse clearly showed how cold it was down in the cells, though Lance forced his eyes at her feet.

"It seems some of you boys have a problem learning the rules," she said mockingly. "Anyone care to tell me who the suda was that spoke?"

None of the men dared to lift their heads. Lance feared Reena since she seemed to show an interest in him, when he tried best to remain as anonymous as possible.

"No one wants to rat out the daring one, huh?" Reena asked as she shifted her weight to one foot and began to impatiently tap the other. "I assume you all admire the bravery of your fellow suda?" Reena asked devilishly. "That is acceptable. However, tonight you will all be beaten for your silence. The first prisoner who tells me who the speaker was will only be beaten for half the time as the others. We will start with you," Reena said as she pointed her finger at one of the prisoners on the west wall.

The man began to weep uncontrollably. "Please, Mistress; it was that fool, Markus. Have mercy on me, I beg you!" the man wailed.

Lance felt a deep anger well up in his belly when the man exposed Markus. His face felt hot, his nose tingled and his only desire was to strike him in the face as hard as he could.

Reena smiled and slowly walked over to Markus' chamber. She placed her manicured hands around the thick iron bars of his cell and leaned her face close to the bars with a sinister smile. "You must be brave, suda."

Markus chuckled. "Only when compared to those that stand outside of iron bars who are deathly afraid of the beasts they cage. If they were not afraid, why else cage them?"

Lance couldn't believe the words that were coming from Markus' mouth! The man must surely have a death wish, but it seemed Reena was not shocked in the slightest.

"Even a proud stallion must be domesticated before he is ridden," Reena stated flatly as she grasped Markus in a fairly complex weave, forcing his hands to his side and hoisting him next to the bars in front of her. "I find a gelding is much gentler and less troublesome to the mares, often obedient to the alpha mare. I abhor disobedience, suda," Reena said with a deadly calm.

As she turned and walked away from the cell, Reena barked out orders down the hall. Soon, two tudas appeared and took Markus from his cell. The tudas wore red silk tunics and breeches and had a small patch of hair that was cut in an exact circle on the top of their heads.

When the tudas left it seemed the entire room seemed to exhale and relax. "I hope they kill that damned fool. Is our lives not bad enough without enduring senseless beatings?" one prisoner yelled.

"Are our lives," Lance corrected.

"What?" the prisoner called out.

Lance exhaled and rolled back over on his cot. The old rickety bunk creaked and groaned as he shifted. "You said, 'Is our lives;' the correct tense should have been 'Are our lives.'"

The man called out a barrage of insults and threats ranging from death and dismemberment to references to Lance's love of small farm animals. Lance ignored the comments, thinking about hurling a spell at the fool, but quickly decided against it.

The fewer people who knew about his spell casting ability, the better. These tuda boys would turn on him in a minute if they thought it might save their own skin. Lance was unable to sleep the rest of the morning as he worried about Markus. Lance had learned not to get attached to other slaves he had met in the cells, since he was frequently moved around and others were often killed. The other prisoners were taken from their cells a few hours later and Reena walked in shortly after. She was dressed provocatively in a low-cut revealing red dress. It was long, to her ankles, and had a narrow slit up the side, revealing a tan, muscled leg. She wore a long golden necklace with a teardrop ruby pendant that hung just at the top of her deep cleavage. Her long brown hair hung loosely around her shoulders and her face was painted brilliantly to accent her bone structure. She placed a small wooden stool in front of Lance's cell and sat down, delicately crossing her legs. Lance could smell her honey-sweet perfume as it lit up the normally dank, stale air of his cell.

"Good morning, Lance," Reena said sweetly.

Lance sat up, surprised that she had called him by name, instead of the suda title. The witches used the title to steal away the slave's identity to mold their minds easier. Lance didn't respond, in case the witch was trying to trick him somehow, though she had spoken to him in this familiar way before.

"Markus is fine; I have not harmed him. Though I have had the other sudas flogged a short while to keep suspicions down," Reena said warmly.

Lance lifted his gaze from her feet to her eyes, purposely avoiding her breasts. "I don't care what you do to him, he is nothing to me," Lance said coldly in hopes to protect his admired friend.

Reena smiled. "If you are to help me in my plotting, it will do us well to work on your ability to lie. Right now it is very poor."

Lance nervously tried to straighten his hair with his dirty hands, then realized that he had none. He awkwardly brought his hands down, trying to downplay his confusion.

Reena smiled. "You amuse as much as you intrigue me."

"How can you be sure I will not betray you to Ramasiel?" Lance asked, cursing himself for calling the mother by her name. He relaxed when Reena didn't appear to notice.

"Because if we succeed and I come to power, I will give you your freedom," Reena said with a smile.

Lance felt his spirits soar, but tried well to keep his hope hidden. "Why should I believe you?" Lance asked.

"You do well to hide your excitement; I almost didn't detect it. As far as whether to believe me, what choice do you have? I can continue to plot without you, though it will take me much longer to overthrow her by myself. When I do take over, and notice I say when, if you have not helped me, I will keep you here as my personal slave, and we both know no mother can have a suda for a slave. Her personal slaves are always tudas," Reena said menacingly.

The truth was right in front of Lance. If Ramasiel remained in power, he had no doubt he would ever escape within five or more years. By then he may have fallen prey to their brainwashing and give up on the idea of freedom. It was well known that the mistresses often commanded a tuda to leave the tower, and they begged and pleaded to stay, that they were sorry for displeasing their master and would work harder to do as they asked. It seemed if he was to escape with any of his sanity, he would have to do it soon. He could feel himself already starting to refer to other slaves as sudas and tudas when he already knew their names. "What do you want me to do?" Lance asked.

"Only one thing for the moment," Reena responded. "I want you to cast a hold spell on me."

Lance was astonished. "I cannot cast such a spell."

Reena's face contorted with anger. "Do not lie to me, suda!" she said as she grabbed Lance by the front of his shirt and pulled his face close to hers. "I saw you examining the weaves I used on Markus and you were testing them for weakness. Your ploys of ignorance will not work on me. Do not think I am placing any trust in you either. You have not an ounce of power that compares to mine, but I do know the extent of yours. I want you to cast the most intricate hold you can. If you hold back on me, the deal is off and I will leave you here in this cell to rot, understand?"

Lance nodded uneasily and began to summon the strands of evocation that he needed to ensnare the witch. He quickly realized that when he cast a spell by summoning strands, his spells could never be even remotely as strong as they could be if he used his innate power. He could not access that power because of the shield that Ramasiel held around him.

As Lance formed the strands he lengthened them and doubled them over, making them twice as thick. He repeated this process several times in mere moments, then wrapped Reena up with hundreds of bars. He allowed the edges of the rings to stay loose and the tendril-like wisps quickly fused together, creating a thick single-barred hold spell. Reena's eyes went wide with surprise as Lance soon severed the linking strands that would ultimately lead to the spells unraveling, making the hold spell that held Reena permanent.

Lance crossed his arms under his chest. "Good enough?" he asked sincerely. "That is the best I can do."

Reena almost choked in astonishment. She had never been grasped by a full-barred hold spell, though it was a small bar, it was remarkably powerful. What made the spell even more spectacular to the mistress was the fact that the hundreds of bars that made up the single bar rotated in opposite directions, making any attempts in instantaneous disruption nearly impossible. What made matters worse was that the suda had severed the free-floating strands, making the spell permanent. If she could not sever the bars, and the suda did not know how to dispel it, she would be there permanently. "You have done well!" Reena said with glee as she managed to sever one of the hundreds of bars that encircled her. "It will take me some time to escape your snare."

Just as Reena finished speaking, Lance tugged on the severed end of the spell and it instantly unraveled and popped into nothingness. "I hope you are not upset I severed the connection. You advised me it would be in my best interest to create the strongest hold I could, and I figured severing the linking strands would make it as strong as possible."

Reena smiled and patted Lance on the head lightly. "You are stronger than I could ever have imagined. How your power was not detected upon your capture is beyond me. Why didn't you resist with your powers?"

Lance frowned. "Resist? I had only seen the spell cast once prior to my capture. The only magic I could cast was a few parlor tricks I had invented as a child."

Reena frowned unbelievingly. "Are you suggesting that not only did you learn to cast the spell by watching without instruction, that you can cast no other spells?"

Lance shook his head from side to side. "Not exactly. I can cast what I think is called the first four tiers of necromancy."

Reena's eyes widened. "How did you learn those?"

"From a book I had. The elves took it," Lance said, showing his disappointment.

Reena was astonished. She didn't believe Lance's story fully, but why would he lie? Reena understood lies were formed for personal gain. She saw no gain Lance could acquire with such a story. She would cast spells in his presence and see if he could indeed mimic them by merely observing. Only the most powerful wizards and sorceresses could learn by observations alone. "Well, we will begin your studies soon, but under no circumstances are you to use any spell unless in my presence. Understood?"

Lance nodded. "I understand."

Reena thought about kissing Lance on the forehead, but decided against it. The suda clearly was attracted to women, but she deduced he was much too intelligent to be charmed by her beauty, and his boyish innocence seemed to be rapidly fading. Merely attempting such a task could undermine his trust in her. "We will speak again soon. In the meantime, do not forget your station."

"Yes, Mistress," Lance said convincingly.

Reena smiled and rose from the stool, setting it back against the wall before walking from the cells. It didn't take the stale air of the dark dirty cells long to overcome the sweet perfume that trailed behind her.

Delania ignored the suspicious stares the royal guards gave her as she strode through the bustling streets of Aquabar. Her long flowing black hair whipped around in the light afternoon breeze and her bright blue silk dress shimmered in the brilliant sun rays of sun jutting out from the billowing cloud cover of the fantastic city. As she glanced around the base of the giant blue tower, she noticed that most of the Aten women were tall, but had dark bronze colored skin and brown hair, which was in stark contrast with her pale sallow skin and jet black hair. Not to mention Delania was at least four inches taller than the tallest Aten woman that she saw walking down the street. It didn't really bother the demon that she looked different, but she had difficulty fabricating a good area she could come from. She knew nothing of human kingdoms, customs or general appearances. The fact that specific types of humans came from certain areas never occurred to her.

Delania pondered the fact as she walked around the base of the tower, but could not locate a door. All she saw was the large thick blue stones that made up the tower walls. She looked up as far as she could see, wondering if she was required to fly up to an entrance when the wall opened in front of her. The startled succubus jumped back and glared at the door that was readily apparent now, which had not been there before. Delania did not detect any magical weaves set about the door, and decided that the door was hidden with superior construction.

"State your name and business or be gone," said the short squat woman who stood in the doorway.

Delania looked her up and down. The woman was about a full foot shorter than her and was as wide as she was tall. Her relatively short brown hair was rounded about her head, giving it the same shape as her body. She wore a plain blue velvety robe that was a size or two too small, making the cherub woman appear even heavier than she was. "My name is Delania. I am here..."

"Come in, I will send for a mistress," the short squat woman interrupted, bidding her to enter.

Delania cautiously stepped inside the tower. Once inside, she was amazed at how the interior was twice as large as the exterior would have allowed; almost as if half of the tower extended into the ethereal plane, or somehow stretched the material realms dimensions. An extraordinary display of power.

The interior of the room was immaculately ornate. Great marble statues of women in poses of power and authority stood about. There were great blue tapestries depicting dragons bowing down to a woman in a blue robe, and what fascinated Delania the most was a painting depicting a woman dressed in a blue dress that looked exactly like herself, battling a succubus that seemed to look just like her as well. The artist couldn't have made the likeness anymore accurate to Delania unless she herself posed for the portrait.

Delania walked over to the painting and gently touched it. The heavy acrylic paste was masterfully mixed and blended, turning the blank canvas into a lifelike image.

"Don't touch the paintings; Mother would be very angry," came a soft voice from behind her.

Delania turned quickly and faced a young woman dressed in a robe similar to the ones she had seen some of the other women on the street wearing. She wore a fine sapphire teardrop necklace around her neck and her long brown hair was braided and hung over her right shoulder.

"It is a fantastic depiction of a riser battling a demon," Delania said, turning back to the painting.

"Not just battling, defeating. Mother has battled many such monsters, but she is no riser, whatever that is," the woman said.

Delania turned slowly with her hands clasped behind her back and regarded the woman a little more carefully. The short squat door girl sat at a small wooden desk at the far wall while this woman stood confidently in the center of the room.

"Don't think of spell casting, or you will be killed, if you are lucky. If you are not lucky, you will be thrown to the sudas. Their wicked violating appendages will make you wish you were dead. Now state your business and be gone. The tower is in no mood for accepting conferences unannounced," the woman said sternly.

Delania arched her jet black eyebrow sharply and turned back to the painting, keeping her hands behind her back. She knew little of the customs of this odd nation, but she was under the impression that since she was portraying herself as a blue, this tower would be more hospitable.

Something seemed wrong to the deadly succubus. "A riser is a mortal who is foolish enough to believe their power can rival an immortal, such as a demon or devil or perhaps an angel or celestial, if they so desire to go that route."

"State your business, bitch, or be gone. I do not desire any misguided stories," the woman said as she clenched her fists tightly at her side.

Delania continued, undaunted. "I know of only a few risers that have faced a succubus and won. I can cite them on one hand, and they all have long ago been thrown into the lake of the damned," she said as she crisply turned back to the mistress.

"I have warned you, feel my wrath!" the woman said as she began forming a complex weave of necromancy.

The dark black strands of snake-like tendrils began to form and whip around at Delania. The succubus almost chuckled at the mistress' weak power. The strands were frail, thin and highly unruly. Necromancy weaves had to be the most disciplined of all. Their power derives from the negative energy plane; few mortals truly understood how to wield them effectively.

Delania easily dashed out a flow of positive energy around the room, causing the snake-like strands to go chasing after them like a hound after a flushed rabbit.

The mistress was undaunted and started again, but Delania was in no mood to toy with the arrogant spawn. She quickly formed a tight weave of several strands of enchantment, settling them on the mistress' head. The magical crown jutted small barbed tendrils into her head, severing her free will. The mistress' arms dropped to her sides and her expression went blank. Delania then walked toward the squat woman behind the desk.

"Please, do not harm me. I have no magical ability, I was sent here by my aunt to maybe learn from Mother," the woman said as she cowered back from the desk.

Delania smiled wickedly and drug her foot around the desk, creating a small semi-circle shaped flame in the wooden floor around the terrified woman. She channeled a strand of evocation into an invisible globe that bordered the semi-circle."You are safe for now, spawn. If you dare step across or reach through this line," she said pointing at the burnt area on the floor, "you will surely die."

Delania watched the squat woman examining the complex weave she had created around her, knowing that the girl did in fact have talent in the arcane arts. Delania admired the woman's quick wit. She might prove useful later.

Just as she started up the staircase on the far end of the room, the door burst open and a woman rushed in. Her bright blue robe was in disarray and her face wore a look of abhorrence. She had tears streaking down her cheeks and was wiping her mouth and spitting on the floor. Delania covered herself in a blanket of alteration and became invisible, controlling the mind of the mistress.

"What is wrong?" Delania said through the mistress.

The woman ran to the mistress and clasped her arms around her and broke down in a wailing sob. "That... She... I was forced to do awful things," the woman said between sobs.

"What were you forced to do?" the mistress asked.

"I tried to wash the taste from my mouth," the woman wailed. "I was held down. I couldn't fight back. It was so disgusting!"

The mistress' face was void of emotion and her body was rigid, but Delania commanded her to speak, hoping the woman was too upset to notice. "What happened?"

"She bedded me!" the woman said and broke down and wailed even louder until she fell to her knees.

Delania pondered the events as the woman wailed in the floor. What did the woman mean by, 'she bedded me?' Delania had never pondered bedding a human female before. The thought disgusted her somewhat, but female bodies were works of art. She wondered if she could fill the void in her life by loving another woman. As she thought about the event, she found herself becoming disinterested. There was something about the way a man would hold her in his powerful grasp and ravage her that seemed much more alluring.

"Why would she do that?" Delania asked through the mistress.

The woman didn't look up from her wailing, she just continued to cling to the mistress' feet. "Because she is wicked and twisted! You promised me that if I allowed you to overthrow Mother; we would become much more powerful and influential. Now that Mother is dead, we have no way to defend ourselves. She would have never let something like this happen, never! Ramasiel threatened to kill me if I did not return and service her again soon! What am I to do?"

Delania recalled the name as the owner of the slave, Lance the handsome one that might possibly love her. She found herself boiling with hate for the wench when she imagined her trying to hurt him. As she looked over at the squat woman, Delania noticed she was starting to sweat profusely. Delania focused her thoughts into a thin needle and entered the squat woman's mind. "Why do you worry?"

The woman's eyes widened when she realized that Delania was inside of her mind. She quickly tried to shut out certain areas to her, but the succubus exploited them immediately. What Delania discovered was fascinating. Apparently this Ramasiel had sent one of her own mistresses, this fat one to be exact, to this tower, the tower of her strongest rival, to become employed there. Once inside, Ramasiel used the fat mistress to plant deceit and mistrust among her mistresses one by one. Once a deep-rooted distrust was established, the mistresses that would not convert were killed. Now the plotting Ramasiel needed only wait until the mistress that Delania had captured matured in her power. Then Ramasiel would control not only her tower, but the most powerful blue tower, giving her twice the voting power in the senate and creating an upheaval with the queen. Had Delania not despised the woman for keeping her Lance, she would have found herself admiring the ingenuity of such a plan. Unfortunately, if this Ramasiel did not relinquish Lance, Delania decided she would have to die.

"The gods. Mortals know what they know and don't know what they do not know. This seemingly contradictory statement is of great importance. I find it odd, that in all of the religions of my world, none of them seem to question who the creator is.

This concern has been cast aside by the ascetic quest for salvation. It has been ignored for by the contemplative mind that should be searching for the roots of the divine power. Who made us, why did they make us? How can so many mortals blindly accept a truth spoon fed to them, without searching for their own answers.

The leaders of the churches are only regurgitating unoriginal spoon-fed facts and lack any substantiate foundation for their rhetoric. A wise man seeks the truth behind the stories he is told. No one questioned where the gods came from. No one questioned how parts of history were missing from their texts, scripts, and minds. Why was I the only one who would look deeper than the surface of basic explanation for the truth. The reason is simple. I had to."

-Lancalion Levendis Lampara

8
A Plot of Witches

The dull murmur of feminine voices echoed throughout the expansive conical chambers. The interior of the structure extended hundreds of feet into the air, similar to an amphitheater, but on a much grander scale. At the bottom was a flat marbled base with an ornate podium in the center depicting a large black dragon coiled about it. An aged woman with long brown hair streaked with silver stood confidently with her chin high. She wore a fantastically designed crimson robe that was gilded with gold and jewels. The fabric of the robe seemed to be alive, somewhat like a flowing sea that tossed and turned in the wake of a violent storm. The woman wore a thin, but majestic crown of platinum and gold, naming her the queen of Aten. Her fingers were littered with rings that had oversized gems at their crests, and a heavy platinum necklace that hung about her narrow shoulders. The bright crimson ruby flickered several magical auras that swirled around the queen, no doubt protecting her from most, if not all forms, of magical attack.

At the queen's right and left stood her two personal bodyguards. They were captains of the royal guard and wore thick heavy plate mail enchanted to withstand all forms of magic, making the women nearly invincible against any wielder of the arcane arts. The guards were tall and strong and their short brown hair barely tucked out from under their great helms. They kept their hands crossed and rested on their great swords that rested blade down in front of them. They wore long capes that hung as still as death in comparison to the wild untamed flowing robe of the queen.

Behind them was a plethora of personal protectors, all powerful sorceresses from the red sept, the queen's sept. The queen always surrounded herself with loyal followers and never in Aten history had a queen been disposed of by anyone charged with her protection.

Surrounding the marble base and podium were hundreds of plush velvety seats of each sept color. The most powerful of each sept sat closest to the base and the weakest of the towers sat at the top. The room was excited with talk, not from the anticipated queen's speech, but of the new, unknown six foot tall woman with long black hair, and pale white skin. She sat in the chair of the former mother of one of the blue septs. The face that held the most contempt and surprise was the hateful scowl of Ramasiel. She glared menacingly at the new unknown Mother and even more hatefully at the mistress at her right hand, Marlana.

The queen's guards hoisted their great swords and held them aloft, signaling for the crowd to become silent. In mere seconds the several hundred excited women became deathly quiet, though Ramasiel's scowl seemed to scream a silent barrage of threats and promises of death.

Delania ignored the woman and pretended as if she didn't even see her, focusing her attention on the vibrant queen and her speech.

"Mothers of Aten, we gather today in the presence of our greatness for proposals of the senate," the queen said as her voice was magically enhanced so everyone from the mothers on the ground floor to the lowest of mistresses at the top might hear. "Let us begin with the yellows," she said as she motioned with her outstretched hand to the group to her right.

A feeble old woman struggled to stand, pushing herself up by bracing on the wooden armrest of her chair. Her long white hair told of her power in sorcery, but her frail body showed that her long life was soon to come to an end. When she finally stood, her voice was surprisingly stern and powerful with only a small hint of rasping. "I have lost yet another suda to the damnable freedom movement rebels. I wish for the crown to use all possible resources to set upon the blasphemous hounds and silence their voices of freedom and the twisted belief that men have the right to think for themselves. Look at the other nations of the realms. They are primarily run by men, and all they know is how to make war.

Andoria is no more, and it looks as if Beykla is poised to gobble up the weakened Adoria. Men have only two thoughts: ravage it or kill it. If this freedom movement continues to go unchecked, the plague of the masculine mind might poison our beloved homeland," the old yellow said before sitting.

The queen nodded slowly and called for a vote. "Then let the mothers of our great nation decide the rebels' fate. I need a vote of five to put into motion the Queendom's unrelenting resources."

Ramasiel fumed. She had several members of her own tower involved in this freedom movement, keeping them from her door, while steering their attacks to her enemies. Over the last year, she had controlled her tower and the blues were keeping the fifth vote from being cast on topics she so desired. Now the mistress she had put in place of the blue was missing, replaced by some dark-haired wench. She didn't know how the blues had managed to discover her plotting was a mystery, but without her ability to block the fifth vote, many of Ramasiel's conspiracies were suddenly in dire jeopardy.

The votes were cast around the room. Ramasiel voted no, but all the others voted yes. The final deciding vote rested on the blues. The strange dark-haired woman stood, as the others had done to cast their votes and the words that came from her mouth shocked everyone in the hall.

"No," Delania said coolly and clearly, knowing her submission of motherhood had been sent three days ago, more than enough time to be recognized with voting authority of her sept.

A quiet murmur began throughout the hall. The queen stepped up to the podium with a look of forlorn and anger on her face. "The vote is cast. The Queendom's resources shall not be set upon the task of hunting down the rebels," the queen said as she turned to Ramasiel and then to Delania. "However, each sept is encouraged to find this freedom cult on their own and any sept, mistress, or mother, who is found to be aiding the rebels shall be shielded from their powers and thrown into the gearian." Ramasiel cringed at the mention of the horrific fate.

Delania leaned over and whispered to Marlana. "What is the gearian?"

Marlana answered softly and quietly as the queen finished her speech. "The gearian is a ceremony where a woman who has been convicted of a crime and sentenced to death is thrown into a pit of ruthless men. The woman is stripped of her powers and the men ravage her every orifice for many days. Some women have been known to live for weeks in the gearian before dying. It is the most horrible and honorless way for an Aten woman to die."

"Sounds delightful," Delania offered as she imagined the event, but instead exchanged the ruthless men with handsome spawns and it didn't seem that bad to her.

"On to other news, I would like to introduce the new Mother of the Blue Sept," the queen said, motioning to Delania. "As you know their tower has been without a true mother, but Delania has made her way to the top, showing great power in sorcery with the ability to rival any who claim the title."

Ramasiel scoffed to herself as she stood. "I object. She is obviously not Aten."

The crowd murmured in confusion. They had suspected with the same vote in regards to the rebels that Ramasiel had the woman under her toe. But with her objection to Delania's appointment, it was obvious the two were not as close as suspected.

The queen arched her silver eyebrow. "It seems Ramasiel objects to Delania's appointment. I need a second objection to deny her motherhood."

Ramasiel and the queen looked around at the other mothers, but none stood or even looked as if they pondered the thought. After a few moments, it was obvious the other mothers gave Delania their full endorsement.

The queen proclaimed Delania the Mother of the Blue Sept and moved on to other topics, ranging from sewer problems to the growing disputes with a great black dragon in the west. When the meeting was adjourned, all of the women made their way out of the amphitheater.

Delania ordered Marlana to shop some prices on sudas,

since the tower's previous ones had been taken by Ramasiel. Delania wasn't overly interested in slaves as perspective mates, but she suspected that if she showed them a little kindness, she could search out this freedom movement and make contact with them again. In the meantime she needed to return to her tower and plot how she was going to steal Lance away from Ramasiel.

Marlana made her way through the crowd of women as she hurried down the cobblestone street outside of the auditorium. Hundreds of merchants, nearly all female, plied their wares from fresh bakeries to golden trinkets. There were a few elven males displaying their merchant passes in the form of a large necklace obviously displayed on their chests. Marlana stopped at a bakery tent and purchased a fresh butter cake, then hurried down the road toward the suda barn. Marlana had been here many times before, purchasing sudas with her old mother. She always found the sights and smells of the place quite discontenting.

Marlana's eyes caught the shining bauble that was set upon one of the merchants wooden tables. The tent was run by a handsome woman with long dark black hair and a tight fitting black leather tunic and breaches. The woman seemed all business and her face occasionally twitched as she nervously inspected the crowd. Her apprentice, a young gray elf, seemed to be enjoying his time and was relaxing in an easy chair with his soft silk walking slippers propped up on a wooden crate. The walking slippers seemed out of place for the hard streets of Aquabar, as did the elven male's carefree attitude when surrounded by thousands of powerful sorceresses who would rather enslave him than frequent his establishment. Marlana decided to stop back by the tent after she had evaluated this week's suda stock.

As the young sorceress neared the suda barn, she took a deep breath to calm herself. She wasn't fond of the large wooden structure since it reeked of feces and urine with frequent sounds of men screaming from the beatings and occasional executions. She paused momentarily and then after collecting herself, she ducked past the sword mistresses into the purveying walkway. Here she could view all of the sudas that were available. There were probably three hundred men crammed into the small pen. They wore only small leather jerkins covering their essentials and their skin was glossy from being oiled up to assent their bodies in hope to increase their value. They were divided by height, weight, and hair color. The colored manacles they wore, ranging from copper to platinum, determined where the starting bids would be. Marlana figured her new mother would appreciate a firm strong body, almost a warrior type, and similar to her height. The taller the suda typically the lower the price, since looking up to a slave seemed to intimidate some of the mistresses and mothers. Yet there were a few, Ramasiel being one, who preferred the largest and strongest slaves to accentuate her power over them. Marlana shivered as she thought of the red mother's name. The horrific deeds the red mother made her perform while she was in her tower made the young mistress want to wash her mouth out again and sit in a warm bath for a week to try and feel clean. Marlana knew there was nothing she could do against the powerful red, but that fact lifted little weight from her shoulders when she recalled how she had so been defiled. It was suspected among many mistresses and mothers that Ramasiel desired the company of women in her bed over men, but it was expected that mothers shared their beds with no one… A mystery that Marlana would have rather remained unsolved.

As she scanned the sudas, the young mistress found a few that seemed to fit her new mother's needs and signed her name under the auction list so that she would receive an invite at the day of sale. When she finished, Marlana quickly departed the revolting barn and headed back toward the market, in hopes of finding the tent with the odd looking elf. Perhaps she could negotiate a sale out of him. She doubted the dark-haired woman expected to sell the elf, or if she even figured she had the right, but if the elf was foolish enough to come into Aten, he wasn't overly intelligent to begin with.

Reena nervously glance around the small room of her

chambers searching for any signs of scrying or magical means of detection. She focused and concentrated, trying to sense even the smallest weave or residue, but found none. After a few minutes of searching, she created a solid complex weave and let it fall over a silver bowl of water. She watched the weaves form what she thought to be a meeting between two places in the world at the same time. Ramasiel had told her to imagine merely taking two ends of a piece of paper and placing them side by side, never making a fold and never tearing it, but using such powerful dweamors still made the young mistress nervous. Before long, an image of a thin gray elf appeared in the bowl. "Kalen?" Reena called out.

The gray elf looked up and gently closed the tome he had been reading. "My beautiful Reena. I had hoped to hear back from you."

Reena gave a quick look behind her and scanned again for scrying, then turned back to the image in the bowl. "Have you made contact with Mother yet?"

Kalen smiled. "I have. She is a wicked one, isn't she? We have a meeting this afternoon in the market when she finishes her meeting with the senate. The arrogant witch is planning to overthrow the queen, did you know that?"

Reena nodded. "I had a good idea, but if she succeeds, I will be moved to mother of this tower and will have no need to plot against her."

"Why not take the throne yourself?" Kalen asked as he rubbed his smooth chin with his delicate fingers.

Reena chuckled. "I'd not sit on it long. There are many that have twice the power I do. I have many years before I could ever consider such a move."

Kalen smiled as he considered that a few years was such a long time to a human. He had been planning his current takeover of Nalir for nearly fifteen years, and he considered the endeavor a hurried one. "If she takes the throne and you need not plot against her, I still want our agreement upheld."

Reena nodded as her beautiful smile turned sinister. "I have many irons in the fire, elf, besides Ramasiel's succession. If she fails, I will still take over the tower from the inside. I will use the suda you seek; he is quite powerful."

"Do not teach him more than is necessary," Kalen quipped. "His potential far surpasses anything you can imagine. He is a lion cub among a flock of sheep, and every moment that passes brings closer the day he will turn from docile feline to unstoppable predator. I have seen it written hundreds of years before his birth."

"I will do as I must to further myself. You forget, I have him now, but I will keep in mind your need of him and monitor what he learns and does not," Reena said with an angry tone. "And I would call him a fox in a hen house at best. He will steal a few eggs when he departs and nothing more."

Kalen was silent for a moment before speaking. "I will tell Ramasiel that I am waiting for one more scroll from you."

Reena shook her head. "Don't do that! The Diltz Quest is rapidly approaching. Not to mention she will blame me for the necklace's tardiness."

"Do not worry, we must not give her much time to examine all of the necklace's auras or she will discover its true function," Kalen said.

"Not giving her much time, or me, elf?" Reena asked suspiciously.

Kalen smiled, revealing his bright white teeth that seemed to glow in comparison to the dull gray skin of his face. "My dear Reena, your point is well made and I am aware you suspect, no expect me, to take whatever means to ensure I get the Ecnal. Trust me when I say I understand that your goals come first because you possess the Ecnal, and I would do nothing to jeopardize your plans, because you alone know how important he is to me."

Reena smiled as she imagined the depths of the elf's plots in his own castle. "Our time runs short, Kalen. Enjoy your visit of my country and remain ever vigilant. Elven sudas are a delicacy to some mothers here," Reena warned as the image of the elf faded from the bowl of water.

Kalen smiled disarmingly as the view of the attractive sorceress slowly vanished from the small mirror that was set on his desk. The mirror was cast in ivory with the carvings of many eyes looking in various directions set about it. The elf

had owned the mirror for some time, but

found he had few people to speak to through it. The mirror seemed to be set on some kind of ley line that floated invisibly throughout the land, and as he tried to contact others he sensed through the mirror, most refused to speak with him. They had warned that those from other planes could sometimes cast spells through the device, but Kalen had tried many times and failed. The only practical use he come up with for casting was when he would create a teleportation weave, he could do so with little or no error with his portal. Creating a portal with no error was important to avoid appearing into the middle of a mountain, appearing hundreds of feet underwater, or slicing the person in half you were trying to teleport to. The more familiar you were with the area, the easier it was to make an accurate portal. Kalen often used the mirror to view the location prior to casting.

The gray elf replaced the tome he was reading and gathered some supplies and went back to the mirror. He had spoken with Kellacun a few weeks earlier when she discovered the whereabouts of the Ecnal and he decided to employ the deadly assassin again, but this time with a much different task.

Kalen sat comfortably in his soft green velvety easy chair and chewed on a cinnamon stick, marveling at the volume of women that surrounded him. Nearly every one of them had a fair amount of skill in the arcane arts and some, he was sure, were quite deadly. The fact that he could easily be in the fight of his life seemed to arouse him and he soon found himself staring at the rear end of the mischievous wererat, Kellacun. She stood next to him, selling his baubles. He really had no attraction for the lycanthrope, but with his heightened level of arousal, the woman was not looking unattractive to him. As Kalen lounged comfortably, he spied men being led around on chains and almost all of them had no hair. He quickly surmised that the men with hair were at a higher level of liberty and were able to walk around on their own, but kept their eyes fixed on the ground. The thought of having his sliver hair shaved and being held against his will quickly made him rethink his wisdom for being here, but when he discovered the Ecnal had been sent here, it ruined his plans to have the death knight come to Nalir and wreak havoc on the king and his armies. If the death knight never came to Nalir, Kalen doubted he could overthrow Hector for some time. If he didn't overthrow the kingdom within five years, he would miss many opportunities to establish his worldwide alliance and further his power. Kalen was a little concerned with some of the sordid deals he had made with the demon Bykalicus. But all in all, he hoped the archdemon's hate for Hector would override any short delays in his promises he might encounter. Not to mention the promises he would soon have to make with one of the most powerful witches in the kingdom. Kalen was roused from his plotting by a sweet and timid voice.

"Have you considered selling the elf?" Marlana asked as she fidgeted with the silver-colored drawstring that kept her silk robe tight around her waist.

Kellacun nearly choked. "Pardon me, Ma'am?"

Marlana smiled disarmingly. "You are here in Aten now. He has no rights, even with his merchant pass. Selling him is as simple as taking the gold I offer and I will take him with me. With or without his cooperation."

Kalen chuckled. "Miss, my name is Kalen Al Kalidius and I am not for sale, though it would so humor me if you tried to take me by force. In fact I urge..."

Kalen's face went to stark amazement as he was hit with a powerful complex weave that formed a web around his mouth, engulfing any sound he tried to make. He quickly identified the source and prepared its counter when the spell disappeared. Kalen was amazed at the woman's prowess; he didn't even see the flow coming. The fearful elf was quickly planning his escape when a second woman spoke up and the gray elf noticed the residual traces of the spell she had cast when he did not see her. He quickly cursed himself for his own arrogance, but remained sitting in hopes to show confidence in front of the vastly more powerful second female. The gray elf examined her carefully as she casually walked up, seemingly more interested in the young sorceress in the blue robe than he or his baubles. She wore a long silk red dress with a low neck line, revealing her deep bronze cleavage. Her long red hair was braided in a single braid that hung over her right shoulder while her blazing green eyes shone with vigor and power.

"Do not dare speak to any woman in this Queendom like that again, elf, or you will pray for death when I am through with you. Second, you will stand when speaking to her and offer her your seat out of obedience and nothing more. Do not confuse my agreement with meeting you as a symbol of equality. You are merely a tool to me that will be discarded when you lose your usefulness," the woman in the red dress said angrily.

Kalen struggled to keep silent and rose from his chair. He had been humbled by the power and speed of the woman's spell, but he would not risk losing the Ecnal and years of planning out of a moment's loss of pride. The bitch would see who was in control soon enough. If he had such the inclination he might rethink betraying Reena and put her on the throne instead of this so-called mother. "My apologies, Mother. I was under the impression I was a guest in this splendid kingdom."

Marlana started to back away when Ramasiel shifted her attention. "Have you been resting that wonderful mouth of yours, Marlana?" Ramasiel asked with a seductive wink. "I am looking forward to our next meeting; it will come sooner than you think."

Marlana ran teary-eyed into the crowd as Ramasiel laughed out loud before turning back to Kalen. "As for you, elf, if I ever hear you refer to this country as a kingdom again, I will personally feed your manhood to you on a silver platter," she warned as venom dripped from her words.

Kalen felt his blood boil, but kept his rage to himself. Part of being a wizard was patience and perseverance. He would endure this witch's verbal tirades, but when he got his hands on the Ecnal, she would experience his power firsthand. Kalen contemplated turning her into a sheep, or a goat, then set her about the pasture for a stud. He would enjoy seeing the torment on her face as she had to submit herself to the beast's pleasure. "Again, my apologies, Mother. I will work diligently at learning your customs while I am here in your queendom."

Ramasiel grinned lightly. "Good, now you have the necklace I asked for?"

Kalen nodded. "Yes, but I am still short a few of the items I need for its completion," Kalen lied.

Ramasiel fumed. "I gave you a deadline, Kalen, I expect it to be met. The Diltz Quest is rapidly approaching and since the queen is yet to have a daughter, she will no doubt use arcane intervention because her womb will soon dry up from old age. I'll not have my plans ruined by some fool elf."

"I will not fail. I can't afford the Ecnal to die," Kalen retorted.

Ramasiel gave Kalen a dark sinister smile. "Elf, if you fail me, the suda's death will pale in comparison to the other prices you will pay."

"The necklace shall be ready. I am waiting on Reena to finish with the final scroll," Kalen responded. A sheep. Defiantly a sheep, he thought to himself. After suffering this bitch's attitude, he might even stroll down to the barn and pleasure himself on her once in a while just for spite.

"*Too many times, those in power lack the real motivation to succeed. Their egos and personal view of themselves counteract their ultimate goal. Had Kalen not been an elf, I doubt he would have had the patience to complete his task. Had he failed, who knows how my life would have turned out? Would I have become the Abyss Walker that so many feared? Would I have destroyed the world for my own personal gain?*

We will never know. Yet of all the truths I learned in life, I kept one near and dear to my heart. A lesson learned without any pain, is often soon forgotten."

-Lancalion Levendis Lampara

9

A Slave's Strength

Delania entered the expansive blue tower and covered the front door in a weave so complex it took her hours to complete. The spell was set to discharge an incredible amount of magical energy, killing whoever set it off. The succubus focused power into runes that would detect the inner light of those that passed by. Delania's first task was to quickly train Marlana to detect such auras in people and she was ordered to purchase only certain auras on her next trip to the suda barn.

When she finished her casting, Delania spent the next few days exploring the magnificent tower. The colors and pleasantries throughout the complex confounded her. Never had she imagined such comforts to exist. There were large porcelain tubs that could be filled with warm water from golden spouts that she could sit in. She had always found water interesting, but scarce little could be found in the Abyss. The succubus would have never imagined heating it inside of a large tub, then crawling inside with no intent other than to just lay there. Spawns were geniuses!

With each new day, she discovered something else that she would have never thought of on her own. And despite the other tower's attempts to infiltrate her sept and her compound, she found it an easy task to fend off the scrying and intruding fools. Delania had spent thousands of years avoiding the complex backstabbing and scheming plots of demons that took centuries to develop and set in motion. These fool spawns spent more than a month working a plot and it was supposed to be well thought out. Delania imagined she could easily conquer the entire nation in no time at all, if she so desired, but what bothered the succubus, was that she had no idea how long she was going to be here, and in truth, why she was here at all. It was obvious that Bykalicus had enchanted the necklace with some spell, but why would the spell send her here of all places, where the demon had no chance of capturing her? When she had the opportunity, Delania was going to research such enchantments. Spawns had these collections of knowledge and writings to refer to called libraries. She knew of such structures, but in the Abyss she had no way of realizing the depths of the writings that were collected. She had spent a few hours in the library of her recently acquired tower and found hundreds of recorded experiences from spell casting to reports of a great black dragon that lived in the deep swamp to the west. Delania had learned that the swamp contained hundreds of wicked beasts that were held in place by a magical barrier. It contained thousands of magical weaves that had been strengthened over time by the mothers of each sept. Delania learned the swamp extended for hundreds of miles to the south and about fifty miles west until it hit the ocean. The barrier didn't stop anyone from entering the swamp; it only prevented the natural beasts in the swamp from leaving. The succubus continued her studies, learning that she was most likely in a human form. She drifted to sleep as she pondered what deviousness the archdemon was plotting and how her coming here would benefit him at all.

Delania lifted her head from the hard oaken desk that sat in the middle of her tower library. Her mouth was dry from the long slumber and she took a long draw of wine from a clear crystal goblet. The air smelled of smoke from the light brown candle that had nearly burned itself out. She wiped the corners of her mouth with her sleeve and stretched, scratching her head with her long black nails, before standing up and placing the book she had been reading back on the shelves that lined the tower library. "Shall I turn down your bed, mother?" Marlana asked.

Delania was startled to hear the mistress' voice, but settled knowing the woman had been loyal so far. The succubus smiled and nodded, following the brown haired mistress down the narrow hall to her chambers.

Marlana opened the heavy wooden door slowly and entered Delania's bedroom. She quietly lit a lantern next to the bed before she pulled the heavy blue blankets down and fluffed the pillows gently. After checking to ensure the bed was turned down perfectly, she turned back to Delania. "Mother, when are we going to replenish our stock of sudas?"

Delania smiled as she sat down on the soft bed. "I have not revealed a great many things to you, Marlana, but this tower is riddled with deceit and treachery."

Marlana felt her face flush and her heart race. Did she know about her plotting with the other mistresses and her meetings with Ramasiel? "What do you mean, Mother?"

Delania's face hardened. "Do not toy with me, witch! I am aware of all the happenings in this tower of past and present. Betray me, and I will make you beg for death. I will not waste time making an example of you or creating some farcical torture to sedate my anger. I will simply kill you and move on. There will be no questioning, no chance to repent or confess. I will simply kill you without warning and without explanation. Do I make myself clear?" Delania said plainly with a cold wicked glare on her pale face.

Marlana wanted to scream in fear, or try to rationalize with the woman, but she dared not, believing every threat the dark-haired mother made. She had never encountered someone so emotionless before. Other mothers were sometimes easy to manipulate based on their reactions to events, but Delania seemed so retracted that Marlana realized that the only thing that could be counted on from the woman was cold, hard punishment. "Yes, Mother," she answered weakly.

Delania's glare softened as she lay back against the pillows and slid her feet under the silky sheets. "Your meetings with Ramasiel will continue tomorrow. Do what you must to serve me, and if you succeed in performing what I ask, I will reward you with the power you killed others to get."

Marlana nearly fainted. The thought of having to pleasure the disgusting mother of the red sept nearly made her legs buckle, but Delania's promise of power made her personal horrors seem tolerable. "What shall I do during my visits, Mother?"

Delania pulled the covers to her shoulders and turned on her side facing Marlana. "You will make her think you are an invaluable agent in her web of sorceresses. You will tell her you have influence over me and we will lean toward some of her plots to bolster your claims. Betray me and I will fulfill my promise to you. To avoid the witch's threats, be sure to tell me everything she tells you. We will work hard to complete all that she asks. Later, I will give you assignments to fulfill while in her charge. The fool has spun the web of her own doom, and I am the widow that is perched upon it to feed."

Marlana curtsied and backed from the chambers. She closed the door and rushed down the hall to her room. She was excited as she imagined what power she could gain from Delania. The woman was unlike any mother she had been around before. Marlana figured the woman had her own interests and they did not include being a Mother of the Blue Sept. She figured Delania was merely using the sept to fulfill some other scheme. That meant when the dark-haired woman was finished, she would leave the tower to her. The thought of being in charge of her own tower made the upcoming visit with Ramasiel something she almost looked forward to. Surely not the tasks she had to perform, but the knowledge she was working toward her time of rule, made pleasuring the mother tolerable. Marlana quickly jumped into her bed and drifted off to sleep.

Lance walked among the crowded streets of Aquabar as he made his way to the market. There were few sudas that were trusted enough to go out into the city unsupervised, and he found himself enjoying the looks of admiration by those who were accompanied by their mistresses and mothers. He was sent out by Reena to the market to purchase her a nice new dress for the upcoming ball that the tower was holding. Lance asked her what kind of a dress she wanted, and she told him she would be pleased with whatever he picked out. Lance was no fool, and quickly recognized the event as part of his training to become a tuda. Reena was becoming nicer to him, frequently patting his bottom or the top of his head. He hated to admit it, but he found himself looking forward to such displays from her and the idea of purchasing a dress that she would enjoy seemed to lighten his step. He envisioned the look on her face and the praise she would give him when he returned with something immaculate and he found himself smiling. Lance cursed himself for being a fool. He refocused his mind to complete the task, not to enjoy it; they were slowly succeeding in training him.

As he made his way through the crowded tents, he came across a large multi-colored one that had hundreds of fancy dresses hanging from wire hangers draped over a long wooden pole. The dresses were of all shapes and sizes and Lance found the dress maker paid him little heed, which gave Lance more time to shop as he once again found himself trying to find a dress he thought suited the mistress.

"Not your color, I'm afraid. Doesn't match your eyes," a honeyed voice called out from behind him.

Lance whirled about quickly, keeping his eyes trained on the ground. "The dress is for my mistress, I am hoping to find one she likes," he said as he stared at the bright blue leather boots that poked out from under a thick blue velvet cloak.

"Why do you stare at the ground? You were not afraid to look me in the eye when we first met. Are you afraid you might give me another dress that was meant for your mistress?" the woman asked.

Lance reluctantly brought his eyes up to meet the woman that was speaking to him. His heart raced when he saw her. She had smooth, sallow skin and long straight black hair. She towered over the other women, and was almost as tall as he was. Her once red eyes were now bright blue and they shined like the morning sky. Her alabaster smile seemed as if it were carved from the heavens. Lance swallowed nervously as he realized he was looking her in the face with hundreds of other women around. He quickly averted his eyes and shot them back to the ground, though his smile did not leave his face. "I am sorry, Mistress, do you really wish for me to speak to you as familiar in front of the entire market?"

Delania's smile faded. It had been some time since she had last seen the dark-haired suda, but how he had changed in that span. "You are the spawn that gave me the dress that time in the alley, are you not?" she asked.

Lance smiled meekly. "Yes, Mistress."

"How much time do you have?" Delania asked.

"What do you mean, Mistress?" Lance responded nervously. "I am here to buy Mistress Reena a new dress she can wear to the ball."

Reena. Delania had discovered that name when she read the minds of the mistresses in her new tower, but she had yet to place a face to it. She contemplated bursting into his mind, but discarded the idea when she realized that such an endeavor would undermine his confidence in her. He had obviously become more slave-like since she had spoken with him last. "I mean, when are you required to return to your mistress?"

Lance frowned. He hadn't considered he could spend most of the day shopping, and Reena hadn't given him any amount of time to return. Obviously he would be expected back by dark. "I suppose I have a reasonable amount of time to shop, why do you ask, Mistress?"

Delania smiled. His deep green eyes seemed so familiar to her, almost like she was looking into her own soul when she gazed at them. "Then I order you to come with me," Delania said flatly.

Lance's face erupted with panic. "I do not wish to disobey you, Mistress, but I dare not disappoint Mistress Reena."

Delania felt her heart flare with heavy jealousy. She wasn't sure why, but the man standing before her seemed almost lost. She had seen souls in the Abyss just before they became lost, and they had some of the similar traits. Strangely enough, the rage she detected in his beautiful green eyes seemed to burn hotter. She guessed there was something more to the meek man who stood before her. "You will not disappoint her. If anyone knows a woman's likes and dislikes, it is me. I shall accompany you on your shopping endeavor and we will find a dress that your mistress will fawn over."

Lance smiled eagerly. He was surely concerned about the strange woman. He recalled giving her a dress, but upsetting Reena would endanger his chances of escape. He needed the brown-haired mistress. Without her, he was lost. If this dark-haired mistress would help him find a spectacular gown for Reena, what could it hurt for him to go with her for a while?

Delania strolled through the market with Lance. They shopped for dresses and spoke with many merchants who found it suspicious that a blue mother was shopping with a suda from a red tower for a red dress, but they did not recognize Delania, so their suspicions were widely speculation. Almost an hour later, Lance and Delania had found a suitable dress and argued price. Lance gave her Reena's size when the price was set and the dress maker set about the task. Delania was sure to pick a dress that was not previously made, so the seamstress would have to make one new, rather than alter one she had on stock. This gave the succubus more time with Lance.

"Now we are finished with the shopping, and your mistress has a most fabulous gown, I implore you to uphold our agreement and accompany me on a secluded walk," Delania said with a warm smile.

Lance was uncomfortable with the way the dark-haired woman described their agreement, but found no valid excuse to avoid the walk so he agreed.

As they strolled from the market, Delania led Lance around towers and to a secluded alley where the buildings were abandoned and run down. "Where were you born, spawn?" she asked.

Lance was taken aback by the odd personal question, but answered shortly after he realized she was truly interested in his answer. He was not used to that. "I was born far to the south, near the kingdom of Nalir," he quipped nervously.

Delania smiled and nodded her head. "What was it like, your home?"

Lance frowned. Another personal question. The other mistresses did not like him to identify with personal events prior to his capture. He paused for a moment before he answered again, waiting to see if the woman did indeed ask about his home. "I didn't get to enjoy it long. When I was six, these men came to my house and killed my mother and father. I ran away before they could kill me."

Delania smiled as Lance seemed to warm up to her. She asked him personal questions about his past to strengthen him against their mind-altering techniques. She found it necessary to re-instill his personal identity by asking him to recall times of his past.

Lance answered every one of the blue mistress' questions and found that he enjoyed answering them. He spoke freely and frequently about events that occurred until just after the dwarves attacked. He and Delania had arrived at an old abandon building on the edge of the city. Its walls were made of stone for the first three feet, and then wood the rest of the way up. The stone of the walls was pale white and chipped in many places, missing as many bricks as it was mortar. The wood of the walls was warped and spread apart, leaving long narrow slits that the warm wind whistled through. The woman led him around the side of building and then to the back, where there was a small wooden door. The door hung weakly on two rusted hinges.

The woman pulled on the door lightly and the seized hinges creaked, throwing bright red rust flakes to the ground. She pulled a second time and slipped inside. Lance stood outside in the dark alley, until he heard her sweet voice urging him to go in. He entered the abandoned building behind her, careful not to step on any rough rocks or splintered wood that might tear his bright red suda robe. The woman led him through a narrow foyer that smelled of old wood and fresh dirt. It led to a large open area that was devoid of any interior structure. The once stone walls were crumbled and piled up in the corners of the rooms along with wooden timbers that once supported the ceilings. The only remnants that suggested the giant warehouse ever had rooms were the small pale white bricks that jutted just above the uneven dirt floor.

Lance spoke out before he thought about it, causing him to cringe and almost cover his mouth with his hand. "Where are we, Mistress?"

Delania smiled. It was the first time the spawn had spoken to her first. She made no mention of the spontaneity of his question and smiled warmly. "This is where I like to come to be myself. Do you have anywhere you go?"

Lance frowned. "Where would I go, Mistress? I am a slave," he said as he lifted his arms, palms up in confusion.

Delania walked closer to Lance and gestured all around. "This is my palace away from my palace. It is a place I come to when I want to forget about my responsibilities at being a Mother of the Blue Tower, and just get to be Delania for once," she said as she clasped her hand gently on the small of Lance's back. "And call me, Delania. I despise the mother or mistress title."

Lance nearly jumped from his skin. He had been calling a Mother of the Blue Tower, mistress! Worse yet, she was touching him in the small of his back! Was she planning to kill him? How did he get himself mixed up in this mess? He was so close to helping Reena and escaping.

Delania felt Lance tense and she took her hand away. She stepped a few feet away and sat down on the edge of a large white rock that had once been the base for one of the inner walls. "Do not fear me, spawn. I mean you no ill, please, sit and speak to me freely as you would another slave," she said motioning to the spot next to her on a second, but smaller piece of stone.

Lance reluctantly sat down, folding his hands together on top of his knees. He looked around the room, purposely keeping his eyes from the blue mother. He didn't speak until the silence became horrifically awkward. "Why did you bring me here, Moth.... er... Delania?" Lance asked, speaking her name softly and meekly.

Delania smiled as warmly and disarmingly as she could. She placed her elbows on her knees and pressed them close together as she leaned forward to talk. Her long silky black hair tumbled around her head, allowing her bright blue eyes to narrowly peer from her part in the middle. She knew this posture pushed her breasts together, giving her already deep cleavage a more appealing look, and she hoped to get a favorable response from him. "I understand your name is Lance."

Lance smiled nervously as she used his name. He hadn't heard his own name spoken by a beautiful woman since Kaisha had said it back in Central City. Oh sure, that witch elf, Overmoon, had used it, but she frequently used that odd title 'Abyss Walker.' Whatever that meant. "Yes, Ma'am, it is, er... Was."

Delania exhaled slowly, as she struggled to think of what next to do. This event was proving more difficult than she had expected. She suddenly rose to her feet and stuck out her hand in attempt to initiate a handshake. "A pleasure to meet you, my friend."

Lance rose and slowly took her hand in his. Her hand was firm, but tender, showing her natural strength as she clasped his. The warmth of her skin sent shivers up his spine as he looked deep into her eyes again. He found himself enjoying the moment. "The pleasure is all mine, Delania," he said more confidently.

Delania smiled again, finding herself doing it more often when she was around the man. She pulled a small wine skin from her belt and offered Lance a drink. "Have some wine, my friend. How long has it been since you had any wine?"

Lance reluctantly took the wineskin and took a short draw. The wine was sweet and tasted warm, making him think of her hand again. He found himself wanting to shake it a second time. Lance wiped his mouth with his sleeve and gave the wine back to Delania. "That wine is very good. It has been too long to remember since I last tasted wine. In fact, I believe the summer is nearly over and fall approaches, making it about a full year since I have been here."

Delania knew of the four seasons that spawns experienced, but she had yet to see much of change in the climate, save for rainy periods. She suspected this place was one of the lands where the weather changed little year round. "What did you do before you were brought here? That is, I assume you were brought here."

"I was a woodcutter. Well, my adoptive father, Davohn, was a woodcutter. I helped occasionally, but I despised a lot of the work he did. I spent most of my time in the Bureland library, studying," Lance said, trailing off, trying to hide the fact he was a spellcaster.

Delania perked up. Her face became aglow with interest. "I loved to study when I was in... the... school I went to. What did you study in the Bureland library?" Delania asked, trying to cover the truth of where she was from.

Lance stammered. "I studied,...uh ...magic spells and stuff."

Delania nearly choked. "You study magic? Are you any good?"

Lance pawed at the ground with his silk red slipper. "I have a few spells that I created, a few I have learned by watching, but I have learned the first four tiers of the Necromidus."

Delania smiled excitedly. She had her reason to begin frequent meetings with him now. They could discuss, and practice magic. "I would like to see one of the spells you have created," she said elatedly.

Lance reached down and handed her a thin wooden stick that was about two feet long. "Here, hold this in your hand as tight as you can."

Delania gripped the stick until her knuckles turned white as she marveled at the complexity of the weaves that swirled around the young mage, but what was the most surprising of all was that she could not determine what school of magic the weaves were from. They looked almost like divine strands, but it was impossible for a spawn to manipulate those weaves, only cast them from their god.

The succubus's eyes widened as the strands came together forming a tight blanket around her hand, forcing the stick from her grasp and sending it flying across the room. "What school of magic is that spell from?" Delania asked eagerly.

Lance smiled in satisfaction as he detected she liked his spell. "It isn't from any of the schools I know of. It is one of my own spells."

Delania shook her head from side to side as she retrieved the stick to study the enchantment residue. "That is impossible, Lance. All arcane spells come from one of the eight schools of magic. They are, necromancy, at which you sound as if you are somewhat skilled at, abjuration, conjuration, enchantment/charm, divination, illusion, transmutation and evocation. You have either created another school of magic, which is only possible by the God of Gods, or you have discovered a long forgotten school.

Lance shrugged his shoulders. "I don't know how to explain it, Delania, only that I am able to do it. What is the most odd, is that I do not manipulate the strands like the other spells I know. It seems to come from inside of me, like sorcery, but different."

Delania asked to see the spell a second time and marveled at its complexity. The strands lacked any real color and seemed transparent with blurred edges, like an artist trying to paint wind.

"So how can you tell the schools of magic apart?" Lance asked after a while.

Delania roused herself from her fascination and smiled warmly at Lance. She had longed for such simple friendly interaction since her creation. "Well, it is complicated. Necromancy, as you know, is made up of dark black snake-like wisps. The strands are somewhat unstable, making them difficult to dispel for any kind of wizard, but easy for a necromancer due to the wisp's predictable pattern. But each school of magic has certain properties that specialty wizards can recognize to their favor."

Lance frowned. "What is a specialty wizard?"

"A specialty wizard is a wizard that specializes in a single school of magic. It makes him, or her, quite limited in their abilities, but also makes them deadly at their own school. A mage is merely a person who studies all schools of magic. He has the ability to cast from all schools, but is a master of none," Delania said.

Lance soaked up the knowledge like a sponge. "What about the other schools?"

"Well, abjuration weaves are smooth, shiny, and metallic looking, and they are almost exclusively yellow. Conjuration strands, the ones that conjure up teleportation portals, are usually in a loop, or ring, and are predominantly orange. Enchantments are green, forming nets and squares, usually centered on the targets head. Evocation, or the manipulation of great energies, are blue. Evokers use the summoned weaves to construct forces of power, like fireballs and walls of fire and ice. Now, illusion spells are tricky. Their strands are always red and their outlines are blurry, like they are vibrating rapidly. But the more powerful the caster who weaves them, the less likely the chance that anyone can detect the strands at all. And due to the blurred outline of the weave they are the most difficult to dispel. Divination spells are always white and they reveal things to the caster, like allowing them to see great distances or reveal a future, though foretelling is reserved for the most powerful and is confusing at best.

The final school is transmutation. These weaves are brown, but have the most adverse effect. Transmuters have the ability to take existing matter, like flesh, or stone, and turn it into something completely different. Once changed, it is changed forever, unless changed back by the same spell. Transmutation weaves are brown and always go into the target. They have to be dispelled before they go into you, or you are most likely going to have a bad day."

Lance spent the rest of his time with Delania visiting and enjoying being something more than a slave. They planned frequent visits in the future and Delania promised to teach him more.

As they started to leave, Delania extended her hand for Lance to shake it. She had seen this practice done before, though she was unsure it was practiced in Aten. She knew Lance was not from here, so she surmised that it might be a safe custom to offer. To her surprise, Lance bypassed the handshake and wrapped his arms around her. He squeezed her tight, but not insomuch she thought it might be threatening. She started to protest, but his arms around her made her feel warm inside. She had never been embraced before and she found her insides buzzing and her heart fluttering. She recalled the incident on her long walk back to her tower. What amazed the succubus even more was that she initially wanted to bed the man, but now she found herself more interested in being around him and hearing his voice, a strange turn of events indeed.

"She had so much power, yet was as a child among vipers. Delania was truly a force to be reckoned with, yet her child-like innocence of the great things of our world surely saved me from a life of captivity. There is no doubt in my mind that I was well on the path of becoming a tuda. Though I surely did not desire to have my genitals mutilated, I definitely, without a doubt, was concerned in what Reena thought of me. Had Delania not stepped in when she did, perhaps I would have become a tuda, or perhaps I would have been slain as an incorrigible suda, but either way I would never again be Lance.

Alternatively, did she save me? Delania taught me the ways of magic. She instructed me in schools of magic, how to cast powerful spells that would incapacitate enemies, and sometimes slay them outright. Through her teachings when the time was right, I emerged from the depths of a slave to become unparallel in the realms with an absolute power. As I reflect back, though I am sure Delania saved me, I have learned that there was no real savior for me. Lance Ecnal perished the moment he was set upon the mothers without children. Because when a man learns to hate, part of him is irreversibly lost."

- Lancalion Levendis Lampara

10
New Beginnings

Amerix slipped from his shackles as a strange horse with a single horn at its forehead crashed into the camp. The soldiers began to shout and scream as they started to don their weapons and armor to combat the equestrian monster. Amerix slid under the cart and made his way to Songsinger; he could feel the sword calling out for help. He was not sure how he heard it, but he knew it nonetheless.

As the old renegade reached up to snatch the sword's pommel, the entire cart lurched with tremendous force. The heavy wooden wheel struck Amerix in the head and knocked him prone. He rolled to his belly and glanced up in time to see the strange horned horse galloping off into the forest with Songsinger in its mouth.

The old dwarf ducked into the thick underbrush and started after the horse into the heavy forest. His old stubby legs were no match for the animal's speed and soon he was out of breath. The old dwarf stood in the forest, slumped over with his hands on his knees. Great gouts of hot breath erupted from his mouth and tiny ice crystals formed on his beard. He was not sure how long he had chased the steed, but it seemed to linger just at the edge of his sight, as if it wanted him to follow. Finally, exhaustion set in and he realized Songsinger was lost. Pangs of regret seeped into the old dwarf's heart as he realized he would not be able to save the orc. He knew the bounty hunter was taking him to Central City and he knew he surely would not be able to save him there. He had no army, no weapons, no armor, and he was hated there.

Amerix stood in the cold winter air amongst the barren trees trying to decide whether he should go back for the whelp and die at the hands of an unworthy foe or whether he should head back to the plateau and find the temple of the rock. Finally, Amerix pushed back south the way he had come. A death in the arena was a good death. The old general hoped he would find a death half as good as the one Vlargcar might have. As the dwarf renegade marched alone in the forest, the only thing warm he felt were the wet tears that streamed down his face. Once again, Amerix felt grief that was transformed into hate. Perhaps he would find another army to lead against the Beyklans. He knew Clan Cutstone in the south had warriors. Perhaps he should pay them a visit.

"What the hell was that!?" one of the men called out as he stared at the gaping wound in his comrade's chest.

"It was a unicorn," Meirgan said with disgust, before spitting on the hard frozen ground. "Never knew that fool dwarf to have one, but it clearly let him escape."

"Should we start after him?" Tallnok asked.

Meirgan shook his head. "No, we barely captured the bastard demon the first time. I already made arrangements at hen ridge. If we could not find Amerix, they have another captured that looks just like him. We have taken too long to get back, and I already spoke of his capture. I am not going to let some stupid pet horse take my glory. We will pass the other dwarf off as Amerix, get the reward and sell the orc to the arena."

The group turned back north and re-secured the orc. Meirgan glanced one final time to the south where Amerix most likely fled. The Beyklan winters were cold. He doubted he would survive on his own.

They took him through the cold dark streets of Central City. Winter had set into the land and light patches of old snow piled up in the corner of houses and under overhangs of large buildings. Few urchins moved about the frigid night, and those who braved the cold turned a timid shoulder away from the men who hauled the heavy wooden cart through the streets. The four men were not known to the citizens of the town, but it was obvious they were the doers of evil and wicked deeds. They were lightly armored, and their weapons were not displayed, but the group had an aura of definitive wickedness that spoke louder than any proclamation they might make.

The wooden cart squeaked and squalled as it was hauled out of the small town and into the dark, leafless forest. There was a rough jolt as the cart came to an abrupt start. The men climbed into the back of the cart. He could hear their wicked laughs as they pulled out their short swords and plunged them into his bare chest. The cold steel burned as it tore through his tender flesh, piercing his lungs and heart. He struggled to breathe as blood filled his throat and his lungs burned.

Amerix jerked up from his bed roll near his camp fire. His old rough hands quickly searched his chest for any signs of the imagined wounds from his dream. Just a dream, he thought to himself. Amerix was guilt-ridden at abandoning the whelp, but he was sure the orc would have a good death.

Amerix traveled south all through the winter and most of the spring, coming to rest at the base of the great plateau where he and the orc had been captured. Before, Amerix had planned to climb atop the plateau to die, but now he had definite plans to complete before his death.

Amerix surmised that if he had not died yet, he was not going to die any time soon, though in truth, he did feel a certain degree of urgency. After all, how long could he possibly live? Five hundred years? He was already fifty years older than the oldest dwarf he had ever heard of. Pulling his heavy blanket around his bare shoulders, Amerix stoked his dwindling fire.

Though he had traveled back far to the south, he found himself frequently chilly at night. As he poked the fire with a short stick, great gouts of orange sparks erupted into the air, and the trees around him took on an amber hue from the glow of the fire. Crickets and other forest insects quieted their midnight calls for a short while before resuming again when the fire died down. Amerix had become accustomed to the surface somewhat, though his dreams were still frequented by nightmares of his ordeals with the orc. Amerix often pondered why he had nightmares about that particular period in his life. He surely had suffered much greater peril in the countless battles he had fought. Yet the brief event where he was a prisoner in a cart with an orc whelp seemed to haunt him.

Amerix got up slowly from his bedroll and hoisted an iron pot from the small wooden stump next to the fire. Its contents sloshed about as he set it on some rocks that sat in the fire. The iron pot quickly heated and the old dwarf rubbed his rumbling stomach. It seemed he was hungrier of late, though he couldn't seem to eat nearly the amounts he had done in his past.

As the soupy concoction heated up on the warm fire, Amerix ran his old knobby fingers through his sliver-streaked beard. His once long thick beard was now straggly and more silver than black. His long hair seemed to have moved halfway up his forehead, leaving a sharp pointed widow's peak and deep bald patches on either side. The old dwarf stirred the soup with a thick stick and poured two bowls full, placing one on the ground on the other side of the fire. He placed the other bowl in front of himself, breaking a loaf of bread in half, setting each half beside each bowl. The old general looked up straining his tired blue eyes into the darkness that stretched out before him on the other side of the fire. He took his thick unkempt beard in his hands and braided it into two distinct braids. He figured it would pass the time when the representative from Clan Cutstone would arrive. Amerix used to wear his beard in this fashion when he was a student at the weapons academy in his home city.

Soon, a young dwarf emerged from the darkness. He was wearing a bright shining suit of chain armor that was brilliantly linked together. His short brown beard was neatly braided into a single braid and he wore a heavy polished iron skull cap. He had a small crossbow tethered to his hip and a great axe strung over his shoulder, the pommel almost dragging on the ground. He was average height for a dwarf and his thick muscled arms protruded from under the heavy chain shirt he wore. If the young dwarf was intimidated by the old scraggly general, he showed no sign of it.

Amerix motioned for the young dwarf to sit, and he did so reluctantly, ignoring the bowl of soup that was offered.

"They denied you, Amerix Stormhammer," the young dwarf said quietly, but sternly.

Amerix showed no emotion at the announcement, but his heart sank a little. He had asked to join Clan Cutstone a week earlier and had camped here, just north of their stronghold awaiting their reply. The old general nodded slightly. "Aye, 'tis no surprise to me."

The young dwarf nodded slowly and sat down by the fire, still ignoring the bowl of soup. "They heard of your exploits with Tharxton."

Amerix did not say anything at the mention of his former king. The young dwarf was not a bad king, and Amerix was somewhat remorseful for the way he treated the boy. "Aye, I did not treat him as he deserved. I hope in time he will forgive me."

The young dwarf frowned. "Forgive you? I am sure his soul screams from beyond the grave a thousand curses on your name," the young dwarf announced sternly.

Amerix could not contain his surprise. He looked up with weary eyes. "He is passed?"

The young dwarf stood up, looking down on the old renegade. "Do you not know? The King of Beykla marched against them. The clan is no more."

Amerix felt rage start to wash through him. He felt the vigor and energy of hate renewing his strength, but he let it go as quickly as it came. "What of the Beyklans?"

The young dwarf smiled softly. "The entire army of thirty thousand strong shares his grave."

Amerix smiled in admiration of his former king. "Tharxton made them Beyklan dogs pay for their crimes, eh? A feat I twice failed at."

The young dwarf sat down again. "There is talk among the humans here that they are going to create a new kingdom from the old. They plan on calling it Southern Beykla with a governing body based on a popular vote. The north is weak and is having trouble governing itself. The south does not share the north's views about our people and prefers to acknowledge our sovereignty, unlike the north."

Amerix growled. "Do not think they like yer clan, fool. They are afraid, that is all."

"Their motives are unimportant. The situation is stable and Clan Cutstone does not need a human killer such as you among us," the dwarf said before softening his tone. "However, the king is concerned that if it does come to war, that you may have already fled when you were needed."

"So, I am a bonnet upon the crib, to be tied when the babe is to be viewed?" Amerix asked.

The young dwarf smiled and tossed a heavy pack down at Amerix's feet. "Think of it more as a razor axe, hung on a warrior's hip. If you are interested, you may keep this equipment that our clerics managed to find for you just before they lost connection with Durion."

Amerix frowned as he eyed the pack suspiciously. "How did they lose the connection to Durion?"

The young dwarf shrugged. "No one knows for sure, but the humans have lost the connection to their gods as well. Some of the elders refer to a prophecy about a great darkness that will come on the land when the faithful lost faith. I am no prophet, but many think your talents may be of use in the times ahead."

Amerix stuffed another mouthful of bread into his mouth. "You'll see me around."

The young dwarf smiled as he disappeared into the darkness, walking back the way he came.

Amerix grabbed the bowl he set aside for the young dwarf and dumped it back in the stew pot. No reason to waste good food, Amerix thought to himself as he opened the pack. To his surprise, he found himself staring into his own reflection that was shining on the scarred, but repaired and polished breast plate he had lost at the bottom of the Dawson River. The rest of the armor was gone, but the sight of the bright symbol of Clan Stormhammer that was set into the breast plate made his nose burn and his eyes sting. Per-

haps being the protector of Clan Cutstone was a new beginning for the old dwarf. Perhaps he could settle some old
scores. His wife was still dead, his son was still dead, and
now they took his green-skinned friend. Aye, he still hated
the Beyklans, and how he longed to kill them to the last.

Amerix donned his armor slowly and methodically.
How he loved its fit. It was when he fastened the strap to his
ram-horned helm that his eyes narrowed and a wicked fire
seemed to return to his cold blue eyes.

Therrig stood defiantly over the bodies of several slain
dark dwarves. Their blood poured out from their grievous wounds and ran down the dark gray rock of the small
ledge he was standing on. Several more of the dark-skinned
dwarves stood with their weapons ready, but were clearly
intimidated by the ease at which their opponent had dispatched their brethren. The odd red-haired surface dwarf
wore their kin's dark colored plate armor that even had the
symbol of their clan on his chest, yet he was clearly not of
their clan. He held a small axe in each hand that dripped
with fresh warm blood and the heavy plated dojair, a kilt-
like armor that covered the thighs and groin, swayed lightly
as he shifted his weight from side to side, taunting them.

"Come on, ya filthy kalistirsts loving gnomes! I'll cut
your innards out and make a rope of 'em!" Therrig taunted.

The dark dwarves looked at each other nervously. They
had been hunting this fiend for almost a year. At first they
thought the random killings of their clansmen and their families were a result of a vengeful spirit, but soon learned that
they were being targeted by a surface dwarf.

They sent patrol after patrol to root him out of the under
mountain, but to their surprise, the monster seemed to know
the passages around the city as well as they. This patrol had
set out with the promise to bring the killer in, but the surface
dwarf had already slain their two best warriors and all that
remained were the tracker and the cook. They had no idea
how he had managed to gain some of their clan's armor and

the surface dwarf fought with a battle prowess they had never seen. A quick glance back and forth and a blood-curdling yell by the surface dwarf sent the two remaining hunters running through the dark passages of the under mountain as fast as their little stubby legs could carry them.

Therrig exhaled slowly and relaxed his arms, which burned from the long battle with the first two dark dwarves. They were skilled foes and their weapons were proficiently made, probably the best Therrig had yet seen of the hated race. He was confident he was beginning to attract the best warriors of the clan and the thought of soon defeating them made him smile.

Once he had defeated the very best, he could stride into the city unmolested and speak with the clan king, to make a bid to either be a general, or become king himself. Therrig knew the dark dwarves lived on the "might is right" principal and if he was mighty enough he would be able to lead them. Therrig smiled as his eyes became distant while he imagined the army of dark dwarves led by his own hand descending down on the despicable Clan Stoneheart and their treacherous general, Amerix. They would pay for banishing him.

The young dwarf knelt down and pilfered through the dead dwarves' pockets, ignoring the cold, lifeless stare from their dark bulbous eyes. He placed the few gold coins he found in his pouch and checked the quality of the armor they wore. After a quick inspection, he decided that the plate armor one of the dwarves wore was superior to the set he was wearing now and quickly donned the plate. He tossed the heavy axes to the ground and tightened the straps down on the side. He was barely able to buckle down the dark dwarves' armor due to their smaller, thinner bodies, but after exhaling deep breaths, he was able to hook the dark metal clasps into place.

Keeping his earned name among them as the head hunter, he cleaved the heads from his victims and ran a rope made of the evil race's own hair, through their mouths and out of their necks, dragging the severed heads with him to toss into a great gorge he had discovered some miles away.

There was no way the dark dwarves would find the heads and it added to the rumor that he was eating them. Therrig realized the dark dwarves fear made him more powerful than he ever could have been. The renegade had learned that they believed he was the embodiment of some great ghost from the past when they originally captured Dregan City. Therrig always smiled when he thought of the fact they were not far from the truth.

Therrig walked for almost two days, dragging the heads along the cavern floor and through narrow passages that littered the under mountain. The passages and trails were endless and a surface dwarf could become lost in them easily. But Therrig had spent his youth playing in the forbidden caverns and the last year familiarizing himself with them once again. They hadn't changed much, save for a small patch of carnivorous fungus that he made a point to avoid.

On the eve of the third day, if a day could be measured in the under mountain, he reached the expansive gorge. It was as if he encountered a massive cavern that had no floor. He found no signs of any civilization here and doubted there was anything at the bottom. He had tossed heads into the gorge many times and never heard so much as an inkling of the cavern having a bottom. Therrig was sure it did; bottomless caverns always had a blast of hot air rising from them, but this one's bottom was so far down, he certainly could not tell if it had one.

The renegade tossed the heads in with a sideways heave and watched in satisfaction as they fell into darkness. He turned and started up the edge of the cavern wall where he had found a small alcove in months past and made it his camp site. The ledge was about forty feet up and was slow going, but the climbing was not treacherous. When he reached the top, Therrig opened a pack he had stolen from a previous victory and pulled out some roasted dolgo seeds. He placed the large brown nuts into his mouth and savored their salty taste as he crunched them slowly. Dolgo seeds were a treat to any mountain dwarf and Therrig had spent months on his last journey to the surface to find some. He had collected enough to have three a day for the rest of the year and used the savory treat to celebrate a victory in battle of his dark cousins.

"Odd place for a mountain dwarf," the sweet, but reptilian voice echoed in Therrig's mind.

Therrig leapt to his feet and searched the area for whoever spoke, but located no one.

"You cannot see me, fool. And if I wished it, you would throw down your weapons," the voice echoed in his mind again.

Therrig realized the voice was in his head and struggled with how to respond.

"You are an interesting trespasser, Therrig Delastan Stormhammer," the voice said again.

Therrig growled with anger. "How do you know that name?!"

The voice hissed in a chuckle. "I know all that your puny mind can possess. Your mental strength is as weak as beovi bones."

Therrig felt rage build inside of him. How dare this thing insult him? He would cut its head from its shoulders like a dark dwarf, though it didn't sound like a dark dwarf, and the mention of the beovi cartilage bones made him think it was a creature native to the under mountain.

"Very good, dwarf. I am from the under mountain, though as I search your mind, I see you have never met my kind," the voice said.

A mind reader, Therrig thought. What creature could do such things?

"I am what your people call a salomin," the voice answered as it slowly drifted into view at the base of Therrig's alcove. The creature was dressed in a dark black robe-like cloak and was as tall as a human, though that is where the similarities ended. Its pink head was long and narrow with six small tentacles that hung down from its upper jaw, hiding its mouth. Its deep black bulbous eyes stared emotionless at the dwarf and its long pink fingers were clasped together in front of it. It seemed to not be wearing any weapons or armor and did not appear to be casting any spells.

Therrig growled and leapt down from his perch with

both axes in his hands. Small rocks and dust kicked up from his descent as he hurled himself in a fury at the odd being. But just as he raised his arms to cleave the monster in two, its voice echoed in his head.

"Stop," the soft reptilian voice commanded.

Therrig felt himself hit an invisible barrier and he complied. His arms froze and his legs stopped. He tried to force them onward and crush the weak being that stood before him, but he could not. "Do not look surprised, fool. I can kill you with a thought," the salomin's voice choed in Therrig's mind.

Therrig struggled with all his might against the power of the being's mind, but could do nothing. And just as abruptly as he was held, Therrig stumbled forward, free from the monster's grasp.

"Attempt to harm me again and I will kill you with your own hand," the salomin warned in Therrig's mind.

Therrig wanted to make one quick strike, but held his hand in case the remote chance the monster could make good his claim. "What do you want?" Therrig asked.

The salomin did not move, made no smile, if it could indeed smile, and kept its hands clasped in front of itself. "I could easily slay you, as any of my race could, but we can only control a limited number of minds. Given mass numbers, we are easily overcome and our frail bodies destroyed. You have a powerful body and fighting prowess, but your mind is very weak. Together, however, we could easily dominate the clan of dark dwarves that you war with."

Therrig pondered the thought for a moment. "I wish to control and lead them to destroy Clan Stoneheart as they have banished me. What do you gain from this deal?" Therrig asked.

The salomin chuckled. "Riches of their treasure, slaves as many as I can control and above all else, chaos."

Therrig smiled and hooked his hand axes on the metal straps that were attached to his belt. "What is your name?" Therrig asked.

The honeyed voice almost giggled in Therrig's mind. "Ayden."

She made her way through the dark streets of Aquabar. Even in the moonless night, the streets were somewhat lit by the hundreds of magical dweamors that dwelled in the city. Though the dweamors were designed to light other areas, the glow often fell on the cobblestone streets below. The woman ducked in and out of alleys as she made her way further from the ominous-looking towers and more toward the abandon sector of old warehouses. The further the woman went into the old city, the less likely she was to run into any night patrols and she allowed herself to slow and relax.

She traveled slowly at a brisk walk for a few minutes before slowing her breathing and removing the cloak that hung tightly over her head. She ducked around the corner of a large warehouse and through the cracked old rotted wooden door. The warehouse was devoid of any interior structures, save for the skeletal remains of walls past that still held on the inside perimeter. Large mounds of bricks and debris were piled up throughout the structure and puddles of water that had gathered from holes in the roof stood like midnight mirrors of the dark night.

The woman slowly and quietly made her way into the room and sat down on a pile of debris and waited patiently. In a few moments a large burly man appeared. He had dark brown hair that hung about his face. He wore a brown suit of leather armor that was ornately crafted and carried a great club that hung from a loop over his right shoulder. He approached the woman nervously. "I am here," he said hoarsely.

The woman smiled, but did not rise. "I have made the arrangements we have agreed on. A woman will meet you in the market two days from now. She will give you a sealed scroll case and a bag of coin. You only need read the parchment inside and the magic will be released."

"How will I know it has worked?" the man asked nervously.

The woman stood slowly and her bright sinister smile

seemed to shine in the dark room. "So this new Mother of the Blue Sept is friends with the resistance leader?"

The man nodded. "Yes, she is very powerful. Though I believe she is more interested in other goals than any of political nature."

The woman laughed. "You think I am concerned with what your puny male mind thinks? If men were even remotely intelligent they would be ruling this country."

The man did not answer the woman's mocking query and shuffled his feet on the dirt floor of the abandoned warehouse. "She is interested in your suda. I think his name is Lance."

The woman perked up. This information was new. "She has been conspiring with one of my sudas? To what end? Sudas have no power."

The man shrugged his shoulders. "I know not why. I suspect that she is sexually interested in him."

The woman nearly swooned with disgust. "How do you know this?"

"They have been meeting secretly for some time," the man said, leaving out the fact they were usually meeting in this very spot. He did not pick this meeting location by sheer accident.

"That is worthless, as well. My sudas know nothing of me or mine. But that damned Reena seems to be fond of them. Perhaps the fool bitch lets her tongue run amok when she uses them for her pleasure," the woman said to herself. "What do you know of her plotting?"

The man shrugged his shoulders and glanced around the warehouse nervously. "I do not know of her plots firsthand, but I do know Lance has mentioned to the blue mother that she does plot something."

The woman smiled. She had hoped Reena would plot something against her. The woman was growing in power and if she was to take over the red tower when she ascended the throne, she was going to have to develop some show of prowess at scheming if she was going to remain a useful ally. "Do you have the scrolls I asked for?"

The man pulled a small case from his breeches and

handed it to the woman. "They were not easy to come by, but I have spent the last few years earning their trust. Once it is broken, I will need to be far away from here."

The woman waved her hand in dismissal at his fears. "Worry not. By the time they discover your treachery it will be too late for them."

The man nodded slowly as he contemplated the woman's words. They didn't exactly reaffirm his hopes, but he did not press her, thinking it was nothing more than her choice of words. The money she was offering him would pay much more than the meager coins the resistance was offering him. He could live like a king for the rest of his life. Perhaps he would travel to Aboe. The rich multicultural society would allow him to blend in with few questions asked of his background.

The woman stood as she placed the scroll case in her side pouch. "Before I go, I want you to know who you are dealing with, that if you think of going against our bargain, you will understand your life will be spent in my tower and no resistance will be able to save you."

The man nodded, but showed no emotion. "I suspect you are the powerful Ramasiel."

Ramasiel was shocked at the man's proclamation of her name. Her shock quickly changed into approval. "You are not as stupid as you seem. Once again, Henrious, you prove I have chosen the best person for the job."

Henrious nodded as he turned and disappeared into the darkness of the warehouse. Ramasiel watched him go and returned to her tower just as she had come. She had to hurry to set this side plot in motion. There was a backstabbing mistress, a damnable blue mother, a suda, and an aging queen that all needed to be dealt with.

Lance eagerly read vast volumes of tomes that lay before him. Reena had taken him to the tower library under some pretense of a task several months ago. When they had arrived she told the other mistresses that he was assigned to sweep the library floors and care for the books to keep them from bookworms and moisture. She told him at night when the other women went to bed, he could examine as many books as he wanted. Lance initially searched out spell books but found they had no instruction on how to cast spells, but had detailed descriptions of their functions and what they looked like. He read those kinds but found himself quickly bored with them and sought out other kinds of books. Tonight he had found some book that was titled 'Prophecies and Predictions.' He wasn't sure exactly what was inside, but the ancient-looking tome was in a poor state of disrepair and had ancient elven runes on the outside of it that looked similar to the ones on his cloak his mother had given him.

The first few pages contained detailed pictures and sketches of a man walking among monsters in a strange world. They bowed low to him and looked as if they were trying to kiss his feet. The monsters ranged from nude women with bat wings and horns to a giant half-man, half-goat monster with bat wings that seemed as if someone had set him on fire. Lance couldn't read any of the text, but the pictures were quite interesting. He thought about copying some of the runes down and asking his new friend, Delania, what she thought they meant. She was very knowledgeable about things like that.

Lance's concentration was broken by the sound of the door lock clanging and the large wooden door creaking open. He quickly closed the tome, picked up his rag and began to pretend he was dusting off the outside. To Lance's relief, Reena rounded the corner of the bookshelf. She wore a soft red silk nightgown that he was sure if he strained his eyes, he would be able to see the points of her ample breasts underneath. But despite his attraction to her, Lance knew she was a deadly enemy.

Reena's face was pale and full of worry. "We must speak, Lance," she said as her voice quivered.

"What seems to be troubling you, Mistress?" Lance asked as he set the book face down on the table in front of him.

"It seems Ramasiel is on to my scheme," Reena said

worriedly.

Lance felt a heavy burden fall onto his shoulders, though he knew he could run to Delania if need be. "What does she know?" Lance asked, hoping Reena might disclose more of her plot in her disheveled state. Lance only new brief details in her scheme and the parts he heard, he didn't understand. The largest confusion he had was why he was to increase his casting ability when he didn't know of any time Reena wanted him to use it, and once he did, he would be slain as quickly as possible.

Reena glanced down at the book that Lance was cleaning. The ancient tome was face down on the table so she picked the heavy book up and turned it over. "You reading this?"

Lance shrugged his shoulders. He didn't want to tell her he had been looking at it, but had learned long ago his ability to lie to her was poor. "I tried to read it, but I can't make out anything except for the title the tower had written on it."

Reena pushed the book aside. "The book has no real meaning. It is of prophecies. Prophecies are not about magic, only the effects of great manipulations of it. Only certain beings can prophesize and almost none of them can understand what they see until it has already happened. And of course, that is too late," Reena said.

Lance glanced at the book then returned his gaze back to hers. "It seemed interesting to me. I gave it passing interest at best."

"Good. We need you as knowledgeable as possible. When the time comes to strike, we will have little chance for pause," Reena said.

"What am I to do? I think I can identify most weaves of basic and intermediate spells. They should not be too difficult to cast," Lance said.

Reena pressed her body close to Lance's. Her hot breath soaked into his face and chest. She pressed her firm breasts against his body and the warmth of her touch against his skin. "When the time is right, I need you to cast that hold spell you cast on me on the queen."

Lance heard her, but was more concerned with her

touch. It used to make his loins burn with hunger for her and an eagerness to please, but now it felt wrong. For some reason, Delania popped into his head. Lance wasn't sure why his friendship with her had anything to do with his attraction to Reena, but it surely kept his head clear.

Lance nodded his head as he tried to hide his discomfort to Reena's touch. "When will I be near her? How am I to know when you need me, too?"

Reena smiled. "Ramasiel will kiss the queen's ring hand. When she does, loose it then. The queen will think Ramasiel did it and attack her. I will take you out of the side door of the royal chamber and teleport you outside of the city limits. There you will make your way east with the rising sun until you reach the city of Lostom. Once you cross the Lostom River, you will be in Kai-Harkia and safe."

Lance did not say anything, he just nodded and shifted uneasily with the woman's body pressed against his.

The mistress mistook Lance's actions as lust and smiled as she left the library, thinking he was closer to wanting to give his life for hers. She knew once he cast the spell, the queen would blame Ramasiel for trying to take the throne. Of course Ramasiel was trying to take the throne, but not by overt force. Ramasiel would be unprepared and the queen would kill her. With Ramasiel gone, she would be the most suited to rule the red tower. Of course Lance would be killed with Ramasiel; the suda was nothing more than a tool. Many had been killed in plots before him and many more would be killed after. It was just the way things were. Reena smiled as she made her way back to her room and wondered if her Markus was still in her bed. She had given him quite a workout, and if he was still there, she planned to work him some more.

Ramasiel brushed her long brown hair with a jeweled ivory brush. She smiled softly and tilted her head to the side and stroked it again. The sorceress stared at her reflection in the mirror with a soft grin. Anyone who knew the woman, however, knew of her ruthless and wicked nature that valued power over any life. She had killed, maimed, tortured, and used countless souls to get what she wanted, and planned to do the same to countless more.

Ramasiel gently placed the hard ivory brush down on the polished cherrywood nightstand and rose from her soft velvety chair. She straightened her bright crimson robes and slowly strode across her room. The chamber was large and expansive, but seemed crowded with the valuable vases, tapestries and other rich artifacts. When she reached the ornate door of her chamber, she opened it, but did not look into the hall as she spoke. "Fetch Reena for me, tuda."

The short-haired man that stood outside of her chamber nodded, but did not look at the beautiful woman and responded . "Yes, Mother."

Ramasiel returned to her cherrywood stand and picked up her brush again, admiring the woman that stared back at her from the mirror.

In minutes a gentle knock at the chamber door turned Ramasiel's soft smile into a sinister grin of wickedness. "Come in, Mistress."

Reena ducked inside of Ramasiel's chamber and peevishly closed the door before coming over to the powerful sorceress. "You summoned me, Mother?"

Ramasiel did not respond right away. She enjoyed watching the mistress wiggle in her dress. After a few moments of brushing her hair, Ramasiel broke the silence. "I have a task for you, Reena."

Reena was relieved. She was worried Ramasiel had discovered her plotting, or her frequent visits to her suda, or any number of the activities she was involved with for which the mother would surely punish her severely. "What is the task, Mother? Please disclose it that I may set out at once."

Ramasiel smiled wickedly. "Kalen plans to double-cross me somehow. The wretched elf is lying about needing other materials to finish the item I asked for. Do you know why?"

Reena's heart raced. Did Ramasiel know about her plan with Kalen? The mother seldom, if ever, asked a question she did not already know the answer to. She was probably hoping she would give her a chance to tell the truth and receive only a small punishment. Reena started to answer, but rethought the situation. If Ramasiel knew of her plot, she would have had her slain, not question her about it. Reena surmised that Ramasiel suspected, but did not know. Reena figured the mother was relying on her fear that she was found out and would voluntarily disclose her own damning testimony. Reena regained her composure and answered, "I do not Mother, but I suspected the same thing. Gray elves are not to be trusted."

"Agreed," Ramasiel answered. "So I have decided to move on with my plan without the elf. I need you to fetch some items for me that I can cut my strings to this elf and add him to my slaves. His arrogance will be fun to break."

Reena nearly choked. If Ramasiel had discovered how to create the necklace without the elf, that crushed both of her plans in a single swoop. "Is it wise to use the resources to create this item ourselves, rather than allow the elf to do our bidding?"

"Normally I would say no. But this instance is different. The elf is up to no good and I can fell several enemies at once by destroying him," Ramasiel said with an evil giggle.

Reena felt her face flush and her body temperature rise. "What shall I do, Mother?"

Ramasiel pulled a small leather pouch and an ivory scroll case sealed with a red wax from the middle drawer of her cherrywood nightstand and placed it on the edge. "This is a map of Kai-Harkia. I need you to take it with you and give it to a suda from the blue tower that will meet you by the market. He will ask for the stolen coins; give him this bag. He has already performed what I asked and the elf will soon be in my custody. The suda needs the money to escape the city, since the elf is blamed for his death."

Reena nodded, quickly took the items and left the chamber. She hurried to complete the task, hoping that the sooner the elf was eliminated, the less likely her scheme was to be discovered. It was obvious Ramasiel had inadvertently thwarted it, but Reena was sure she would create another. Lance's magical prowess created many opportunities.

"I surely recall my horrid period of slavery in the wicked city of Aquabar. The women there plotted against each other with such deceit that even the demons and devils would have found themselves at home in the revolting city. Treachery was not just a way of life; it was an action that was expected. I cannot imagine such a lowly existence as theirs must have been.

Even as a slave, there were few men I could call friend, or at least a good acquaintance. I need not fear betrayal by them, though surely some were as conniving as the women they served. But the poor sorceress knew no friendship other than the backstabbing ally they worked with long enough to achieve something they both wanted. Delania was a succubus from the Deep Abyss. She had no friends and made little attempt to make any. But when she was presented into the world of the living, the first thing she sought out was that which had eluded her since her creation, friendship.

Even now, looking back at that horrid time of my life that ultimately changed me, I often wonder what would have become of half of the women there if they had left the web of deceit and treachery they lived in. I surely think their wickedness was nothing more than an attempt to thrive in the culture in which they lived. Poor Reena; she was good at heart at one time before she slipped into the delves of wickedness. I wonder if history will say the same of me."

- Lancalion Levendis Lampara

ᔑ 11 ᔑ
Arc of the Pendulum

Dark rolling clouds stretched across the evening sky. The cool mountain wind seemed to slide off of the rocky peaks to the east like a lard-covered egg slipping from an iron skillet. A fog was beginning to settle in the plains and the army of nearly fifteen thousand was not concerned. They had marched for nearly two weeks without food, without water, without rest. They neither cheered nor jeered, as this army was made of the dead.

Their rusted mail clung to rotten, festering corpses that marched forward following the will of their creator. Their creator rode atop a decaying equine corpse. The monstrosity had no eyes and was as bloated as it was muscled. It had no need for encouragement and was not skittish. It moved as uniformly as the soldiers behind it, in a dull, lifeless march. The beast atop the undead steed moved freely, making him stand out like a bright green leaf sitting atop a murky puddle.

Trinidy gazed out at the army he had created. It was larger than the army he used to attack the vale, but the death knight knew he was soon reaching the limits of his power. There was no being on the prime realm that could create a fraction of the undead he had, yet the defiled champion knew he needed more. He had stumbled across an old battle field in a lush valley in the Pyberian Mountains. It seemed as if the majority of the dead had been killed by a beast of colossal proportions. Yet to the death knight's dismay, he could not locate the creature.

It took the death knight nearly a week to animate all of the bodies. Trinidy could animate more, but when he tried, others he had already created fell apart. He just simply could not control enough weaves to create another single apparition.

The death knight paused on his horse and turned to

face the rotting army that was stretched from one horizon to the other. His blue glowing eyes scanned the army with great scrutiny. Though he commanded all of them, the death knight could not give them the ability to make decisions. They only attacked if he ordered, and that was erratic at best. He had no unit cohesiveness, and could not facilitate all points of the battle. That was how his army was decimated at the elven vale. The mere thought of the elves sent hate ripping through Trinidy's soul. He had been tricked by that foul demon Bykalicus, he was sure of it. He had once been a beacon of light for those who were in need, now he was a vile black spot on the horizon of good, yet the thought of being insignificant angered him. He would turn that black spot into a plague on the earth that had not been seen, nor would ever be seen again. Oh, he would do as he must and right that which was wrong, but after that task was completed, he would spread his armies and become a cancer that would envelope the world.

Trinidy felt a tickle deep inside of him when he imagined the sky blackened and the earth rotted. He knew he was evil, and he knew it was wrong to be evil, but he didn't care. Somehow the demon had changed his heart. Trinidy vowed to himself when he finished this task, he would show the demon what true evil really was.

It was the hate inside of him that spurred the first few tentacles of necromancy from him. Trinidy watched as his arms involuntarily moved and his fingers danced, sending out wave after wave of necromancy. The dark snake-like wisps of energy melted into the ground and the death knight felt himself animating another corpse. Trinidy started to sever the weaves thinking it fruitless, when he paused. This creation was different than the others. He could feel its conscious thought. No, maybe not a thought, but more of a drive. The death knight's rotted face cracked and hundreds of black stinging insects erupted across his cheek, running from his nose to his ears and back into his lifeless eye sockets when the apparition's violet hand erupted from the earth. It had long black razor-sharp claws and its tight skin held the beast's flesh in place. When it pulled its head and upper torso from the earth, Trinidy nearly laughed with excitement. The undead monster had long needle-like teeth and its eyes were gray and lifeless. It had long black hair that hung from its pustule-filled head in thin greasy locks. It wore no armor and wielded no weapons unlike the other creations Trinidy had made, but the dead knight knew this beast needed neither and was three times as deadly. It was soon after that Trinidy recognized the monster. He fought its kind in his life. The beast was called a ghoul, an undead monster that was as ferocious as it was cunning. These monsters could paralyze victims immediately with its tainted bite and devour them alive with its insatiable hunger for live flesh. Ghouls hated all living things and Trinidy knew they could sense their heartbeats, just as he could.

"Go to the central ranks, my pet, while I make the rest of your unit," Trinidy commanded silently.

The beast did not reply, but obeyed with eagerness. The other undead soldiers gave no inclination of the new monster added to their ranks, but Trinidy could detect a lust for flesh coming from the ghoul.

The death knight focused his powers consciously this time, and created another ghoul, then another. The dark violet-skinned monsters hastily made their way into ranks after they were created, awaiting their master's command to march forward and kill anything that was alive.

The rest of the night and the following day, Trinidy spent creating five hundred ghouls. When he was finished, he began his march further east, but stopped frequently whenever he sensed more bodies in the ground. It was then it occurred to the death knight that he had stumbled on the old battlegrounds of the Adorian Civil War. The country's king had died with no heir to the throne and all of the nobles produced who they felt should be king. The small factions fought amongst each other for several years until two powerful candidates arose from the masses. They each built armies with the east, opting to create his own kingdom, calling it Andoria. The west refused to accept the sovereignty of Andoria and ordered the new kingdom to relinquish its land. Naturally, Andoria refused and the war began.

Trinidy felt his ambitions soar when he imagined the possible number of dead he might come across as he made his way across this land. The last thing he recalled when he was alive was at least twenty thousand dead from both sides and the war was just beginning to heat up. The death knight imagined the plague he could bring about with an army touting those numbers and he immediately began imagining ways to create more powerful undead beasts.

The following day Trinidy created a creature similar to the ghouls but he called them ghasts. They were more monstrous in appearance and had a stench that he was sure could nauseate even the most strong-willed fighters. Plus, the ghasts had a more potent form of paralyzing power that the undead knight suspected could even overcome an elf's immunity to such magic. Trinidy created a unit of ghasts. They were more taxing on his powers and took a week to finish four hundred of them.

Trinidy marched on for the rest of the day when he encountered another battlefield containing several thousand dead. This time he summoned raw energies from the negative material plane and infused it with the souls of the dead. The result was an intangible form that had the ability to pass through solid objects and drain the life force of their victims. Trinidy imagined that those slain by these beasts would become one in a matter of hours. But to Trinidy's dismay, these beasts were destroyed by daylight, so he named them shadows. His unit of shadows was his most powerful by far, but they forced the death knight to march only at night, as the shadows were hid in the earth during the day. As he made his way slowly across the lands of Andoria, Trinidy created an army of undead that was larger than any army of the living had ever seen. Soon he would reach this wrong that he had to right, and he would unleash his hate on the world.

"I am not taking orders from a damned boy!" Doogan Raymer shouted to the other northern nobles as they sat in their council room atop the Dawson River Inn. The room was a posh one, decorated for the king himself with the Beyklan symbol of a long sword piercing the center of a golden crown tilted on its axis on lavish crimson tapestries.

"You think I enjoy it, fool?" Kareeg Hut shouted as he slammed his large fist down on the polished oaken table. I own more lands than any noble here and my brother was slain in the battle of the Torrent Manor. I despise taking orders from a boy as well, but I risk more than any of you here," he said as spittle sprayed from his mouth and stuck in his coarse brown beard.

"Yes, you have more to lose than we. So you have said several times tonight. But not withstanding, we all have our livelihoods to consider," Edgar said with an eerie calm.

"You have no authority here, Edgar," Doogan Raymer growled. "You might as well be spying on us for the boy king. Your only concern is your damned church of Surshy."

The other nobles in the room murmured in agreement.

Edgar's eyes narrowed in a deadly glare. "Careful who you are damning, Raymer. I think Surshy has more authority to carry that threat than you can ever fathom."

Kareeg waved his hands in an attempt to diminish the unspoken threat by Edgar. "This is foolishness. We all have our agendas and they are on the table. We have taken oaths not to profit from this trying time. Edgar," Kareeg announced, pointing to the high priest, "has made it known he wishes to oust Stephanis as the observed royal religion and in his place, add Surshy, the Goddess of Water. We all have agreed to this. What other plot could he serve that would effect us? He needs us to make the vote happen, just as we need him to sway the king in our endeavors."

The other northern nobles murmured in agreement and whispered amongst themselves. "And what if one of us makes an overt move against another?" a nobleman called out with many others shouting words of agreement.

"Then we will address this at our monthly meetings. If need be, the nobleman will be stripped of his lands and titles," Raymer said sternly.

The nobles all talked amongst themselves for several minutes before eventually agreeing.

"Clan Stoneheart is no more, our scouts report that the dwarf is dead. Our king is dead and the entire western army was defeated. I say we rebuild the Torrent Manor and start mining the mountains," another noble put in.

"And what of the Western Army? It is no more. How will we defend ourselves from the war-prepared Adorians? Sure, they do not have the military we do, but any army can defeat city militias and undefended towns," Hut argued.

"We can send the central army to cover the west," another noble suggested.

"Are you mad? Who would defend us from the south? You know the southern nobles are probably meeting just as we are, on how to strike us, not to mention the general of the southern army has made it known he does not acknowledge the boy king's crown. Besides, you know how those murdering dwarf-loving bastards are. They think we were wrong in killing every last one of Clan Stoneheart when it was the bearded hellions that killed every man, woman, and child of the Torrent Manor. Had the dwarves sacked Motivas or Portia, I think they would not be as sympathetic," Hut responded passionately.

"We obviously must appease the south somehow," Edgar stated flatly.

"The only thing that will appease those bastards is their own sovereignty," a noble called out.

"Fine, give it to them," Kareeg blurted out.

"Have you gone mad?" Doogan Raymer shouted with the agreement of the room.

"It's not a bad idea, really," Edgar responded. "They have one army, a plethora of poor noblemen in comparison to us. By giving them their sovereignty, we can eliminate the threat of the southern army, move the central army to cover our western fronts and start mining the Pyberian Mountains. In several years if the south doesn't beg to return to us after we refuse to trade with them, we will have replenished our armies and we will crush them just as we have done all of our enemies in the past."

The room was silent. The priest had presented a solution that seemed to solve all of their problems at once. Only

Kareeg owned lands in the south and he was in the process of selling them. Though they all detested giving the poorer southern nobles anything, they agreed uniting the kingdom under the boy was futile at best. But in ten or so years, the boy king would be a man who could unite the kingdom and reclaim its lost land.

"All in favor of the plan presented by Edgar?" Doogan asked.

In unison all the northern nobles raised their hands. Edgar imagined it was the first time in history the selfish pig-hearted fools had ever agreed on anything.

Ramasiel focused her mind intently on the red pulsing weave of illusion. She was skilled at illusions, but this spell was difficult and the importance of it required her to cast it perfectly. Marlana shook nervously as the spell took hold and the unstable strands blended into her body.

Ramasiel smiled when she was done casting and dabbed the sweat from her brow with a moist towel. "You look good enough to eat," Ramasiel said jokingly as she stared at Marlana who now looked like an exact replica of her.

"Did it work, Mother?" Marlana asked doubtfully as she stared down at her still blue robe she had wore when she came in.

"Perfectly," Ramasiel said as she ran a lustful finger down Marlana's cheek and into the front of her bodice. "Now, you will not be able to see the illusion that envelopes you unless you look into the mirror. It is important than you say as little as possible. Even though you possess my voice, you do not have the mannerisms that are necessary to fool many that have been close to me. Do as I told you and let Reena think you are me. She thinks I discovered her first plot and will be eager to allow me to spoil this one."

"How does this help us, Mother?" Marlana asked.

Ramasiel merely smiled and patted the blue mistress' bottom with a cupped hand. Ramasiel was no fool, the more uncomfortable the woman was, the less she would evaluate the importance of her role. "It will allow me to be in two different places. While you are being me in this foolish ceremony, I will be working to oust the blue mother, Delania. Once she is gone, I will make you Mother of the Blue Tower."

Marlana quickly dismissed her fears and focused on the power that was soon to be hers. "I will do as you instructed me to."

"Good, now go, my pet. Fool that stupid donk of a queen," Ramasiel said stroking Marlana's cheek as she left the red mother's chamber. Marlana blushed when Ramasiel referred to the queen as a donk. Ramasiel hated referring to any woman as male genitals, and reserved the insult for those she truly hated.

Marlana made her way down the corridor and routinely ignored the comments and questions from the other mistresses. Marlana felt she might blow her cover at first, but as she held her scowl, the mistresses apologized for interrupting the mother's duty and hastily curtsied away.

It was a short ride to the palace from the red tower and the carriage ride was finer than any ride Marlana had ever experienced. She sipped fine red wine on her trip to calm her nerves and felt a little tipsy when she stepped down from the carriage.

Though she had seen the palace many times from outside the walls, she was amazed at how beautiful it was when she was standing this close. The golden dome shaped towers and structures were littered with fantastic carvings and artwork. The walkways on the exterior were paved with colored crystal-like glass that seemed to give the illusion that whomever was walking on them was in fact striding across a pool of enchanted water.

There were many well-muscled Dall-Kal-Mour walking around performing various tasks about the outside of the palace. Their chiseled bronze-skinned chests bore a thin glaze of sweat that accented their near perfect physique. They had more hair than Delania had ever seen on a male and their breeches were even made of silk. The carriage came to a stop just outside of the long glass-covered walkway that led to a large open staircase. At the top of the stairs were seven huge polished marble pillars that were large enough that twenty men holding hand in hand could not reach around. The pillars extended some sixty feet into the air and held aloft the heavy marble ceiling that was covered in a mosaic of artwork devoted to glorifying the queen and her legacy.

Marlana stepped out of the carriage next, as did three other mistresses, three tudas and the suda that Delania was interested in. The three tudas knew their place well and kept the sights of the palace out of their eyes as they stared expressionless at the floor. But the suda glanced around whenever he thought he might steal a glimpse of the palace's grandeur. Marlana thought about ordering the suda back to the carriage, but Ramasiel told her everyone in the carriage was important to her plot, regardless of whether that person was aware of it or not.

"Shall we enter, Mother?" Reena asked as she gently placed her hair behind her ear as the warm breeze hastily blew it across her face.

Marlana struggled to keep her composure, but Reena seemed to be too caught up in her own plot to notice. "Yes, but I want you to lead us. If you are to succeed me in the tower one day, you will surely need to familiarize yourself with the palace," Marlana said as she struggled for an excuse to have the mistress navigate them through the expansive palace. Marlana had never been in the palace and surely could not navigate through its winding corridors, but she was hoping that Reena could.

Reena gave Marlana a quick sidelong glance, and then started up the stairs as Marlana followed. Reena led her and the others up the many flights. When they reached the top, two mistresses of the sword checked them for weapons. When they searched Marlana, they pulled out a wooden box that Ramasiel had given her. The red mother did not say what it was, only that it was a gift for the queen. Marlana assumed that it was the necklace that had been mentioned, though knowing the red mother, it could have been anything.

As the dark-haired sword mistress opened the wooden box, her face went pale, though she said nothing. She hastily closed the box and handed it back to Marlana. "What is this, Mother?" the sword mistress asked.

Marlana smiled disarmingly. "It is merely a gift for the queen," she said meekly.

The sword mistress arched her eyebrow suspiciously, and reluctantly handed the box back to Marlana. "You will hold all gifts for the queen until after the meeting. You will be allowed one mistress with you. But, Mother, you know more than all else that only one slave is permitted inside the council chamber."

Marlana nodded sternly and struggled to create an annoyed tone. "Do not lecture me. I do not have time for fools to state the obvious. I have a mistress that can do that," she said before turning to Reena. "Reena, come with me and bring the suda. The others can see that we receive only the finest accommodations that the power of our tower deserves."

Reena eyed Ramasiel suspiciously. "Yes, Mother," she said with a light curtsy.

The sword mistresses gave Marlana an angry glare, but stepped to the side, allowing the three to go inside. When they stepped through the ornately carved wooden doors of the council chamber, Marlana was taken aback by its complexity. It was nothing like the senate meeting hall, designed for mere numbers and no comfort. This lavish chamber had ten large stain glass windows that rose up on each side of the room like rays of light extending from the earth into the heavens. The seating area was made of dark wood so polished you could see your reflection in it.

The entire chamber floor was covered in a thick white carpet that was clearly enchanted as no dirt from any of their soft walking shoes would stick to it. There were many thick timbers made of polished oak that rose between each finely cut stain glass window. The timbers stretched upwards, then curved over the room, following the pitched ceiling as it angled overhead. There were several huge crystal chandeliers that hung down from polished brass chains over the room, setting the room aglow with a flickering light that seemed more suited for a dancing hall than senate meeting with the queen.

The three made their way through the center of the polished benches and sat near the back corner, next to a small wooden door. Ramasiel had told Marlana that the door lead to a chute that ended in the laundry room. Marlana hoped that they would not need such a harrowing escape, but was thankful for the information. She had informed the other mistress to wait there with the tudas, just as Ramasiel had instructed her to do so. They sat down on the cold, hard wooden benches and waited as the room filled up with mothers from other towers and senate members. Marlana feared that if her heart pounded any louder, the others might hear it. All she had to do was what Ramasiel had told her and she would be fine.

Lance marveled at the enormity of the great palace. He focused his thoughts and frequently examined the complexity of the many hundred spells that bounded this structure together. The magical weaves had been severed for the most part, making them permanent. He suspected that if he could unravel one of the hundreds of magical weaves, he could bring the whole chamber down on them. The tudas kept their heads low and did not dare look around, but Reena suggested that Lance steal as many glimpses as he could until Ramasiel corrected him. Though the punishment would no doubt be sever, Reena promised that the wicked woman would not be alive long to exact it. Reena had instructed him that as soon as Ramasiel placed the necklace around the queen's neck, he was to cast a full bar hold on the queen. Reena would capture him before any of the other sorceresses could retaliate against him and she would expose the wicked mother's attack. Reena would explain that he was nothing more than a victim and she would take him back to the tower. Lance wasn't sure that the women would be easy to forget that a suda could cast such spells, and worse, cast one on their queen. But Lance had no other recourse of escape and any chance was better than rotting in a cell as his mind was slowly warped and altered by their endless torturing.

Lance caught Ramasiel looking at him several times and seeing him looking around, yet she did not say a single word. There was something different about her, but he could not figure out what.

They made their way through the immaculate palace. Huge tapestries adorned to show the queen's power and glory decorated the halls like the fertility tree the women back in Bureland would dance around while they hoped to conceive a child. To Lance's surprise, there were many sword mistresses about the palace. They paid little heed to Ramasiel, Reena, and him and he thought they may have even given them a wider berth. Lance wondered exactly how much power Ramasiel possessed to command such profound fear and respect.

It wasn't long before they entered an expansive chamber with magnificent stained glass windows that were tall and narrow. There were many wooden timbers that stretched to the ceiling that held aloft numerous crystal chandeliers. The ceiling seemed to be a great mosaic painted by an artist who wielded magic rather than a paintbrush. Ramasiel led them to a bench in the far right rear of the room next to a small door. He sat on the floor next to Reena and put his head down as the room filled with women wearing every kind of colored cloak. He saw some with blue, some with green, he even thought he saw one with black, but dismissed it as a dark blue.

Soon the chamber was full of women from all colors of septs. There was a soft murmur of hundreds of female voices conversing at once and the flickering lights from the candles in the chandeliers seemed to combine with the sunlight that filtered through the stain glass windows, giving the room a rainbow hue.

Suddenly all of the women stood. Ramasiel took more than a passing glance at Lance as he sat with his head down, looking out of the corner of his eye. She would stare at him for a brief time, and then back at the wooden box. When Lance felt her look straight ahead, he focused his eyes more carefully on the box. He could tell there was some kind of a magical aura inside, though he could not make it out with looking at it. He struggled to see the colors of the aura when a trumpet sounded. All of the women bowed their heads as a woman with a heavy voice called out.

"Hail the great Queen of Aten. May her wisdom bring enlightenment to us all as we struggle to perfect our imperfect souls. Through her wisdom, our country prospers," the woman shouted.

The women sat back down after the thick-voiced woman finished her proclamation. Lance could not see where the queen was, though he figured she was in the middle of the room in front of a podium. All of the great speakers that ever spoke in Bureland stood in front of one.

Marlana marveled at the beauty of the queen. She was definitely getting older, but her presence commanded respect and held such authority that it seemed she would be less beautiful if she were younger. She wore a plain white robe with a high upturned collar. She wore a long string of diamond earrings that dangled from her ears and her long brown hair was wrapped around her hair in a conical bun. A platinum tiara littered with the finest precious stones sat on her brow. Her fingernails were long and painted a soft white color, the same color as her silk slippers, but her light brown skin named her as a full-blooded Aten. "My fellow sisters and daughters," the queen began, "it is no secret that I have yet to conceive a child to be heiress to the throne. I have purchased three Dall-Kal-Mours, and I am proud to say they serve the crown well. I will be holding a Diltz Quest at the full moon of this month in hopes of selecting the finest specimen to create your new queen. Hiramem tells me my successor will rule with an iron hand and bring about great power to our queendom. I will be accepting gifts from the towers in hopes they may be taken to the temple that Kobli will bless me with a great daughter. Will the first house in Aten approach?"

Marlana gulped and fought back the urge to turn and flee. But instead, she forced one foot in front of the other as she stood from her bench and made her way to the aisle. Reena followed with a large grin on her face. It was then that Lance discovered what was wrong with Ramasiel. She was enveloped in a finely cast illusion web. Lance struggled to see through the bright red weaves as Delania had taught him, but he could not tell who the woman was inside of the illusion. It was not Ramasiel, he was sure of that, but was that part of Reena's plan?

Marlana knelt at the feet of the queen and slowly pulled a polished wooden box from a small leather pack that was fastened to her belt. Her brightly lacquered nails shone red like the evening sun, reflecting the light of the chamber as it flickered from the hundreds of candles that lit the room.

"Ramasiel, I have never seen you so humble," the queen said suspiciously as she took the small wooden box.

Reena glanced over to Marlana and watched a small trickle of sweat drip down the side of her face and fall on the carpet in front of the queen. She felt her heart rise up into the middle of her throat and she started to cry out when she saw the outer ring of a powerful illusion spell that surrounded the red mother. As Reena strained her eyes, she could see the faint outline of a blue dress and Marlana's worried face. Ramasiel had foiled her plan again! Reena started to shout a warning to the queen, but another broke the soft ambiance of the chamber.

"Imposter!" a sword mistress screamed as she rushed into the chamber with her sword drawn. Her heavy plate armor clanged as her heavy footfalls thudded down the center of the walkway in the expansive chamber. Another sword mistress rushed in behind the first with a crossbow drawn. The heavy-hafted weapon was cocked back with a deadly bolt ready to spring forth and end a life.

Lance looked up from his kneeling position to see two of the sword mistresses rushing with their weapons drawn toward the queen. One had her sword out and the other had a loaded and cocked crossbow. Lance could see many more as they charged down the hall with their weapons drawn.

The queen jerked her hand back worriedly as several of her mistresses rushed forward with spells ready. Their hands were aglow with powerful sapphire weaves of enchantments. Lance immediately recognized they were beginning to cast hold spells, if needed.

"What is the meaning of this intrusion?" the queen demanded.

Reena was too dumbfounded to speak, and was further confused when a familiar voice echoed throughout the chamber. "Beware, Your Highness. There is a plot to take your throne!"

All eyes turned to the front of the chamber as a woman dressed in a ruffled red robe strode into the room. Her long red hair was unkempt and mussed. Her nose had been bleeding and she had a swollen eye that was sure to change colors by morning. The shoulder of the robe was torn, revealing her bronze skin. As soon as the woman entered the chamber, the queen's mistresses wove tight blue rings around Reena and Marlana. The sword mistresses rushed up to them, preparing to strike them dead with a command from the queen.

Reena struggled to force a wedge into the rings that surrounded her as Ramasiel made her way up to them. The captured mistress glanced over at Marlana, who was on the ground quivering with fear.

"If you are Ramasiel, who is this?" the queen asked as she gestured to Marlana, who cowered on the floor.

Ramasiel quickly hurled a small globe of abjuration at Reena and Marlana. The finely woven golden net encircled them and faded into nothing, though its effects were snugly in place.

"She is trying to take your crown!" Reena shouted, but no sound came from her mouth.

"Your Highness, this fool mistress of mine had a suda that she had been bedding accost me, though I assure you he is just beginning to see the error of his ways," Ramasiel said as she gestured to the befuddled Reena and the cowering Marlana. "The woman that looks like me is a servant of the blue tower that Mistress Reena had been conspiring with. She cast an illusion around her to disguise her as me to get close enough to use her necklace. Once the necklace weakened you, the wretch of a doppelganger planned to disguise herself as you," Ramasiel said as she gave Reena a wicked, satisfied smile.

"This is an outrage!" the queen shouted. "Sword mistresses!"

"Yes, your highness?" the sword mistresses asked as they saluted the queen by bringing the hilt of their swords across their hearts.

"Throw Reena into the gearian and kill the blue mistress!" the queen commanded with a murderous scowl.

"The relation of sex and religion has been an intimate one since the beginning of time. Many secular religions use sexual intercourse as a way of magic orgiastic, or it is an unintended result of an orgiastic event.

Often the very vows of marriage revolve around a transition from prostitution to legally constituted marriage. Many will abhorrently disagree with me, but let's examine the foundation of many basic marital vow principles.

A woman that cannot support herself is married away to a man. She receives compensation in the form of shelter, food, clothing, and love. It is her duty to provide the man with children through procreation. In a very basic way, she is providing intimacy in exchange for love and other indemnities. This could easily be viewed in the opposite fashion, except men seldom ever need anything other than the physical drive itself, to be intimate.

Though many believe this truth may darken the sanctity of marriage, I argue the differ. Understanding the basic way that we are motivated to act does not cheapen any of our institutions any more than discovering how to cast a spell belittles the power of magic. It is simply a truth, that if understood, can be used as a tool to sharpen the knowledge of our lives. Often a man must be intimate with a woman to fully feel his love for her. Often a woman must feel fully in love with a man, before she is intimate. One of the sad paradoxes of the mortal realm."

-Lancalion Levendis Lampara

12

Faithfully Betrayed

Delania tightly wove her long black hair into a thin braid as she stared at herself in the clear looking glass. She loved to stare at her image in the tall mirror, though she still had not gotten used to seeing the form that looked back at her. The succubus had been in the realm of the living for almost a year, but she was still not accustomed to her own appearance. She aptly pondered how she came to this situation, and how it played into the hands of the archdemon that placed her here. But soon she found her thoughts drifting to her only friend, Lance. He had told her he would be at this meeting and he was going to carry out the plan that would ultimately lead to his freedom. He warned her not to interfere, that it was all worked out regardless of how it might appear, and as much as she worried about him, she trusted him. Trust! The word seemed inconceivable to her some short months ago. In the Abyss, trust is built on the necessity of plotting alliances, and betrayal is expected in short order. But here in the mortal realm, she had learned that there are those who can be trusted.

Delania finished braiding her hair as she fawned over the mental image of Lance's square jaw when he smiled. Every image of him was near perfection, like he was carved from alabaster, or was a Breedikai himself. She tried to imagine what he would look like if he were allowed to grow hair, and the infinite looks seemed to lull her into a deep longing for him. She quickly finished placing the colored pastes on her face to accentuate her natural beauty like the other spawns and gave herself a quick once-over in the mirror, straightening her dress several times. She snatched her dark blue velvety shawl and headed to the door of her chamber. As she stepped into the long curved hall, one of her mistresses came running toward her. Her forehead was dotted with perspiration and she wore a concerned look on her face.

"Mother, please hurry. We must have you at the palace in thirty minutes. The queen does not tolerate tardiness and if you do not go, it will seem that you do not wish her to sit on the throne," the woman said as she snatched Delania's arm and pulled her down the hall.

Delania quickened her step and followed the woman. "Why would the fool coot think that I do not wish her to sit on her own throne because I decided not to attend her self-serving party?"

The mistress was oblivious to Delania's question. "Here is a gift for her, it should suffice," the mistress said as she crammed a small wooden box that was covered with small carvings of animals and covered in polished lacquer. "Try not to speak to anyone unless you have to. We both know how unskilled you are at our country's etiquette. Honestly, I still have no idea how you became a mother of this tower."

Delania followed the woman down the stairs and into the lobby of her tower. "Well, I think I have explained it before. It was really quite easy. You see..."

The mistress cut her off. "It was a figure of speech, Mother. I, oh, never mind. Normally you can take one tuda into the royal chamber, but since you do not own any, you will have to take just a mistress. All four of them, excluding myself and Marlana, are waiting for you at the carriage. You may choose one there if you like, but I do recommend you take at least one."

Delania paused in front of the door as the mistress gave her a once-over and straightened her sleeve that had become wrinkled from pulling her so hastily. "Now remember, above all else, do not speak to any suda or tuda in the chamber. I know how you think they are intelligent and have worthwhile thoughts and noteworthy ideas, and even though I might agree with you on rare occasion, the other mothers, including the queen, do not."

Delania smiled and patted the mistress on the shoulder as her deep blue eyes gazed down at the smaller woman. I will be fine, Arluda. Tell me again why Marlana cannot be here?"

Arluda frowned lightly. "I am not exactly sure, Mother. I think she is up to no good. Perhaps you should question her with a truth globe when you see her next. I know she does jobs under the table for you, but those who are out of sight are the most likely to stab you in the back."

Delania started to protest that the fool woman would be struck dead if she even so much as thought something of that nature but instead smiled with admiration at the mistress that always seemed to help her of late. "Since I can choose any of my mistresses, I choose you."

Arluda gasped. "Mother, I am not ready, nor do I have the training..."

Delania cut her off. "You are ready, and you will accompany me. Get an overcoat and let's go. You yourself mentioned the importance of punctuality, yet you stand there with your mouth open as if trying to catch a fly or a honey bee."

Arluda started to protest, but the stern look on Delania's face clearly showed there was no debating the issue. The young mistress sighed and grabbed her plain blue cloak dejectedly. "Yes, Mother," she said as she started out the door.

The two women arrived at the palace just as the sword mistresses were starting to close the gates. The armor-clad women gave Delania's carriage a few disparaging looks, but allowed them to pass. As they entered the palace, Delania was unimpressed with the decor, but Arluda was as wide-eyed in wonder as a small child in a sugar store. Delania chuckled to herself, and when Arluda noticed her demeanor was entertaining to the blue mother, she quickly regained her composure.

The pair made their way through the winding passages and corridors of the palace, until they entered the great chamber. A dark-haired tuda offered to show them to their seats and Delania allowed him, much to the disgust of many of the mothers who had already arrived. After they were seated, Arluda leaned over and whispered in Delania's ear. "I think we made a mistake by accepting the tuda's offer to be seated."

Delania smiled, but kept her eyes forward on the procession that was taking place just before the queen arrived. "Maybe to the other mistresses, but if the queen wishes me to be seated by one of her tudas I can think of no better way to humble ourselves before her crown."

Arluda pondered the wisdom for a moment, and then shrugged her shoulders as she watched the queen enter the chamber. The aging woman gave a small speech and asked for gifts. Arluda produced the small lacquered box she had given Delania and started to rise when the blue mother grabbed her arm and forced her to sit. Arluda was surprised at Delania's strength. "What is it, Mother?" the young mistress asked.

Delania frowned lightly. "That woman that seems to be Ramasiel is not. It is Marlana hidden behind a weave that is much too complex for her to cast. In fact, whoever cast it is as skilled, if not more skilled, than I."

Arluda frowned and focused her eyes as she strained to see the bright red rings of the illusion spell that Delania claimed was around the red mother. She could not see anything out of the ordinary no matter how hard she tried. "Marlana? Are you sure, Mother?" Arluda asked.

"Why would she be disguised as Ramasiel, and in the queen's presence, no less?"

Delania shrugged her shoulders as she strained to hear the conversation. "I have no idea, Arluda, but it seems we are soon to find out."

Suddenly the crowd began to mumble to themselves and several sword mistresses burst into the room. Some had their swords drawn and others had loaded crossbows. Behind the armored women, was another woman dressed in a bright red robe that was torn on the sleeve. Her long red hair was mussed and it appeared as if she had been hit hard in the face. "There is the real Ramasiel," Delania said.

Arluda whipped her head around to watch the disheveled woman march up the center walkway of the chamber. "How can you tell? She looks the same to me."

Delania didn't take her eyes off of the scene as it unfolded. "In time, you will be able to see and identify such complex weaves, but in the meantime, enjoy the show. I am sure this will be some spectacle."

Ramasiel straightened her torn sleeve as best she could and stood angry in front of the queen. "Gearian? I demand she is executed immediately!" she screamed.

The queen leaned back slightly and placed her aged hands on her hips. "I appreciate your embarrassment, Ramasiel, but you shall not make any demands in this chamber!"

Ramasiel calmed herself and ran her red polished fingernails through her hair, placing the bulk of the fiery locks behind her ears. "I am sorry, Your Majesty," she responded. "This betrayal goes beyond embarrassment. This deplorable act demands justice."

The queen glanced down at the cowering faces of Marlana and Reena. The pair was held fast by the thick green rings of enchantments, but they lacked the lust for murder in their eyes that the queen had become accustomed to seeing in those that plotted to take her life. Wise from years of service to the crown, the queen shifted her suspicious looks from Marlana and Reena to Ramasiel. "Do tell me what you have discovered of this plot, Red Mother."

Ramasiel quickly regained her composure, ignoring the mumbling voices of the hundreds of mothers and mistresses that had gathered in the chamber. "I am not sure, but obviously they sought to frame me. I learned that they purchased the necklace they were about to give you from one of the freedom movement. The necklace has some kind of enchantment on it that would weaken you. They sought to somehow slay you at a later date, as the cursed item cannot be removed. When, where, or how, I have not learned. Perhaps if you hand them over to me, I can use my skills at persuading them into telling what they know."

The queen waved her hand in dismissal. "Your interviewing techniques lead to the deaths of those you interrogate. They are as worthless as arcane talent in a suda," she said, glancing back down at the two captives. "And since this attack occurred in my chamber, under my rule, I do not need to consult anyone on their fates."

The crowd mumbled to themselves as the queen motioned for a sword mistress to approach.

The short brown-haired woman's armor clinked together as she walked up to the queen. She lowered her head and kneeled before the aging matriarch and her long brown hair tumbled over her head, hiding her face. "My sword is yours to command, Your Highness."

"I command you to draw your sword and run it through the heart of the woman that deceived me through the fraudulent use of illusion magic. The other, though obviously included in this plot, will have a brief interview under a globe of truth, and then she will most likely be thrown into the gearian."

The woman bowed a little lower in acknowledgement of the queen's orders, and then stood. The chamber became deadly silent as the sword mistress drew her long sword from its scabbard. The long polished blade sang as it was drawn and the bright torchlight of the room danced and flickered in its reflection. The sword mistress slowly leveled the tip of the sword and gently pressed it against Marlana's breast, directly at her heart. She lowered her head slightly and closed her eyes. "May the gods have mercy on the soul that I send to them."

Marlana struggled to escape her bonds, to shift her weight or hurl a spell, but she could not move or speak. She was as helpless as a baby held in the mouth of a shark. Her mind frantically scrambled to wedge energy into the bars that held her but a sharp pain in her chest broke her concentration.

The sword mistress flexed the muscles in her arm and drove the sword into Marlana's heart. The razor-sharp blade easily pierced her chest and erupted from her back. Marlana gurgled in response as bright crimson blood pooled in her mouth and ran down her chin, soaking the front of her blouse. The sword mistress ripped her long sword free from Marlana's body as hastily as she plunged it in. The enchanted blade was not soiled from Marlana's blood and it still shone in the room's torchlight. The sword mistress sheathed the spotless sword before bowing back at the feet of the queen while Marlana quickly bled to death. The blue mistress struggled in vain against the hold spell and felt herself becoming overcome with terror and horror as her warm sticky life blood drained from the hole in her chest and soaked her gown. In a few moments, Marlana felt cold and tired, and then she was gone.

The crowd said little and watched in awe at the spectacle that had just occurred. It had been at least ten years since someone had tried to take the throne by force and never in any of their recollection had a mistress tried to do so. It was obvious that a mother was behind the attacks and the obvious suspects were the mothers of the red towers, and the mothers of the blue towers. Ramasiel was head of all of the red towers, and the blues had not named their representative, but they all agreed that Delania was most likely the most powerful.

"Take her vile body from my chamber and toss it into the sea. As for the other, take her to a cell, have her interrogated, and then regardless of the outcome, throw her in the gearian.

Regardless of what she says, even going along with such a scheme deserves a slow horrible death. Ramasiel, you will return to your tower and stay there. It is obvious there is much more to this than meets the eye. You may take your suda…," the queen said motioning to a horrified Lance. "… but if he is harmed, I will consider that you are somehow involved in this," the queen ordered as she and her mistresses stormed from the chamber.

Delania watched in interest as the events unfolded before her.

"Mother, shouldn't we say something on Marlana's behalf?" Arluda asked nervously as the queen announced that the blue mistress was to be killed.

Delania frowned as she considered the events that were unfolding before her. "No, Arluda. I think this plot is of Marlana's own making. What unimaginable treasures she was promised to try to carry out such a foolish endeavor is yet to be seen, but any attempt on my part to intervene would surely cast an eye of suspicion on our tower."

Arluda shifted her gaze from Delania back to the queen and the two captured women, then back to Delania. "Perhaps the queen will think that you were involved by letting her die, thinking that you are letting any secrets she might know die with her."

Delania never took her gaze from the scene as the event unfolded. "The queen already suspects us, unless she is a fool. Trying to hide suspicion would surely foster it even more. No, we will do nothing except cooperate with the queen and her supporters."

Arluda turned her head and winced as the sword mistress stabbed her long sword into Marlana's heart. But Delania, merely watched in interest at the queen's, Ramasiel's, and Reena's facial expressions as the blue mistress died. It seemed to her that she was not the only demon in the chamber. No, it seemed to Delania that Ramasiel was probably more suited for the Abyss than most of the demons that dwelled there.

"Arluda, as we leave, inquire about purchasing that suda that was with Reena and Marlana," Delania ordered.

Arluda held her queasy stomach with both hands. "Why, Mother? You have not owned a suda yet, why buy this one?"

"My reasons are my own, Arluda, but I do believe he has information regarding the poorly planned attack on the queen. Surely Ramasiel would have planned something far more complex and covert. I suspect that the suda could give us valuable information," Delania lied. She really wanted to get Lance away from the red tower before he was caught up in their scheming and was slain.

"How much shall I pay?" Arluda asked.

Delania didn't hesitate as she answered. "Pay her whatever she wants. Ten thousand gold coins if she so demands it. If she gets nosey as to our intentions, spin a plot for her to think over, but keep it simple. If you reveal too much, she will suspect we are up to something. Keep it simple and she will try to understand the hidden secret that does not exist."

Arluda pondered a story to invent in case the wicked red mother asked. "What makes you so sure she will suspect something if it is elaborate?" the young mistress asked.

"Trust me, Arluda. I have been dealing with her kind on a much grander scale my entire existence. Because she schemes and backstabs, she expects everyone else to do the same. We will keep our story vague and uninteresting. She will suspect that we are hiding something and will spend days trying to discover what."

Arluda nodded slowly. "You think this suda is that important?"

Delania just smiled as she kept her gaze fixed on Lance. "I heard a wise woman say he was a viper among babes."

Arluda turned and appraised the suda with a new light, then looked back at Delania. "I do not think he is much of a viper at all, Mother."

Delania nodded her head slowly. "You know, I think you are right, Arluda. He is not the viper that he was thought to be. I believe he is something worse, something much, much worse."

Ramasiel stormed from the queen's chamber to her carriage. She wore a stern visage with a glimmer of satisfaction. The encounter didn't go as well as she had hoped, but it surely was a victory. She had not anticipated the queen would have Marlana killed, and she underestimated the queen's distrust in her, that much was sure. Now she had a problem with a suda that had no reason to be loyal to her, and she was sure the weak-minded fool would crack under pressure if the queen's mistress interrogated him. Men were so stupid.

Lance followed Ramasiel from the queen's chamber and into the courtyard toward her carriage. He was unsure of what exactly had just happened. Surely the women were weavers of complex plots of deceit and backstabbing, but he was not sure if what unfolded was going to be beneficial to him. He knew the gearian was a place where convicted women were taken to be raped and killed, and that surely was not in Reena's plan. Lance was sure Ramasiel had discovered Reena's plots and foiled them. He was not sure who the woman was that was disguised as Ramasiel, but the illusion spell was woven with the utmost skill. Now he was being taken back to the dungeons of the red tower, and if things were going the way he suspected, he was sure he would be killed. The thought didn't scare him. Death would be a form of freedom from these malicious she-devils. Though Lance didn't fear death, he did find himself being saddened by the thought he would not be able to see Delania again.

Lance was roused from his thoughts by a soft young woman's voice. "Mother Ramasiel."

Ramasiel paused as she was just starting to get into her carriage and turned to see Arluda standing a few feet away. Ramasiel motioned for the mistresses that were handling the carriage to load Lance up and turned to face the young blue mistress. "Who are you, and what do you want?" she sneered.

Arluda gulped and cleared her throat. She was surely intimidated by the red mother's power. "Mother Ramasiel, my mother understands you have a suda in your possession that may be linked to the small betrayal in your tower. Instead of killing the pitiful creature, she would like to purchase him from you."

Ramasiel thumbed her bottom lip as she mulled over the proposal. The queen would surely know if she killed the suda, but the old witch said nothing about selling him. The fool would be out of her hair, and the blue tower would appear to be trying to hide something by purchasing him. "There are hundreds of sudas in the slave barn, why does your mother want this one?" she asked with an arched eyebrow of suspicion.

Arluda was prepared for the questions and was quick to answer. "My mother fears that one of her mistresses was sending Marlana to conspire with your Mistress Reena under the guise as she was going to spy on our tower for you. Though Marlana is dead, Delania fears that the conspirator in our tower is active and well into her plotting."

Ramasiel nodded. She had not entertained the idea that Marlana was working for another, just as Reena had been. But who? "Surely she is prepared to pay a hefty price, for the suda is the gateway to my own mutinous fools."

Arluda stepped closer and smiled as she glanced around for any wards or other scrying devices. "This is true, Mother Ramasiel, but Reena has been dealt with, where our mutinous fools have not."

Ramasiel placed her hands on her hips as she contemplated a price. A normal suda of his level of training would cost about thirty gold coins. "My price is three thousand gold coins and one vote of my choice in my favor in the upcoming council meetings."

Arluda steadied herself to not be overcome by the unbelievable amount the red mother asked. That was about one year's earnings for an average tower. "My mother has instructed me to pay any price you ask, and not barter, so when do you want to make the exchange?"

Ramasiel glanced around, and then back to the carriage where the suda was being held. She didn't want the fool to even set foot in her tower. She was sure she would most likely kill him anyway out of sheer anger, and that would surely set her against the queen before she was ready. "We can make the exchange now, if you wish. I have little desire to delay, though. I have many pressing matters that need tending to," Ramasiel offered, glancing back at the many sword mistresses that started to move from the chamber into the courtyard.

"I do not have the coin with me now, but I can arrange for it to be delivered," Arluda responded.

Ramasiel smiled and opened the carriage door. The door was made of red stained leather that bore countless designs and symbols. "Send the suda out."

A few seconds later, a confused Lance stepped from the carriage. Arluda noticed he was somewhat despondent and his blue eyes seemed dull and lifeless.

"You have been sold, suda," Ramasiel said as she roughly grabbed his chin in her hands, lifting it up so that it met her deadly emerald eyes. "You will go with this mistress. If you prove to be lacking in your training and bring embarrassment on my tower, I will buy you back and you will beg me to kill you."

Lance did not respond, but kept his steel eyes locked on the wicked red mother's. He could detect a wickedness and disgust from her that he hoped he was able to emulate in return.

Arluda took Lance by the sleeve and pulled him from the courtyard into the cobblestone street. The evening twilight was rapidly approaching and the cool night air was beginning to wash over the city. The streets began to empty as sudas and mistresses returned to their towers from their errands.

Ramasiel ducked her head and sat down in her carriage. She smiled wickedly at the three red mistresses and one large burly man that were inside. "Henrious, back for one more job?" she asked with a sly smile.

The large man nodded his head, but did not look into the face of the red mother. "Yes, Mother," he said with his deep coarse voice. "It would seem gold coins don't go as far as you would like when you are buying estates and titles in foreign countries."

Ramasiel patted his knee lightly. "Carry out this job, and I will send another thousand gold coins to your manor."

Henrious' eyes lit up with greed at the promise of such a large sum. "I would kill my own mother for that price."

Ramasiel waved her hand and chuckled. "No, no. All I need you to do is kill the suda that just left our carriage before he gets to the blue tower."

Henrious frowned. "What am I to do with the mistress? She surely has some magical talent. I have no skill in the arcane arts."

"Do not worry, Henrious. I will send someone right on your heels to help you. He is a gray elf and his name is Kalen. He will deal with the mistress while you kill the suda," Ramasiel said as the carriage halted near an alley by two abandoned warehouses.

The ex-Diltz Quest gladiator leapt from the carriage and disappeared into the dark alley.

Ramasiel glanced over at the mistress in the carriage with a long blond braid down the middle of her back. "Is the gray elf still staying in the room above the Reagle?"

The mistress nodded. "He is, though, I think he will be angry that you have sold the suda he wanted."

Ramasiel waved her hand in dismissal. "Tell him if he wants the suda, he is being taken to the blue tower by a young mistress. If he can kill the mistress, he can have the suda."

The mistress nodded and stepped from the carriage and started toward the Reagle.

One of the other mistresses frowned in confusion. "You want the suda alive to be interrogated about the depths of Reena's betrayal, yet you send the renegade to kill him and the elf to kill the mistress. How will that work?"

Ramasiel smiled as she revealed her web. "I sold the suda for three thousand gold coins. I paid the fool Henrious to kill him. Thus Delania won't have him and neither will the queen. The elf will be enraged the suda is dead and most likely kill Henrious after he kills Arluda. I will inform the queen that Arluda stole the suda from me to cover up her own role in the plot to kill her and that the body of Henrious proves that the blue tower was plotting with the freedom movement. I do not have to pay Henrious for killing the suda, and I will offer the gray elf as a suda gift for the queen. You know how she loves elves. I will contact the elf and tell him his only chance for freedom is to help me overthrow the queen. With his ability with the arcane arts, I will be able to kill the old bat in no time. The blue tower will be out of the way, and my tower will be cleared of suspicion."

The mistress smiled at the way her mother used people to achieve her own ends. "But what if the suda is not slain and Kalen gets him?"

Ramasiel sighed. "I still report the suda stolen and that the elf conspired with the blue tower to do so. I will offer the blue mistress' body as proof. I will capture the elf, get the suda back, and still offer the elf to the queen."

The mistress nodded again. "But what if Arluda kills both Kalen and..."

Ramasiel cut her off. "Shut your fool mouth. I grow tired of your 'what ifs.' Kalen is much more powerful than Arluda. Besides, if every plan was airtight, what would be fun in that?"

The mistress did not dare respond as they rode back to the red tower to see how the night's events would unfold.

Kalen muttered a curse to himself as he wove a globe of illusion, making him appear as an Aten woman drabbed in a bright yellow robe. He randomly sculpted the weaves to create some symbols that he surmised might be of some significance. He figured he was walking into some trap that Ramasiel was weaving. He didn't know what she had been up to of late, but how could he? He could not move around in this country and all of his attempts to hire or create contacts were met with laughter or threats. Kellacun stayed with him in the room, posing as his owner, and fortunately for him, the black-haired wererat had stayed true to her job. Who said there was no honor among thieves? Many of the women had offered her a noble's ransom to purchase him. Kalen would surely be able to deal with the first few who tried to take him by force, but he had learned that the power of the women here was much too great to hold out very long at all.

Though his magical disguise was not perfect, he had no desire to fool anyone he made contact with. All he hoped to do was slip by any street women he might meet until he could strike at the blue mistress and take the suda. Kalen imagined the chaos as the death knight stormed Hector's castle and slay him. Kalen would then emerge and give the death knight the boy. The foul monstrous creation would kill the Ecnal, and then he would cease to exist.

Kalen would then assume the throne, and his rule would begin. He almost chuckled aloud as he hurried down the cobblestone streets of Aquabar. He had endured much from the hands of the wicked women of this country and as soon as he was King of Nalir he was going to lead a crusade against the damnable country.

He ducked in and out of alleys paralleling the blue mistress and the suda. Why the mother left her mistress to walk on her own was beyond him, but Henrious was not going to wait much longer. If that damned elf that Ramasiel spoke about didn't arrive soon, he was going to have to strike. The night had taken hold of the city and the tudas were lighting the street lanterns. Henrious figured he would rush the mistress and cut her down first, then kill the suda. He knew he would be seen, but since he worked for the freedom movement, he could duck into the undercity and make his way out.

The large man drew his sword as he leaned his back against a large two story brick building. He pulled a vial of a black syrupy substance and poured it down the blade of his sword. The thick liquid quickly covered the polished blade, making it nearly impossible for the weapon to reflect any amount of light. As he moved again, trying to match the mistress's speed, he pulled his dark brown cloak up and covered his long wavy brown hair. One quick stroke was all he needed.

Reena awoke in a dark chamber chained to a small wooden plank. The plank was old and worn and there were large spaces between the boards. A thick large metal plate held the plank together at the top and the bottom. The rusted plate had a crusted bolt at each board, holding it fast. The wood smelled of dried blood and body odor and was still a little damp. The red mistress winced in pain as she strained her neck to look around. Her fingers were numb, but she could still move them, despite the tight iron shackles that were cutting off the blood flow to her hands.

She blew a lock of her hair from her face as she called out. "Hello? Is there anyone there?"

No one answered her, but she could hear several feminine voices overhead. She tried to slow her breathing and listen to what they were saying, but she could not understand them. Reena cocked her head to the side and glanced upwards at the wooden ceiling of her chamber. It was probably ten or so feet above her and small beams of bright light shone through the cracks. She could see several people moving around, causing small bits of dust and debris to rain down on her from above. She turned her head and tried to avoid the falling pieces, but she was held fast. She started to call out again when she heard heavy footfalls thudding down the stairs to her right. The footfalls paused and the jingle of keys preceded the sounds of a door being unlocked. The old portal creaked and groaned as it was pushed open and a deep guttural voice coughed.

"You finally awake?" the man asked.

Reena squinted, but could not make anything out of the man save for his silhouette. "Yes, who are you?" she asked.

The man coughed and slowly stepped in front of her. He was barely over six feet tall and his skin was bronze like that of a Dall-Kal-Mour, but his hair was sleek and black. His sable mane was pulled tight across his head and tied into a pony tail that dangled all the way down his back to his buttocks. The beginning of the ponytail started at the crown of his head, so it appeared as if the hair erupted like a small water fountain. "My name is Dargruden. Perhaps you have heard of me."

Reena's heart sank and bile rose into her throat. Dargruden was the keeper of the gearian. It was said he was as evil and ruthless as any man in the history of the world. Reena fought to hide her fear and disgust. "I have heard of you, suda," she said, hoping the title might put the man in his place. To her disappointment it seemed to have the opposite effect.

"I am no suda, bitch," he said as he spat at her feet. "I am master here. You'd better start learning that."

Reena felt her fear being washed away by anger. "You will have no power over me, fool. As soon as they place me in the gearian I will kill the first man who tries to touch me. Regardless of what happens to me, the first one will die," she said with as much ferocity as she could muster.

Dargruden just chuckled and patted his thin, tight stomach. "Do you think you are the first woman to have been given to me? I have executed mothers with ten times your power. Do you think these men, *these beasts*, this country has created cares if he risks his life for the feel of a woman's breast? I have seen men who hunger so much for the feel of a woman that her skin is literally torn from her bones as she screams and fights as fierce as you claim you will do. But who is to say you will have that opportunity? Perhaps I will keep you shackled to this plank and use you for a few years."

Reena chuckled and tried to take a different approach. "Do you think the company of men is strange to me? I have bedded many sudas of mine."

Dargruden smiled and folded his chiseled arms across his thick powerful chest. "A different tactic. You would hope to dissuade me from using you for pleasure by telling me it is not torture for you. I will remember that. You are a dangerous one, aren't you?"

Reena didn't respond. She had never spoken to a man with such powers of observation.

Dargruden smiled widely, exposing his thick broad teeth. "Who said anything about having men bending you over anyway? Perhaps I might have the pack mule in for a romp. Perhaps I'll sell tickets to the mistresses of other towers who despise Ramasiel and all those who ever worked for her. Or perhaps I will line up all of the sudas in the gearian and have them pleasure themselves one by one. Perhaps I will insert a Borkin into your mouth and allow three to have a go with you at once. Perhaps three at a time until you either choke to death on their fluids or bleed to death from their ravaging. You see, Reena, do not try to play mind games with me. Here, I am the master."

Reena nearly broke into tears as the man spelled out all the colorful possibilities of her torture. Dargruden was silent for a moment before he started for the door of her chamber. "Go ahead and cry, Reena. I would get all of my sobs out now if I were you. When I give you to the men, any cry you let out in their presence will only excite them into a frenzy," he said as he closed the door of the chamber. The echo of the heavy door closing was a gong of finality that the red mistress could not deny. She cried fiercely until she fell asleep.

"Love. What begets it? What becomes of it? How does it be-gin? Many have spent their mortal lives trying in vain to find it and others have ended their own lives when they lost it. It can-not be bound, captured, or created. It just happens. Or does it? I say that it can be created, though not within yourself, but within another. The conditions must be right for it to exist beforehand, but it certainly can be created. The process does not involve undy-ing devotion, though a level of devotion is needed, and it does not require arrogance, though a certain level of that is needed as well. Surely beauty is in the eye of the beholder, but without a measure of it, love will not grow.

Love is a culmination of those things and more. If you are wor-shiped by another, you will not love them. If you have no confidence in yourself, or self-worth, they will not love you. And the most and least important of all, beauty. If you have it, the spark may begin, but if you do not, it cannot. Physical beauty is necessary in the beginning. Once love grows, beauty may fade, but not before. It is this delicate combination that teeters on the edge of disaster that seems to drive the very world we live in. A scary thought. What is the most amazing is that given all of the possible variables that can occur, and what variables need to occur, love still often finds a way. I found love once. But just like countless men before me, losing it nearly cost me my soul."

-Lancalion Levendis Lampara

13
The Fall of Lostom

The evening sun fell quietly in the small farming community of Lostom. The orange sun was setting in the western horizon and small bugs danced across the tops of wheat fields, highlighted by the waning light. A cool breeze blew out of the north sending waves that rode from one field to the other. Men and women toiled about, performing various chores and preparing for the end of another long hard day of work.

The hamlet was divided by a small river that was really more of a creek. Those on the west side of the creek called it the Adorian River and those on the east side of it called it the Aten River. The muddy brown creek flowed from the south to the north and emptied into the bay, leaving a small cloud of silt and debris that was quickly swallowed up by the large body of salt water. The village was really two separate villages, but kept the name Lostom. The west side was composed of women from Aten, though they kept their beliefs under check for the most part.

They did not kill, capture or enslave any male that they came across, but did keep indentured servants of peasants or others who worked for the mistresses for a given period of time as they hoped to earn enough money to buy some land. The women of West Lostom were usually tolerant of their eastern neighbors and frequently went as far as to hold banquets and feasts, inviting the males of the east side for dancing and dinner. Though the males frequently attended, it was apparent that they were still uneasy given the deadly reputation of the sorceresses.

On the west side, Marzahna the Wise had built a respectable tower of about fifty feet and filled it with several mistresses and a score of indentured servants. She was a stern woman, but fair. In her youth she had been a mother of a yellow tower in the city of Aquabar, but gave up her position when she fell in love with one of her sudas. It was forbidden by law for her to bear children since she was the mother of a tower, so she and her love had moved to West Lostom and planned on spending the remainder of their lives there. Her love died three seasons past and the aging woman was just beginning to hold festivals again. She missed her love dearly, but knew that it was time for her mourning to end.

She had purchased enough ale from Dalzon, another small town about fifteen miles inside of the Adorian border. Though the country was no longer in its bloody civil war, it was weak and vulnerable. Almost eighty percent of child producing men had been killed in the war and all that remained were old men or young boys who were unable to work. In Dalzon there was a dwarven brewmaster named Gorsan who cared little for the politics of war and kept his business running well. But what angered Marzahna was that the ale she had ordered should have arrived by wagon yesterday. She was planning her festival to celebrate the life of her dearly departed love, and she found the delay to be insulting.

The old sorceress gazed out of her window to the east and started upon the Brightson Keep. The Duke of East Lostom, Darren Brightson, was away on a fishing trip in the bay and was not due back until the morning. Marzahna was deathly afraid of the water, never having learned to swim, and often thought the young duke a fool for frequenting such adventures. Tonight his keep was well lit, with bright torches set about his walls. She could not see much else, since the keep was atop a great hill and was several miles away.

Marzahna sat down on a plush chair on her balcony and gazed longingly at the picture of her departed love. She stroked the picture with her thumb as a single wet tear slid down her old wrinkled face. How long did she want to live without him? In her youth she had never imagined she would face such a dilemma, but when he fell ill, she contemplated passing with him. She spoke of her thoughts with him and he forbade it. He told her the warm kiss of the evening sun would comfort her as he sent it from beyond until she could join him. As the evening sun fell behind the western sky and the orange and yellows were replaced by dark blues and violets, the calm was interrupted by the thunder of hoof prints.

Marzahna held the portrait to her bosom and glanced at the rider with little interest as he ran through the streets of East Lostom. He was apparently shouting something that seemed to rouse some of the townsfolk. As torches begin to light up and dogs began to bark, Marzahna became more interested. She wondered what wonderful news was being spread about the city. She knew the duke's wife was with child, but they were not expecting the child for another season yet.

Thinking of the duke's wife, Marzahna glanced back up to the hill where the keep was, but to her surprise she could not see it. Oddly enough, it seems they had extinguished all of the torches. As she strained to understand why the keep had extinguished its lanterns, she saw deer skittering through the streets of East Lostom. What was odd to Marzahna was that it was not just a few feet into the street; it seemed as if there were thirty or more. As she watched in confusion, she witnessed wolves, coyotes, foxes, raccoons, rabbits, and even squirrels running together into East Lostom as if they were running from a forest fire.

"Earl!" the old sorceress called out.

A middle aged man ducked out from behind the thick yellow curtain that was draped over the entrance to her balcony. "Yes, Mother?"

Marzahna stood and leaned against the stone rail of her balcony. "Look, Earl. All of the forest creatures seem to be running from something. What do you think is going on? Even a band of ogres wouldn't scare up that much wildlife."

The balding man stepped to the rail and gazed out as thousands of birds of every type took flight from the trees about a mile east of the city and scattered over the tower. "I am not sure, Mother. But whatever is causing it, surely cannot be good."

Marzahna nodded. "Summon the serving men and tell the mistresses to lock up the tower."

Earl nodded and started to leave when Marzahna snatched his arm. "Earl, be hasty. I do not have a good feeling about this."

The middle-aged man did not need the voiced concerns of the powerful sorceress to be hurried in his duties. He quickly ducked back behind the curtain and his hard wooden shoes clicked across the stone floor of the tower as he rushed to carry out his command.

The screams of the villagers in East Lostom prompted Marzahna to grab her staff from under her bed. She and the other mistresses were prepared to kill any foe. She stood defiant on the balcony of her tower as she witnessed thousands upon thousands of soldiers erupt from the forest and wash over the buildings of the east side. To her surprise the soldiers did not loot any of the houses after they had killed the inhabitants; they merely trudged forward, almost as if in a death-like trance.

"What is it, Mother? Brigands?" a mistress called out as she emerged from behind the balcony curtain.

"It appears as if the armies have reassembled and for some reason find it necessary to attack our beloved community. No fear, Mary. I shall deal enough death to the infidels that they will go wide of our home. It will not be profitable for them to...," Marzahna trailed off.

"What is it, Mother?" Mary asked as she stepped to the balcony.

Marzahna felt her knees buckle and she had to support herself by leaning on the balcony rail. The cold hard rail suddenly felt weak and vulnerable. "May the gods give us a merciful death," she said with a cracked voice. "Hell hath opened up and its cursed souls come for us."

The cool embrace of the night washed over Trinidy as he rode atop the skeletal steed. He ran his hand across the smooth yellow bones of the monster's neck and smiled at its beauty. The death knight recalled in the past he abhorred creations such as this, but now for some reason he really appreciated the apparitions. They did not complain, were always loyal, and would serve without fail to the best of their ability. The undead were superior to real soldiers in every way. Trinidy's dark, rotted face cracked as he smiled. Large black bugs erupted from his mouth and skittered into his nose or his empty eye sockets. The death knight was pleased at himself. Though he was forced into servitude on this realm, he was not in the Abyss being tempted by demons, and, best of all, he was using an evil magic to work the will of his god. Who would have ever thought to give evil a wound from their own weapon?

Trinidy's old rotted saddle creaked and popped as he leaned around to his left. His glowing blue eyes caught the shadows as they emerged from the earth. The creatures seemed to climb from their daily slumber like a mermaid as she struggled from the ocean, but once they were atop the surface, they moved with a deadly grace.

The death knight surveyed his ghouls, wraiths, wights and other creations like a proud father overlooking his family. His army was mighty. Mighty indeed.

"The vile ones approach, Master," the snake-like raspy voice echoed in Trinidy's mind.

The death knight turned his attention to the west. As he blocked out his thoughts he could hear them about twenty or so. Thump-thump, thump-thump. Then there were another twenty reverberations, but larger. "They are riders on horses, my pet," Trinidy thought back. "No doubt sent to surrender themselves to my mighty army. Perhaps they want to give me what I seek. We will hear what they have to say."

The shadow squealed in disgust. "Their taunting is unbearable, Master. Let us go end their blasphemy!" they called out in unison. Trinidy turned and revered his creations with an angry scowl. They had never as much as disagreed with him before. "We will hear their terms, understand? If a single one of you cannot obey my commands, I will destroy you all!" he screamed at them through his mind.

The shadows squealed again in fear and ducked down low to the ground in subservience. "We will obey, Master."

Trinidy smiled slightly and faced the riders as they approached through the dark forest. They were all dressed in full plate armor with a yellow lion on their chests and carried the same lion on a white banner. Trinidy recognized the banner as that of Adoria. "However, if they do not present acceptable terms, my pets, kill them."

"Sir! Sir, wake up," the messenger said as he rushed into the large bed chamber of Duke Darren Brightson.

The middle-aged duke sat up from under his silk sheets and rubbed his tired eyes. He reached over to his nightstand and picked up a small chalice of cool water. As he sipped the refreshing drink to wash the grime from his mouth, he held his hand up, halting the messenger in his tracks. When he finished sipping the water, he sat the chalice back down and wiped his mouth with his hand and promptly wiped it on his shirt tail. "What is so important, messenger, that I am roused from my sleep?"

The messenger held a candle in one hand and straightened his night cap with the other. "Sir, the patrol sergeant reports that the Andorians have somehow mustered another army and are marching on us right now!"

Duke Brightson leapt from his bead. "They what? How can that be? For the last three months all that remained were a few random patrols of soldiers. It is impossible that they would be able to have enough numbers to make an army, let alone organize one."

The messenger shrieked as the hot candle wax dripped down the side of the candle and onto his hand. He quickly switched hands and stuck the burned one in his mouth. "I am just telling you what the patrol sergeant told me to tell you. He said he saw them through the big eyes."

The duke kicked his feet off of the bed and ran his hands through his hair. "Fine, fine. I'll be up in a minute. How far away are they? Three, four days?"

The watch stuttered and kicked at the thick ornate rug on the floor. "Sir, he said they could hit us in about an hour."

The duke jumped up and started donning his armor.

"You two had better not be playing a prank on me like the time you claimed the Kai-Harkians were coming out of the mountains in troves of thousands."

The messenger turned and hurried out of the chamber. "No, Sir. This is no joke," he said sincerely.

The duke finished getting ready as his two attendants came in and helped him into his armor. He was still more than able to put his armor on by himself; it just was quicker to place on if other people assisted with some straps.

When he opened the door to the watch tower, the night was unusually cool. A cold, artic wind was washing in from the bay. Duke Brightson stepped to the upper battlement as he just finished strapping on his gauntlets. "What do you have, Ian, another trick from the witches in the tower?"

The grizzled old patrol commander shook his head and motioned his hand to the two large black spy glasses that had been tied side by side so that both eyes could look through them at once. "Look for yourself, Sir, though all you can see are the silhouettes, it is obvious they are Andorians. But..."

The duke frowned. "But what?"

"Well, Sir. They have no fires, no tents, no supply wagons, no siege engines, no archers, and as far as I can tell, no horsemen," Ian said.

The duke stepped to the big eyes and looked through them. About three miles to the west he could see a large group of men in a small clearing. They were surely Andorians by their armor, but they were moving differently. "Are they drunk?" he asked.

Ian shrugged his shoulders. "I do not know, Sir. They do move oddly, but if they are intoxicated, where are their supply wagons? I have scanned the area all around, and there is nothing. I do not think they intend to make war with us, but rather are looking for employment. Do we have the resources to hire a few thousand soldiers? It surely would bolster our power to the witch, Marzahna."

The duke took his eyes away from the spyglasses. "I think I might at least be able to house them in various places of the keep, but they would need to find jobs to supplement their income. Perhaps we could re-open the trade docks."

Ian rubbed his chin as he contemplated the idea. "Not a bad idea, Sir. Perhaps I should ride down with a few men and meet them. I will carry a banner of truce and see what their intentions are. If they are foul reasons, I will let them know that when they attack in the morning, we will resist."

The duke nodded. "Agreed. Take our finest knights to make an impressive show. I will order the watchmen to light every pyre on the walls. This will light up the keep and display our thick stone walls. Few soldiers will want to try to get in these impenetrable barriers without siege engines. Our archers would slaughter them."

Ian nodded and started toward the stairs. "I will return soon, Sir. Keep watch in the big eyes. If I lower the banner when I start riding back, they want a fight and we can get our preparations made."

The duke nodded. "A fine idea, Ian. But, only a fool would risk his life trying to sack this keep with nothing more than foot soldiers."

Ian agreed as he closed the door to the battlement. Duke Brightson turned and started watching the soldiers though the big eyes. They surely didn't move like soldiers. They seemed to stand more like statues, then walk like their arms and legs were stiff. No matter, if the fools attacked his keep, his archers would cut them down like dogs.

Ian trotted his horse through the dark forest on an old deer trail. He and twenty of his best knights rode single file toward where they last saw the many soldiers that seemed to be marching toward his Duke's keep. It was unusually dark and he frequently had to pause to duck a limb or branch. His heavy plate armor creaked against itself as the men made their way down the meandering trail. When they reached the base of the small hill the horses refused to press on further. Their eyes were wide with fear and Ian's horse laid its ears back, pawing at the ground and snorting uneasily.

Ian patted his steed's neck and tried to calm the barrel-chested stallion. "Easy, boy."

"What is it, sir?" one of the knights called out from behind the patrol leader.

Ian turned backwards to the knight. "I'm not sure, but

the horses are uneasy about something. Perhaps they have war dogs or wild wolves," he said quietly.

Ian paused a moment, calming his horse, before forcing the animal to move forward. The stallion reluctantly complied, slowing occasionally to toss his head in disagreement. As the group advanced, they were overcome with the foul encompassing odor of rotting flesh. Many of the soldiers covered their mouths and vomited uncontrollably, barely able to remain on their horses, and the ones who did not vomit, gasped in disgust at the noxious fumes. Ian vomited several times, covering the front of his armor and saddle in what was his supper. The burn of his stomach acids scorched his throat and the rotting fumes made him dizzy. As he fought to regain his composure, he spied movement in the trees in front of him. He strained his eyes in an attempt to make out who was approaching, but it was too dark and he was too distracted by the horrific odor that assailed him and his men at every turn.

"Why are you here?" Trinidy asked as he approached the armored men. To his surprise, he found that the men did not respond to his question; they seemed disorientated as they coughed and gagged. Sickness, he thought. Maybe a plague of some kind. The death knight almost laughed out loud as he imagined how his army was immune to such things that had defeated many great armies of history's past.

Trinidy shifted his weight and stepped forward from beside a large tree. "I asked you why you were here."

The men did not respond, but Trinidy could easily hear their incessant heartbeats. Thump-thump, thump-thump. Though he did not know why, the sound seemed to infuriate him, but Trinidy kept his hatred at bay. "Sir, are you ill?" he asked with a noticeable strain in his voice as he fought the urge to kill the men.

The leader of this group was wearing heavy plate mail that bore the signs of many battles. It was as well used as it was ornate, and the death knight guessed him to be a skilled warrior among his people. Trinidy stepped closer to the warrior. When the middle-aged man met his eyes, his uneasy demeanor changed from cautious to hostile and the sick man charged on his horse.

Ian struggled to lift his head. The feeling of nausea lasted for a few minutes, but seemed to be lifting. He could still hear his men coughing and regaining their composure when a tall figure stepped from the tree line. The man was dressed in full plate armor, but the armor was old and rusted. It had large patches of thick black crust that seemed to cling to it in places. On the shoulders and near the breast plates were small skull-like carvings which Ian could not tell if they were real skulls or not. The man wore a great helm that covered most of his face, but the part of it he could see was sent directly from his nightmares. The man's face was dead and rotted, covered in yellow and dark blue patches of decaying flesh. Many black stinging insects skittered from out of the beast's mouth only to scramble excitedly across his face before ducking into either his nose or his eye sockets. The man had no eyes, but only empty recesses housing a small blue glow that permeated a sense of intense evil. Ian quickly drew his sword and charged the foul creation. The bright polished blade seemed to gleam in the night, though there was no moon to light it. "To arms, men!" he shouted as he urged his stallion forward despite the equine's snorted protest.

Trinidy stepped back from the charging man and sent a metal command to his ghasts that were waiting in the midst to attack. It was not that Trinidy had any fear, or was worried the old fool might cut him down. He was more interested in seeing his pets work firsthand. Though he was sure a death at the hands of the ghasts was akin to being damned, he tried to offer peace to the men, but they chose war. No, the dead knight thought, they choose death.

Ian rushed forward with his enchanted broadsword blazing. The weapon had a weak enchantment on it, but the razor-sharp blade was as light as a small wooden stick. Ian could wield it with amazing precision and skill. As he rushed onward into battle, the undead beast stepped back and hundreds of other hellish monsters erupted from the shadows. These beasts were once men, at least they looked as if they had once been alive. Their skin was a dark violet that seemed stretched and tight. Large creases of cracked flesh dripped pockets of yellow ooze that secreted a horrific smell. The beasts carried no weapons but their pale white eyes darted around excitedly as they rushed forward.

Ian brought his broad sword down into one of the monsters. The enchanted blade easily sliced through the ghast's skull, sending out a spray of black bile and yellow puss. Ian quickly shifted his weight and turned his stallion. The well-trained war horse kicked out with both of its rear feet, catching two of the ghasts in the chest. The ghasts' ribs popped from the force of the blow as they were lifted from their feet and sent tumbling into the darkness. Another ghast lashed out and its razor-sharp black claws scraped across Ian's leg plating, leaving four long deep grooves in the thick armor. The patrol leader responded with a backhand swing which severed the ghast's head from its body.

"Flee!" Ian shouted to his men who were in full combat with the horrible beasts.

The knights quickly complied and turned their steeds back the way they came. As Ian spurred his stallion on, he noticed that three of his knights were lying still on the ground. They had not suffered wounds that were life threatening, nor debilitating, yet there they lay paralyzed.

Two others struggled to get their horses to move as the animals acted as if their hind quarters were paralyzed. Ian sliced his way to the downed men, cutting down ghast after ghast. The dark-skinned monstrosities growled and hissed as the man fought his way to one of the knights whose horse had been paralyzed. Ian reached down and snatched the man by the wrist as he rode by and with a mighty groan, hoisted the heavily armored man to the rear of his stallion. The knight quickly tossed his shield and grabbed the saddle with one hand and swung his sword with the other, slicing as many of the undead monsters as he could reach.

As Ian darted back over the small hill, he glanced back hoping to see any of the four knights that had fallen, but he saw only a sea of rotting enemies. As much as Ian wanted to turn around and fight, he knew he had to return to the keep and warn the Duke. Not only was this enemy intent on sacking the keep, they were surely capable with the numbers they possessed. Even worse, these enemies could not be intimidated, bribed or bargained with.

Trinidy watched in satisfaction as his ghasts overcame the knights. The undead monsters overwhelmed their enemies with sheer numbers as their paralyzing bites and claws felled the knight's steeds, making them easy targets to be run down. The ghasts quickly ate the men that were paralyzed, consuming their hands and feet, then arms and face. It seemed to Trinidy that the monsters had an inborn sense of how to consume their paralyzed victims in a way that prolonged their life the longest, thus extending an unthinkable torturous death. Though the ghasts were skilled in their trade, Trinidy was not happy with the numbers he lost overcoming four men, albeit well-trained and well armored ones. The the ghasts showed their lack of versatility in that they were not fast enough to run down a war horse.

As the soldiers' war horses thundered away, Trinidy sent a mental command to his shadows. The two thousand squeals of delight made the death knight crack a smile. He did not need to siege this keep. His minions of the shadow could not be stopped by walls of stone and steel. He would march his army of death onward at a stumbling-like pace. And when he arrived at the keep, he would use their supplies to arm and armor his skeletons and zombies. As if on command, black tendrils of powerful necromancies erupted from the death knight and surrounded the bodies of the dead knights that his ghasts had just slain. The scattered bones of the recently slain soldiers quickly formed together and in moments, four new undead monsters joined his ranks. Trinidy smiled as he imagined finishing his mission of righting that which was wrong. He would soon be free of that dastardly pull that he felt even now, driving him further to the west.

Ian thundered the short miles from the hellish encounter to the front walls of his keep in what seemed like hours to the seasoned soldier. The portcullis watch quickly recognized him and the heavy gate was slowly raised. The iron entrance creaked and groaned as it was hoisted up just enough that Ian and the other fifteen knights could duck under. As soon as the last knight had cleared the gate, it began to lower equally as slow.

Ian helped lower the knight from the rear of his horse before dismounting himself. The stable boy quickly led the gallant stallion to the stables to be brushed and walked as Ian removed his helm and met the duke as he strode across the courtyard. The duke read the worry in Ian's face and noticed that four of his best knights had not returned.

"I guess the encounter did not go well, Ian," the duke asked somewhat jovially, despite losing four of his trusted friends. "Who was lost?"

Ian paused to get his breath and waved his gauntleted hand in dismissal. "Sir," he said as he struggled to get his breath. "We are in dire straights. This army is much greater than we had anticipated."

The duke cut in. "How many? Four, five thousand?"

"No, Sir. You don't understand. There are too many to count, maybe ten thousand or more, but sir, they are not an army of men. They are an army of the dead! Rha-Cordan has cursed us and our defeated enemies have risen up to crush us!" Ian yelled as he grabbed the duke by his shoulders. "Sir, if we do not flee, these monsters will kill us in short order!"

The duke pulled himself free from Ian's ranting. "Pull yourself together, Ian. What has gotten into you? Even if there is an army of dead, I have seen skeletons and zombies fight. They have no coordination and if we kill the person who is in control of them, they all fall apart. Don't you remember the Battle of Calito?"

Ian gulped and slowed his breathing. "Yes, Sir, but there are more than zombies and skeletons; there were these horrid beasts that had elongated claws and needle-like teeth. They carried a stench that was more powerful than anything I have ever experienced. The mere smell of them made our stomachs churn into knots, doubling us over involuntarily. And to make matters worse, when they bit or clawed the men, it paralyzed them with some sort of venom substance," he said as he wiped beads of nervous sweat that formed on his brow.

The duke patted Ian's shoulder reassuringly. "Ian, we will defeat them, but I will send a messenger into the city to warn the villagers. They will not have time to come here, but I know the witch will house them in her tower until I can defeat this minor problem."

"But, Sir," Ian said as his voice cracked as he pleaded mournfully. "These undead ate the men. They ate them, Darren. They ate them alive!"

A trumpet of warning sounded from the south battlements just above the portcullis. Both Ian and the duke glanced that way. "Hurry and dispatch the rider, Ian. The first trumpet has sounded. Their masses should be on us in less than an hour," the Duke said as he grabbed the patrol leader's shoulder. "Be steadfast, my friend. As long as these monsters cannot get into the keep, we can defeat them easily."

As silent as death, they slipped around dark trees and through the underbrush. Their amorphous forms glided across the dense forest quicker than the most agile deer. They had no eyes, no face and no mouth and as many of them walked through the trees as went around them.

Thousands of Trinidy's shadows moved as fast as their supernatural legs would carry them. They surrounded every wall on the outside of the keep and waited, undetected, as they squealed in anticipation of extinguishing the life of every soul that dwelled there.

After they were all in place, they felt the command from Trinidy ordering them to attack. Just as they started forward, a single rider on horseback erupted from a small set of wide wooden doors that had been closed in front of the large portcullis. Several shadows started toward the rider, but his swift horse quickly outdistanced them. The shadows, realizing they could not catch the lone human, refocused their efforts at the thousands of hapless souls that were trapped inside.

Ian hastily fastened the girth strap to his thick leather war saddle. Its features had worn smooth from countless battles of the past. He quickly double-checked his gear and gave his stallion an inspection to ensure he had not suffered any injuries from the sprint back to the keep earlier in the night. Though he was sure the stable boy had inspected his steed, Ian considered the animal a friend as much as a piece of property. When he was satisfied the animal was in good condition, he mounted up. The leather from the saddle creaked and groaned from the weight of the heavy rider as Ian hoisted himself up. His stallion flicked his ears and stomped in anticipation, sensing Ian's fear. The animal had been with Ian for over twenty years and knew when his master was about to ride into battle. But what the stallion did not understand was that this time, Ian was riding from battle. The portcullis was raised enough for Ian to get under it, and then he waited for it to close and the outer gates to open. The thick wooden door-like walls were closed when danger was afoot, to be a preemptive barrier before the enemies could focus their siege weapons on the iron gate.

Once the doors opened up, Ian spurred his stallion to

run like he had never ran before. As he rushed headlong into the cool night he felt a pang of guilt at leaving his keep behind. He had tried to convince his friend that fighting this force was futile, but the duke would not hear it. Ian knew as he glanced back at the rapidly shrinking stone fortress, that he would never see his friend alive again.

The Battle of Calito was nearly lost because whenever a soldier fell in battle, the necromancer used his foul magic to animate his corpse. Fighting your companion that has just perished before your eyes forced many soldiers who survived to go mad. What bothered Ian even more was that there were little over eight hundred at the Battle of Calito. But here he had seen thousands upon thousands of the undead beasts. But never in his day had he encountered beasts as foul as the ones that attacked him and his men today.

No, Ian would not die tonight, not by being eaten alive. He would try to warn as many as he could, then he was taking his friend's fishing boat and sailing north. Ian wasn't sure how long these monstrosities would occupy Lostom, but as far as he was concerned, the town was already lost.

"Kill them all," Trinidy's voice echoed in each of the shadows dark twisted minds. The evil creations squealed in delight and rushed forward. Their intangible bodies easily melted through the thick stone walls of the keep and silently began killing the inhabitants in the courtyard.

The duke was looking through the big eyes at the mass of undead soldiers marching his way when the first scream echoed through the night. He turned toward the sound, but saw nothing in the courtyard. He started to look through the big eyes, when a much louder blood-curdling scream pierced the calm of night. The duke rushed to the edge of the battlement and glanced over at the pandemic scene. His men swung their swords futilely at these odd black shapes that resembled shadows more than monsters, yet their weapons passed right through the beasts, only to have the monsters reach out and touch their victim. When the single black claw made contact with the man, he screamed and dropped to the ground while the beasts kept touching him over and over again.

The duke drew his enchanted sword and watched in horror as his men were helpless against the undead monsters. He tried to understand how the creatures had gotten inside. If he could find where the breach was, he could shut it down and perhaps destroy the existing ones that were already in the keep.

He ran down the dark stone stairs of the battlement with his sword in hand. As he neared the bottom, the screams of his men grew louder as the shadow figures killed them. As he burst through the bottom doors of the battlement, he felt a stab in his ribs by a horrible cold. He reflexively swung his sword in a backhanded motion. The sword hit the shadow and went right through it as if the beast was not there. The duke felt weak and staggered back against the wall of the stairwell. His legs were suddenly sluggish and he was dizzy.

The shadow took the shape of a man and slashed out at him again. The duke ducked under the attack and stabbed in with his sword, and again the weapon went right through, as if the creature was not even there. The shadow clawed at him a second time, and the duke managed to avoid it, only to be grabbed from behind by two dark arms that erupted from the wall behind him. He felt his body spasm from the intense cold and his strength waned. He tried to stab back at the shadow behind him as he fell to the hard stone stairs, but the sword merely clanged off of the stone wall. The shadows avoided the enchanted sword as the duke fell dead. In a matter of minutes the wicked shadows had managed to kill over a thousand soldiers, adding the numbers to Trinidy's massive army of death.

A short time after the last man was slain, Trinidy arrived at the keep. He was pleased at the silence he heard from the forest. There were no beating hearts to mock him. No man drew breath within a mile around him. Even the animals have fled from his army of undeath. Who could stand against him? His enemies would cower before him and beg for mercy. This right he was to wrong would be only the first, Trinidy thought to himself as his skeletal soldiers slowly worked at breaking down the doors to the keep.

"I have the power to abolish evil altogether!" Trinidy yelled into the night. "What is evil?" the death knight asked his shadows.

"Evil is in the hearts of men!" they echoed back in their squealing unison. Trinidy smiled and folded his arms across his rusted and scarred breast plate.

Then we will cut out their hearts, the death knight thought. "If evil is in the hearts of men, I will roast every heart of every man over the fire of justice! Let only undead walk the earth. I will abolish sickness, death, pain, misery, suffering and evil all in a single sweep! Kill every man woman and child you see, my pets!" Trinidy shouted to his army of death.

"Yes!" We will end all evil by ending all life!" the shadows shrieked, the zombies moaned, and the skeletons clicked, as they started west toward the small hamlet of Lostom.

Ian rode as fast as his horse would carry him. He gripped the reins of his stallion with both hands and stood up in the saddle with his head low, cushioning each thunderous step of the horse with his legs. Great clods of dirt and sod flipped up from behind the charging steed as he made his way toward the first few buildings of Lostom. No one was on the street, save for a few chickens that were roosting on a hitching post and some watch dogs that lazily lounged on the porches of their master's homes.

"To arms!" Ian shouted as he rode by the houses. "To arms. The dead are coming. Flee to Marzahna's tower!"

A few houses began to light lanterns and look outside. Dogs began to bark at the commotion as their keen noses began to smell the unnatural smell of death that was rapidly falling down on them, despite the strong westerly winds keeping the undead army's odor from preceding them.

"To arms! The Battle of Calito is upon us again!" Ian shouted as he rode through the town square and turned north toward the docks.

The mention of Calito was fresh in the townsfolk's minds. The battle had not occurred that long ago and even a few of the townsfolk were retired soldiers that bled the ground red fighting the undead of the necromancer, Randolph Forlinger.

Ian kept shouting as he reached the docks. He jumped from his steed and quickly took off the saddle and bridle. He tossed the tack into a large one-sailed ship and smacked the horse on the rump. "Go on, you fool. Get moving. You can move twice as fast without carrying me and my armor so you should be able to outrun these demons!"

The stallion tucked his butt from the smack, but otherwise turned and stared at Ian as if he had gone mad.

"Go on fool, you haven't much time!" he said as he began to unwrap the mooring line of the boat from the dock's bollards.

The horse glanced back at the town that was alive with bustle as people began to look outside and see what was going on. A few pointed to the keep, that was normally well-lit, and wondered why it was black as night tonight. Others screamed from their bedroom windows demanding quiet, but Ian did not have time to explain. His warning was the best he could give.

As he tossed the forward mooring line onto the forecastle of the single mast boat, he noticed his horse had followed him and was nosing around the bollard, trying to figure out how the rope pertained to him.

"Damn you, you fool horse! The beasts are going to be on you soon if you do not get going!" Ian shouted as he tried in vain to shove the nineteen hundred pound animal. "Suit yourself, you damned fool. I'm not getting myself killed over no damned horse!" Ian said as he skittered across the gang plank and began to remove is armor. The horse merely watched him walk across the thin weak board and nosed at it, then snorted in protest. "You can't get in the boat, you fool beast!" Ian shouted as the villagers began to scream in horror as the shadows cascaded down on the city. "Hurry up! Those hellions will be here soon!" Ian shouted as he adjusted the rigging and raised the sail.

The stallion smelled the edge of the dock and snorted again, before raising his head and turning his ears toward the city where several shadows and ghasts had started down the long dock. The stallion reared up on its haunches as it had been trained to do in battle and prepared to defend his knight.

"NO!" Ian shouted futilely. "I do not need defending!" he screamed at the horse as if the animal could understand him.

The shadows floated across the top of the wooden dock and the ghast's razor-sharp claws clicked and clacked as they ran at unearthly speeds toward him.

Ian glanced at the safety of the ocean and then back at his trusted friend that had served him through countless battles, including the Battle of Calito. The proud stallion flicked his tail and stomped the wooden dock as if daring the monsters to come forth. With an angry groan, Ian fastened a loop with the forward mooring line and lassoed the bollard. The ship lurched and the dock shook as the large vessel was jerked to a stop. "I'm coming, you damned fool horse!" Ian shouted as he ran across the tight mooring line without thinking that he still had his leggings and greaves on and if he fell into the bay, he would drown.

Just as he reached the dock, the mooring line groaned and creaked as the sail from the ship caught air. The taut line dripped water from it as it was stretched to its limit. Ian ran from behind and leapt over the huge war horse's rump on pure adrenaline, a feat he had never before had the leg strength to do, let alone perform it wearing his leggings and greaves.

Once the stallion felt Ian on his back, the animal relaxed and Ian felt his trusted friend waiting for a command. Ian felt the only way to save his horse was to run him off the end of the dock. Once in the water, the animal's training for war would change to survival and the stallion should be more likely to avoid the undead rather than stay and fight, like he was trying to do now. Ian planned on cutting his leggings and greaves loose once in the water and swimming to his ship and sailing away to safety.

Ian grabbed a fist full of his stallion's mane and turned the animal around. He gave him a quick kick in the flanks and the powerful war horse erupted into a full run. Just as Ian and his stallion ran down the dock, the first shadow swiped its claws at the horse's rump. The monster's dark amorphous hand hit only air as the stallion thundered down the pier, leaving deep splintered grooves from the his powerful hooves. Ian held to the mane tight and gripped his horse's waist with his legs. Just as he was about to reach the edge of the dock, the mooring line snapped.

The force of the stretched line rocketed into the dock like an iron missile, splintering the bollard and sending shards of wood flying through the air. Ian ducked his head as tiny pieces of dagger-like wood stuck into his flesh and his hopes of survival began to float away with his boat. Ian felt the horse's powerful legs flex as he reached the edge of the dock. He kept his head down and prepared for the cold rush of water, knowing that if he fell from the horse he would drown.

Ian heard a loud thud and a small splash as he was violently thrown from the back of his horse. He tried in vain to keep hold, but he could not. Ian felt himself flying through the air for a time before suffering a hard blow to the back of his head. He saw bright flashes of light in his closed eyes, and then lost consciousness.

"Hate. It is a simple word with such profound meaning. It is an emotion so solid, so powerful, that it can drive one to perform great feats of strength, bravery, or foolishness. Hate slowly clouds the mind so that when one realizes they have it, they care little how it guides them.

The smart use it to their advantage and the wise recognize and shape it, but try as they might, once hate begins to grow, it cannot be abolished.

What few men know is that hate is akin to a fire. It needs fuel to burn. Often memories of the event that created it do not suffice to feed its wrath. So hate begins to consume other aspects of one's personalities. Perhaps first it takes their ability to trust. Then it takes their ability to reason. Hate is a timeless creation of demons and devils.

My father was a man so pure that even with his beloved wife slaughtered in front of his face and with his impending death before him, he would not allow his faith to be lost. But when he was surrounded by the emotion's endless barrage in the pits of the Abyss, the black vile wrath took hold. Once it has you, there is little anyone can do to defeat it. Hate consumed my father, the purest man I knew.

Yet, I cannot fathom how I defeated it when it consumed me. I was surely no pure man. I was selfish and full of fear. Perhaps the love of my life helped me defeat my hate, though she was used to implant it. And though I overcame my hate before it consumed me, I can feel it there, in the bottom of my soul festering and waiting for the time it will rise again to wage a war to consume me.

But I scoff at the dark feeling as it tries to mock me. You see, I surprisingly discovered in order to defeat my hate, ironically, I had to learn to hate it."

- Lancalion Levendis Lampara

❧14❧
A Tower of Iron

Mary's long blonde hair hung in front of her face and blew with the cool breeze of the northern wind. She frantically held the heavy wooden door of Marzahna's tower open as few townsfolk had managed to escape the onslaught of death. She held her robe closed with the other hand, though given the circumstances, she doubted anyone would take notice of her small clothes.

Screams and sounds of terror echoed through the city streets on the east side of the town and were beginning to permeate into the east. Though many more townsfolk were going to make it across the river, Mary had orders to only keep the tower open for a few minutes longer. The yellow mistress tried not to imagine the horrific sounds of those who begged to be let inside but would die at the door.

As Mary hurried the townsfolk inside, she thought she saw something move in the night just south of the tower. She stepped out a little, still holding the door with her left hand and holding her bright yellow robe tight with her right, and glanced toward the place she saw the movement, but she couldn't see anything. A stark scream a few dozen feet in front to her north turned her attention, but she saw only a man stumble and fall. Then another scream and another townsperson fell. Mary struggled to see why they were falling. The ghouls and ghasts were still about a hundred yards away. Mary summoned a small weave of evocation. The bright blue ball of magical energy swirled in front of her briefly before rocketing into the air. When the ball reached about twenty feet, it exploded in a bright flash of yellow light that illuminated the area around the tower. To her horror, Mary clearly witnessed the gruesome death the townsfolk had been suffering. Many dark shapes of amorphous necromancy ducked and darted about, stabbing into the townsfolk with wicked attacks that snuffed out the life force of their victims. Mary quickly recognized them as shadows.

Mary snatched one of the women who were running by. "Listen to me!" she shouted as she firmly gripped the terrified woman by the arm. "Find one of the mistresses and tell her Hiramem's prophecy is upon us!"

The woman nodded franticly and nearly jerked her arm free as she rushed into the tower. Mary hoped she would deliver the message, though it mattered little. She remembered the prophecy from the old queen's advisor well. "There will come a day when the heavens turn their back on us and the shadows will rise to claim our lands. Only one who is humbled among us can be our salvation when he discovers who walks for death." Mary was certain the heavens had turned their back on them, as every priest in every country as far south as Nalir had reported they are lost to their gods. And now, an army of undead appears from nowhere and descends on her country's borders.

Mary stepped from the door and called forth more intricate weavings of evocation. She summoned a bright blue globe of fire that thinned out into a shield of flame. Another globe elongated and formed a flickering cobalt sword of magical energy. Her robe shifted and formed a barrier of armor made of pure energy. Mary was not the mother of this tower, but she was one of the most skilled evokers in the area. Though she had battled shadows before, she had never faced this many.

Mary called out a roar of defiance at the undead beasts that seemed to avoid her, picking on townsfolk, rather than attacking her. "Come on undeath! Does my heartbeat not anger you?" she shouted as spittle sprayed from her mouth and her fiery sword and shield flickered in the dark night. But to her dismay, the shadows fled from her, keeping their distance.

"To arms!" the man screamed as his heavy war horse thundered past under the rented room of Gorsan, the brewmaster. He had arrived in town a few hours before amid a flurry of forest creatures that seemed to be in a rush to get to the west. The dwarven brewer found it odd the animals would do such things, but he never really made a note of the habits and rituals of surface animals and found them to be more of nuisance than anything.

Gorsan shot straight up from his bed and his skin crawled when the rider screamed something about the Battle of Calito. The dwarf remembered the wicked necromancer Randolph Forlinger that attacked his town some years ago. He had created an undead army of mammoth proportions. The mere mention of Calito sent the dwarf into a tizzy. He hopped up from the bed and his short stocky legs thudded on the hard floor of the room he had rented. He quickly pulled an old crate out from under his bed and blew the dust from it. After fumbling with a key he wore around his neck on a leather tether, he opened the case.

The old wood creaked and revealed a suit of dirty plate armor, that at one time must have been magnificent to behold. But now, it was in disuse and poor repair. Gorsan almost smiled as he gazed down at the emblem of Clan Stoneheart and his days of study under the great cleric Fehzban Stoneheart. Fehzban was not much of a tactician and was always trying to get the king to let him join their army. Gorsan left long before the cleric was even allowed to see a battle, but his friend wrote him many letters keeping him abreast of events in the under mountain. Gorsan remembered that his last letter mentioned he was promoted to the rank of commander and the young king had the council's approval to sack the Torrent Manor.

A shriek from outside and the barking of dogs roused the dwarf from his doldrums. He quickly donned the old plate armor and sucked in a breath as he tried to fasten the very last hole on his belt. "Seems this darned suit of armor has gotten smaller in me old age," he muttered to himself as he finally got the belt fastened. Gorsan had barely taken a step when the old leather belt snapped, sending the buckle sprawling across the room. The corroded brass ring clanged across the hardwood floor. Gorsan paused a moment and contemplated a plethora of curses he wanted to utter, yet he found the most difficult thought to be which colorful adjective to use first.

Another scream, this one from downstairs in the inn, reminded the dwarf that Calito may be on him again. He quickly waddled back to his crate and hastily pulled out scroll cases and silk tunics until he found an old platinum flask. He smiled and kissed the cool metal mug that was carved on the outside of it and popped the top. After a long draw, he wiped his mouth with his sleeve and relaxed. "Nothing like a kiss from the great mother earth!" he said as he re-corked the flask and fastened it to his loose, unfastened belt. "Now, I think I have a sword or something around here."

Gorsan spent the next few minutes looking around the room, trying to find his sword when he remembered he traded it a year or so back for his beautiful platinum flask. The puzzled drunkard rubbed his greasy hair with his calloused hand and let out a light belch. He gazed around the room trying to think of what he could use to club zombies with, when he spied the bed post. He waddled over to the large bed and grabbed the thick wooden leg. He tugged with all his might, but could not pull the leg loose.

Gorsan cursed, spat, kicked the leg, and cursed some more and tried to think of a way to get the wooden bed post loose. After a few minutes of pondering his options and an occasional pick at his nose, he waddled to the wooden closet where he had hung his cloak the previous night. The dwarf opened the door and snatched his axe that was resting against the wall. He started for the bed, when Gorsan realized he was holding a much better weapon in his hand. He muttered another curse under his breath and gathered up all of his scroll cases. He fastened them to a leather thong and tucked them into his side belt pouch. As he started toward the door, he cursed again and turned back to the closet.

His old friend Fehzban had given him his cloak and told him it had magical properties that would protect him against the walking dead if he ever faced them again. Gorsan squeezed his armored body into the cloak and stepped into the hallway of the inn. The hallway had the heavy stench of decaying flesh. Gorsan crept down the stairs as something moved to his right. He turned and felt his heart rise to his throat. There he stood face to face with some odd, nearly transparent, undead monster. The beast, which floated above the ground, had no eyes and no mouth, but clearly mimicked the human form. Its edges seemed flat while odd black wisps seemed to rise off of it like steam, then duck back under and into the body of the creature.

Gorsan could feel the evil resonating from the creature, but to his surprise, it merely squealed an odd sound and moved past without trying to harm him. The dark amorphous mass of black wispy energy floated down the hall slowly before melting through a wall. As Gorsan made his way down the old rickety stairs, he could hear the screams of the poor person who was in the room the shadow had entered.

As Gorsan made his way into the street it was sheer pandemonium. Villagers screamed as they were eaten alive by ghasts and ghouls. Ivory skeletons clacked their way through the streets, chopping up the already dead bodies of slain townsfolk. Rotted walking corpses lumbered through the alleys as occasional pieces of decayed flesh fell from their fetid bodies. The sweet foul stench of death hung in the air, and bright green and yellow flies swarmed the maggot-filled soldiers. Gorsan ignored the scene and tried to make his way west, to the yellow witch's tower. Several of the undead beasts eyed him suspiciously as if they expected him to be alive, but whatever magic the cloak possessed, it was obvious they either did not see him, or they thought he was one of them. Either way, the chubby dwarf made his way west with the heart of the rotting army.

A bright flash of energy lit up the night sky as a thick bolt of evocation rocketed from the top of the tower and incinerated several shadows. The undead beasts howled and shrieked as their intangible forms vibrated and seemingly unraveled into nothing but small wisps of black smoke. Mary glanced to the top of the tower at the powerful yellow mother, Marzahna. She wore her battle robe and was covered in many powerful spells that protected her from the magic that created the walking dead monsters. Mary smiled with renewed vigor and charged the shadows, but she was unable to reach any of them, as they fled from her, but then circled around.

Another blast of energy hit several more shadows to her left. She turned to see another mistress who was casting a second powerful evocation. When she was finished, the spell created many bright blue bolts of energy that blasted out from her hand and incinerated a few more shadows, yet they did not try to advance.

"What are they waiting for?" Mary asked as she backed to the door to try to fend off the hellish beasts, knowing the walls of the keep were too thick for the shadows to get through.

The other mistress answered with another powerful evocation, and Marzahna growled as she held her staff up above her head. She started chanting a powerful spell that Mary had never heard before. Soon she was covered in a bright yellow globe of abjuration, transparent with a metallic luster.

"It appears our leader of undead shows himself!" she shouted at a hapless looking dwarf who was running toward them. He was wearing heavy plate armor that was tarnished and dirty. His front chest plate was not fastened to his belt and looked as if the buckle was broken. He wore a dark brown cloak that barely fit him and he waddled at them as quickly as his short stubby little legs would carry him.

"Woe, Woe!" Gorsan screamed as he neared the base of the tower. "It's me, Gorsan!"

The mother relaxed slightly, before focusing her powers back into the ranks of the undead with a new fury. "How are you not harmed, you bearded drunkard!"

Gorsan slowed and placed his thick chubby hands on his knees as he tried to get air in his weak, tired lungs. "Flattery will get you nowhere!" the dwarf struggled to say as he sucked in great amounts of air.

Mary stepped forward with her fiery sword blazing. "Gorsan, get in the tower. You will be safe there."

The dwarf shook his head and held up his hands. "No, no. I think these vile creatures cannot see me," he said as he held his arm in front of his dark brown eyes to shield the bright light the sorceress's fiery sword and shield produced.

The shadows began to tighten the circle around Mary as they squealed in excitement, but would scatter as Mary rushed in to cut them down. As soon as the mistress went forward, dozens more moved in behind her in a attempt to tighten the circle around her.

"It looks like you are the one that needs to get out of here, Mistress. I'll be looking for ya in the morning to see if yer tower is intact. Otherwise, good luck my lady," the dwarf said with a bow as he disappeared into the darkness.

Mary had little time to contemplate the selfish dwarf as the shadows began to dive in at her in attempt to touch her with their powerful soul-draining claws. She ducked low and slashed several of them, forcing the necromantic beasts to keep their distance.

Marzahna fired spell after spell into the undead masses, but for every four of the foul undead monsters she incinerated, ten more took their places. She glanced down at Mary, who was well known for her skills in evocation, as she kept the beasts away from the door of the tower. Marzahna applauded the woman's bravery, though the yellow mother knew the shadows did not need a door to enter the tower, they would simply move through the walls. She knew that stone walls needed to be at least ten feet thick to thwart a shadow from passing through, though fresh dirt of six feet would suffice. She figured the dirt acted like a grave, keeping the shadows out, but there were ghouls, ghasts, skeletons, and zombies with this group, so they could easily claw through dirt. Whoever had created this army was powerful indeed, and the mother knew the leader would soon show his face. That was the only way she could understand why the monsters had not entered the tower. A few moments later, her suspicions were confirmed.

A monster of a man walked from the darkness of the undead masses. He wore a great helm that seemed to resemble a skull, more than a helmet, with a great blue plume that dangled down the back. A pair of blue eyes glowed out from the inside of the helm that made Marzahna shudder from fear as she gazed into them. He wore full plate armor that was covered in dark black patches of corrosion and odd jagged spikes. Many small skulls were affixed to the armor that seemed more life-like than carvings. The monster wore a long blue silk cape that was tattered and torn and carried a massive shield and a thick broad sword. Marzahna wanted to shout a warning to Mary, but knew it would do little to aid her against the monster. Instead, she began to prepare her own spells to defeat the apparition, though she doubted she would be able to stop it. The weaves of necromancy that surrounded the creation were so complex; they almost resembled those of a divine power.

Marzahna began to weave a myriad of protection spells around her. She had memorized a few, but had to rely on some of her older scrolls to cast the others. When she had finished casting them, she glanced back down at the base of her tower in hopes of seeing Mary, but instead she saw only the undead monster that was adorned in the plate armor. He held his sword out in front of him and pointed it at her.

Trinidy noticed one of his zombies acting odd. It was the short one that carried equipment and armor that was not in as poor repair as the others. The death knight's other zombies were busy killing the townsfolk, but this one was up with the shadows and appeared to be conversing with one of the sorceress outside of the tower. Trinidy had never known any of his zombies to have any cognitive thought.

"Come here, ghast," Trinidy commanded to the nearest one.

The hungry beast scurried over and looked up at his master with an insatiable hunger to slay the living. "Yes,

Master?" the creature answered back.

Trinidy pointed to the short zombie. "That zombie is acting peculiar. Bring it to me."

The ghast turned and regarded the zombie, then looked back at the death knight. "Yes, I will obey," the ghast said as it bounded off to fulfill its command.

Satisfied the ghast would carry out the order, Trinidy turned his attention to a woman in a yellow robe, standing in front of the tower, waving a shield and sword of evoker fire around at the shadows as they encircled her. He slowly stepped from the shadows. Her heart pounded when she looked at him. Trinidy felt empowered by her fear of him. He stared deep into her eyes and he felt her resolve begin to melt away.

"You stand in defiance of me, the crusher of evil. Your wicked heart thumps its sinister tune as you destroy the beauty I created. I will give you one chance to denounce your wicked nature and ask for forgiveness. How do you plead?"

As Mary fought the shadows, they surprisingly backed off and widened the circle they had fought so hard to tighten. She stood defiant among them with her disheveled hair clinging to her sweat-covered face in wet strands. She wiped a lock of hair away from her face with her sleeve as the shadows began to part in front of her, making a walkway. A few moments later, Mary could see the silhouette of a large man walking toward her. As it neared, she felt the air go cold around her, like a cool front that preceded a northern storm. She tightened her grip on her fiery sword and planted her feet squarely to fight the new enemy. The yellow mistress strained her eyes in the dark night to see the armored figure approach. He was well over six feet tall and wore plate armor that was covered in a charred, black, crust-like patches. Many small black insects erupted from the ground where he stepped and his sinister eyes were a deep azure glow that sent cold chills down the yellow mistress' spine. Mary felt herself being frozen with fear as she tried to back away from the approaching apparition. When the monster was about ten feet away, it opened its decayed mouth to speak, to reveal dull black centipedes that crawled into its nose and eye sockets.

The beast said something that she could not understand in a dark and sinister tongue. The undead monster's voice was deep and guttural, making Mary feel unclean just from having heard it. The beast finished talking and stood motionless in front of her. Mary fought the urge to run. She knew the shadows were so thick that she would be slain before she could make her way through the masses. If she tried to fight her way through this monster, the shadows would most likely strike her in the back. She had no other option but to fight. With lightning speed, Mary lunged in with her sword. The blue fiery sword slashed down at the death knight's neck with blinding speed. Just as the magical sword of energy would have hit the apparition in the neck, it moved, drawing its broad sword and deflected the blow.

Mary's eyes went wide with surprise and horror. It was impossible to deflect her evoker's sword. There was nothing within it to deflect. Mary had little time to ponder the event as the death knight shifted his weight and struck back.

Trinidy smiled as the woman raised her sword and slashed in. He could feel the energy crack and pop as he parried the magical blade. He had never seen such a weapon, but his magical blade evaded it in short order. The woman was a poor swordsman, probably relying on the blade to win her battles. She had overextended herself and was now off balance. She was able to do little else than to parry his counterattack except deflect the blow with her shield. The force of his strike would most likely knock the woman from her feet, and from there, he should have little difficulty dispatching her. Evil was always stupid when it came down to it.

Trinidy launched his blade at the woman, and just as he expected, she raised her shield arm up to deflect the blow. But to his surprise, his broad sword sliced right through the fiery shield and through her arm. The force of his strike carried the blade deep into her shoulder. The blow knocked the woman from her feet and sent her crashing to the ground. Bright red blood erupted from her severed arm and a darker violet blood bubbled from the sucking chest wound in her shoulder. Her eyes were wide with surprise and horror. Trinidy smiled as bright red blood poured out with each fleeting beat of the evil woman's heart. But as Trinidy watched her bleed out, she started to reach for her sword. He almost admired the courage in the woman. Evil usually begged for mercy, when faced with adversity. The death knight placed his heavy armored boot on the woman's wrist just as she was about to reach her sword. She looked up at him with rage in her eyes and a powerful stare of derision. Trinidy nearly pitied the woman as he brought his sword down on her neck, severing her head. But he was sure not every being was pure evil. But killing them was the only way to ensure it was destroyed.

"Save her arm, her head, and her body," Trinidy commanded to his undead. With a cracked a smile, he added, "I will have a use for her later. Her talents are much desired."

Gorsan waddled his way through the undead masses and tried to make his way to the docks. If he could find a small ship, or even a rowboat, he could make his escape. The cool, salty breeze washed away the pungent stench of death that overwhelmed the city streets. Though he could see the amber glow of dawn, the dwarf knew the sun would not rise for a few more hours. Just as he started on the docks, he felt an iron-like grip that seized his arm. He turned and flinched at the sight of a rotted tight skinned ghoul face. Its eyes were dry and sunken with a yellow puss that dripped from them. The monster's mouth was full of hundreds of needle-like teeth that had pieces of fresh meat stuck between them, and the dwarf knew that Lostom had little livestock to be eaten. The monster's hair was long and black and hung from the ghoul's head. The creature had horrible breath that smelled like the combination of coppery fresh blood and a bloated goat.

"The master wants to see you," the monster said.

Gorsan glanced back at the dock, and then back at the ghoul. He knew ghouls could paralyze their victims with a single scratch, and if this one's grip got any tighter, its claws might pierce his skin in between his armor plating. Gorsan took one final glance at freedom, and resigned to go with the beast. He wasn't sure if zombies were able to speak, so he just nodded and followed as the ghoul led him away from the docks and back toward the tower. The chubby dwarf cursed his luck and his uncle Fehzban. It seems the damned cloak worked too well. It even fooled the necromancer that was leading this army of the dead.

The death knight stood below Marzahna's balcony. She could hear the screams of the men and women that were in the tower as the shadows overcame them. An uncharacteristic sadness besieged her and she fought back the tears that welled in her eyes. She would not bargain with this beast; it did not deserve such satisfaction and she knew that the lives of her and the people in the tower were forfeit. She would die with dignity, like a true mother of a yellow tower. She channeled a weave of evocation, creating a dark blue globe of energy that flattened out in front of her. She stepped onto the shining round circle and eased herself slowly to the ground. Several shadows squealed in protest as they reached the balcony to find that the woman had floated down. The shadows quickly turned and went back into the tower, eager to find the last few heartbeats that had eluded them thus far.

Marzahna stepped from the energy and stood directly in front of the death knight. She had never seen such a fiendish beast. It seemed as if it came directly from the deep Abyss itself, though she knew the Abyss held no undead, Rha-Cordan would not allow it.

"Another brave soul; odd for those who are wicked," Trinidy said.

Marzahna was surprised the apparition could speak, and recognized its dialect as Abyssal, the language of demons. "There is only one wicked heart here, monster, and it is yours," she said with confidence and power.

Trinidy chuckled as he rested his arms on the pommel of his broadsword. "You are something, bitch," he said. "You are the first I have come across that can speak in the tongue of righteousness. Have you come to ask for mercy?"

Marzahna smiled confidently. "Yes, I have come so that you may do just that. The God of Death will love to torture your soul for stealing thousands of those already in his grasp."

Trinidy growled. "Rha-Cordan has no power over me, wench! I am performing the will of Merioulus. I am going to finish righting that which is wrong. When I have done that, I am going to rid Terrigan of your kind."

Marzahna pulled a small stick from under her belt and shouted a command. The stick rapidly grew into a powerful white oaken staff. Its head was a likeness to an acorn and it glowed with a white hot power that made the death knight shield his face. "If you are to rid Terrigan of my kind, then you may start with me!"

Trinidy backed away and growled in frustration. He could not approach the white light and it burned his skin like the sun had done when he first came back to the world of the living. "What foul sorcery is this, woman?"

Marzahna smile confidently. "It is the power of the sun. Sha-Shor'Nai, the God of Light, who commands you to crumble!" she screamed as a white snake-like tendril erupted from the staff and encircled the death knight.

Trinidy writhed in pain as his skin smoked and burned. Black insects erupted from his mouth, eyes, and nose and fell to the ground, quivering in the troughs of death. The staff set out such a light that it turned the darkness around the tower courtyard into daytime. The shadows squealed in pain and scurried to the edge of the staff's power, and the ghouls and ghasts were immediately incinerated. They tried to flee the white hot power, but crumbled before they could take a step.

Rage filled Trinidy as he was burned inside his armor.

He focused his mind on the staff and the energy and allowed it to enter him. In moments, the white tendril turned gray, and the light dimmed. The shadows squealed in delight and moved closer as the edge of the faded light.

Trinidy felt his soul touch the white-hot tendril and cool it.

Marzahna felt her heart sink. Never had she seen a being of such power that could withstand the might of the God of Sun. This staff had been handed down from cleric to cleric for thousands of years, and had defeated even the mightiest liches, vampires, and other undead monstrosities, yet against this new foe, it failed.

Trinidy rose to his feet and weakly laughed as the white staff turned black in the woman's hands. The light was gone and though she slew hundreds of undead, hundreds more surrounded her.

The death knight drew his sword and weakly leaned on it. "Save her body, my pets. I have a use for her," Trinidy said as he turned his back and staggered back into the masses of his army.

The woman's screams from the hundreds of shadows' slashes echoed in his ears. He focused his thoughts on her heartbeat. Once the shadows had killed her, Trinidy focused his thoughts on her no more.

The smile quickly faded from the death knight's face as he watched one of his ghouls bringing a small, squat zombie toward him by the arm. The zombie did not move like the others. Instead of having a lumbering slow movement, this one seemed to waddle and spent a great deal of effort to maintain his balance. Though his skin was rotted and his clothing was old and torn, Trinidy could clearly see something was amiss with this undead soldier.

The death knight closed his eyes and tried to send out black tendrils of necromancy to surround the zombie and give him a command, but he was still much too weak from the sorceress' staff. The pure white energy from the God of the Sun took most of his power to corrupt. Trinidy paused.

He did corrupt the staff didn't he? It was clearly a holy staff of power, created from the most powerful high priest of an order and given to a defender of the faith. He had seen only a handful of those kinds of staves when he served Dicermadon before the Abyss. It must take a formidable darkness to corrupt such purity. Trinidy puffed out his chest in pride at his power. The fact that he corrupted the powerful holy staff with darkness seemed to have no effect, as he was lost in the enchantment of how powerful he really was. He had stood up to one of the most powerful creations from a church of the land, and defeated it single handedly. Pride of his accomplishment overshadowed the implications to the death knight. He knew he was not evil, and even if he was, he would still do the works of righteousness.

The ghoul practically dragged the zombie before the death knight. Trinidy was roused from his visions to self-greatness and looked down at the odd zombie. He could not detect any signs of life, no heartbeat, no smell of breath, and he had no desire to taste the zombie's blood. *Taste his blood?*

"What is your name?" Trinidy asked, knowing that zombies have no sense of self.

Gorsan felt sweat drip down the side of his face. This beast spoke in that ancient language Fehzban was always trying to get him to learn. He recalled some of the language, but he doubted he could speak it with much proficiency. What was he to say? The mere look of the undead knight sent rivers of fear raging down his spine and into his ever-weakening legs. "Gorsan, Master," he replied in his best imagination of what a zombie should sound like.

Trinidy almost chuckled. Somehow a fool dwarf had managed to magically disguise himself as an undead. He was using some form of divine magic, as Trinidy could not see any arcane illusion weaves surrounding the halfwit. The death knight leaned closer and decided to toy with the fool in celebration of his great victory here in Lostom. "Strange, my other zombies don't have any names."

The ghoul growled and started to salivate as he stared at the dwarf, imagining he might actually be a tasty snack.

Gorsan fidgeted. "Uh, that's, well... have you ever asked

them their names? For example...," Gorsan said as he pointed to a zombie that was standing in rank and file while half of its face hung down and dripped dark black ooze from a wound it suffered fighting the villagers, "that one's name is Steven."

Trinidy turned his head and glanced over at the zombie with the half-severed head. The fool dwarf had chosen a zombie that obviously lacked the physical ability to talk if he ever possessed it.

Trinidy chuckled again. This dwarf was resourceful. "Did you know zombies do not fear?" the death knight asked as he ordered a zombie to approach. The zombie obeyed the mental command and lumbered over.

Gorsan watched the zombie approach and made a mental note of how the beast moved. The zombie staggered over and paused in front of the death knight. Trinidy drew his sword and let the powerful evil blade cackle and pop in the air next to him. The dwarf slightly shied away from the blade as the cold enchantment from it obviously burned his face.

Trinidy held the blade for a moment before making a lightening quick slice that severed the zombie's head. The zombie didn't flinch, or cry out. It merely stood as it was commanded for a few seconds before it toppled over. "You see, it did not fear my sword, it did not feel pain, and it was under my complete command. It cannot talk, nor does it know its name. I do not know how or why you have these abilities. But, you will remain at my side until I can determine what to do with you. If you obey like a real zombie does, I have no reason to dispatch you. Though, if I suspect you are not one of my undead soldiers, I will make you become one."

Gorsan nodded as he gulped down a hard swallow. "I will obey, Master," he said meekly.

Trinidy nodded in satisfaction. "Now go and bring me every one of the sorceress' bodies and pile them at my feet."

Gorsan nodded. "Yes, Master," he said as he quickly hurried off to find the woman's bodies. Once he was a fair distance away from the death knight, the other undead paid him no heed. It was apparent only the death knight suspected he was not undead. Curse the luck! He should have made a break for the boat. The dwarf cursed under his breath and grabbed the charred remains of one of the women. He could not make out who she was, but he could tell she was one of the mistresses. He dragged the body over and set it at the feet of the death knight and set out again. Even in death, the damned women were causing him troubles.

Trinidy glanced down at the dark, twisted form of the yellow mother, Marzahna. She was much more beautiful when her body was not corrupted with her evil mortal heart. The death knight channeled an intricate weave into her body. The weave was more complex than he had ever cast, but the magic seemed to guide his hand. In moments, the dark twisted skin of the woman tightened and stretched across her face, giving her a skeletal appearance.

The black snake-like tendrils of necromancy continued to pour into the woman's body until her eyes shot open. Though the rest of her body was obviously dead and decayed, her eyes were a perfect beautiful brown. Trinidy smiled at the first lich he had created. She would be a general in his army and create undead of her own. She would retain her powers in the arcane arts, and she would answer only to him.

"What do you command, Master?" Marzahna asked in an old dry voice.

Trinidy was pleased with his work. "After I raise your mistresses as liches, just as I have done to you, we will seek refuge from the cursed sun. At nightfall we will march against the city to the west; the city that houses and protects the wrong that I must right."

Marzahna looked to the west. "That is the city of Aquabar. It is the capital of Aten and is occupied by tens of thousands of powerful sorceresses. They will be a difficult lot to defeat, master," she said emotionlessly.

Trinidy nodded. "Perhaps, but I cannot be stopped by any other than the one I seek to destroy. And even his power is pale when compared against my own. After I am finished with him, I will raise an army of these undead sorceresses, which I will call liches. Then I will loose them upon the world."

Gorsan heard the death knight and shuddered at his words. His clansman Fehzban was a keeper of the heart of the rock. Though Gorsan had never seen it, he knew the artifact was a potent tool in battling undeath. He would have to march with this army for a time until he could make his escape.

"Self deception. It is the bane of the foolish, and a tool of the wise. If a man focus on the good things in his life, he can deceive himself into being happy. If a man does the same with the negative aspects, he can achieve a state of despair.

Self deception begins innocently. It is formed when a reality is not known, but surmised. The person then creates a theory about the unknown truth. Instead of looking for the certainty, they begin to try to validate their theory instead. They begin to bend the facts to support their own idea, or ignore contradictory evidence completely.

Once a person has deceived themselves, it is nearly impossible to convince to the contrary. To do so would require that person to understand they have lied to themselves. This is a betrayal that the human mind simply will never recognize. No, there is nothing more dangerous than a man who is self deceived."

-Lancalion Levendis Lampara

ᴄ 15 ᴄ

The Mantle of a New Crown

Edgar, the young boy king's advisor, scanned the room that was filled with the pompous northern nobles. The cleric despised every last one of them, placing their faith in their own politicking rather than a faith in a much higher power. The cleric did not mind that they schemed; all great men did. What bothered Edgar was that they schemed only for wealth, land, and titles. Titles were given, they could be taken away as could lands, and wealth. But faith is a driving power that no man can give you and no man can take away. Faith is a supreme power that lesser men could not afford themselves. And that is exactly how he looked upon the nobles, as lesser men. They were a means to an end, and the cleric was close to achieving that end.

Darious, the young boy king, had found little time to grieve over the loss of his father. Edgar had him mulling over everything from taxes to the country's religion. Though he was only eleven, the boy remembered many of his father's teachings about how to be a king, much to the cleric's dismay, and he often feuded with the overbearing advisor. The northern nobles had given him no respect and short of causing a civil war among them, were forced to obey the king with threat of military action. Though the nobles commanded large forces themselves, they did not dare risk their lands, and titles, over a dispute with a child.

So they bargained with Edgar, who seemed to have a great deal of influence over the boy. Edgar proposed that the nobles should be allowed to impose martial law on all dwarves within the kingdom north and south and any who disobeyed would face criminal action taken against them. The northern nobles knew that a few of the southern nobles would choose to fight rather than agree, would have their lands forfeited and they could split it up fairly amongst themselves.

In return, the northern nobles agreed to vote on the church of Surshy as the countries official faith, thus thrusting the advisor into an even more powerful position. What confounded the cleric was that every cleric priest and even the paladins had lost their spell casting ability. They could not call on even the smallest amount of power from their god, and they felt empty from their prayers. At first many of the clergy felt they had been shunned by the gods and had taken their own life. But though Edgar was a man of faith, he was also a man of practicality. Drastic times called for drastic solutions and suicide seemed a permanent solution to a temporary problem. As he contemplated the event, he concluded that with the other churches not having any ability of divine power, all the power that remained was political, and there was no other cleric with as much skill in that field as he.

The cleric smiled as Doogan Raymer and Kareeg Hut took their seats at the meeting in Dawson. The simple location of the meeting was strategic to Edgar and the northern nobles, because Dawson was the northernmost city and made it more difficult for all of the southern nobles to attend. The south, though they objected to the location, was overruled by the king, stating that in this time of war, Dawson was the safest place.

There was three loud knocks as the king tapped his oversized crown on the heavy oak table. The dull murmurs subsided as the boy looked over the crowd. There were only a small handful of southern nobles present, and most of the north. There were representatives from many churches, including some that Darious had never heard of, and they all quieted as the young king command their attention.

"I would first like to thank everyone for coming," the young king said as sternly as he could. Many of the nobles balked, knowing he should have never thanked anyone, that he was the king and his word was law. The young king was oblivious to their subtle scoffs and continued. "We have much to discuss. I would like to open the first topics with refreshments."

The other nobles were astonished when many scantily

clad serving wenches, not long out of their teen years, burst into the room serving wine and roasted beef. Most of the nobles smiled cheerfully as the appetizers were presented, though the few churches that were run by high priestesses did not appreciate the gesture of the girls. By their reaction, they found it demeaning to their faith. Edgar smiled, knowing in that serving a simple meal he had turned some of the southern churches against most of the southern nobles. Though the southern nobles were goodly men, past meetings had shown they were easily swayed with wine and women.

Kareeg Hut and Doogan Raymer eyed Edgar with a smile of approval. It would seem to them that the king's advisor was a skilled schemer, where Gregory Herwain and Jordan Gersian, the two most powerful southern nobles, were angered by what they viewed as a flagrant attempt to appease them.

When the girls finished serving the meal and flirting with the nobles, they departed the room. A few of the high priests were perturbed at the delay in the meeting the meal caused, but they could not deny how much they enjoyed such pleasantries after their long journey north. When the last plate was pulled, young Darious stood and outstretched his hands. "Nobles and clergymen, I welcome you to the first Beyklan council meeting under my rule. I extend my deepest apologies to the southern nobles that had to travel so far to attend, and hope this meal was ample in placating the journey."

A few of the southern nobles smiled in agreement and Gregory Herwain, known in the south for saying much and doing little, went so far as raising his cup and toasting the king. Jordan Gersian, on the other hand, suspected the king was going to announce many things he was not going to like. Though Darious was but a boy, his advisors were not.

"The first order is to determine what to do with the Torrent Manor. Should it be raised again, or left as a sanctuary for those who fought and died there?" Darious asked.

"It should be razed to the ground!" Jordan shouted as he stood. "The Torrent is a bitter reminder to our nation what results from greed and tyranny!"

"Greed and tyranny?" Kareeg Hut exclaimed. "How about murder and deceit from the dwarves! They tunneled under the keep, backstabbed the men, raped the women, and decapitated the children. The Torrent should be kept as a holy place to remind us of our victory over the bearded demons and the sacrifice of those who died there!"

"It matters little really," Doogan the skilled tactician put in. "The Torrent was built as a keep to monitor the dwarven actions and a place to launch military forces against them if need be. Since the dwarves are no more, I see little need to invest a single coin from our coffers in rebuilding it."

Many of the other nobles mumbled in agreement, but Kareeg's face grew red with fury.

"How dare you suggest such an atrocity? How can you turn your back on your own people who bled to the ground and gave their lives there?" Kareeg exclaimed as he pounded his fist into the table.

"No one would have bled or died there had the north's greed not overcome their senses!" Jordan exclaimed.

Jordan's comments brought fury from the north as they shouted back, erupting the whole room into a screaming match. Even a few of the church leaders tossed in their views, especially the leaders from the church of Stephanis, the current religious faith of the country.

Darious hammered the table for several seconds demanding quiet, before the nobles calmed themselves but kept their murderous glares on their red and angry faces.

"It would seem tempers flare at the Torrent, so I am going to offer this solution," Darious said as sternly as his pre-pubescent voice would allow him. "The entire Western Army was defeated in the battle against the dwarves. There were only a few clerics and wounded that survived when the mountain came down on them. It's true, the Torrent was built to monitor the dwarves, but with our borders unsecured, it can act as a guard point to govern the west. It will be rebuilt, not as a testimony to the dwarven defeat, but as a backbone for the western defense," the young king said and then turned to Kareeg. "We will construct a great monument to account of not only the sacrifice of those who died at the

Torrent, but of those who died in the Pyberian Mountains as well."

"Who will station this keep, sire? And how can this small structure effectively defend the west from a possible Adorian invasion?" Jordan asked, knowing the only force to send was the Central Beyklan army.

Darious surprised everyone in the room, even Edgar, with his response. "A few weeks ago, I ordered the central army to march to the west and craftsmen have started amassing materials to start the build. The great keep should be finished by the end of the year."

Jordan quickly pulled some parchments from his leather case and began examining them. He checked locations, cities and estimated a time of arrival. If the army was on the schedule he said it was, he would need to announce the south's independence soon very soon.

"Sire, do you mean to say you have already dispatched the Central Army to the west?" Doogan asked, a bit caught off guard by the young king's bold move. Doogan, being the tactician he was, was amazed and even proud of his young king. Perhaps he was not the boy fool the northern nobles had thought.

"That is correct," Edgar answered for the king. The cleric was no fool to politics and knew the south wanted to pull away. The unannounced move of the Central Army would make them need to act hastily if they were going to unite and form their own country. Edgar knew that if the south was united, the north had little ability to oppose them for many years to come. So he felt the push a rash action would only help. Even if the south managed to pull away, they would have little ability to deal with it now.

Jordan eyed Edgar suspiciously, but kept his nose in his notes. He was concerned with the way Edgar answered for the king. The boy was young and impressionable. It would not take a scheming advisor much effort to sway his youthful views.

"Is there any discussion as to the movement of the Central Army?" the young king asked the room.

The nobles mumbled amongst themselves, but had no

real interest. The southern nobles had much interest, but dared not speak of it for fear of exposing their plot to secede from the north.

"Good," Darious said as he drummed his fingers on the hard surface of the large oaken table. "The next order of business is to address the loss of divine power with the churches. It had been brought to my attention that every church in the nation has suffered the same effects throughout the kingdom. Though there are rumors this event is more widespread than here in Beykla, they are not substantiated and are merely rumors. For that matter, I assume that the gods must be angry with us as a nation. I suggest a vote by the nobles, who represent the will of the people, to vote on the national faith whether it remains the Church of Justice, or a new one."

"The Church of Justice had watched over the people of Beykla for nearly a century!" the high priest exclaimed as he stood up from the table, his bright orange and violet robe shaking as he sternly pointed his finger at the advisor.

Edgar smiled deviously and folded his hands together. "Obviously your church has failed in its duties and now our kingdom suffers."

A light-skinned man dressed in a dark black robe chuckled. He had a bald head and many odd tattoos on his face and neck. "Surely you are not suggesting that the apparent abandonment from the gods is a direct result of the actions by the Church of Justice," the man said softly.

Edgar waved his hand in dismissal. "No, no. But what I am saying is that as the faith of the nation, they should have been more insightful in predicting this problem."

"There was nothing to predict!" the High Priest of Stephanis shouted. "I suspect this tragedy is a direct result of greed from you and the crown!"

The room gasped and Edgar snarled back. "Are you making accusations against the king? That is treason. I'll have you drawn and quartered!"

The high priest folded his arms across his chest. "I am no fool, Edgar, unlike some in this room," he said, glaring at the high priest. "I did make accusations. I made them against you and the old king, neither of which are violations of law. The gods are all disgusted at our nation and are punishing us for your wickedness."

Edgar tightened his fists. "Fool! If you cannot see the clear picture of who is righteous between our people and the bearded monsters, then perhaps you lack the wisdom to lead the faith of this nation."

The high priest kicked over his chair. The room went silent as it bounced across the stone floor. "How dare you make such preposterous assumptions? It is apparent to me that you have already decided to move against Stephanis. I will not stand here while your backstabbing, double-dealing, pig-minded schemes use and manipulate our young king!" he said as he turned and addressed the king with a softer tone. "Sire, you are king in a trying time, and your age is not a benefit to you. Kings are not always remembered by the lands they conquered or wealth they built. I hope your majesty can see the orc in peasant's clothing that stands next to you and preaches faith, when his own agenda rules his heart. I am taking my leave, Sire. If you need me, I will be in my church," he said before turning to the room a second time. "I can see this will soon be a nation of lawlessness and debauchery. Do not be surprised to see my faith departing this land of filth. If you all had any resolve, you would leave. If this fool's church gets named as the faith of the kingdom, there will be a terrible plague brought on our lands."

The king watched the high priests leave with interest and slight confusion. He understood what the high priest had been saying, but was a little unclear on his intentions and his warning. He looked up at Edgar, who flashed a warm smile of reassurance before he readdressed the crowd. "Clergymen, I do not ask to have the king decide on the nation's faith, but propose that we as a nation vote on it. Each noble understands what his people's views are and should cast his vote based on the wants of the masses. When we are finished, we will count the votes and the winner will have been selected by the will of the people."

There were a few seconds of soft mumbling as the room talked over the proposed idea, before they agreed it was a fair method of selecting the nation's faith. Edgar smiled triumphantly. He had already worked it out with every one of the northern nobles to vote for the church of Surshy, his church. Edgar knew he would win the vote. Each high priest would vote for himself, and the southern nobles, even if two thirds of them picked together, were out numbered by the northern nobles three to one. Short of a miracle, his faith would be elected the faith of the nation, and he would be in charge of it. The Church of Stephanis would have little proof he maneuvered politically to win the vote, and would soon be out of the kingdom on its own volition. Once he was head of the kingdom's faith, he would begin working on a resolution as to why no cleric or priest could cast any divine spells. Everything was going according to plan.

Jordan Gersian sat in his carriage as it quickly traveled south. He was three days ride south of Central City and had been on the road nearly two weeks. They were making remarkable time and once the king had announced he had already ordered the Central Army to move, it was readily apparent that the king was, at the very least, suspicious that the south might try and secede from the north.

The early movement and the far meeting place all the way north into Dawson was proof enough. If the central army managed to move west, no doubt some of the northern and eastern armies would shift to the central zone. The Southern Army was just south of Motivas, the southern most Beyklan city. By the time they formed a south and east army, there would be little time to move toward the center of the country to entrench against the north. Without a fair show of force in the center of the kingdom, they would not get the nobles there to support the secession. Without the nobles' support, their success would be difficult.

To make matters worse, the king announced the Church of Surshy as the country's new religious faith. The clerics of Stephanis had already left the chamber and of course the heads of each church voted for themselves. There were similar views in the south, with most voting to retain Stephanis, but what surprised Jordan the most, was that every one of the northern nobles voted for Surshy. Even the two northern rivals, Doogan Raymer and Kareeg Hut, voted together. Jordan was sure that was the first time those two had agreed on anything. That cursed Edgar had the boy king in the palm of his hand, and he was beginning to squeeze.

"What ails you, Sir?" the middle aged man asked. He had served Jordan for most of his life and counted the noble as friend as much as employer.

Jordan looked up from his frown and leaned back against the soft leather seat in his carriage. He exhaled slowly and visibly relaxed. "We are at a trying era, Sedan. Time will tell if we are fools, traitors, or both."

Sedan smiled as he reached under the seat and pulled out a small wooden chest. He gently opened the lid and pulled out a dark-colored bottle of wine and two crystal goblets. He handed one goblet to Jordan and popped the top of the bottle. A small mist from inside of the bottle rose from the cherry liquid as it was poured into both glasses. "A drink, Sir. Whereof we cannot foresee that which is around the bend and not look back at the road we left without stumbling through the one we are on. What we must do is merely be steadfast on the road we travel now, and enjoy our trip. No amount of worrying will get us home any sooner. I have sent three different pigeons with the instructions for our house. There is little else to do."

Jordan held the cool crystal goblet in his hand and stared at the liquid for a few seconds before taking a drink of wine. "Well spoken, Sedan, but I have much at stake here. At the worst, my head will be given to the axe man's blade."

Sedan smiled warmly as he took a sip and savored the taste of the expensive wine. "Perhaps, but at best you stand to achieve so much more. Only great men take risks, Sir. Fools like me settle for a life of mediocrity."

Jordan smiled and leaned forward, toasting his goblet into Sedan's. "Only time will tell which of us is the greater fool, my old friend." With that they both had a hearty laugh.

Amerix sat on an old rock that was worn and weathered from hundreds of years of rain and snow. He ran his calloused hands over the rock's smoothed surface and marveled at the stone. Durion, the god of the mountain, made dwarves; at least Amerix believed he did. But what bothered the renegade general was that the huge rocks that made up the mountains became smooth as they aged. But Amerix had seen his reflection as he got older and his face became anything but smooth.

The old dwarf began to ponder what deep meaning the way rocks aged and how it compared to his life when he became distracted by a deep rumble in the west. The old general glanced up at the darkening clouds that were beginning to form and grumbled. "That's the third damned storm this week. How is a dwarf to enjoy the warm breezes of the surface world with those cursed bulbous clouds spitting on them? It's no wonder the pink-skinned human dogs have a vile temperament."

Amerix glared menacingly at the approaching storm for a few more moments before hopping down from the rock and wandering back down the side of the small mountain peak. Though the Lalin Plateau loomed just behind him, this small peak managed to jut above the deep green tree line and gave the dwarf a fine spot for sitting, drinking, and thinking. As he made his way down the trail that ran on the side of the giant boulder, he could hear several dwarves chuckling and mumbling to themselves. Amerix smiled and looked forward to meeting them.

Though they regarded him as a dangerous beast at their doorstep, Amerix still looked forward to their company. He often found himself speaking to plants and bushes as if they had personalities. Talking to real life brethren was always a warm welcome. Amerix chuckled and found himself hurrying his pace to meet the others when their words stopped him in his tracks.

"I don't know why we are to find the old fool," one dwarf said. "He is more of a liability than anything. He will never

lead any of our brethren into battle as they would sooner follow the woman folk to their duties."

"Aye, but the fool humans don't think so. All we have
to do is convince the old coot that he is invited to lead our
cause. Them fool northerners think they killed him when
they captured that orc that turned into some gladiator champion. When they find out he is alive and leads Clan Cutstone
against them, it will give the humans here in the south time
to bargain, or whatever they intend to do, and we can keep
our home without fear that the pink-skinned bastards will
try to do to us what they did to the Stonehearts," the other
dwarf said back.

"I don't like the thought of the evil monster even pre-
tending to lead our clan into battle. Our king should suffice
enough," the first said.

"We are a clan of miners, not warriors. Look at Clan
Stoneheart. They were miners and craftsman and they
were slaughtered in their homes and now they are all dead.
Clan Stormhammer was a clan of warriors; Amerix is proof
enough of that. No one would fear our king, but look at how
Amerix led the Stonehearts. He turned a clan of artisans into
vicious killers. The north has no choice but to think he has
done the same to our clan," the second responded back as
they walked right past a hidden Amerix.

Amerix felt his heart sink. In the past he may have been
angered by what he heard, but in a way, the two dwarves
were right. He was a killer. But they spoke of Clan Stoneheart being wiped out in their homes. He knew he lost the
battle of Central City, but he did not know the humans in-
vaded. Amerix wondered how many dwarves escaped, if
any. And they spoke of an orc; he was sure they referred to
Vlargcar. Why the humans kept the whelp alive was beyond
his old mind, but the fact that the only true friend the dwarf
ever had might be alive was more than enough reason to war
against the northern humans.

When the dwarves were well over the pass and far out
of earshot, Amerix stepped from the bushes and brushed
the many bugs off of his shoulders and out of his long silver
streaked beard. Those fool messengers would not find him

in his cave. He would make his way back north and rescue his friend, but first he would travel to the Cutstone mine and speak with this fool king directly. They would think of him an old withered dwarf no longer.

Vlargcar's bright blue eyes stared at the three men that stood before him in the dry dusty arena. They were unskilled at best and had been dressed in patchwork armor that was either too big or too small. Thick leather straps held the armor in place, which seemed to restrict movement more than protect them. The men had fear in their eyes, but they seemed more interested in achievement. Though he was not sure why the men were pit against him, Vlargcar cared little. He would offer them a chance to surrender. If they did not accept, he would kill them, just as he had done all he faced.

"Throw down your swords and you will be spared!" Vlargcar shouted in his guttural orc language.

The men all flinched when he spoke and seemed to quickly become more uninterested in fighting. Vlargcar cocked his head to the side as he tried to understand what he could have said to scare them. After a few seconds and the men did not throw down their weapons, he reached up from behind his back and drew his great sword with his right hand and pulled his long sword from his belt scabbard with his left. He had spent many months perfecting the two bladed fighting prowess, but he had grown much since then and felt he could wield much larger swords with equal proficiency.

When Vlargcar's swords were freed from their scabbards, the men screamed and ran. Two of them threw down their swords as they ran and the third seemed to afraid to even think of tossing the weapon down. Vlargcar watched with amusement and confusion. Perhaps they had heard what he said after all.

As the men ran back toward the rusted iron grate that had led them into the arena, a heavy volley of crossbow bolts filled the sky from small battlements around the arena.

The heavy shafts slammed into each of the three men, killing them. They twitched and moaned in the agony of death as bright red blood streamed from their wounds. Vlargcar slowly walked up to the three dead men, while keeping an eye on the battlements. He had never seen anything come from them before, and wondered why they shot the men. The shots were fairly accurate and the heavy shafts proved to be quite deadly.

The ever-growing orc cast a suspicious eye at the stone towers and he walked toward his grate as it was being raised. Though he was sure they would not shoot at him, he still was cautious as it appeared the men were running toward their grates when they were cut down as well.

Vlargcar had always seen the large sandstone colored towers that were positioned in six different equally spaced areas around the arena, but he had never known anyone was inside. The thought was somewhat chilling and unnerving. If he was ever to escape, he would either have to find a way to do it from the inside of the complex, or somehow create some diversion where the men inside of the battlements were forced to flee.

As the orc walked from the arena and down the cobblestone ramp to his cell, he happened to pass a large human man with long brown hair. He had a stubbly beard and a stern glare on his face. The human carried the largest sword Vlargcar had ever seen and stood a few inches taller than him. The human gave him little more than a passing glance, but Vlargcar could tell the warrior studied him more in that glance than most of the guards in the complex. The orc made mental notes about the way the man walked and his muscle size in hope to determine what hand he favored. Amerix had taught him to notice such things and he was sure the human was doing the same to him.

"Move along, Jude," one of the guards said as they pushed the giant man in the back.

The swordsman whirled and struck the guard in the face with his elbow. There was a sickening pop as the guard's jaw was shattered. The large man glared down at the unconscious sentry, then gave a long angry stare at the other two, before turning and starting toward the weapons room.

Vlargcar was not sure what the guard said to the large man, but he figured out the last part was the big man's name. The ever-growing orc said the name to himself over and over until he remembered it. For some reason he figured Jude would be important to him somehow.

Jude was led down the corridor to another fight. He had started to fight last each day, which always seemed to attract the largest crowds and more difficult fights. Jude had learned to control his rage over the last several months and had started using it to his advantage. He learned that the feral rage only lasted a little over a minute, but during it he was stronger, tougher, faster, and he felt little or no pain. His mind was somewhat clouded and his agility was slightly slower, but the benefits seemed to far outweigh the hindrances.

He was not sure what he was fighting today, Copel had not stopped by to talk to him as he usually did, but Jude figured it was something large or ferocious due to the loud roar of the crowd. The fact that Copel did not stop by and the exceptionally loud roar had the large swordsman on edge.

As he was staring toward the weapons room, he spied the largest orc he had ever seen coming from the arena. He was nearly as tall as Jude and probably twice as wide. The strength the creature possessed must have been phenomenal. Jude gave a quick glance at the green-skinned monster, measuring everything about him from his walk to the weapons he carried, but what caught Jude's eye the most was the monster's bright blue eyes. Jude slowed and pondered how many poor slaves the orc had killed when he felt a dull pain in his back as he was shoved from behind.

"Move along, Jude," the guard behind him commanded.

Anger roared through the mighty swordsman. Though he was in shackles, Jude whirled and caught the man square in the chin with a rock hard elbow. Jude felt the man's jaw pop as he rammed it to the other side of his face. The guard fell to the ground unconscious and Jude glared at the other two. They backed away cautiously and placed their hands on their weapons, but they did not draw them. They were no fools. They knew that if given a reason, Jude could easily kill them without breaking a sweat. The large man had gained quite a reputation for his fighting prowess and they did not wish to test him.

Jude glared at the guards for a few fleeting seconds then returned on his long walk to the arena. He was not sure what he was fighting today, but he was sure it would require every ounce of his strength and skill.

Kalen made his way through the dark streets of Aquabar. He had been trailing the blue mistress, Arluda, and Lance for some time. He was amazed at how weak and pitiful the Ecnal was when he finally laid eyes on him. The gray elf almost chuckled to himself that he had risked his life and spent years formulating a plan that was built around this human boy. He was not even striking to say the least. He was dressed in the dark brown suda garb and his bald head showed signs of black stubble that was beginning to grow. Kalen could tell the mistress was not overly skilled, and he would have made his move much earlier, except that there was another man that was following them. He was dressed in dark brown tuda robes, but Kalen could easily tell he was armed. The gray elf did not know of any mothers who used tudas to kill or assassinate other mistresses, thus the man's intentions were unclear to him. So Kalen followed close by, watching the man, determining when the best time was to strike.

As the night progressed and Arluda neared the blue tower, Kalen moved in. He had prepared several spells for such an encounter and it appeared the man in the tuda robes had lethal intentions. Kalen suspected that the man was sent by Ramasiel to kill Lance before he could get the boy out of the country, despite his claims he would kill him when he returned to Nalir. Kalen summoned a globe of a bright yellow abjuration. The bright magical sphere bulged and surged until it completely surrounded him. Once the gray elf was satisfied, he wove the strands together and moved from the rooftop with his silent spell intact. With the spell, he omitted no sound and could move at a full sprint as quiet as a breeze if need be.

The man in the dark brown robes moved stealthily, but could not match the gray elf's pace. When Kalen was about thirty feet behind the man, he began his second spell. Kalen quickly summoned a web of thick brown transmutations. He had practiced the spell many times at Hector's castle and had even practiced it on Spencer once or twice. When he gathered a thick enough web, he sent it out at the man who had drawn his sword and peeked around the corner.

The magical energy slammed into Henrious as he took a deep breath and prepared himself to charge the mistress and the suda. Henrious turned to see a small man, perhaps a woman with masculine features, standing behind him. The man was about four and a half feet tall and a dark black cloak hung about him. He wasn't sure what the man had done to him, or if he was sent from Ramasiel. Just as Henrious started to speak, he felt his body spasm into horrifically painful convulsions.

Henrious fell to the ground and the man rushed over to him. Henrious tried to swing his sword, but the small man easily snatched it away. The man pulled his cloak back, revealing a dark gray face with sharp pointed ears. Henrious cried out, but to his surprise, he did not utter a sound. He tried to make a fist to strike the elf, but his hands had hardened and started to turn black. His fingers had all but disappeared and his knuckles elongated and split down the middle. Henrious watched in horror as his arms became thinner and long coarse white hairs began to sprout from them. He could see his mouth stretch and lengthen in front of his face and felt his ears become heavy and laden with hair.

In moments, Kalen smiled at the large ram that was taking shape before him. It was mostly gray and white with huge thick horns that were beginning to sprout from the side of his head. Kalen smiled as he kneeled down and patted the wide-eyed head of the rapidly fading Henrious.

The gray elf quickly summoned another weave of magical energy but this one started as a small dot in front of the ever-changing Henrious. The magical dot stretched until it was about four feet wide, and elongated vertically until it formed a bright orange portal. On one side was the alley they were standing in, and on the other side was a dark room that was covered with hay and straw. Kalen guided the portal until it engulfed the almost transformed Henrious, and then dispelled it. As he hurried toward the blue mistress and the Ecnal, he imagined how happy the man would be when he learned he would be the animal that ravages that backstabbing Ramasiel when he captured her. The gray elf grinned from ear to ear as he imagined the disgusted look on the witch's face as the ram pleasured himself again and again on her.

It did not take Kalen long to catch up with the blue mistress and the Ecnal. Kalen knew he did not have long before his silent spell wore off. As the pair turned around an old abandoned grocer, Kalen hurled ten thin green strands of an enchantment weave that struck the Ecnal in the chest. The green strands of the hold spell quickly surrounded and held him.

Lance glanced down at the ten shimmering rings that encircled him. He had never quite seen a hold spell fashioned in this manner, but he quickly recognized it for what it was. Before Lance could call out a warning to Arluda, a gray elf stepped out from behind the corner of the grocer.

"I have no quarrel with you, Mistress. But, I will not leave without the boy. If you fight me, I will kill you," Kalen said with a deadly confidence.

Arluda glanced around nervously. She had no idea how this elf had eluded capture in this city and she could sense his power was much greater than hers. She hoped that if she stalled him, the suda would be able to escape. She did not know how skilled the suda was at magery, but Delania had told her he had the potential to be more powerful than anyone she had ever seen. Arluda elected to stall. "I may not have a quarrel with you, unless you work for an enemy of mine," Arluda said as she scanned the rooftops, looking for more foes.

Kalen relaxed when he realized that she was indeed afraid and appeared willing to bargain. "I work for no one other than myself, and have my own agenda here. Right now, my only agenda left is to capture this suda and return home with him. He has committed a crime in my lands and I will bring him to justice," Kalen lied.

Arluda began preparing herself to summon the power of evocation and hurl at the elf in the form of a spell called burning hands. "What am I to tell my mistress, elf? She paid a high price for this suda. I think she fancies him."

Kalen glanced around before regarding the woman again. He began to suspect she was stalling. "Last chance, witch. Either turn and walk, or die."

Lance watched the swirling bars of energy as they floated by. They were surely enchantment strands just as Delania had taught him, but they moved differently than evocation strands. Lance noticed that the only way to sever them was to slow or speed up each one until the seams were lined up, then he could force a wedge between all of them. With practice, that would take no time at all, but he had never practiced such things.

He knew the elf was going to attack Arluda, and he was not going to be this close to freedom to have it stolen away from him again. Lance summoned the power that was inside of him. He quickly wove a net of the clear magical strands that caused the person to only be able to belch when they opened their mouths. Though the spell did not last long, it should be more than ample for Arluda to dispatch the elf.

Arluda said nothing. She doubted she would be able to walk away and get to Delania in time to catch him. If he managed to survive in the country for any amount of time, he probably had the ability to teleport. Once he teleported, it would be nearly impossible to determine where he went.

She doubted she could defeat the elf either, so she elected to send a cry for help on a small wisp of evocation. The spell could carry her message for miles and the tower was only a few hundred yards away. "Delania, we are under attack by the old grocer," she whispered. She watched her words scurry away on the bright blue wisp of evocation.

Kalen recognized the spell Arluda had cast. "No one will get here in time to save you, witch," Kalen said angrily as he began to summon a powerful necromancy. But before he could utter the commands of the spell, Lance encircled him with one of his own. When Kalen commanded the wisps to attack Arluda, they fizzled and quivered into nothingness as a series of loud belches erupted from his mouth.

Kalen's eyes went wide in shock and when he tried to speak the incantations of his spell, only belches came out. Kalen knew the witch did not cast a spell and the boy was held. The gray elf hastily scanned the rooftops as he ran around the corner and ducked into the building.

Arluda had seen the necromancy forming and awaited the horrible death she was about to endure, but to her surprise the elf belched instead of commanding the weaves. When she realized the spell fizzled, she ran over to Lance who was lining up the hold spell and severing the strands. "What happened?" she asked with short quick breaths.

Lance watched the strands pop into nothingness like a soap bubble and snatched the mistress by her arm. "The fool underestimated us, nothing more. Let's hurry to the tower before he finds a way to dispel my little trick and comes back for us."

Arluda nodded and they hurried down the alleys.

Kalen ducked in and out of alleys for the rest of the night, but the bright orange glow of the morning sun had already taken hold of the eastern skyline and the stars had been washed away by the ever-growing morning sky. He had tried to dispel the odd incantation that was on him, but he could not even see the weaves, let alone identify the seam in them. He hoped they would wear off, but that was over an hour ago, and nothing had happened. Without the power to speak he was limited to a few choice spells, and he had not prepared any of them. He had already eluded several morning patrols of the sword mistresses and was taking refuge in an old wooden cart that had a tarp thrown over it. He figured he would not be captured here and settled down to sleep off the spell.

Just as he tucked his legs up to his chest to sleep, the tarp was ripped off of the cart. His tired eyes struggled to see into the blinding morning light, but the blow to the side of his head rendered him unconscious.

"You think he saw us, Mother?" the blonde haired mistress in the bright red dress asked.

Ramasiel smiled as her dazzling green eyes looked the elf up and down. "I do not think so, but it matters little."

"What are we to do with him?" the mistress asked as she began the spells to render the resourceful elf helpless.

Ramasiel grabbed the edge of the tarp and tossed it back over the cart, covering the elf. "We will present him to the queen as a gift and appreciation of helping quell the rebellion of my tower. Of course, we will omit the fact the elf is a powerful mage. Once he is in the queen's palace we will buy his loyalty with the promise of freedom."

"What of the suda that got away and what about Henrious?" the blonde haired mistress asked as she motioned for three tudas to pick up the handles to the cart.

"I will pay my street urchins to find and kill the traitor, if he is still in the city. As for the elf, once he helps me take over the throne, I will grant his freedom and tell him the blue mother, Delania, was responsible for his capture. He will stop at nothing to kill her, and I will aid him in growing into his already formidable magical talents. In the meantime, I will enjoy the three thousand gold crown payment that the blue tower owes me for the purchase of the suda," Ramasiel said as she patted the top of the tarp that lay above the unconscious elf's head. "There are prices to be paid for failing me, elf."

"Men do not look for the correct answers in life, they simply look for one that is plausible. Men often seek the truth, not to understand, but to simply have it. They would rather spend their time on basic pursuits of the body.

I have seen many sheep in my day. Most of them were men that were respected among their peers. The regurgitated spoon fed rhetoric to the masses, but never educated themselves in the first place.

I often asked this question in my travels; Who is more foolish, the fool or the fool that follows him?"

-Lancalion Levendis Lampara

⟨16⟩

Vnderground Memories

The slow rumble of the large river that flowed down the center of Dregan City echoed from the giant cavern that the city dwelled in. Therrig checked behind him a final time to ensure General Artamanake and his soldiers of the dark dwarf clan were with him. He stared at the iron visage of Artamanake making sure the salomin still held him in his power before he set foot inside the city. Therrig wasn't sure where the dark dwarven king would be, but he guessed the ebon skinned leader would have taken refuge in Stormhammer Hall, where the old king had lived.

They emerged from an old passage on the north side of the city and started down a small passage. Artamanake was in the lead and strode confidently down the ledge toward the large expansive palace that was carved in the side of a giant stalagmite. Behind him, Therrig followed cautiously and behind him were the general's soldiers. They were not under the salomin's mind control, but followed the general's commands as best as their bodies would allow. Therrig was sure that if the general commanded the ebon soldiers to choke themselves to death, that the fools would tie a leather cord around their necks to make sure they achieved the feat after they lost consciousness. Therrig hated such blind loyalty and considered it a fool's honor.

As they reached the bottom of the ledge, many of the dark dwarven guards hurried to meet the general, thinking he had captured Stormhammer's ghost.

"Generals, generals. Yous have captured the ghosts!" one guard called out.

Artamanake narrowed his white pupiless eyes under his dark black lids. "Fool! Isa' have dones no such things. The ghosts of Stormhammers will be the new kings. Nows bow to hims, or feel mys wrath!" the general commanded.

The two dark dwarven guards regarded the general suspiciously then glanced back to Therrig. Just when it looked like they were going to raise their axes against them, Therrig saw one of the dwarf's face lose its expression and he bowed low. Therrig recognized the look immediately, knowing that Ayden had entered the fool's mind and taken control. Therrig glanced back at the general and breathed a sigh of relief to see he was still under the salomin's control. The red-haired dwarf wondered just how many minds Ayden could control at once.

The second guard looked bewildered at the other as he bowed to the surface dwarf that had claimed the life of many of their kin over the last year and a half. He reluctantly bowed too, but kept his hand near the haft of his axe, just in case a problem arose and Artamanake ordered him to kill the last Stormhammer.

The general growled at the soldiers as he pushed by and Therrig didn't even look at them. He had never been royalty, but he imagined that he should feel as if he was above looking on the simpleton soldiers.

Artamanake led them through the streets as hundreds and thousands of dark dwarves came from their homes and businesses to stare at the sight of the great General Artamanake leading the ghost of Stormhammer to the palace. Therrig couldn't make out what they were saying, but he saw more than a dozen of the ebon dwarves get overcome by the salomin's mind power. Each of the dwarves dropped to their knees and bowed low to Therrig, exclaiming him the mighty savior of their clan and some called him the king of all dwarves. Not all of the dwarves remained under the salomin's power and some rose just as abruptly as they had bowed, seemingly embarrassed or confused by their actions.

As they started up the tall wide stairs of the palace, Therrig was awestruck at the remaining beauty of the structure. The stairs were old and unkempt, with many chips and breaks on their crowns, but they were constructed with a plethora of colored stones that the dark dwarves were unable to see because their vision allowed them to see in total darkness. The top of the palace had huge pillars that were twenty feet wide and rose over a hundred feet into the air. The pillars had carvings of fruit and plant life that created a small garden around their base. Though many of the plant statues were broken or missing, Therrig could clearly recall how they looked in their great splendor when he was a child.

The pillars were set into the side of the great stalagmite and two iron portcullises were held aloft over the only entrance into the heart of the great structure. Therrig glanced around to see where the salomin was, but could not find him. He guessed the creature was invisible somehow, but the dark dwarves could see body heat, so he must have somehow managed to hide his. Of course, Therrig wasn't even sure the odd creatures had body heat.

The guards at the gate tried to stop Therrig's entourage at first, but they were quickly overcome by Ayden's power, and after they bowed before them, they quickly got up and escorted Therrig's group through the palace.

Therrig was amazed at the incredible craftsmanship it must have taken to carve out the interior of the palace, as it was more magnificent than the exterior. Therrig had never been inside the palace when he was a boy and he felt the sting in his nose as the childhood emotions started to well up in his eyes. He quickly turned the pain into rage, and then held his desire to cut the ebon-skinned monsters down from around him. He focused his murderous thoughts to his revenge on Amerix and Clan Stoneheart.

Artamanake and the two palace guards led Therrig and his group up a thousand feet winding staircase that opened up every thirty feet or so into some chamber of the palace. One was the kitchen, another the smithy. There were many of these rooms, and the look of fear and surprise on the dark dwarves that worked on these floors helped sedate some of Therrig's murderous fury.

When they reached the top of the stairs, two huge oak doors opened up, pulled by a large rock-like creature that stood nearly twelve feet tall. It had no head to speak of and its thick stone arms had a hand with three triangle-like appendages that bent and moved like fingers. The room echoed when its heavy feet pounded the ground as it stood behind the left door awaiting the group to enter. Therrig watched the beast cautiously as he and the group walked in.

On the far end of the room was an old dark dwarf with a surprisingly full white beard. He was dressed in full plate armor and had a bright pink silk cape that hung down from his back. Therrig let out a small chuckle at the king's cape, knowing the fool could not see the color, knowing only surface races wore the soft fabric and it was rare and expensive. Next to the king was another dark dwarf that was dressed in a form of chain armor, but he wore a bright silver holy symbol of Kobli, the goddess of pain and torture.

The king stood angrily and tossed the pink cape over his shoulder. "You dares not tos bow ins my presences, General Artamanake? Ands further, yous bring theses unholy heathens into mys personal chambers! Do yous wish mes to brings down mys wrath upons you fors your disrespects?"

Therrig chuckled again as the bright pink cape shimmered and shook as the king angrily gestured as he shouted at the general. "What now, Ayden?" Therrig asked mentally to the salomin.

"I cannot enter the chamber. The golem of earth and stone does see with mortal eyes, therefore I cannot deceive him. The high cleric can see through the golem as he sees through his own eyes, therefore if I enter in the room, our plot will be discovered. I am going to order the general to attack the cleric and kill him. If Artamanake succeeds, the golem will go out of control. At that time, flee the tower and we will have to gain control of the masses another way," Ayden answered.

Therrig frowned as the general and the king traded verbal blows. "What if the golem does not go out of control?" Therrig asked back.

"If the golem merely goes inactive, then I will control the king's mind and resume the original plan," Ayden answered back.

Artamanake turned to his soldiers. "Kills the highs cleric, hes is controllings the king's mind against the king's will."

The soldiers nodded and charged the high cleric without pause. As soon as the soldiers stepped forward, the golem sprung to life. It brought its thick massive arms down like a hammer and crushed a dark dwarf as he charged. Bright crimson blood erupted like a bursting pustule and splattered across the smooth stone chamber.

The golem's second fist swung like a giant club and hit three of the charging dwarves, sending them flying into the air like tiny pebbles. Their bodies hit the hard stone floor and tumbled a bit before laying lifelessly still.

The cleric backed toward the corner of the king's chamber, grabbing his holy symbol and chanting words that Therrig could not understand. In moments, a great gout of intense flame erupted from the ceiling of the chamber and rocketed down on the mass of dwarves that were charging him. About twenty of the dark dwarves screamed in pain as they were burned alive with a fire that was so hot, five others that were near it caught fire and their armor melted to their skin.

The cleric started another spell when he was overcome with sheer numbers. He managed to draw his hammer and split the skull of three other of his brethren assailants, but their skill and numbers were too much for him as he was disemboweled. Therrig watched intently as the golem froze and seemed lifeless when the high cleric was slain. Therrig turned to the king, who was already removing his crown and starting to kneel. "Thank you for saving me, great ghost of Stormhammer. Take my crown and lead my people to greatness!" the king shouted as he held the crown aloft.

Therrig walked over and took the golden crown that he recognized as the one that King Midagord Stormhammer wore. Therrig held the crown up and gazed on it worshipfully for a few seconds before placing it on his head.

"Welcome, King Therrig. You command one of the largest clan's of dark dwarves in the under mountain. What enemy will we crush first?" Ayden asked in Therrig's mind with a humorous sarcasm.

"The Stonehearts," Therrig said out loud as he laughed with a murderous glee. "We will kill them all!"

Delania was sitting at her study brushing her long black hair. She had plastered her face with the pastes the other women here used and colored her nails with a bright blue lacquer. She was amazed at how the simple pastes and lacquer made her feel more beautiful, but feeling beautiful in and of itself was something she was yet to become accustomed to. She was wearing a fine evening dress of a bright blue with a light green sheer shawl that hung about her shoulders. She meticulously tied a thick blue ribbon in her hair and gave herself a once-over in the mirror. She smiled at her reflection.

Delania raised her thin hand up and slowly patted the area on her head where her small upturned horns used to be. She was careful not to muss her hair as she touched her head. It was odd not having her horns. She had always felt they were a testament to her power, as only a few demons had horns that protruded like that. Most of the others had horns that turned down or straight out. She had seen the avatars of Rha-Cordan and they always had upturned horns. Though theirs were much larger in comparison, Delania had always felt a likeness to them. But what amazed her was that she did not have any of the features that set her apart as a demon and she felt more whole now than then.

She often wondered what Lance would think of her had he seen her in her natural form. Her smile faded from her face and was replaced with a sorrowful scowl as she wondered how long she would have this form. Another day? Another year? The rest of her life, if indeed she did have a life? Delania was a succubus; she was created and therefore did not have a soul. Would she age and die as a mortal that had a soul? Or did she gain a soul when she appeared here on the mortal realm? Perhaps that was Bykalicus' plan: make her a mortal, and then when she died in a few short years, he would have her weak mortal soul.

Delania's excitement and anticipation at having Lance to herself was washed away by the impending dread that seemed to hang above her head and she was helpless to avoid it. She stood from her looking glass and started toward the door to her chambers. How do mortals get by in their lives with such uncertainty?

As she started down the long winding staircase of the blue tower, Arluda's faint whisper reached her ears on the wisps of a rapidly fading evocation strand. Delania quickly recognized the spell as a wizard's whisper, or sorcerer's song, but she could not make out what Arluda was saying. Her voice sounded somewhat in duress, but focused.

Delania quickly alerted at the image of Lance in her mind and began weaving a loop of divination. The magical strands formed a small window that the succubus used to look down on Lance. After a few moments she saw him held with an enchantment weave of a hold spell. The spell was just as effective as its evocation cousin, but because it was made from an enchantment, it had to be broken differently, making the spell seem impenetrable to a low-tiered wizard.

Delania's heart raced. What was going on? Where was Arluda? The blue mother quickly harnessed many threads of abjuration. The bright orange magical weave quickly formed a small portal that the succubus jumped through. She purposely summoned the portal a distance away just in case she needed to prepare some powerful spells to fight whatever enemy that might have him. She could risk getting herself captured along with him; then they both would be in a dire position.

The cool night air washed over her as Delania stepped from the portal into the alley. She was slightly worried her portal might open somewhere more conspicuous than an alley, but to her pleasure it did not. She quickly moved through the streets when a gray elf ran by her in the alley. He was belching uncontrollably and ducking from building to building. The blue mother felt her emotions rise when she recognized the odd dweamor as the strange school of magic Lance could manipulate.

Delania hurried through the alleys when she met up with Arluda and Lance as the pair rushed toward her. The blue mother wasted no time and could tell by the look on both of their faces they were eager to be back in the tower. Delania summoned another portal and the three stepped through as quickly as they could.

Lance stepped through the portal, and though he was freed from the vile Ramasiel, he felt his heart sink as he glanced around the tower. It was much similar to Ramasiel's tower, save that it was adorned with blue rather than red. Two mistresses dressed in blue robes eyed him suspiciously as they set polished candle ware on a smooth oaken table. Lance wiped the sweat from his forehead with his dark brown suda robe's sleeve and wondered where the cloak was his mother had given him. He had last seen it some months ago in Ramasiel's tower.

A few seconds later Delania burst through the portal. She did not say a word as she rushed toward Lance. The sight of his chiseled features and bright emerald eyes seemed to excite her to a state of euphoria that she had never felt before. Her belly wrenched up in knots with an odd hurting-hungry feeling of genuine emotion.

Arluda was the last to step through the portal and collapsed on a small divan that was in the lobby of the tower. Her chest heaved from the running and she looked at Delania and Lance in equal confusion and awe.

Lance turned to see Delania as she stepped through the portal. He looked on her for the first time in months. Her bright blue eyes seemed to glow in the dimly lit room and her long sleek black hair was tied up in a bright blue ribbon that not only matched her robe, but seemed to match her eyes. She had pasted her face and cheeks with colors that seemed to accentuate her features, making it appear she wore any pastes at all. Her presence seemed unyielding, yet strangely comforting. Lance stared deep into her eyes and wanted to say something, but no words came from his mouth. It seemed Delania wanted to say something too, but instead she grabbed him and hugged him. Her warm body being pressed against his brought flashes of memories from his childhood. He recalled how his mother hugged him and made him feel safe when he was scared. Lance recalled he had spent his entire childhood and his early adult life with no one to hug him, no one to love him. It was in that moment he recognized his feelings for the blue mother. But his untrusting mind quickly regained control. Why did he feel this way? It was probably an effect of the endless torture and pain he had endured from the wicked women of this country. Did he really love her, or did his broken down will and need trick him into thinking he did?

When Delania lifted her head from his shoulder and stared deep into his eyes, his thoughts of his pain, his suffering, his loneliness all drifted away into an unconscious part of his mind. Now all that existed was her and him. He ignored the two mistresses that were looking at them oddly as they stood next to small night table. He ignored Arluda as she flopped through the rapidly closing portal and collapsed on the divan. All Lance knew was an angelic song from the soul of the woman that stared at him with an endless ocean of deep blue. He could feel her hot breath on his face and the smell of her sweet perfume seemed to envelope him in an inescapable snare. Not only did he stare into the loving eyes of his best friend, he stared into the eyes of the woman he loved. Lance inched his face closer to hers and she moved equally close. Their eyes rapidly darted across each other's face as their lips were so close together that when he inhaled, he breathed her breath. Then they kissed. He could almost feel her love, her pain, her joy erupt from her lips. The moment seemed to last for an eternity and was over too quick at the same time. Their lips slowly and gently pulled apart, but their eyes stayed locked in a lover's gaze. Lance thought he might suffocate from the intensity of his emotion for her.

Delania reached up and stroked his soft cheek. "You are free, my friend. You are finally free."

"And the God of Creation shall be released from his eternal bonds by the hand of a slave. He shall wear his mask even after he is named, though he will not know himself before the fall of the scorpion..."

-Prophecy recovered in the lair of Mersaat,
Great Blue Dragon

Glossary

Aboe- (a-bow) Kingdom on the southernmost peninsula of Terrigan. The kingdom has little or no army, but does not fear being conquered due to the great mountain reaches that surround its borders. Kingdom is wealthy and home of merchants and pirate alike. Of all the kingdoms in Terrigan, it is the most racially diverse with humans, dwarves, and elves holding political offices.

Adoria- (A-door-ee-ah) Kingdom just west of Beykla. It waged abloody civil war against its western half, Andoria.

Alexis Alexandria Overmoon- (a-lex-us / al-ecks-zan-dree-uh /over-moon) Daughter heir of King Christopher Calamon Overmoon. High lord of the Minok Vale. She travels with Apollisian Bargoe, the paladin of Justice, trying to learn the ways of justice to aid her when she becomes queen.

Amerix Alistair Stormhammer- (am-er-icks / ali-stair / storm hamer) Dwarven general of Clan Stoneheart, formerly of Clan Stormhammer. His clan was wiped out before him, when he was a young man, by dark dwarves and a white dragon. He fled with a few survivors and was welcomed into Clan Stoneheart where he excelled in the art of war.

Androdius- (an-drode-ee-us) Evil black dragon of immense power that lives in the swamp west of Aquabar.

Apollisian Bargoe- (A-paul-issi-in / bar-go) Paladin of justice that was sent from his order in Westvon keep to oversee the negotiations between the humans and the dwarves from Clan Stoneheart, in attempt to derail a conflict, when he was caught in the middle of the war.

Andoria- (an-door-ee-ah) Formally western Adoria, this kingdom's brief history came when it declared it's independence from Adoria. It waged an eight month long war with Adoria, but was eventually reconquered.

Aquabar- (awk-wuh-bar) Capitol of Aten, which lies near the great swamp and the Mountains of Meara.

Arluda- (are-loo-duh) Blue mistress and friend of Delania.

Artamanake- (art-man-uh-key) Dark dwarven general.

Aten- (A-ten) Queendom to the far west that is ran solely by women. Males of any race are considered inferior and are immediately made into slaves, or killed at birth. Only a choice few males are kept alive for reproduction purposes only. The women of Aten are adept sorceresses and keep a rigid society of backstabbing and political maneuvering.

Ayden- (A-den) Powerful salomin that used Therrig to gain control of a large clan of Dark Dwarves.

Barbetin- (bar-bet-in) Also known as the Lake of the Damned. It is the lake in the Abyss that damned souls are thrown into to be tortured for eternity by the demons that swim among it.

Beovi- (bee-o-vi) Subterranean fish that live in the deepest freshwater caverns of the underworld. They are a delicacy to dwarves, dark dwarves, dark elves and other subterranean races. These fish can grow to unlimited size, depending on the lake or river in which they live.

Beykla- (bay-kla) Human kingdom on the northeastern corner of Terrigan. The kingdom is well-to-do, militantly powerful, and well patrolled. It has never, in its long history, been conquered.

Blue Dragon Inn- Inn in Central City that is closest to the Dawson River and the Dawson River bridge, where Lance, Kaisha, Ryshander, and Apollisian battled the dwarven horde, until the king arrived with re-enforcements.

Borkin- (bore-kin) Small wooden device that is inserted into the mouth that keeps the wearer from closing their jaws.

Bureland- (bur-land) small hamlet, in the southern part of Beykla, where Lance spent most of his childhood and early adult life with his adoptive father, Davohn.

Brohe-tah- (Bro-tah) Orc word equivalent to comrade. The orcs use in reference to another that he or she likes as a friend. Though the orcish language does not have a single word for friend, it has over a dozen for enemy.

Breedikai- (bree-da-kii) Original gods, or gods that were created. They have no soul and most dwell in Meri-oulus.

Bykalicus- (bye-kal-eh-kus) Powerful archdemon that controls much of the Abyss.

Cadacka- (ka-doc-uh) Black ceremonial robe worn by elves when they have lost a loved one and are mourning. Most elves never remove the cloak once it is donned.

Calours- (ka-loo-ers) Non sedimentary rocks found in the underworld. Subterranean races, mostly species of dwarves, use them to cook meat on.

Calito, battle of- (kuh-lee-toe) Battle that took place in Adoria near the town of Dalzan Adorian knights fought against an evil necromancer named Randolph Forlinger who commanded over a thousand undead soldiers.

Carcarass- (kar-kar-us) Training school that raises and trains Atenborn pureblood males to be slaves as they age.

Central City- City just south of the Dawson Stronghold that is in the center of the Beyklan nation.

Christopher Calamon Overmoon- (Kris-toe-fur / Kal-a-mon / over-moon) High king of the Minok Vale.

Clan Cutstone- Clan that makes its home under the La-lin Plateau in Southern Beykla.

Colonel Mortan Ganover- First lieutenant of Duke Do-lin Blackhawk, and acting mayor when the duke is gone. He is considered responsible for the slaughter at Central City by the dwarves due to his inability to act on the paladin Apol-lisian's recommendations.

Commander Fehzban Algor Stoneheart- (fez-ben / al-gore) Commander and loyal follower of General Amerix Stormhammer. He was tried and convicted of treason after the Torrent Manor and the Central City campaigns.

Copel Nin- (cope-ul) Fat keeper of the gladiator slaves in the arena in Central City. Copel was once a gladiator champion but in the fight he earned his freedom he was severely injured, ending his career as a fighter. He was hired by the duke to be the keeper of the slaves. Copel always worked hard at the job but as he aged, his injury and time took its toll on him, preventing his ability to stay in shape. He soon became fat, but he enjoyed his job at the arena as he longed for the days to hear the roar of the crowd once more.

Council of Wise- Consists of ten elders that sit on the governing seat at Minok Vale, though not all ten are usually present at meeting, There has to be at least six to hold a vote.

Cranetium- (krane-tee-um) Official title given to an elven high mage. The title means little to other elves, save for the wizards and sorcerers of their Vales.

Dadramedion- (day-drom-uh-dee-in) Powerful archdemon and enemy to Bykalicus.

Dall-kal-Mour- (doll-kal-moo-ur) Title given to bloodborn men from Aten. They are the only males that are allowed to reproduce. They are expensive slaves and only the highest ranking or wealthy own them. It is a status symbol for Mothers or heads of septs to own more than one, since they will never give birth.

Dalzon- (dal-zohn) Small city in the northwestern side of Adoria.

Darayal Legion- (dar-ray-all) One hundred of the finest elite elven rangers that patrol the Minok Vale in pairs. They are skilled swordsmen who wield a weapon in each hand during battle. They are as feared as they are awed.

Darious Theobold- (dare-ee-us / They-bold) Eleven year old son of King Theobold.

Dark Dwarves- Dwarves that live solely in the underworld. They have pupil less eyes that have adapted over time to see in the dark by detecting heat patterns. They hate bright light as it is painful for them, and have turned to wicked and evil ways as a society.

Dargruden - (dar-grude-in) Dall-Kal-Mour that runs

the gearian.

Darren Brightson, Duke- (Dare-in / bright-sun) Duke of the Adorian lands just to the east of the northeastern border of Aten. Governs over the small hamlet of Lostom.

Darrion-Quieness- (dare-ee-on / kwee-eh-ness) Great white dragon. Oldest of all white dragons and most powerful. His lair is in the mountains of Nalir, but he roams all over the realms. He often leads lesser races against heir enemies, and takes the majority of the treasure after the victory. His last major campaign was in aide of the dark dwarves against the dwarven Clan Stormhammer.

Davohn Ecnal- (da-von) Adoptive father of Lance. He is a woodcutter that made his home in Bureland and found Lance when Lance was only six years old. He raised him as his son until Lance left when he was seventeen.

Dawson River- Largest river that runs in Terrigan. It stretches from the Sea of Balfour, north of Beykla, all the way through the southern Kingdom of Aboe.

Dawson Stronghold- Capital of Beykla, this port city is the largest hub in the Bay of Balfour.

Delania- (duh-lane-ee-uh) Beautiful succubus that dwells in the Abyss.

Dicermadon- (die-sir-ma-don) God of gods, Dicermadon plots with demons to kill the son of a goddess, drawing the wrath of the gods that he governs.

Diltz Quest- (Dilts) Ceremony in which Dall-Kal-Mours, Aten full-blooded males, compete in a gladiator competition to be selected as a mate for the queen.

Dolgo seeds- (dole-go) A tasty mountain nut found on the steepest slopes of the highest mountain. Considered a delicacy by all dwarves and mountain people.

Dome of the Rock- Ancient dwarven temple that was supposedly built by Durion, the dwarven mountain god. The temple is rumored to be atop the Lalin Plateau.

Donk- Aten word for the male reproductive organ. It

is an insulting word in their culture and is associated with mental weakness and stupidity.

Doogan Raymer- (doo-gun / ray-muhr) Northern noble from Dawson. Doogan is a conniving tactician who has made his estates through double dealing and backstabbing. He shows his family tree as being distantly related to the king, and hopes to one day return his house the throne.

Dorcastig- (door-cast-ig) Tall muscled priest of Rha-Cordan. Follows under Resin Darkhand. One of the priests that participated in the DeNaucght.

Durion- (doog-a thee-in) Dwarven Mountain god.

Dregan City- (dree-gan) Home of the Clan Stormhammer before it was wiped out by the dark dwarves and a white dragon.

Drunda- (drun-duh) The god the orcs follow. It is not known if he actually exists, or even if he is male.

Dweamor- (Dwec-mer) Another name for a spell.

Earth Oath- Oath an elf makes that they will give their lives trying to uphold.

Ecnal- (eck-null) Surname given to all orphans of Beykla before they were killed by unknown assassins.

Elder Bartoke- (bar-toke) Elder of the Minok Vale, member of the council of the wise, and Keeper of the sealed passings.

Elder Darmond- (dar-mond) Elder of the Minok Vale, member of the council of the wise, and Keeper of the passings.

Elder Humas- (hue-mass) Elder of the Minok Vale, member of the council of the wise, and Keeper of the passings.

Elder Varmintan- (Var-mint-ton) Elder of the Minok Vale, member of the council of wise, and Keeper of the passings.

Erik Stromson- (stahm-son) General of the Beyklan Western army and hero of the orc wars.

Eucladower Strongbow- Oldest Elder of the Minok

council of wise and Keeper of the passings.

Famen's Tree- (fay-mens) Large tree three miles east of the Dawson River bridge. The tree was named after Jeddis Famen, a Central City militia leader that held off an orc attack. After the battle he led a group of militiamen after the fleeing orcs, and managed to slay one of the orc leaders as they fled. He nailed the orc's head on a spike to the tree as a message to any other orcs. That was the last orc battle against Central City during the Orc Wars. The people believed the orcs were afraid of him, but in truth they were massing to finish the elves at the Minok Vale.

Flunt- God of Fire, and one of the four elemental gods.

Freedom Festival- Holiday celebrated in Beykla to commemorate the end of the twenty-year-long orc wars.

Garlibane- (gar-lee-bane) High mage and Elder of the council of wise in Minok.

Gearian- (Gear-ee-in) Collection of incorrigible sudas that exist for the sole purpose of raping and killing women in Aten who have been convicted of the most serious crimes. The women are stripped of their power and thrown into the pit for spectators to watch as they are raped repeatedly over many days until they are killed or die.

General Laricin West- (lair-iss-in) Late general for the northern Beyklan army that was responsible for scattering the orc horde, in the battle that was later referred to as The Quigen. General Laricin and his men fought to the last man, keeping the orc horde from wiping out what was left of the elven resistance.

Gorsan- (gore-sahn) Dwarven brew master and distant relative to Fehzban. Gorsan lives in Dalzan and sells dwarven ales to the locals.

Gregory Herwain- (her-wane) Southern noble who is chairmen of affairs in southern Beykla. He is leader of House Herwain that is well-known for saying much and doing little. He hosts the monthly meetings of the southern nobles in the city of Motivas at the house of affairs.

Gweits- (ga-weets) Tiny insect-like demons that dwell on the rocky floor of the Abyss. They feed on flesh, and burrow under skin with their horrific claws and hooks.

Heart of the Rock- A gemstone mounted on a gold ring that is said to have magical properties that can prevent the wearer from being harmed by dragon's breath.

Hector De Scoran- (heck-tor / day-skore-an) Evil warrior wizard that is king of Nalir. He believes that Lance was prophesized to destroy his kingdom, and will stop at nothing until the boy is dead.

Henrious- (Hen-ree-us) Ex-Diltz Quest gladiator and Dall-Kal-Mour that helps Tonya of the White and the freedom movement.

Hiramem- (her-uh-mem) Old female sorceress that lives in Aten. She often works for Ramasiel in the red tower and has a limited ability at foretelling. She often uses old chicken bones, stones and other small objects that she tosses about on a board with elven skin stretched over it. She is from Beykla originally. She grew up in Sineuvia.

Hourid Thigguard- (hor-id / thig-guard) Master of arms and father of Mylaneia.

Ian Silverman- (E-uhn) Human knight under Duke Darren Brightstar. Fought in the Battle of Calito. Has two sons, Ian Silverman II and Myer Silverman. Both are adventurers and Ian does not agree with their lifestyles.

Ickten Norris- (ick-ton) Ranger that works for the Hentridge farm south of Central City. He is an expert tracker and skilled swordsman. His favored enemies are orcs.

Illilander tree- (ill-lee-land-er) Largest trees in the realms. Over five hundred feet tall.

Jordan Gersian- (jor-dun / Ger-see-in) Southern Nobleman that is leading the plot to pull southern Beykla away from the north.

Jude- (Jewd) Mercenary swordsman from Bureland. He sold his sword to fight brigands, polecats and other minor enemies of Bureland. He is also Lance's best friend.

Kai-Harkia- (Kay-hark-ee-uh) Mountain kingdom northwest of Beykla. Its people are dark-skinned, dark-haired, heavy-chested, nomad swordsmen. They seldom form static villages, though some do exist.

Kalen Al-Kalidius- (kay-lin / al-kal-id-ee-us) Grey elf ex-stepson of King Overmoon of the Minok Vale. Kalen has turned to the shadow and hungers for power, hoping to take over the throne of Nalir when Hector dies.

Kalistirsts- (kal-eh-stirsts) Underground mole people with no eyes that live in the underworld.

Kalliman Theobold- (kall-eh-man) King of Beykla.

Kalliman Castle- (kall-eh-man) Castle and home of King Kalliman Theobold.

Kareeg Hut- (kuh-reeg) Nobleman that owned more land than any other noble in all of Beykla. His lands were in the north that extended from just south of the Torrent Manor all that way west to the border of Beykla and all the way east to the Dawson River right up Dawson itself. His brother was a Captain that was stationed at the Torrent Manor when it fell. He hates the dwarves more than any other Beyklan.

Kellacun- (kell-eh-kun) Wererat assassin that worked for the guild in Central City before it was destroyed. Now she works for Kalen in attempt to kill Lance.

Kingsford City- Largest city in Terrigan. Capital of Ladathon.

Kornicus- (corn-uh-cus) Demon imp servant of Delania.

Ladathon- (lad-uh-thon) Southern country, south of Tyrine, where mysterious animals live in thick jungle. Kingsford City, the largest city in the world, is its capital.

Lancalion Levendis Lampara- (lance-uh-lion / lev-un-dis / lambpar-uh) Birth name given to Lance Ecnal.

Lalin Platue- (lay-lin) large plateau that is the middle of Southern Beykla. It is covered by a thick lush forest and is nearly impossible to scale its thousand-foot-high sheer rock walls. Stories tell of ancient ruins at the top, but few have climbed to its summit to validate the claims. What makes the plateau so unique is that the Dawson River runs through the inside of it in a great river cave.

Lance Ecnal- Adopted son of Davohn Ecnal. Lance's birth name is Lancalion Levendis Lampara. His natural mother was Panoleen, the goddess of mercy. Lance is prophesized to bring plague and death on the world, though he sees himself as nothing more than an orphan trying to discover his past.

Leska- (les-kuh) The Earth Mother Goddess. She reins over all living things while they are alive, including plants and animals. She is one of the four elemental gods.

Lostom- (lose-tom) Small Hamlet on the border of Aten and Adoria.

Lostos- (low-stoes) Name for the underground complex of the severed heart guild of wererats in Central City.

Lukcrey- (lou-kear-ee) God of Luck and Mischief.

Lunarian- (lou-nar-ee-in) Enchanted wells that priestly elves or other good forest creatures bless by the powers of Leska to rejuvenate and to heal one another.

Lyndall- (lin-doll) Gladiator champion in Central City. A skilled swordsman that had fought over two hundred forty fights. He is only four fights away from earning his freedom.

Malwinar- (Mal-win-are) Elf wizard assistant to Garlibane.

Markus- (Mark-us) Suda in Ramasiel's tower who is secret lover with Reena.

Marlana- (Mar-lane-uh) Backstabbing mistress of the blue sept that conspired with Ramasiel to overthrow the mother of the blue sept in order for her to control a second vote in the senate.

Marzahna- (marr-zohn-uh) Mother of the yellow sept that was banished for wanting to marry. She built a smaller tower on the border of Aten in the hamlet of Lostom.

Mary of the Yellow Robe- Mistress of the banished yellow mother, Marzahna.

Master David Hentridge- (hint-ridge) Leader of small mercenary guild that is disguised as a farm, just south of Central City. King Theobold uses them to hunt and kill orcs that he does not want the public to know exists, keeping their awareness of the actual amount of the green-skinned beasts that still live in his kingdom.

Meirgan- (Mare-gun) Ruthless bounty hunter from Beykla.

Merioulus- (mare-ee-oh-you-lus) City of the gods. Set on a form of the Astral plane.

Mersaat- (mare-sat) Great Blue Dragon that lives in the Desert of Tyrine. A scroll was stolen from his lair by a hapless thief. The scroll was sold several times until it ended up at the great library in Kingsford City where Ladathon scholars identified the text as draconian. What made the scroll unique was that it was written in humanoid size. Few humans know draconic. It gave credibility that there is a secret sept of priests that worship the great serpents, but it led others to believe that once the beasts fully mature, they gain the ability to transform into a manlike creature. All of these theories are yet to be proven.

Mershul- (mur-shul) God of serpents, some believe the god does not exist and is only worshipped by a cult following known as the sept of serpents. Mershul is also the term referred to for men who go into berserker rage in battle. The rage is so intense the men do not feel pain, can continue to battle long after their body has died, and have a hard time differing friend from foe on the battlefield. Mershuls are as feared as they are respected as warriors, though they never fight with comrades as a Mershul often claims the lives of those around him while he is in his rage, unable to determine friend from foe.

Midagord Milence Stormhammer- (mid-uh-gord / my-lence) Amerix Stormhammer's deceased father.

Minok Vale- (my-nock) Name of the elven sovereignty that is set in Beykla.

Motivas- (moe-ta-vis) Southern most city in Beykla. City is built on a large brick foundation that is rumored to be ruins of an ancient civilization.

Mountain Heart- Home city of Clan Stoneheart, located in the Pyberian Mountains.

Mount Steeple- The largest mountain on Terrigan. The mountain is rumored to hold the roadway to Merioulus as its peak cannot be seen as it ascends into a permanent veil of clouds.

Mowaka- (moe-walk-uh) camouflage cloak-like blanket that elven archers, and sometimes rangers, use to spy on their enemies.

Myer Silverman- (my-er) Son of Ian Silverman of Lostom.

Mylaneia Thigguard- (my-lane-ya / thig-guard) Young daughter of Hourid Thigguard, and courtier of Tharxton Stoneheart.

Nalir- (nall-er) Evil southern empire made primarily of swamps and quagmires. A militantly powerful nation that worships most of the evil gods.

Necromidus- (neck-rom-eh-dus) A collection of the first four tiers of necromancy spells.

Oswald Thorrin- (oz-wald / Thor-in) Captain of the royal Beyklan guard and bounty hunter, though he only collects on lawful bounties set by the magistrates.

Panoleen- (pan-oh-leen) Goddess of Mercy that was banished from the heavens.

Pav-co- (pahv-coe) Fat wererat guild leader in Central City.

Pyberian Mountains- (pie-beer-ee-an) Mountain range in the northwest corner of Beykla, near Adoria.

Quadry Proudarrow- (Quad-ree) Darayal Legionnaire

of the Minok Vale.

Quigen- (kwi-jin) Elven word for sacrifice. Most widely known as the name of the great battlefield where General Laricin West scattered the orcish horde by fighting until every man in his army fell in the Serrin plains.

Ramasiel- (ram-uh-zeal) One of the three mothers of the red order in Aten. She is a powerful sorceress and a political power in Aquabar.

Randolph Forlinger- (ran-doff / four-ling-er) Powerful necromancer that was defeated and slain at the Battle of Calito.

Reagle, The- A fancy clothing store in Aquabar that makes dresses and other articles of women's clothing. It does not make any article of clothing that could be used in an intimate way to make the women more attractive. Atenians believe that men have no right to be attracted to women, that the act should be gratifying to the woman only.

Reena- (ree-nuh) Third sorceress, also called third sister, of the red sept in Aten. Second only to Ramasiel herself.

Rha-Cordan- (rah-kor-don) God of death and dying. Not inherently evil, he reins over the placement of souls when they enter the afterlife, though he has been known to be incredibly vengeful to those who prolong their lives through magical means.

Salomin- (sal-low-men) Subterranean humanoid species with powerful mind-controlling abilities. Also known as mind eaters.

Serrin Plains- (sare-in) Dangerous expansive grassland just south of Minok Vale where most of the evil races that live in Beykla dwell.

Sha-Shor'Nai- (sha-shore-nigh) God of the Sun and Light.

Silas Proudarrow- (sigh-less) Darayal Legionnaire of the Minok Vale.

Stephanis- (stuh-fawn-is) God of Justice.

Stieny Gittledorf- (stie-knee / get-tull-dorf) Halfling thief who became mixed up with the dragon Darrion-Quieness.

Stormghast- The great stone doors that seals Mountain Heart from the dark uncharted reaches of the under mountain.

Suda- (sue-duh) Title given to all non-eunuch slaves in Aten. A suda is looked at as a lower form of a man by the tuda, or eunuch.

Surelda Al-Kalidius- (sir-el-da / al-kuh-lid-ee-us) Ex-wife of King Overmoon and mother of Kalen, Ultsa, and Ulma Al-Kalidius.

Surshy- (sir-she) Goddess of Water. One of the four elemental gods.

Takash- (Tah-kosh) Place in an Aten tower where the sudas are brainwashed.

Tallnok- (tal-knock) Young wizard that works for the Hentridge Farm south of Central City. Occasionally hires himself out for specific jobs.

Talwin- (tall-win) Young apprentice war wizard that joined the Western Beyklan army instead of staying with the mage guild in Dawson.

Targavian Hollen Stoneheart- (tar-gave-ee-in / hall-in) New general promoted by Tharxton after the betrayal of Amerix and his officers.

Terrigan- (ter-eh-gun) Name of the continent that all known civilizations exists.

Tharxton Stoneheart- (tharx-ton) Young king of Clan Stoneheart and political rival with Amerix Alistair Stormhammer.

Therrig Alistair Delastan- (ther-ig / al-eh-stair / del-eh-stan) One of the few surviving members of Clan Stormhammer.

Thomas Smith- (Arwar)-(are-wahr) Blacksmith that was worked at the Torrent Manor before Amerix attacked.

He was head of the ambassador's liaison between the two peoples and he learned dwarven from his many dwarven friends at Mountain Heart before he retired and moved back to Poria.

Tonya- Former Mother of the White Tower, who staged her death so that she could anonymously lead the freedom movement of Aten.

Torrent Manor- small keep northwest of Central City that was built specifically for enforcing the trade embargo on the dwarves that dwelled in the Pyberian Mountains, and the Adorians in the civil war.

Trinidy- (trin-eh-dee) Dead paladin of Dicermadon that was raised from the dead by evil priests of Rha-Cordan, creating the first death knight.

Tuda- (too-duh) Title given to all eunuch slaves in Aten.

Tyrine- (tie-reen) Kingdom south west of Beykla.

Valley of Mist- Lush green valley just below the entrance to Mountain Heart in the Pyberian Mountains.

Vendaigehn- (vin-day-gun) Type of horse from the plains of Vendaiga. The steeds are marked with white spots on their flanks, and are taller than most horses with longer, thinner legs. Legend says that Vendaigehn steeds are the offspring of a Pegasus and a unicorn, though that has never been proven.

Victor DeVulge- (day-vul-juh) Slain squire of Apollisian Bargoe.

Vlargcar- (va-larg-car) Orc whelp saved by Amerix when he and his mother was ordered killed by their tribe.

Vrescan Alistair Delastan- Therrig's father who was killed fighting side by side with Midagord Stormhammer in defense of Dregan City.

Walter Thigpen- Middle-aged royal guard crossbowman and longtime friend of Captain Oswald Thorrin.

Westvon Keep- (west-van) Large keep and hamlet to the far east in Beykla on the banks of the Dawson River.

Whisten- (wiss-ton) God of Air, and one of the four elemental gods.

Yahna- (ya-nuh) City in the heavens where mortal souls, blessed by their gods, dwell.

Yohr-Acht- (your-awk-tuh) Great green dragon that makes his lair atop the Lalin Plateau.

About the Author

Shane Moore grew up on a farm in rural Illinois. An only child that was six miles from his nearest peer, Shane often created wild tales of heroes and villains during his many trips into the deep woods that surrounded his rural home.

Shane was accelerated in his class and started his senior year of high school at age sixteen. After graduating and getting a waiver for his age, Shane joined the United States Navy to pay for college. He participated in campaigns; "Provide Hope" and "Secure Democracy" during the Yugoslavian civil war. Shane received several naval awards and citations and was one of the highest trained members of his ship.

After getting out of the service, Shane began college. He was soon hired by the Carlinville Police Department, beginning his multiple venue police career. Shane retired as a detective for the Gillespie Police Department after serving twelve years. His police career was quite notable with awards for bravery and with one life saving medal. He was named Officer of the Year in 2005.

A lesser known truth about Shane is that he played eight years of semi pro football with the Central Illinois Cougars. Shane is the team's all-time tackle leader and holds the record for most special teams tackles in a season and the most tackles in a game. Shane received many awards including Defensive Player of the Year in 2005.

January 14th, 2008. Shane retires from his police career to be a professional novelist.

Mr. Moore resides in Central Illinois with his son, Dakota.

SHADE MOORE